Claire Challis has been Editor and Dep[...] [...] of
the best-selling women's m[...] [...]
decade, from fast-paced wee[...]
fashion monthlies.

She is now a writer and jo[...] [...] rich,
glam and infamous . . .

Fabulous has been on the sidelines of the biggest on and off-
pitch stories to hit the high-octane world of premiership
football – and now she's ready to share all the glamour, the
gossip and the own goals . . .

The Beautiful Game

A Wag's Tale

CLAIRE CHALLIS & *FABULOUS*

headline
review

First published in 2008 by Headline Review
An imprint of HEADLINE PUBLISHING GROUP

1

Cataloguing in Publication Data is available from the British Library

ISBN 978 0 7553 1826 1

Typeset in Bembo by Avon DataSet Ltd, Bidford on Avon, Warwickshire

Printed and bound in Great Britain by
Mackays of Chatham plc, Chatham Kent

Headline's policy is to use papers that are natural, renewable and recyclable
products and made from wood grown in sustainable forests. The logging and
manufacturing processes are expected to conform to the environmental
regulations of the country of origin.

HEADLINE PUBLISHING GROUP
An Hachette Livre UK Company
338 Euston Road
London NW1 3BH

www.headline.co.uk
www.hachettelivre.co.uk

To Lena, who would have found
it all a right good do.

Huge thanks to my agent Pat Lomax and my editor Carly Cook for all your support, inspiration, energy and encouragement. Between the early morning phone calls, late night meetings and weekend emails I think we can safely say we've got speed-novelling down to a fine art. High five!

Also a big thank you to everyone at the Bell Lomax Moreton agency and Headline for your hard work and overwhelming enthusiasm.

All my love and thanks to Stu, for your round-the-clock football fact-checking and (fictional) character assassination, but most of all for being my 24/7 soulmate. And to Mum, Dad, Hev and all my closest friends for dealing with my new-found flakiness with patience and good humour. May I never utter the words 'I'll have to be quick, I'm on deadline' again.

And of course, thanks to *Fabulous*. Babe, without our marathon champagne-fuelled chats and your eyewatering insights this book would never have been written, and I might still be in possession of at least a smidge of respect for the footballing profession. I might also still believe that old adage: never believe what you read in the newspapers. Because as we and all our readers now know, the reality is much more outrageous . . .

Fabulous

A huge thank you to my family and to my real friends (you know who you are). Darlings, without your support I wouldn't be where I am today – or half as fabulous XXX

Prologue

My name is Louise and I'm a full-time WAG.
During the past few years I thought I'd seen it all, but <u>nothing</u>
compares to your best friend's husband-to-be getting arrested
outside a brothel — on his wedding morning.
Poor Jodie. Such romantic plans — but such a sordid day.
Welcome to my world . . .

I tweaked the curtain and peered through the crack, blinking as the June sunshine poured through the huge windows, and took in the madness unfolding below.

A stream of TV satellite vans was snaking its way down the poplar-lined avenue. One after the other, ITV, BBC, Sky News, Five, even CNN satellites were gathering in the ancient courtyard and negotiating with the *Hello!* security team. Further back, I could see paparazzi zigzagging across the Abbey grounds, climbing up trees, over walls and one even hanging from a tree branch, all intent on getting the money shot.

'Oh. My. God.' I breathed deeply, and looked anxiously

back into the room. Jodie was pacing up and down in her champagne-coloured Vera Wang wedding dress, a flute of Laurent Perrier rosé in one hand, and a mobile phone in the other, her voice turning the air blue as she screamed insults down the phone.

'Do you really think I care what fucking colour the candles are at this point? You're the bloody wedding planner – sort it!'

She hung up and tossed her phone on to the bed. I turned around slowly and exhaled. 'Blimey, babe, it's mental outside! Totally mental.'

She joined me at the window, standing on tiptoes to avoid being spotted by the news crews below. 'Oh, I know, babe, it's getting worse. It's like bleeding Armageddon down there. Is nothing else going on in the world or something?'

Despite the four-letter tirade and her furious demeanour, Jodie was still stunning. Her distressed glamour contrasted vividly with the ugly scenes outside – and the unpleasant story being pieced together here in the hotel suite.

I gave her what I hoped was a reassuring smile. 'Nothing as interesting as you, babe, that's for sure. You always have been front-page news.' As I took one last look out the window, I saw a cameraman take a pop at one of the security guards, sadly he was no match for the burly guard, who promptly KO-ed the pap with a sharp left hook and stuck a boot in for good measure.

It was a far cry from how Jodie's wedding day had started.

I'd tiptoed through from my adjoining room in the converted Abbey at 7 a.m. to wake her up. Drinking a bottle of champagne, we'd sat in her room, me and her mum and dad, all perched on her bed with her still in it, sun streaming in through the window as it lit up the beautiful fourteenth-century bedroom inside.

Jodie had picked up the TV remote and her mum had given her a 'look', in that mum kind of way. 'God, Jodie, you are addicted to that bloody thing! Why don't you just lie back and enjoy some peace while you can? You won't get a minute to yourself once the magazine people start pulling you this way and that.'

Clearly, Jodie selling the exclusive pictures of the wedding for a record £1.3 million still jarred with her mum. She was miffed because security concerns, the number of celebrity guests required and the thought of how some of her long-lost relatives might behave had led to some eleventh-hour tactical 'un-inviting'.

Jodie had batted her hand dismissively. 'Come on, Mum, I've said all week that the only thing I want, is for it to not be raining. I'm just checking the forecast, don't worry, I'll keep it on mute.'

Her mum, looking slightly surreal in one of the pink Juicy Couture tracksuits Jodie had had customised with 'Team Bride' in silver script on the back, had raised her eyebrows at me. Her dad – already in his suit trousers, worn for the moment with an M&S sweatshirt – had looked out of the window at what was clearly a blazing hot June day and chuckled indulgently.

'I think you're all right on the rain front, darlin'.'

Suddenly, Gary's football mug shot filled the screen. 'Turn it up, babe,' I said excitedly. 'Your wedding's only gone and made the national news!'

Jodie scrabbled for the remote and the newsreader's clipped tones filled the room.

'. . . Gary Webber, who has been arrested on the morning of his wedding . . .'

We all stared at each other in shock.

'Hang on,' I said slowly. 'Did they just say he's been arrested?'

'. . . Webber was picked up outside a brothel in the early hours of the morning . . .'

I looked at Jodie. She'd gone as white as a sheet. Her mum reached for the remote and switched it on to mute again. Images of Jodie and Gary posing for pictures at some red-carpet do flicked silently across the screen. Jodie reached across the bed for her mobile. No one said anything – all we could hear was the dial tone of the phone Jodie was ringing. There was a click as it was answered.

'Jodie? What you doing phoning me? You should be getting all tarted up for your big day!' I cringed. Peter Quick, Gary's agent, was a right oily prat.

'Peter, what's happened to Gary?' said Jodie flatly.

Peter snorted with laughter. 'I dunno, Jodie. Last I heard

he was tucked up at home yesterday evening. Whassup? – Can't you live without him until this afternoon? There's only a few more hours to go until you've got him for life, babe!'

'It says on the TV news that he's been arrested,' said Jodie, again in a monotone voice.

There was a stunned silence. When Peter finally spoke, he was brisk and businesslike. 'Right, leave it with me.' He hung up.

Jodie stared at us blankly. 'Well, that's an interesting start to what's supposed to be the best day of my life. Jeez, I need a fag.'

Blimey, I thought to myself, was that all she was going to say? I shrugged helplessly. The hotel was all non-smoking – and the terms of her contract with *Hello!* meant she wasn't allowed outside this morning, in case she was photographed by a crafty pap. Hanging out of the window with a ciggie was clearly not an option. Jodie laughed shrilly. 'So what now?'

Her mum stood up decisively. 'Well, you, young lady, are going to get in the bath. Hair and make-up's arriving in half an hour, and until we know exactly what's happened, there's no point getting upset, is there? We might as well carry on as planned.'

She nodded at me over Jodie's head. 'Meanwhile, Louise here can try and find out from her young man what he knows about everything.'

I nodded, glad of something to do. 'Yeah, of course. I'll give Ad a call and get to the bottom of it. You know what the press are like – in the absence of a real story, they just make it up!' I said brightly, wanting desperately to believe it was true.

As her mum plucked Jodie's champagne glass out of her hand and ushered her towards the bathroom, I dialled Adam's number. I'd be lucky if he was up, I thought, even with the prospect of being Gary's best man in front of him.

To my surprise, Adam answered almost immediately.

'Adam, have you heard about Gary?' I whispered urgently.

'Yes, babe, calm down, it's OK – I know what's going on,' he said calmly. 'Gary's been arrested but we're gonna get him out.'

'Well, this is just fucking great, isn't it?' I hissed back. 'Adam, I don't know what world you're living in, but Gary getting arrested on his wedding day is definitely *not* OK. And nor' – I took a deep breath, trying to control my temper – 'is Jodie being left to find out about it on the frigging news! Why were we the last people to hear?' (As usual, I added under my breath.)

'He couldn't call her – he was only allowed one call so he rang me, the daft git. And he wanted me to call Raymond Moore straight away.'

My heart sank. Raymond Moore, PR guru and tabloid aficionado, known as 'the Silver Fox', had been involved in most of the biggest tabloid scandals over the past twenty years or so – and, allegedly, was responsible for burying even more to protect his clients. The fact that he was involved showed exactly how explosive this situation was.

'The cops've taken Gary's belt, his shoes, his phone – everything,' continued Adam. 'I was waiting to find out more before I called you. I'm just going down there now.'

'Not before you've told me what's going on.' I heard Adam sigh and I bristled. 'And I want the truth, Adam, not some sugar-coated fiancée-friendly version you and Gary've dreamed up.'

'I wouldn't do that!' he protested. 'Look, I heard that Gary was at home having dinner with his mum and dad when Mitch rang up, pissed out of his head, saying he couldn't be best man. Gary went off on one about it, saying Jodie was going to do her nut – but Mitch wouldn't have any of it. So Gary's dad says go and get him, bring him back, sober him up and he'll be right as rain tomorrow.'

I groaned with frustration. I should've known Mitch, Gary's wayward brother-in-law and the second best man, had something to do with this.

'Go on, Adam, I haven't got all day,' I said impatiently, then felt guilty for getting narky. It wasn't Adam's fault, after all.

Adam paused. 'So, Gary goes to Mitch's favourite dodgy cop-off joint and asks the bouncers if Mitch is in there, and they tell him he's left ten minutes before. Gal can tell they're lying, but while he's there arguing the toss, he hears this 'click

click click' and realises he's been done – someone's tipped off a journalist and a pap photographer. So Gal sees red, picks this photographer up by the scruff of his neck and punches his lights out. The journo calls the cops and Gary's hauled in for ABH. He's innocent, babe – well, of being in a brothel, at any rate.'

I sighed and rubbed my temples.

'All right, Adam – well you'd better get down there. Keep me posted.'

'Will do. And don't let Jodie speak to anyone until Raymond calls. Not even *Hello!* I love you!' He hung up.

'Love you too,' I said to the silent phone.

I trotted over to the bathroom door and knocked tentatively.

'Jodie? Babe?' I opened the door a crack. Through the steam I could see her reclining in the enormous free-standing bath, up to her neck in Molton Brown bubbles.

She smiled and raised her champagne glass to me. 'Only good news allowed, babe.'

I took a deep breath. 'Well, Adam reckons Gary hasn't done anything wrong other than – well, choose the wrong best man.'

Jodie snorted. 'I told him that weeks ago! That's why he ended up having two, of 'em!'

I smiled in what I hoped was a calming manner. 'Yes, I know. Well, it seems Mitch went out on a bender, and called Gary saying he was pulling out. Gary went off to the brothel to find him and he got himself arrested for lashing out at a pap.'

Jodie sneered derisively. 'How fucking convenient for Gary. Though I have to commend the boys on coming up with that story so quickly. It's almost plausible. I don't think Raymond bloody Moore could have done any better.'

I coughed nervously. 'Well, actually, I think Adam *has* called Raymond – apparently he's on the case with the papers. He says don't speak to anyone – not even *Hello!* – until he's called you.'

Jodie laughed bitterly. 'Oh does he indeed? Well, that's just fucking perfect, isn't it? After years of sniffing around for business, the Silver Fox finally gets his mitts on Gary – on his wedding day. It's almost bloody poetic.'

I sighed. 'Look, Jodie, maybe you should wait before you judge Gary too harshly. Adam wouldn't lie to me.'

Jodie looked at me pityingly. 'Look and learn, Louise, look and learn. The question isn't *if* they'll spin you a line at some point in their sorry little lives – it's *when*.'

Just then there was a knock at the door and Jodie's dad opened it to the hair and make-up girls – friends from Jodie's days as a national soap star – who rushed into the room, pulling their kit cases behind them.

'Omigod, you should see what's going on down there! It's totally unbelievable!'

'They reckon the TV people are all sending helicopters over and everything!'

'Where's Jodie, is she all right?'

Behind them, a porter was struggling under the weight of a huge delivery of flowers. Not, as I'd expected, our bouquets and the buttonholes, but two enormous posies from separate TV companies, obviously hoping to get an interview with the bride-to-be. I took them from him, and busied myself ordering room service coffees, getting the girls set up and the flowers out of the way.

Just as I was rummaging around to find a plug socket for the hair dryer, the bathroom door swung open. Jodie was stood there, wrapped only in a towel, another one swept around her head, turban-style.

Suddenly she darted across the room, and stood staring at the TV screen curiously.

'Oh my God. That's my first ever drama teacher!'

On the TV screen, a heavily made-up woman with henna-dyed hair and impressive jowls was talking self-importantly about Jodie. 'You know, Jodie's a lovely girl, and I'm sure she'll come through this,' she was saying earnestly.

Jodie shrieked, clutching at her towel turban. 'I haven't seen her for over twenty years! What the bleeding hell does she know about me?'

The camera moved over to someone else on the couch, a skinny, chavvy-looking woman with lank, dirty-blonde hair and a hangdog expression. Jodie let out another ear-piercing shriek.

'Ha! I went to school with her. She was the class bike . . . I haven't seen her for years either!' She grinned at me wickedly. 'Wow, time hasn't been kind to her, eh, babe?'

The woman was talking in a broad Cockney accent about what a lovely couple Gary and Jodie were, and how she wished she was going to the wedding. The bizarreness of the whole situation seemed to appeal to Jodie, and she cheered up a bit. Well, a lot actually. It was almost as though she realised how, in the grand scheme of how life dealt out luck, she hadn't done too badly. Not to mention the fact that she, not Gary, was now the centre of attention, even if her moment of glory had come at a price.

'Come on, Jodie, let's get going,' said the hair stylist firmly. 'I don't care whether you do go through with it or you don't go through with it. You're gonna have great hair for it.'

Jodie grinned and flopped into a chair. As the hair straighteners heated, and an assistant set about steaming our dresses, it seemed like a normal scene being played out on the morning of any girl's big day.

Suddenly Jodie's phone rang in her lap. She looked around at us, horrified. 'It's Gary!'

The make-up girl backed off and, after a moment's pause, Jodie answered it, looking round at us bullishly.

'What's going on, Gary?' she said, calmly but coldly, picking at an imaginary hair on her white towelling robe.

Gary's voice, tinny from the phone reception, rang out around the room.

'Jodie sweetheart, it's nothing like what they're saying . . .'

She looked up at the ceiling. 'Whatever it is, I just don't believe you. How can I? What kind of disrespectful twat does this to his bride on HER FUCKING WEDDING DAY?'

She stood up, scattering pins and curlers around her, and stalked around the room. Lunging for the nearest breakable – a crystal vase containing an elaborate flower arrangement – and flung it against the wall. We all flinched as it smashed into smithereens, sending grasses, petals and water flying.

'Aw, c'mon, darling, ask Adam. Ask Mitch.'

Jodie snorted. Her disregard for Mitch was well known.

'You know what really gets me, Gal?' she said dangerously. 'It's not the fact that you could be so bloody stupid on such an important day. It's not even being there in front of all our friends, family and GOD vowing till death us do part. It's the prospect of doing our first dance to 'Angels' when you've just spent the witching hour with a bunch of SLAGS!'

Gary's voice turned falsely bright. 'I swear on your life, I've done nothing wrong.'

Jodie's face darkened. 'Don't swear on *my* life, you selfish bastard,' she hollered. 'I know you're lying to me, just like you always do.'

Gary stuttered with panic. 'N-no, babe! I swear, not this time!'

I winced.

'WHAT DO YOU MEAN, NOT THIS TIME?' bellowed Jodie, her face almost purple with rage. 'For Christ's sake,

Gary, can you not even get an apology fucking right?'

There was a momentary pause, and then Gary spoke again, this time in a soothing tone. 'Look, come on, darling, we're getting married! We're gonna go party, we're gonna go off on honeymoon, have us a bit of sun and fun, come back and start a family. It's gonna be great!'

I shook my head silently. For Gary to pull the family card, I knew he must be desperate. Jodie'd been on at him for years to have kids.

'So I'm gonna get ready, and go to the church – I'll even be there on time!' Gary continued. No one laughed. Suddenly his voice broke. 'The thing is, darling – are *you* gonna be there?'

There was a long, long silence. Jodie carried on picking at her robe. Finally she looked up and round at us all. 'I just don't know, Gary. I haven't decided yet. You're just gonna have to turn up and see if I'm there, aren't you?' She chucked the phone at me dismissively. 'Right, who's for more champagne?'

I looked uncertainly at her dad. As usual, Jodie hadn't eaten a scrap but this must be at least her fourth glass of bubbly. He shrugged as if to say 'whatever makes her feel better'.

Phones were now ringing all over the room as journalists tried to get an exclusive interview. The *Hello!* team, who already had all our numbers in their contract, were persistently calling us one after the other.

Jodie's phone rang again. 'It's Tara,' I said, handing it to her, then immediately regretted it.

'Tara, don't cry – I haven't cried yet! You'll start me off!' she wailed. After only a couple of minutes she handed the phone back to me. 'Don't let me talk to anyone else, babe – I can't cope. Turn it off.'

'So, what you gonna do, babe?' I said lightly.

'I dunno,' said Jodie, looking at me uncertainly. 'What d'you reckon?'

I sighed. 'Babe – I hate to say it, but I think you've got to believe Gary. Ad swears he's done nothing wrong. Think about all those misunderstandings that happen thanks to the press.'

I twiddled my own Tiffany diamond solitaire engagement ring and thought of all the dramas that me and Adam had been through – and survived. Just.

'Maybe it's not his fault?'

She looked at me sagely. 'Or maybe it is. Y'know, babe, that's the difference between you and me. You're a believer in happy ever after. I've got used to looking at the worst-case scenario. Life with Gary has taught me that.'

I shook my head at her sadly. 'But he loves you, Jodie, and you love him, don't you? That's all that matters.'

She snorted derisively. 'Babe, if only. There are other things that exist outside your cloud-cuckoo land of hearts and flowers. Like self-respect, and pride. There comes a point when even the big houses and the flash cars and' – she looked

14

around her defeatedly – 'the fancy weddings don't compensate for losing those. Or at least, they shouldn't.'

'But you don't have to lose any of it, babe. Just believe in the man you love.'

I looked back into the room at our dresses hanging up in the corner. Her gorgeous strapless one with swathes of ivory taffeta, and my dark red one, the exact same colour as the velvety red roses that would make up her bouquet.

She followed my gaze, and wandered over to her dress, fingering the fabric thoughtfully. She turned to me, touching her sparkling engagement ring, an odd, far-away look in her eyes.

'I'll tell you what, babe. I'll get my make-up done, put my dress on, get gorgeous and see how I feel. That's what it's all about, isn't it?'

Suddenly I felt sick, but nodded mutely. 'Yes, babe. That's what it's all about.'

Chapter 1
Kick Off

The close-up of the sports presenter flicked over to live footage of the Reebok Humber Park stadium. On the TV screen, Adam – my Adam! – stood suited and booted, all cute and clean-shaven and looking a bit bashful, surrounded by men whose wide, wolfish smiles seemed at odds with their sombre dark blue suits and ties. Blinking in the glare of the flashbulbs, Adam was holding up a Leeds City club T-shirt for the cameras. To his left, his new boss went to shake his hand and Adam, a bit bewildered, let go of the shirt and nearly dropped it.

I giggled and turned to my mum next to me on the sofa. 'Oh, bless, Mum, look at him. He's all nervous!'

Mum smiled and patted me on the knee as she got up to go. 'Well, love, he'd better get used to the attention. There's no more quiet life for you two now!' She bent over to kiss me on the head. 'We'd better get off – I need to get your father's tea on.' She turned to my dad, sitting on the opposite sofa, still engrossed in the sports news. The story had now moved on to a test match and Dad seemed totally absorbed. 'Come on, Malcolm. Lou, we'll see you tomorrow at some point, no doubt.'

I smiled up at her as she bustled off and stretched contentedly out into the space she'd left on the sofa. Mum and Dad only lived a ten-minute drive away from our three-bed new-build semi on a posh new estate just outside of town, and popped in most days. Despite Adam's success as a midfielder for Cardiff Rovers, and our lovely new home, we still only lived around the corner from all our family and old friends, so even though people might assume our lives had totally changed when Adam signed for the club eighteen months ago, in reality we were still nearly the same Adam and Louise we'd always been.

I say nearly, because obviously the money had changed things a little bit. I still couldn't get my head around it, really. Our families had never had much – not that we were poor or anything, but they scrimped and saved like anyone else. When we started going out with each other at school, neither me nor Adam had ever had any cash to speak of – just the odd few quid from my Saturday job at the beautician's. Adam was always too busy with training and try-outs to get a Saturday job. But then, just as I went full-time, he got signed up and it seemed we didn't have to worry any more. Not that we were mad with our money – but it meant when we moved out of home, we could afford to buy our own place instead of renting a poky little flat like most of our friends. We found our dream house – only small, but it was really exciting, and to me it was all I had ever wanted. Me, Adam and our own perfect, lush little home. We got to choose all the furniture for it, and not even by saving up madly and buying things on the never-never like our parents – we just bought it all outright. If, say, we wanted a table, or a new sofa, I'd be like 'Can we afford it?' And Adam would laugh and say, 'Well, yeah, babe – let's get it!'

It was a bit beyond me still – but it wasn't just the house. It really did seem that anything we wanted, we could have. One minute I was going to work by bus, and the next minute Adam gave me this car – a brand-new Vauxhall Corsa from the team's sponsors. Instead of going into New Look and just choosing one top, I could now go into Warehouse and Miss Selfridge and choose anything I liked (even though at the till I was always scared someone was going to tell me my card wouldn't work or that I was buying too much). I'd even sneak a couple of bits in for my best mate from school, Sara, so she didn't feel left out! Me and Sara'd known each other since we were three, and she was so excited for me. And we started going out to restaurants every now and again, and instead of worrying about how much, say, a steak was, we could just have it – and a bottle of champagne too! I couldn't stop pinching myself, even eighteen months on.

It wasn't just the material stuff, though – me and Adam

were really in love, and though I'd often get a 'look' when I told salon clients I was living with a footballer, he was nothing like the players you read about in the papers. Mostly Adam just liked coming home and snuggling down in front of a DVD with me, or having a family Sunday lunch round his mum's house. People always said we were dead cute together. And it was true: not only did we look like we belonged together – both tall, me with long brown hair and blue eyes and him with slightly darker hair and dark brown Labrador eyes – but we were so obviously in love it seemed to be infectious, and you'd often catch people looking at us and smiling to themselves. I still worked part-time in the beauty salon (not Saturdays any more – they were match days!) and was doing a sports therapy course. I loved testing out my new massage techniques on him after college. But most of all I loved keeping the house nice for him and making our own little nest. He'd leave little romantic Post-it notes all over the house for me, and buy me flowers and stuff. It was just all so perfect.

I sat up and hugged my knees, with a sudden pang of – I wasn't sure. Nerves? Excitement? Fear? Because now, Adam had been signed to a major club up north – the biggest break he'd had yet in his career. It meant he was going to be playing in the Premiership, and he was going to be earning mega-bucks. It also meant moving our perfect life somewhere else, away from our family and schoolfriends, away from Sara and our girly chats, and away from our cosy little house. I looked around the living room longingly and took in the squashy Ikea sofas, the Habitat coffee table, the Marks and Spencer's side lamps and the Laura Ashley curtains and matching cushions. I loved this house – silly, but we always said it loved us too – and the thought of leaving it made me feel unbearably and unfathomably sad. Adam had said we could keep it, but that just seemed crazy – I mean, who has two houses at the same time? It wasn't as if Cardiff was a place for a holiday home – and whenever we came back to visit, we could stay with our parents, after all.

Suddenly my mobile rang, my latest Sugababes ringtone overriding the background murmur of the TV. It was Adam. My heart leapt.

'Ad! How are you, babe? We've just been watching you on the news!'

'Hiya, gorgeous, I'm cool, I'm cool. How was I? How'd I look? I felt like a right prat with all those football bigwigs around me!'

'You were great, baby, just great. Mum and Dad came round to see you too – we're all so proud of you!'

'I nearly dropped the bloody shirt. What an idiot. Did it look stupid?'

'Babe! No one noticed!' I cringed at the fib. 'You looked like the superstar footballer I know you are – and now the whole world is gonna know it too!'

'That's the whole point, Lou,' snapped Adam. I flinched – I wasn't used to him being mean to me. 'The whole world *was* watching. Well, six million people at least. If *you* noticed, you can guarantee someone else did!'

I flushed bright red. Why was he being like this?

'Babe, honestly. I hardly even saw it – and no one will have been looking at you as closely as me! Everyone else will have just been looking at you lined up alongside all those important people and being dead impressed by you!'

Adam grunted. I took a deep breath – he was obviously just nervous and needing some TLC.

'As if anyone's going to even clock a little thing like that when you've just signed a mega-bucks deal for a Premiership team! You're one of the top footballers in the country – no, the world, now. You're living every bloke's dream out there, babe!'

I felt Adam relax over the phone.

'Good. Because this is it, babe. This is the big time. And it's gonna be everything we've ever dreamed of.'

I reached the hotel in Leeds flustered and close to tears after having got lost a couple of times. It was right in the middle of the city centre, and I found all the one-way systems and dual carriageways really confusing. I'd only ever really driven around Cardiff before. It didn't help that all my bags stacked up in the back of the car meant my view through the rear window wasn't the clearest . . .

Not sure of where to leave the car, I pulled up outside the imposing front entrance and a man in a top hat and tails approached the driver's door. I opened the window, startled.

He smiled warmly and doffed his hat. 'Madam. Are you a guest here?'

I smiled back distractedly. 'No. I mean, yes. I'm going to be living here for a couple of months. My boyfriend is already here.'

I cringed. I sounded naive and young even to my own ears!

He smiled. 'Well then, madam, if you'd be so kind as to give me your keys, I can arrange for your luggage to be brought in and for the valet to park your car for you.' He looked over my shoulder at the piles of bags behind me (I hadn't had enough cases for all my stuff, so some of my bits were packed into carrier bags).

I smiled, suddenly relieved. 'That would be great, thanks.' Handing him the keys, I practically skipped through the revolving doors and across the marble floor to the grand mahogany reception desk. A five-star hotel – and it was home for the next few weeks! How cool was *that*?

Adam had been up here for a couple of weeks, tying up legal issues and getting fitted with kit and stuff. I hadn't wanted to let down the salon at the last minute so had worked a couple of weeks' notice before leaving Cardiff. Ad's phone calls were full of how amazing the hotel was – the gym, the pool and the people. I hardly got a word in at all! It was apparently not just the hub of all club meetings and business deals, but a celebrity favourite that drew movers and shakers from almost every industry. He kept texting me with famous faces he'd seen (I hadn't heard of half the people, but I got excited for him regardless!).

But now, my excitement didn't last very long. The receptionist couldn't find me on the system and there was no record anywhere that I was expected.

Close to tears again, I tried to call Adam. The call went straight through to voice mail – not surprisingly. Pre-season training had started in earnest, and he was working out every waking moment to make sure he was as fit as possible for his first few sessions with his new team-mates. He seemed a bit paranoid about fitting in and measuring up to everyone else. I guess I could understand it – I mean, he was playing with all his present-day heroes now. I'd got here early on purpose – I'd wanted to surprise him by being in the room and unpacked and settled by the time he got back, instead of arriving mid-evening like he was expecting. He'd promised he'd make sure the hotel knew I was coming, though.

I turned back to the receptionist. 'Look, please. Our room was reserved by Leeds City Football Club. They know I'm arriving at some point today, just not the exact time. You must have a number for the person who booked it?'

The receptionist shook her head pleasantly but firmly. 'I'm so sorry, but our policy is not to let unauthorised persons into rooms booked by the club. As I'm sure you can imagine,' she looked at me knowingly, 'we get quite a few young women trying to find their way into footballers' bedrooms.' She held a hand up apologetically as I opened my mouth to object. 'Now I'm sure you are just exactly who you say you are, but if you wouldn't mind waiting in the lounge until Mr Jones gets back, I'm sure we can have all this cleared up in no time. We can look after your . . .' she cleared her throat as she looked at the tower of bags precariously piled on the brass luggage trolley, 'baggage until then.'

I glared at her angrily, powerless to do anything but what she said. In a futile act of fury, I pulled several of the carrier bags off the trolley as if to show I didn't trust anyone with them, and stomped through to the lounge, where I flopped into a high-backed armchair, blood boiling.

As I sat, furiously texting Adam about my plight, I was aware of someone staring down at me. I looked up and saw a stocky, rugged-looking man standing in front of me. He was black, in his mid-thirties and wearing expensive baggy jeans, white T-shirt and designer tracksuit top and trainers. Although I was sure I recognised him, I couldn't place him. 'You don't look like someone who's happy to be here,' he said kindly, eyes twinkling. 'Someone should tell the manager – I'm sure it's against hotel policy.'

I snorted angrily. 'It's because of hotel policy I'm here in the first place,' I ranted. 'My boyfriend has been here for a few weeks, the club knows I'm coming, but just because their flaming computer system hasn't got the right information on it, they won't let me into my room. Or any of my stuff,' I finished lamely, waving a weak hand at the bags that surrounded me, flinching as I noticed that at least two were from the local corner shop in Cardiff. Class. 'I look like some kind of bloomin' bag lady!'

The man laughed. 'You must be Adam Jones's missus. It's Louise, right?' I looked up at him, startled that he knew of me. 'I'm Gary Webber, one of his team-mates.'

'Oh, right – of course,' I said, suddenly feeling really stupid as I realised who he was. Gary Webber was one of Adam's idols – he had been around for ever, but even though pundits kept predicting his retirement, he always seemed to produce amazing form just in time, and get re-signed. 'Sorry, I didn't recognise you.'

He laughed even louder at that. 'Oh, no. Oooooh, no.' I gazed up at him, puzzled. He was cracking up, and shaking his head as he looked at me.

'What?' I said, frowning and suddenly feeling really self-conscious all over again.

'I've just realised how well you're going to get on with my other half, Jodie,' he said, still chuckling. 'I think me and Adam could be in for some trouble. I must tell her to look out for you at the match on Saturday. I'm off now, but I'm going to get you a drink before I go and have a word at reception on my way out. Should all be sorted in no time. See you Saturday, gorgeous.'

With that, he gave me a wink, flicked the top of my head affectionately and sauntered off. I watched him wander down the bar, flabbergasted. Well, at least some people around here were friendly!

Within minutes I had a flute of champagne fizzing away in front of me, a bowl of olives, and a shiny door card sitting snugly in its cardboard wallet. Hallelujah! I took a deep sip of the champagne and got up, suddenly feeling much happier. So what if it had all got off to an awful start? It could only get better from now on. I quickly sent my mum a text about meeting Gary. She had to tell my dad – he'd be well impressed! Then, gathering my bags around me, I stood up, leaving the rest of my drink. Wouldn't do to greet Adam stinking of booze, after all . . .

Smiling to myself, I walked over to the lift and tried to press the call button without putting any of my bags down, but failed. As a trainer spilled out and landed on my foot, I swore under my breath. However, before I could put the bags down, a tanned, toned, muscular forearm reached over my shoulder and pressed the button for me. I turned round in surprise to say thanks, but shock made me speechless. Before me, dressed in white T-shirt, lemon Pringle jumper, grey combat trousers and trainers was Jonnie Renton. *The* Jonnie Renton, no less – club captain, up-and-coming England player and heartthrob of all my friends back home. Instead of thanks, no noise came out of my mouth, and so I stood dumbfounded, gaping gormlessly like a goldfish.

'Been shopping?' he said, giving me a sexy wonky smile and nodding at the bags.

'No – I'm, er – I'm just moving in,' I stammered, praying for the lift to arrive.

His eyes danced in amusement. 'Oh, right. Don't you generally need removal men for that?'

I laughed awkwardly, feeling like a right prat. 'Yes – no – I mean . . . I'm Adam Jones's girlfriend, Louise. We're staying here until we find somewhere more permanent.'

'Oh, right!' he repeated. There it was again, that wonky smile. I felt myself starting to get flustered and my nervous rash was threatening to appear at my throat. 'Then no doubt my wife Tara will be in touch with you very soon. She takes her role as head of the wives and girlfriends very seriously. She's probably already sorting you out store discounts as we speak!' I looked over his shoulder nervously. How would it look if someone saw me chatting to Jonnie? I'd heard how possessive some footballers' wives could be (it always sounded a bit OTT to me, but who was I to judge!). Where was the bloody lift?

As if by magic, the lift appeared and I gratefully stepped into it, dragging the bags with me. I looked up to thank Jonnie, and to my horror he was leaning on the door to prevent it shutting.

'So where are you thinking of looking to live?' he continued conversationally. 'I guess it's early days for you, but we've been here a while now and can probably give you some pointers. I mean, what's your priority? Good nightlife, good schools, proximity to the club? There're loads of great places within—'

I looked at him in horror as he chattered away. This couldn't be happening to me. I was standing in a lift with a load of corner-shop carrier bags and a nervous rash, all dishevelled after a five-hour drive and a row with reception, and Jonnie Renton was propping the door open and advising me on property?

Jonnie shifted on to the other leg and the lift door started to close. He stuck his foot in to stop it, but it kept closing. In panic, I shoved one of the carrier bags against it, which worked – to a point. The lift door now was opening and shutting insistently on Jonnie's foot and my carrier bag, while he, seemingly unperturbed, carried on chatting and smiling his wonky smile. Suddenly he stopped and looked searchingly at me.

'Look, Louise, why don't I help you carry these up to your room?'

He leant forward as if to get in the lift. I was in a quandary. What if someone saw him getting in with me? What would they think? I wasn't sure why, but again I had the instinctive feeling that it wouldn't be good.

'No! I mean, thanks so much. But you know, I'll be fine – and Adam'll be back soon, and I really want to get showered and . . .' I stopped short. What on earth was I babbling on about?

He winked at me, and I thought I was going to pass out. 'No worries, babe.' He stepped out of the lift and the doors shut behind him. I had leant back against the wall and was heaving an exaggerated sigh of relief when all of a sudden the doors only went and opened again! Jonnie was still standing there, still smiling that ridiculously sexy smile. 'See you Saturday.' The doors shut again – this time, for good.

I couldn't ever remember being so relieved.

Adam and I lay on our king-size bed, surrounded by bags, clothes, toiletry bags and room-service debris. Unfortunately, the bed was the only thing that was king-size – the room was tiny, and with both of us and all our stuff in it, on top of the bed was the only place you could actually move.

He leaned over and touched my face softly. 'I'm sorry again it was such a trauma for you getting in here,' he said. 'I really did tell them to expect you.'

I rolled over and gave him a tender kiss on the lips. 'I know that, silly. Anyway, this lot has made up for it!' I giggled as I looked at the unfinished plates of Thai prawns, dim sum and sushi, and the bottle of champagne, huge bunch of flowers and cute card that Adam had left waiting for me in the room, telling me how much he loved me and how much he'd missed me whilst we'd been apart.

He kissed me back and looked searchingly at me.

'I'd never want to hurt or upset you, babe, you know that, don't you? You know I really love you?'

I looked at him, confused. 'Of course I do, Ad. What's wrong?'

He frowned and lay back, looking up at the ceiling.

'Nothing. It's just hard, y'know. The rest of the players are so good. I'm worried I won't keep up. I'm worried I won't fit in.'

I hugged him tightly. 'Babe, you're just as good as them if not better! And of course you're going to fit in. You'll be one of them before you know it.'

I didn't realise just how right I was.

Chapter 2

'OK, Jodie, I'll see you in half an hour.'

I ended the call to Jodie, pulled off my new Marni blouse and threw it on the floor in frustration. I looked around our hotel room at the chaos surrounding me and felt hot tears well up in my eyes. Clothes were everywhere – spilling out of drawers, hanging over the wardrobe doors, and strewn over the as-yet-unmade bed. Under the discarded outfits, piles of neatly folded T-shirts and jumpers jostled for floor space with designer shopping bags and shoe boxes. How on earth was I meant to pull together a look in this kind of chaos?

I sat down on the bed, defeated, as the incessant chatter of morning TV enveloped me and threatened to drive me even further over the edge. I was loving our new life, I really was. Adam was doing really well at the club, I'd got two new friends, Tara and Jodie, and I wanted for nothing. Clothes, shoes, beauty treatments – I'd even started having my nails done instead of doing them myself (the biggest kind of splurge, considering I was a trained beautician!).

But – and it sounds really spoilt – I was missing our little house in Cardiff. Constantly. I was fed up with the four walls of the hotel room and I'd had enough of Adam telling me off every time I went shopping, or when I went back to Cardiff and brought back something that reminded me of home. 'Don't buy any more clothes!' was the last thing he'd say before he went out to the club every morning – not because he was being tight with his money, but because there was no room to put anything else! I was sick of living in one tiny room, sick of spending loads of time on my own every day watching boring daytime TV meant for housewives, and sick of eating room service. I mean, sometimes you just want beans on toast, don't you? I'd even grown to resent all the fabulous people hanging out on my 'doorstep' – I couldn't nip to Sainsbury's for some normal-price water or some magazines without staff and guests knowing my business. Yep, I'd had enough all right – even if our current dose of five-star luxury was all being paid for by the club.

Although Adam wouldn't admit it, I knew he'd had enough too. We'd been here six weeks now, and although he got out of the hotel more than me, for training, it was still his home once he got back after his nutritionally controlled lunch at the club every day (the club insisted the team ate in the posh café there so they could make sure they were eating all the right stuff – I thought it would be more helpful just to tell us girls what to cook, but we didn't seem to figure very much in the grand scheme of things – it was all about the boys). I could tell it was getting on top of Adam. Not only that, but he felt like he was living under Big Brother. In the past when he felt a bit low, he'd always liked to sit in front of the telly with milk and cookies – but as it turned out, with the club paying our bills, they were also checking out what we were eating, drinking, and doing. Chocolate biscuits weren't on Adam's diet plan – so he'd had his knuckles rapped, good and proper.

And there was another pressure. Our all-expenses-paid time was running out – and fast. The club had promised to pay for bed and board for two months, when we would either have to move out into our own place or start paying our own hotel bills. The problem was, I hadn't got a clue where or how to start looking. It might sound stupid, but it was really scary having to find the perfect place for us to live in a town I didn't know. The club employed a 'fixer' to help new players find somewhere to live, but there were several other new players who needed homes – including two foreigners – and because Adam was a new, relatively unknown UK player, we were way down the waiting list for assistance.

I was just no good at this house-hunting thing. I didn't have a clue what the 'right' kind of place was for a successful footballer like my Adam. So instead of getting out and looking around properties in the mornings like I was meant to, I'd wander the streets miserably for a while before heading back to the hotel to wait until Adam finished training so he could come with me. Like the other footballers, he normally liked to have a little nap after training, but with the room in such a state and no prospect of finding a home any time soon, he was now having to spend most afternoons traipsing around town, going from house to house with me. It wasn't doing our relationship any favours and we'd started bickering for the first time ever – even about what houses we liked!

And for once, not even a phone call to Mum and Dad was any help – I'd tried asking their advice but as far as they were concerned, as long as you had a roof over your head and a manageable mortgage, you'd done all right. And that wasn't even half the challenge I was facing. The problem was, it wasn't even like I had two or three different properties to choose from. It was a huge city, with an old town, a modern centre and lots of different areas surrounding it. And some of those areas were cool, and some weren't. Listening to everyone, it seemed *where* you lived was even more important than what you lived in! And in some careers, you could buy an eight-bedroom mansion and others a two-bedroom penthouse for the same money. It was so confusing – I couldn't work out which was which, or what would suit Adam best. There was the flash city-centre bit, next to all the bars and restaurants, which seemed to be all dead modern blocks of flats and apartments. That was a good area, if a bit busy – but Adam seemed quite taken with it. Then there was a more leafy, older-looking bit that had older townhouses set back from the road a bit but with small gardens and metered parking. To be honest, it didn't really do it for me – why would you want all the bad things about living in the city with none of the good? But again, Adam said he wouldn't mind being near where it all went on. Then there were all these other suburban areas with huge gated residences – three or four modern houses behind big electronic iron gates, massive gardens and about six bathrooms per house! I quite liked those, but they seemed awfully grown-up and a bit scary. Also, each of the areas was meant to be better for something – one had good schools, another was nearer to the club, another one was near to the golf course. It was all just dead confusing.

Even the girls' intervention hadn't really helped. Tara had rung me earlier in the week wanting to know how I was getting on, and when I'd admitted I was as far off as ever, she'd stepped in and taken charge. 'Right, babe, get yourself over to mine tomorrow morning. This is ridiculous – we're going to get this sorted,' she'd ordered. I must admit, I'd breathed a sigh of relief, and called Jodie to let her know – I didn't want her to think I was going off with Tara or anything. So the next morning, I'd picked Jodie up in my zippy new red Audi A3 (we'd had to give the Corsa back when we'd left Cardiff) and sped around to Tara's.

'So, babe, first off we need to write a list of priorities for the area you want to end up in,' Tara had decreed, as I looked helplessly at the sheets of property details spread around me on the kitchen table. 'Of course, there are some areas that just nobody would dream of moving to, so we can strike those off before we've even started,' she added, ripping up a pile of papers without even reading them. 'Then we need to get some viewing appointments sorted. You can get a feel for the city as we drive around.'

I looked up at her gratefully. She made it all sound so easy!

'I don't think you can dismiss half of Leeds that easily,' objected Jodie. 'Just because you don't like an area doesn't mean Louise will feel the same.'

'Jodie, it's all very well for you to make a statement by moving to a more down-at-heel area on the basis that it's cool and up-and-coming,' said Tara starchily. 'But Louise isn't well known like you, and needs to build a profile. She needs to be careful of what messages she sends out.'

I put my head down and carefully studied the sheet I was holding. Clearly with both Jodie and Tara along for the ride, this wasn't going to be as straightforward as I'd hoped.

Once Tara had rewritten my lists according to what she thought we needed (Jodie had tutted, but I was frankly just glad someone was taking charge), booked two or three appointments, and her kids were happily eating the lunch that the nanny had carefully prepared, we all piled back into my car and drove out to the first viewing – a big five-bedroom house in the suburbs.

'Are you sure about this?' I said uncertainly, checking in my rear-view mirror as I pulled out on to the dual carriageway. 'It seems really big for just me and Adam.'

Tara sighed impatiently. 'Louise, it's not just about you and Adam, is it? You have to consider buying somewhere for you both to grow into. It's in a very classy area and close to some great schools.'

Jodie leant forward from the back seat. 'Watch out, babe – she'll have you planning two point four kids before you know it!'

Tara gave her a frosty look. 'Well, family is very important in football,' she said snippily. 'Which is something you and Gary might like to think about whenever you decide it's time to grow up.'

Jodie patted Tara on the shoulder. 'All in good time, Tara, babe, all in good time.'

I smiled to myself. Tara and Jodie might be the best of friends, but Jodie's fame and effusive self-confidence were a constant irritant to Tara, and didn't sit easily with her role as Chief WAG.

Just then, a car pulled into the outside lane behind us, and drove right up the rear of my car, flashing its lights. Instinctively, I went to brake.

Tara looked in the passenger-door wing mirror. 'Don't slow down, Lou! He's got a camera. It's a bloody paparazzi. He must have followed us from home.'

In the back seat, I was dimly aware of Jodie ducking – I

figured it was to hide, but I could hear her reapplying her lippie in her compact.

'What should I do?' I said to Tara in panic. Tara, too, had her head down.

'It's OK, babe, pull into the inside lane and let them get past,' called Jodie. 'Once they see we're not playing ball, they'll be off. Bet they can't believe their luck, getting both me and Tara in the car at the same time!'

'I knew we should have come out in your car, Jodie!' piped up Tara, still with her head on her knees. 'All this, just because you wanted to have a drink at lunchtime!'

The photographer's car pulled alongside us, and out of the corner of my eye I could see a camera being held out of the window and snapping away. The photographer was shouting out Tara and Jodie's names as we sped along. It was dead scary.

I spotted a slip road coming up. 'Shall I take the next exit?' I yelled desperately.

'Yes, do it!' shouted back Tara. 'But don't indicate first or they'll follow!' As we pulled off, I breathed a sigh of relief, but my heart was racing and my hands were clammy. If that was what being famous was all about, I was pretty glad to be a nobody!

When I'd told Adam about all the properties from that afternoon, he hadn't seemed keen. Mind you, I'd only had about five seconds flat to tell him, in between him coming home from training and shooting off out again. I frowned. Before, I'd loved the start of the season, when Adam had finished his long and punishing pre-season training and had a bit more free time. Generally he'd have had Mondays and maybe even Tuesdays off, and most afternoons, and we'd have got to spend loads of time together. But now he was spending most of his time at the club doing extra training and then going straight out on 'bonding' nights with his team-mates. I couldn't blame him for trying to fit in – but although he was dead busy, he had people fussing around his every move, so he was always occupied without ever having to think for himself. In fact, for the players, being at the club was a bit like being at school. From the moment they arrived at ten in the morning, they had everything planned for them. Their kit was always washed and laid out, they'd have their own towels with labels on – they even had pegs with their names on! And with the club flunkies doing stuff like ordering suits for him and making his social arrangements, I felt a bit left out and – well – lonely.

I shook myself. What an old moaner. I should be counting my blessings, not sitting about whingeing! I glanced at my Tag watch – my gorgeous twentieth birthday present from Adam – and looked around despairingly at the discarded heaps of clothes. I was going to be late and still had no idea what I was going to wear. I know it seemed brattish with all that to choose from, but it was hard keeping up with the other girls. Tara and Jodie were always turned out so nicely, and amongst the others there was real pressure not just to look good, but to have the latest stuff and put it together properly *and* look good. Which was harder than it sounds . . .

Decisively, I pulled on a pair of boot-cut Citizens of Humanity jeans, a black scoop-necked Gap T-shirt and a black blazer with gold buttons from H&M. Classic and comfortable – it wasn't quite the cutting-edge glamour I was after, but at least I'd look good. And we were only meeting for a quick bite of lunch, after all.

Grabbing my black patent Miu Miu bag and slipping on my zebra-print Pierre Hardy wedges, I picked my way gingerly out of the room. As I opened the door, I felt my phone vibrate with a voice-mail message. It must have come through when I was on the phone to Jodie earlier. As I listened, my heart lifted. The property fixer was free that afternoon, and he had a flat to show me he thought was right up my street. Maybe now, finally, we'd find somewhere to call home.

'I don't care how much it costs. We need to get that bed up north, into an underground car park and up to the sixteenth floor. I thought you said you were specialists?'

I paced back and forth outside the apartment block and kicked a granite flowerbed in frustration.

'Look, I honestly don't care how you do it – I've given you the number of the concierge, you'd be better off speaking to him. But whatever happens, we need that bed here tomorrow!'

I hung up and looked down the road expectantly. Adam was on his way, straight from training, so we could both walk into our new home – our new home! – for the first time together. Trust the bed men to spoil the moment. Our specially made orthopaedic water bed was proving more hassle to move than all the rest of our stuff put together. I'd had to find a specialist removal company, and even then they were creating a fuss over how to get it up to our new penthouse flat. Of course, I'd had no help from the club. The minute I'd clapped eyes on our new place – I got butterflies as I thought about us finally moving into it – I'd been left to arrange everything, from signing the rental agreement to moving all our stuff up from Cardiff. It was dead stressful – but at least it had given me something to do. And now – finally – we were moving in!

I jumped up and down excitedly as I saw Adam's black Hummer appear around the bend. He honked noisily and I ran across to greet him. He was grinning from ear to ear, and when he jumped down from the driver's seat he picked me up and spun me around before giving me a huge kiss. His eyes were shining and he looked happier than I'd seen him for weeks. I hoped he stayed that way. This was the first time he'd seen the flat, so I was nervous as well as dead excited. It was a brand-new penthouse on a gated development just outside the city centre – a bit of a drive from the training ground or Humber Park, but Adam reckoned it was better for us to be near all the shops and the nightlife as we were getting to know everyone, rather than further out of town.

He grabbed my hand and squeezed it hard. 'What are you waiting for, babe, let's go check out our new pad. I'll race you!'

I squealed and tried in vain to catch him up as he sprinted towards the glass-fronted doors. Of course, he hadn't got a key yet, so there was no danger of him getting to the flat first – but I wanted to be there to show him in. Slightly out of breath from the sprint, I swiped the key card and entered our special code and showed Adam down the spotlit, carpeted reception hall to the lift at the end. He looked puzzled.

'Just the one lift? I thought you said we had our own private one?'

I smiled smugly. 'We do. Just wait and see.'

'OK, Sarah Beeny, I believe you.' As the lift door opened, Adam pushed me playfully in the small of the back and blew a raspberry on my neck.

The buttons shown on the lift only went up to fifteen, and I could tell Adam was still wondering what on earth was going on. 'So, Mr Jones, once you're in here, you have to press floor fifteen, but then use this little key here, and it'll take us up to floor sixteen.' I looked at him proudly. Adam grunted as the lift lurched upwards, but I could tell he was impressed.

Once at the sixteenth floor, the lift doors opened, and even though I knew what was waiting there, I still gasped in awe. To our right were ten carpeted stairs leading up to a mezzanine floor and the front door of the penthouse, and hanging in front of us in the stairwell was my surprise housewarming present to Adam – a six-foot framed photograph of us both, taken at his sister's wedding the previous summer. It had been a searingly hot sunny June day, and the heat had made it look almost soft-focus. Adam was looking down at me tenderly, and I was looking at the camera, squinting a little against the sun. We both looked young, a bit vulnerable, and utterly in love – and it was our favourite ever picture.

'Awww, babe,' said Adam, obviously touched and a bit lost for words. I could have sworn I saw tears in his eyes. But I was too excited to waste any more time over the picture. We both climbed the stairs to the front door, our feet padding on the carpet as if we were already inside – which in a way, I suppose, we were. The door was a grand black Edwardian-style affair, flanked on both sides by a round box hedge in a silver pot. At eye level, faux-Grecian flames 'burned' excitedly on either side, as if pleased to finally welcome us.

I gave the key to Adam – my hands were shaking too much to turn it in the lock! – and he swept me up and carried me squealing over the threshold. As I kicked in mock protest, Adam, still holding me, looked around the open-plan living and dining room, taking in the white leather sofas, the smoked-glass dining table, the seven-foot suspended aquarium, the leopardskin chaise longue and the state-of-the-art plasma screen and stereo system. I could tell he was pleased.

'Well, say something!' I shrieked impatiently.

Adam swung me around again and growled passionately, 'Where's the bedroom? Bed or no bed, we need to christen our new pad!'

I shook some KP nuts into a bowl and placed them on one of the side tables, stopping on the way to admire the pink Stargazer lilies we hired someone to arrange around the flat for us every three days. I still hadn't got over the novelty of having fresh flowers all the time – nor, I thought with a giggle, the hassle it was letting anyone into the apartment! Adam called it Fort Knox – and what with the CCTV, the intercom, the complicated entry system, not to mention a grilling from the security guard every time someone he didn't know tried to get in, it did feel a bit like that.

I hummed contentedly as I opened a packet of M&S breaded prawns, laid them out on a baking tray and checked the oven temperature. All ready to go.

Adam appeared from the bedroom, his skin still shower-damp and smelling of freshly applied aftershave.

'So, all set for the party of the year?' he said, kissing my head. 'I could murder a beer.'

He opened the door to our bright red Smeg fridge and took out a bottle of Stella, using the novelty 'goal' bottle-opener my dad had given him the previous Christmas. I laughed and tried to grab the bottle off him. 'We're having

Laurent Perrier rosé, Ad – I've got the glasses out ready and everything!'

He lifted the bottle up, expertly avoiding my grasp, and with the other hand took a handful of crisps from a bowl on the side. 'I've got time for a cheeky one, haven't I? I don't know why you've bothered with the food, it's not as if the girls will touch it.'

'Jodie won't,' I agreed. 'But she'll make out she's had loads. And it's only a few nibbles, anyhow – if they weren't there for her to ignore, she'd feel uncomfortable about it. Anyway, the rate you're going, there'll be none left,' I said pointedly.

He didn't seem to hear me. Instead, he was looking around the living room, frowning. 'D'you think those sofas are a bit naff?' he mused, almost to himself. He turned to me sharply. 'Louise, you haven't gone and made us look like pikeys, have you?'

I was stunned and speechless. 'Adam! You love those sofas!'

But again, he wasn't listening. He picked up one of the champagne flutes and twizzled it. 'And are these the best glasses we've got? We're not in Cardiff now, you know!'

I couldn't understand what he was on about. Why the sudden change of mood? But before I had time to respond, the intercom buzzer rang, and I checked the CCTV before speaking into it. 'It's cool, Jim, these are our guests for the evening. You can let them up.'

I watched on the CCTV camera as the distorted black-

and-white images of Tara, Jonnie, Jodie and Gary – bickering already, by the looks of it – walked over to the lift. It was only a small housewarming, but I couldn't wait to show off our new home to our friends.

An hour later, and the party was in full swing. The lads had been playing around with the Bang and Olufsen sound system since they arrived, largely ignoring my carefully chilled pink champers in favour of the Stella, and instead seeing how loud they could get the bass without breaking any windows. As Adam went to change the CD to a Snoop Dogg album, all of a sudden there was a loud, distorted thud from the bass and he looked up, mystified as to what had happened. Jonnie and Gary burst out laughing.

'Waay, geezer, you went in a bit strong on that one!' crowed Jonnie, slapping him on the back and taking a long swig of beer.

'Yeah, mate, you want to try putting that kind of welly into your crosses, not your speakers!' laughed Gary, and chinked bottles with Jonnie.

Adam chuckled self-consciously and went red, hiding his head as he tried to readjust the speaker.

I looked over fondly from where me, Tara and Jodie were lounging around on the sofas. Bless him – he looked all embarrassed. But ribbing each other was just what lads did, wasn't it? He'd soon feel comfortable enough to give as good as he got. I turned back to the girls, who were gossiping about clothes, Tara's kids and the club's other WAGs and making inroads into a second bottle. Jodie, as usual, was a couple of glasses ahead of me and Tara. Jodie seemed to save all of her calorie intake for alcohol, and though she never seemed to eat – she was the world champion at chasing a piece of iceberg lettuce around a plate – she could sink a bottle of bubbly without it even touching the sides.

Tara, however, was no boozer. In fact, I'd never seen her have more than a couple of sips of buck's fizz, and tonight I was starting to understand why. Not even halfway through her second glass, and she was starting to slur her words and her eyes were rolling a bit. I couldn't help but giggle – she was normally so in control!

She leaned forward playfully – but very clumsily. 'Now, missus, don't you take the pish out of me. I may have gone a bit squiffy, but . . .' Her face suddenly dropped and Jodie gave me a look over the top of her head and pointed frantically at the bathroom.

'Tara, why don't you go to the bathroom with Louise?' Jodie said, as if she were talking to a small child. She nodded conspiratorially at me. 'Go on, Louise, you're good in situations like this.'

I pulled a face in response but dutifully pulled Tara up. Her long, thick, honey-blonde hair, normally swept glamorously away from her face and bouncing with health and vitality (Tara was one of the few WAGs who didn't need hair extensions, and it was a bone of contention amongst many of the other girls), now hung limply in a middle parting over both her shoulders, and her long, lithe limbs were floppy and flailing at odd angles, like pipe-cleaners.

I looked back over my shoulder at Jodie in mock horror as Tara, legs wobbling like Bambi, staggered over to the bathroom. She knelt immediately on the slate floor and crawled over to the toilet. Just in time, I pulled her mane of hair out of the way before she threw up noisily.

Lifting her head after the first wave, she looked at me over her shoulder. 'Louish. Louish! Don't tell Jonnie. Don't tell Jonnie!'

I stroked her back reassuringly. 'Don't worry, Tara, of course I won't!'

'Gerroff, Louish,' she mumbled, batting my hand away from her back, before promptly throwing up again.

The door creaked open and I looked up, expecting Jodie's curiosity to have got the better of her. But peering around the door was not Jodie – it was Jonnie. I grinned sheepishly. 'Er – Jonnie. I think Tara's had a bit too much champagne . . .'

He smiled grimly. 'Tara, I can't believe you!'

'I'm shorry, Jonnie,' said Tara, voice echoing from down the pan. 'I'm really shorry.'

He stepped over to the toilet, wrinkling his nose. 'Babe, you know you can't deal with alcohol!' He started rubbing her back gently. Tara's hand resumed its ineffective batting as she started puking again.

I looked at him sympathetically.

'I wouldn't do that if I were you, Jonnie.' I giggled. 'But it might be a good idea to hold this.' I handed him Tara's hair, and went back to the party.

Chapter 3

From the start, it became very clear that there was more to being a Premiership WAG than met the eye.

Not just turning shopping into a military manoeuvre (I'd very quickly had to lose my fear of flexing my credit cards – spending money wasn't just a pastime, it was part of the job spec, and something I'd found surprisingly easy to get used to!). Not just all the attention from the press, the fan mail (Adam's and, weirdly, mine). Not just the pressure to *never* wear anything that a fellow WAG had worn before – or, even worse, that *you'd* worn before. Not just the need to have your hair, nails (fingers and toes), tan, eyelashes and teeth done every week – and by the right people. Not just the need to make sure that when you went out, you were in the right place and with the right people. Nope, it turned out that even my new friends were high-maintenance.

After my first day at the hotel when Gary had promised to introduce me to his girlfriend, I'd had a text that same evening from a 'Jodie' who I guessed must be her, saying she was looking forward to meeting me. So, when Saturday's friendly match came around I was a bit less nervous than I might have been, despite the fact that it was my first public outing and I was dead nervous about letting Adam down. I'd also had a call from Tara, who was Jonnie's wife, being all sweet and lovely and saying she'd look out for me at the game. Still, walking into the players' lounge for the first time on my own was really nerve-racking. I hadn't dared say anything to Adam – he'd been preoccupied with it being his first game, and had been obsessively working himself up to match day with such focus that sometimes I wondered if he was even aware I was there!

I was dead early – it was only half one! – but I figured better that than walking into a full lounge with all eyes on the newcomer. I'd got really dressed up – I knew the girls up north went all-out for glamour – and I'd got a new chiffon Jaeger shirt on under a black waistcoat, skinny black jeans and some chrome-heeled Gucci shoe-boots (my S&M boots, as Adam called them). I'd had my hair done and was wearing full slap. I wasn't taking any chances.

I walked into the plush bar area, with its subtle grey sofas, chrome and glass tables and oversized palms, and got myself a vodka and tonic. I was in dire need of some Dutch courage – this was all a bit different to the more down-at-heel surroundings I'd been used to back home! Sitting at a table towards the back of the room, I busied myself with playing on my phone, and took sneaky looks around the room to see what was going on. A succession of wives, girlfriends, kids, families and puffed-up sports agents trickled through the door, and I entertained myself wondering who they all were. I recognised a lot of them – after all, many of Adam's new team-mates were household names, and their wives or girlfriends were now regulars in women's magazines – and I was a bit taken aback at how, well, *flashy* they were. They were all sat in groups (thank goodness I'd taken a seat at the back, I thought, rather than risk accidentally sitting in someone's regular spot) and there was a bit of a cliquey atmosphere between tables – a lot of unsubtle looking up and down and discussing what each other was wearing.

After a bit, a well-preserved lady with short, layered, highlighted hair and minimal make-up, invited me to join her. She and her friend – Jonnie's mother, as it turned out – were babysitting some of the kids, Tara's included. Though undeniably well groomed – and really lovely – unlike some of the others in the lounge they were much more dressed down than me, in designer jeans and T-shirts or shirts, and I started to feel a bit uncomfortable. But I needn't have worried. Minutes before kick-off, two girls burst in, and as all heads turned they introduced themselves dramatically, enveloping me in heavily scented hugs and covered me in glossy-lipped air kisses. Tara and Jodie were swathed in va-va-voom glamour, but also gorgeous and welcoming, and I suddenly felt totally at home. These girls were going to be my friends, I could tell.

And I was right. From that first match day, we've been inseparable, and spent hours every day together – brunching, shopping, lunching, shopping, sitting around each other's living rooms and gassing away, or taking Tara's kids out to a park or the zoo. What we were really doing was filling the hours until our husbands or boyfriends came home and needed fussing over.

The girls are gorgeous – if a bit 'special'.

With Jodie, to all intents and purposes what you saw was what you got. Former star of TV soap opera *Temperley Road*, she had played a tough-talking, salt-of-the-earth barmaid for seven years, and had more or less morphed into her on-screen character. (Not that I imagine there were too many differences between them to start with.) In fact, she only left the series when Gary, her old-timer footballer (well, he was thirty-four, but in football terms that was well beyond retirement age and practically pushing daisies), got transferred to AC Milan four years ago. He'd seen out his contract before coming back to the UK, and since then, despite having had a lot of work *done*, Jodie hadn't done a lot of work herself, only the odd voice-over job. Not that she'd admit to having ever even considered cosmetic surgery. Jodie claimed she was 'all God's own work' – she never dieted, worked out, or had any 'unnecessary' pampering. Yet though she drank like a fish, she never seemed to eat (poor Gary – Jodie still couldn't believe she was expected to touch food, let alone cook him a filling meal every evening!); though she was 'soooo unfit', she referenced her personal trainer *a lot* (especially when we were discussing other girls' figures – i.e. much of the time); and though she maintained she couldn't stand being 'messed about with', she had all the best of the north's mobile beauticians on speed dial.

But in a way, you couldn't blame her for not giving anything away. In her TV heyday she'd been a bona fide star, a bit of a national treasure. The fact that she was now going out with one of the UK's favourite ex-England footballers meant she was still tabloid gold. Along with her exotic looks – shiny black hair, olive skin, feline green eyes, high cheekbones and tiny figure – she had a natural talent for a headline-grabbing soundbite, which of course made her prime pap material. She was often followed around by loads of photographers (and even though they only seemed to turn up when she was dolled up to the nines, she vehemently denied she'd ever tipped any of them off . . .). She drove a Range Rover with blacked-out windows, which at least meant she could get around town in relative anonymity.

Yet the paps followed her every move. Not that Jodie couldn't give as good as she got – it was just that when you were speeding along a motorway at seventy mph, there was little you could do to get people off your back other than blow a kiss or give them the finger. However, with Gary she had no such inhibitions. They were a nightmare together. They were either love, love, love or hate, hate, hate, and could go from one to the other in a split second. And the trouble was, not only were they so striking together, but they were totally unselfconscious about where and when they fell out. The first time me and Adam witnessed one of their spats was the first time the four of us were all out together, at a charity dinner – big do, red carpet and all the rest. I couldn't wait! It was the kind of thing me and Sara had read about in gossip magazines for years, and suddenly not only were me and Adam invited to one, we were VIP guests! As I stepped into my full-length Maria Grachvogel one-shoulder chiffon dress in cornflower blue, I vowed to call Sara up tomorrow and tell her all about it. I'd neglected her a bit since the move, and I didn't feel great about it.

But right now, I was so excited I almost felt sick. Adam drove us in the Hummer, Gary next to him, me and Jodie in the back. There was a noisy buzz in the car. Me and Jodie were leaning forward so we could chat with the boys and it was a laugh, you know – just a lot of banter. All of a sudden, though, it all kicked off between Jodie and Gary.

Gary turned round to say something and ended up with his face practically buried in Jodie's cleavage.

'Cor blimey, sweetheart, you nearly had me eye out there!' he sniggered. Jodie giggled and looked at me coyly.

'He's such as charmer, my Gal, isn't he?'

Gary turned and nudged Adam. 'But then I guess most blokes get an earful off their missus,' he said, guffawing with laughter. 'I just get an eyeful! Mind you, cost me enough. I reckon you could get three of these babies,' he slapped the dashboard of the Hummer, 'for every pair of Jodie's tits!'

They both roared with laughter. Jodie's face fell and her brow furrowed dangerously. She punched Gary on the shoulder.

'Fuck off, Gary. The only surgery you've paid for is the plate in your fucking head where your brain should be.'

Gary suddenly stopped laughing, and turned around with a snarl. 'Sweetheart, if I'd never met you I'd be retired by now and living the life of fucking riley on the savings.'

Jodie slapped him again. 'And if I hadn't met you I'd be with someone actually famous who could keep me in the lifestyle I kept myself – and I'd look ten years younger to boot!'

Gary turned round a hundred and eighty degrees. 'Jodie, you look ten years younger than when I met you, thanks to all the bloody surgery!'

That was it for the night. When they finally stopped screaming at each other in the car, Jodie turned to me and it was 'he said this, he said that, he's bringing stuff up from years ago' (er, hello – I'd been sitting next to them, so I knew exactly what was going on – and it hadn't sounded like that to me!), and Adam was having to deal with the same kind of thing from Gary in the front. Anyway, this carried on out of the car park, down the red carpet (even between gritted teeth as they smiled for the photographers), through reception drinks and into the ballroom for dinner. It had proper kicked off. Even when we were in the middle of dinner – all sat there in our finest dress – they didn't stop taking a piece out of each other. It was so embarrassing I actually made them go into the kitchen at one point to sort themselves out. Gary looked like he wanted to kill her, and Jodie looked like she wanted to kill him. How it never got out, I don't know – but this was a lesson I was learning fast. It was the power of the tabloids. They had loads of stories they just sat on, and they could bring you down whenever they wanted to – but if, like Jodie, you played the game, you got more chances than most.

Where Jodie really *was* low-maintenance, though, was clothes. My God. Of all the most glamorous people I knew, Jodie sure did hate shopping and fashion. She was a walking directory of top jewellers and had a collection of posh watches that was probably worth more than most people's houses, but clothes she just seemed to find really dull. We'd go out shopping, and whereas me and Tara could shop until we dropped, Jodie would get bored within about half an hour and demand we stopped for a drink. She was what I called 'retail lazy' – because she didn't understand it, she didn't like it. And because she didn't like it, she didn't do it. Which made life extra-difficult for the rest of us, because instead of looking around and finding stuff she really liked, she'd just copy the best of what we'd all bought, wear it first (and, though none of us liked to admit it, often wear it best), get papped in it and then render that particular item unwearable for the rest of us for ever.

It was a while before I discovered she had VIP 'arrangements' with certain shops like Mango and Zara, where if she phoned ahead, they'd shut down the whole place and let her and a friend in – and shop for free.

The first time she mentioned it, I thought she was kidding. We were walking past Topshop, and I said that even though I supposed I should be a real designer label queen, it was still my favourite store.

'Oh, babe, I can't bear it,' she said, squinting into the store. 'Look at how busy it is! I'll tell you what, let's go for a drink, I'll give them a call and see when they can let just us in.'

I stopped right there in the middle of the street. 'What do you mean, just us?'

Jodie had smiled like it was the most normal thing in the world. 'Well, just us. The best thing is, it'll all be for free – and that kind of shopping, babe, is the kind I'm more than happy to do!'

I was absolutely gobsmacked. I still didn't believe her, but didn't want to look like an overexcited teenager, so I nodded like it happened to me every day of the week. Sure enough, just one quick call and a couple of glasses of champagne later, and we were the only people in Topshop apart from the staff and a *very* excited manager, who was standing in front of us wringing her hands and glancing nervously over our shoulders at the shoppers locked outside, looking in curiously.

'I'm afraid I can't give you any more than half an hour, ladies – not mid-afternoon. But should you want to come back another time after hours, we'd be more than happy to accommodate you whenever is convenient. And it goes without saying that whatever you find to your liking is yours with the compliments of the store.'

Jodie had grinned and wandered off absent-mindedly, but I think I wasted about ten minutes of my trolley dash thanking the manager!

It was amazing. I just couldn't believe it. We had the run of the whole place, and everything was free! It was brilliant. I started slowly wandering round the store, feeling really self-conscious and like all the staff were looking at me (I was half expecting someone to tell me to put it all back!). I picked a top, and a pair of trousers and a necklace off the accessory rack next to the changing room.

Inside, Jodie was standing in just her fake tan and white G-string, rifling through the armful of clothes she'd taken in. She looked at me in horror. 'Babe! I didn't call in a favour for you just to pick up a poxy top! Come on, we're running out of time!'

I ran out of the changing room in a panic, feeling like a right fool. How was I to know we literally could take anything we wanted? I swept around the store, pulling tops, skirts, coats and trousers off the rails, cheeks burning with the embarrassment. I felt really cheeky! Plus, I was sure the staff knew I'd never done this before — I must have had it written all over my forehead.

Back in the changing room, Jodie was still half naked and looking through her pile of clothes with dismay, chewing gum loudly. Her eyes lit up as she saw my haul. 'Oh babe, you've got such great taste,' she said. 'Mind if I try a couple of bits on myself?'

Of course, she nabbed all my best stuff — and then picked up some of the other stuff I'd chosen on the way to the till, and so I still ended up with a load of clothes in my wardrobe with tags on that I didn't like, but what the hell? It was dead exciting, and fun, and I loved her for it.

Tara, too, was lovely — ninety-nine per cent of the time. She looked like an all-American cheerleader — except she was from Bromley. She *was* all natural — apart from a couple of subtle boob jobs, of course, which had turned her flat little 'boy' boobs into a pert pair of 32D knockers in a matter of months. Her long, thick honey-blonde hair framed a delicate heart-shaped face, big brown eyes and bee-stung lips, and her petite size-eight figure was thanks to a speedy metabolism rather than strict diet — even after two kids. She'd done a bit of modelling in the past, but since she met Jonnie in a bar in London, she'd focused all her impressive energy resources on being an über-WAG — some kind of superhuman wife, mother and official clothes-horse.

She always had the latest of everything, and would go to extraordinary lengths to secure it. (And, I suspected, keep it secret from Jodie before she got wind and bought it before her.) It wasn't enough to get on the waiting list – Tara had to *be* the waiting list, and she showered the retail assistants in the area with gifts, flowers and cards to keep them sweet. They gave her an extra 10 per cent discount on top of our mandatory 40 per cent – she'd send them a five-star spa day to say thanks. They got her the latest Louboutin shoes before they'd even hit the shelves – she'd send them a box of twenty-four personalised cupcakes in return.

Although, to be fair, this extravagance did extend to friends and family too – apparently Tara's Christmas presents were so generous they bordered on embarrassing. For Jodie's birthday, we all went to a swanky restaurant for lunch – well, obviously not the boys; we were lucky if we spent one lunchtime a week with our other halves – but us girls and the kids too. We had the best table, Cristal champagne, and Tara had even arranged for a 'Happy Birthday Auntie Jodie' cake. The tab must have been in the thousands but she picked it up without even flinching.

Tara was also a great shopping companion, if a bit danger-ous. Like, take the first time we went shopping together. We went into a posh department store – you know, like Selfridges, with high-street concessions on one floor, more pricey brands on the first floor, next to a whole section that I'd never even stepped in that held all the super-expensive designer stuff. I automatically went to go straight to the ground floor, but Tara stopped dead in her tracks.

'Babe, where are you going?' she said, looking a bit confused.

'Oh, nowhere – just looking,' I said meekly, and followed her, bag hooked into her elbow, nose in the air as if excitedly catching scent of her prey, up the escalator to the first floor.

What followed was literally a supermarket sweep. I picked up a couple of things (having put a lot more back after seeing the prices!), but by the time Tara and I crossed paths again, she had armfuls of clothes.

'Babe! Is that all you've got?' she tutted. 'That's no fun! Look at how much I've got to try on! Come on, you *must* be able to find something else?'

It was like deja vu. With that, she unceremoniously dumped her stuff on a slathering shop assistant and dragged me around the store by the hand, picking up tops, trousers, skirts and scarves like there was no tomorrow.

I won't deny, it was a real giggle trying stuff on. I'd never really experimented with clothes – I like them, and I liked to look sexy and on trend, but Tara was something else. She really knew how to put stuff together, and wasn't afraid to try what seemed like really way-out ideas but which, nine times out of ten, kind of worked.

'You see, babe, you've got a lovely little figure there,' she said at one point, looking at me appraisingly as she tweaked a top I'd tried on and retied the scarf I was wearing with it. 'You should cut loose a bit more. It's not as if it'll matter if

65

you decide you don't like something when you get it home, after all!'

'Why, what's the returns policy here?' I asked innocently.

Tara looked at me, wide-eyed in shock. 'Babe! You don't need to *return* stuff. Just don't wear it!'

I blushed and looked down at my scarf, pretending to adjust it. How wasteful! I could never do that – no matter what Adam earned. My mum would go mad if she knew!

But by the time I got to the till, I'd still got a bigger pile of stuff than I'd ever bought before – and all of it much more expensive than I was used to, too. In front of me, Tara seemed unconcerned at her huge splurge and didn't even check the amount before she punched in her credit-card pin number. As the assistant packed up her stuff, Tara was already bored and looking around again.

'I'm just going over there a minute, babe,' she said, pointing over at the designer section. 'Come over when you're done.'

I nodded mutely, trying to ignore the rising panic I felt. My mouth was dry and my forehead was burning up. My palms were clammy and sticking to the hangers I was clutching, and I couldn't escape the feeling that I was about to do something really wrong. The minute she'd wandered off, I couldn't ignore it any longer. Smiling apologetically at the shop assistant, I shot off around the store, putting back half the items I'd planned to buy. By the time I returned to the till, I'd lessened my load – and lightened my conscience – considerably.

It was still more than I'd ever spent on one shopping trip, but once I'd found Tara again, I was feeling a lot better.

'What d'you think of this, babe?' she said, holding up an Alexander McQueen leather jacket. The tag swinging nonchalantly from it read £1,900!

I swallowed hard. 'It's gorgeous, babe, but . . .'

Tara held it out as best she could with its security tag locking it to the rail, then put it back dismissively.

'Yeah, I guess you're right, babe. I couldn't manage it today anyway, not with all those other bags to carry.'

Days later, when I admitted to Tara that I'd never really 'done' proper designer shops, it was like a red rag to a bull. She arranged for a driver to take us in her Merc to a posh shopping street in town. He drove us from one to the next – literally door to door! – and she introduced me to the manager of each, getting me a VIP discount card in the process. We spent, and we spent – even with 50 per cent discount in some places, we must have totted up thousands. I started to feel a bit sick, but Tara was a pro at knowing what I'd look good in and what would be good to wear on various occasions. I had to stop myself in the end, though, I was feeling way too guilty – but Tara kept shopping for Britain, sprinkling a little bit of her princess stardust on everyone we spoke to. You could see them all melt whenever she smiled at them or spoke to them.

But that was Tara all over – Miss Perfect. Bubbly, unflappable, kind – she had it all, and she was married to one of the sexiest men on the planet. She was the perfect material for Chief WAG – and she reflected her husband's role on pitch behind the scenes – in the players' lounge, and popping into our homes and checking up on us throughout the week.

She had no airs and graces, though – she'd often invite me and Jodie around for girls' nights in at her and Jonnie's mansion outside of town, and for a 'treat' we'd have Marks and Spencer buck's fizz, prawns and sauce, or maybe even a ready-meal steak-and-chip dinner. (Well, me and Tara would – Jodie would make do with the buck's fizz). Tara was queen of the ready meal – she was notorious for her inability to cook, and Jonnie was about the only footballer I knew who got home and not only cooked himself dinner, but would occasionally even knock something up for the kids too! Tara was totally unapologetic about it, and shrugged it off as something she was too busy to learn how to do. One Saturday lunchtime I was round there and we even had a ready-meal jacket potato with cheese! Another time, Jodie was teasing Tara and so Tara challenged Jodie to make a meal for us all. We won't be repeating that experiment again. Jodie brought a tin of tuna, a tin of tomatoes, and some peas, mashed them all up together and served it between the three of us! She couldn't understand why we were so unimpressed . . . and hungry.

The only problem was, sometimes you couldn't separate who Tara thought she should be from who she actually was – I guess she had so many different characters for different people, understanding her was a bit of a minefield.

Because the other one per cent of the time, when she wasn't being totally lovely, she could be quite a weirdo, really. Like, on the face of it, she really didn't need to worry about Jonnie. Despite being lusted after by women all around the country – not just those into football! – he seemed besotted with her. Yes, he was a natural-born flirt but he would never miss the chance to be attentive. If the four of us went out for dinner, for example, he'd be all over her – stroking her back, her hair, fawning all over her, making sure she had everything she wanted. But she'd almost get a bit annoyed with him, and shrug him off in irritation. Same when me and her were out shopping – he'd constantly be on the phone to her, and she'd always be rejecting his calls dismissively. Once, when we went out for a few drinks, just the two of us – when she was obviously going through a 'footballers' wives should be seen to be out and about' phase – he turned up, dressed as a tramp, to check up on her! I thought it was really sweet, but even though he paid our bill on the way out, she acted like she found it really annoying. What's that they say about treat 'em mean? Guess it was working for Tara.

But anyway, other times she'd act all jealous and weird. I went round one afternoon – like I often did – and Jonnie answered the door in a tight white vest which showed off his beautifully honed bod and rippling six-pack, I didn't know where to look. I mean, it was a very nice sight, but he was my mate's husband and it wouldn't do to start lusting over him, even for a split second! But then later that afternoon, sitting in her plush living room with a cuppa while the kids watched some video on TV, Tara was really staring at me, winding her hair round her finger thoughtfully.

'What?' I asked, pushing her affectionately.

She was unmoved and carried on staring. 'You know, Louise, I sometimes wonder why I'm friends with you.'

I looked at her in disbelief. She carried on twisting her hair around her finger, still staring.

'Well, look at you.' She looked me up and down appraisingly. 'Tall, brunette, big tits. You're just Jonnie's type. And here you are, coming round every day, seeing him practically in the altogether, flaunting it at him.' She laughed a tinkly, humourless laugh. 'Like I say, sometimes I wonder.'

Like *I* say, weirdo.

Chapter 4

'Jodie! Louise! Hang on, babes!' As Tara's dulcet tones rang across the autumn afternoon, me and Jodie turned to see our friend tottering over from the car park, all bright Hollywood smile and honey-coloured highlights. Her long, sunkissed limbs were showcased in a blue-and-white-striped T-shirt, tiny white hot pants, and silver Vivienne Westwood platform wedges. A harassed-looking nanny trailed behind her, pushing baby Teja in a Bugaboo pushchair with one hand, the other pulling along Tara's three-year-old daughter Delilah. (Tara always played down the extent of her domestic 'help', but as a permanently immaculate mother of two, there had to be more to her glorified babysitters than she made out.) Hooked in the crook of Tara's elbow was an oversized new silver limited-edition Balenciaga handbag. I sighed in envy. Our favourite boutique, Elena's, had only been able to get hold of one of the bags, and as wife of the club's captain and renowned shopaholic, Tara would have been top of the lengthy waiting list. Jodie let out a gravelly laugh, her poker-straight shiny black hair swinging around her shoulders as she shook her head incredulously.

'How the bloody hell did you get your mitts on that, Tara? That'll be one in the eye for our new friend the ex-glamour girl.'

Tara frowned as she leaned forward to give me an air kiss in a cloud of Coco Chanel perfume.

'What new friend?'

I dug Jodie in the ribs as she hitched up her J-Brand jeans, smoothed down her tight white Joseph T-shirt and ruffled Delilah's blonde hair affectionately. As self-appointed chief WAG, Tara took the care of new arrivals very seriously – it wasn't so long since she'd taken me under her wing, after all – and I didn't want her to think I was trying to muscle in on her territory.

'Shut up, Jodie, you're just stirring it.'

Jodie raised her green eyes in mock outrage, so that they nearly disappeared under her heavy fringe, and bent over to lift the front of the pushchair as the nanny struggled to pull it up the stairs. I turned back to Tara, who seemed to have forgotten about the rest of her entourage.

'It's Jez Steadman's first game today, and he was telling Adam that he was worried about his wife Pattii fitting in,' I explained. 'Despite how she comes across in the press, he reckons she's really quite shy and a bit nervous. Adam asked me to keep an eye out for her, that's all.'

Without missing a beat, Tara smiled sweetly. 'Well, I'm

sure we'll all do our bit,' she said briskly. 'Of course, I've already called Pattii this week and she seemed to be settling in just fine.'

With that, Tara slipped past the nanny, strutted up the stairs and was first to reach the players' lounge. A busy hubbub escaped through the open door – the away team's coach had obviously already arrived and the players' friends and families were all chatting on one side of the lounge as wives and girlfriends from both teams checked out what the others were wearing. As we crossed the room to our table – the best one, of course, befitting Tara's place in the WAG hierarchy and, as her best friends, mine and Jodie's by association – the chatter subsided and one by one the assembled crowd turned and looked at us expectantly. I couldn't work out why until Tara, still in front, came to an abrupt halt. As Jodie and I fell in on either side of her, we too stopped in shock.

Bold as brass, on *our* table, sat a vision of OTT Page 3 glamour. Wearing white high-heeled boots, a Diesel denim mini, tiny white vest, and bathed in an almost iridescent orange glow, Pattii Steadman was chatting animatedly on a pink sparkly mobile phone, inspecting her French-manicured nails and fluffing her elaborately coiffed blonde hair extensions as she spoke. I inhaled sharply. Not only had she committed the grave mistake of taking Tara's table – something the bar staff would no doubt have warned her against – but she seemed totally unconcerned about it.

Beside me, I felt Tara stiffen. Her eyes were glinting dangerously, and though she was smiling, it was fixed and forced. Shifting her bag on her elbow, she touched me lightly on the arm and spoke loudly enough for those around us to hear.

'Girls, this must be Pattii Steadman. Come and introduce yourselves.'

Pattii looked up, waved flirtatiously and closed her phone. 'Hey, girls,' she trilled, pulling a glob of chewing gum out of her mouth and sticking it under the table. 'Thought I'd make myself comfortable! Would have waited for you but figured, get stuck in, girl — so I've already started on the booze,' she giggled.

Tara looked with distaste at the large glass of white wine on the table, the rim smudged messily with frosted, sticky pink lipstick. She discouraged us all from drinking before a game, claiming it was bad for the players to come off the pitch to a group of half-cut wives and girlfriends — though we suspected it was more likely a symptom of her general control-freakery.

'Hi Pattii,' she said coolly. 'Glad you're making yourself at home.' She nodded over at the head barman, who was making a fuss of Delilah as another tender made her favourite strawberry smoothie. 'We'll have the usual, please, Nick.'

She turned back to Pattii, who was cooing showily over Teja — no doubt filling the buggy with white wine fumes.

'We should go out on to the terrace and get to know each other there,' Tara said primly. 'I think we could all do with some fresh air.'

As the team jogged out on to the pitch, I couldn't help but marvel – not for the first time – at how *slim* all the boys were compared to the lower-league players who'd been Adam's team mates until recently. No wonder he'd felt the pressure to do all that extra training when we first arrived. I mean, all footballers were fit – but at this level, they were like whippets! The games were so much faster too, like a streamlined version of all the other leagues.

Pattii elbowed me roughly, jolting me out of my daydream. 'Not very good-looking, is he?' she said, nodding at Jez. Me and Jodie looked at her, confused. It was true: with his ginger hair and protruding overbite, Jez wasn't the bonniest on the pitch – but he was her husband!

I was the first to speak. 'What do you mean?'

Pattii looked out on the pitch and laughed. 'Well, when we met, I did have to ask myself the question: could I sleep with him? Then I thought, of course you can, Pattii, he's a footballer, isn't he?'

I stared at her incredulously. Was she for real?

But Pattii carried on, unperturbed. 'I had to think about it all night, but then I thought, well, despite his looks, he's such a nice guy, I guess I can.'

I was staring at her open-mouthed. Jodie laughed in

disbelief, narrowing her almond-shaped eyes and treating Pattii to one of her famous filthy looks.

Catching her disdain, Pattii smirked. 'But that's better for me, isn't it?' She turned to me. ''Cos, like, I'm in a much better position than you two.'

I had no idea where this was going. 'Why?'

Pattii crossed her arms in triumph. 'Well, your Adam's so good-looking, everybody wants him. And Jodie's Gary might be past it but he's still a looker, right?' She turned to Jodie, who sniffed dismissively. 'All those hangers-on and football groupies – they must be round them like flies on crap.' She paused triumphantly, savouring the punchline. 'But no one's going to want my Jez, are they?'

I was dumbfounded. Jodie was quicker to react, and leant across me and grabbed Pattii's arm firmly. Pattii suddenly looked intimidated and tried to shake her off. She failed.

'Don't get too comfortable, babe,' spat Jodie threateningly. 'Jez is a footballer. It doesn't matter what he looks like. Everybody's going to want him. And the better he does, the more they'll want him. So be warned. A footballer's wife can never afford to let her guard down.'

After the match, we moved back to our table in the players' lounge to wait for the boys to come out. They'd won, and when they started straggling in from the changing room, all in their identikit blue suits with club emblem embroidered on the top pocket, they were buzzing and full of comradely banter. They made quite a sight, all good-looking guys (well, most of them), glowing and in their prime. Sometimes, I still had to pinch myself when I remembered that I was now a part of this glamorous world.

Adam, Jonnie, Gary and a couple of the other lads came over and crowded around the table. Gary slumped down into the seat next to Jodie, and Adam leant over the back of mine and gave me a kiss. 'Hi, baby. Good game, eh?'

'It was fantastic!' I said excitedly. 'You played so well. Your corner set up that first goal. You're turning into the team's good-luck mascot!'

Adam gave me a dirty look and glanced around shiftily. 'Shhh! Keep your voice down, Lou, it was a team effort.'

I looked at him quizzically, feeling a bit crushed. Was Adam embarrassed of me? But before I could say anything, Jonnie came over and slapped Adam on the back. 'Well played, mate, well played. Think you're finally finding your feet, eh? You'll be man of the match before you know it!'

Adam coloured, looking well chuffed. My heart swelled with pride for him.

'Yeah, well, you'll have to pick up a bit of speed before you do,' butted in the club goalie, Craig. 'Forrest Gump could have overtaken you on that break upfield.'

There were a few chuckles at that one. Adam went red and tried to laugh it off. 'Yeah, well, I was trying to make you look better, mate – couldn't have you being the only one coming up the rear!'

'Don't worry – he's used to it' snorted Gary, looking up from texting on his phone. 'Coming up the rear's one of his favourite pastimes!'

The boys all roared with laughter. Gary stood up, standing on Jodie's foot. She yelped and looked up at him accusingly, but he seemed not to notice. 'Who's for a beer, anyway? I've just seen the gaffer leave – let's get them in!'

Tara coughed delicately and looked meaningfully up at Jonnie standing next to her. It was unofficially frowned upon for the lads to drink in the players' lounge, and she obviously thought that as captain he should be setting an example in the manager's absence. She put her hand around his leg and stroked it. 'So, what are we all going to do to celebrate the big win?' she said brightly. Jonnie looked down at her, a bit irritably I thought, and shook her hand off his leg. I was shocked. Normally, he was all over her!

'Oh, I think we're going to do our own thing tonight,' Jonnie said distractedly. He called over to Gary at the bar. 'What d'you reckon, Gal?'

Jodie stood up, brushing down her jeans elaborately. 'Well, after that little display, if the plans involve Gary, they don't involve me,' she said crossly. 'I'm off. Tara, babe, you can get Gary home if he needs it, can't you? Bye, all.'

She picked up her red Hermès Birkin bag and kissed me and Tara goodbye. I stared at her open-mouthed. Jodie really had a brass nerve. I would never walk out on Adam like that!

Jodie swept out, pointedly ignoring Pattii, who was draped over the other sofa alluringly. I frowned as I followed Pattii's gaze over to where Adam was leaning on the bar with Gary, Jez and Craig. Surely she wasn't eyeing my boyfriend up?

Gary, apparently unaffected by Jodie's huffy exit, was busy showing the lads something on his phone. They were all laughing crudely. He looked up as Jodie swanned out, and nudged Adam.

'Oh well – one down, three to go!' I was sure I heard him say, as they all trooped out of the lounge together.

Charming!

I looked around the table in despair. My 'bonding' lunch for the girls hadn't quite gone to plan.

Pattii, at the end of the table, was draining yet another glass of pink Laurent Perrier, clearly drunk and with mascara smudged under one eye.

Jodie, along the table from her, had turned her back on Pattii, and despite matching her glass for glass seemed to have remained sober. Her mood had darkened with every glass, however, and her initial dislike of Pattii – which I'd hoped this lunch would help dispel – seemed to be getting worse. Jodie had a long-standing feud with one of Pattii's glamour model friends, after the friend claimed in a newspaper interview that she'd been on a date with Gary when Jodie first met him, and that, along with Pattii's brash, loud-mouthed manner, hadn't gone down well. Jodie even called her 'Fatty' behind her back, which had made me laugh but which I privately thought was quite mean.

Tara was sitting bolt upright, looking at Pattii with undisguised disdain and pursed lips. She, too, had been sniffy with Pattii from the off. So far she'd made no attempt to babysit Pattii as she'd done with me when I first arrived, and seemed quite happy to pass all responsibility over to me – but I figured she was just preoccupied and had hoped, as I had with Jodie, that she'd see fit to include Pattii in our little friendship group. It seemed the nice thing to do, and would certainly make my life easier!

But it wasn't just the guest list that hadn't worked. My carefully planned lunch – with three courses ordered in from a chic caterer in town, bottles of Laurent Perrier rosé, and carefully arranged floral table centrepieces and scented candles – had gone down like a lead balloon. I'd thought that using one of Tara's favourite suppliers and having Jodie's favourite fizz would be a good idea, but Tara's face had fallen when she'd seen the display. 'How fantastically elaborate,' was her initial response, and although Jodie had smiled encouragingly, I could tell she thought it was too OTT as well. And then Pattii had arrived and the atmosphere had plummeted by about fifty degrees. Now, I just couldn't wait to get rid of everyone.

'Jusht going to the lav,' said Pattii, standing up and swaying dangerously. As she minced off to the bathroom, Tara ostentatiously glanced at her eighteen–carat gold Franck Muller Long Island Master Banker watch and popped her phone in her bag. 'I think we'll take this opportunity to make a move,' she said, looking knowingly at Jodie. Jodie winked at her ostentatiously and gave me a wide smile.

Tara leaned over and grabbed my hand. 'You know, Louise, there was no need to go to all this trouble on our account. We are your friends and you don't need to impress us.'

The bathroom door slammed shut and she lowered her voice as Pattii's footsteps approached. 'But what you do need to do is follow the social code around here. Who you make friends with other than me and Jodie is up to you, but in my position I need to be a bit more choosy. Fortunately, this was all behind closed doors, but . . .' She looked up as Pattii staggered in. 'I should *not* be having lunch with the likes of Pattii Steadman.'

I nodded, feeling really stupid and burning up at my gaucheness. Pattii, apparently unaware of any kind of awkwardness, approached swinging a fancy paper carrier bag tied with ribbon.

''Ere, Louise, babe, I just found this! 'S got my name on it. There's one for you two an' all! What is it?'

I looked up miserably as she waved a gift bag full of expensive cosmetics under my nose. 'Oh,' I said quietly. 'Those are your goody bags.'

Ever felt totally stupid?

★

The coach pulled in to the hotel car park and Pattii turned to me, eyes shining with excitement.

'Here we go, girl – let's get glammed up and get on it!'

I giggled. Despite the lunch disaster, I'd spent quite a bit of time with Pattii over the past two weeks; taking her shopping and sorting her out the same discounts Tara had helped me with, even organising a joint personal training deal with her and working out together twice a week. As far as Tara and Jodie were concerned, I was doing it to please Adam – he was pally with Jez, and keen that me and Pattii got on well. But to be honest, I did enjoy her company too. Yes, she was rough as old boots, and she quite often said things that made my eyes water, but she was also good fun and lively, and things were never dull when she was around!

But neither of the girls were on the wives' and girlfriends' coach for tomorrow's away game in London – Tara was travelling down separately in the morning, something to do with a birthday party Delilah was going to, and Jodie was off on some mysterious meeting and coming down with her. So that left me with Pattii.

She'd brought her live-in nanny along with her, as we were spending tonight in our specially allocated hotel (the boys were all holed up together in another hotel and under pre-match surveillance), and we'd planned to have a little girls' night out in town.

Now, I realise a night out with the girls isn't such a big deal for most people. I mean, everyone likes to let their hair down every once in a while, don't they? Get glammed up, meet your mates, have a gossip and a bit of a boogie and all that. But most people aren't living with a footballer . . . It seemed that what was OK for the lads was definitely not OK for us girls, and a lot of the players took a pretty dim view of WAG nights out. And although Adam was spending a large chunk of his time out on boys' nights, not answering his phone, getting home at 4 a.m. steaming drunk, he seemed to be adopting this attitude too. We'd never had a problem with us each doing our own thing before now, but peer pressure was definitely getting to him. And I, like most of the girls, hated it, but couldn't be bothered with the inevitable row if I said anything about how unfair it was.

But, with all the boys cooped up, there would be no resistance to us going out – no sulks, no moods, no whining. What's more, I'd never really been out in London before, but Pattii was a born-and-bred Cockney, and claimed to know all the best places to go.

Over a late lunch with Natasha, the straight-faced Russian nanny, and Pattii's five- and four-year-old boys, Robbie and Jason, we planned a strategic shop and chatted over what we fancied doing later. At least, we tried to plan – but the kids were obviously feeling fractious and were intent on playing up. They were driving Transformers through our place settings, tearing up bread rolls and deliberately kneading them into sweaty little pellets. Pattii was getting more and more annoyed as Natasha – a tall, graceful natural blonde (the exact opposite of her boss!) – sat sullenly texting and dodging flying dough balls.

'Natasha, how about you take your eyes away from that bloody phone and help Jason chop up his food?' snapped Pattii, turning her own attention to Robbie. As Natasha tried to feed Jason a piece of sausage, he burst into indignant howls, and the nanny looked up at Pattii helplessly.

'Jason, what's the matter now?' said Pattii irritably.

'I don't want it,' he wailed. 'I want that.' He pointed at Natasha's bowl of pasta.

'Don't be silly, Jason, eat up your sausage,' snapped Pattii.

'Don't want it. Want that,' he insisted, wailing loudly again.

'Oh, for goodness' sake,' said Pattii, and leaned across the table, swapping Jason's plate of cut-up food with Natasha's rather more appealing bowl of pasta. Natasha stared at her new baby dinner mutely, simmering with anger. 'Now, the lot of you, eat up – me and Louise have got some shopping to do.'

We went to our rooms to get ready, and I sighed as I ran myself a bubble bath in the luxurious pale limestone bathroom. I still couldn't believe I was staying in this amazing hotel room, all on my own, when it wasn't really a special occasion or anything – but sometimes, all the getting ready really was a pain. I'd only done my hair and make-up for the coach ride a few hours ago, and looked more glamorous than I ever would have at home for a night out with Sara and our other mates in Cardiff. But here I was having to do it all over again — twice in one day! The trouble was, Tara had warned me about the paparazzi and I was terrified that the first time I got my picture in a magazine — which I was secretly quite hoping for soon — it would be when I was looking anything other than perfectly groomed.

Just as I was applying my second coat of mascara, there was a knock at the door.

'Louise, it's me, open up!' I could hear Pattii giggling outside, so I went to let her in. She squeezed through the door surreptitiously, and looked at me with a wicked glint in her eye. She waved a bottle of pink Dom Perignon under my nose.

'Let's get the party started!'

She sashayed into the room and I couldn't help but laugh. She had squeezed her shapely curves into a bright red lurex catsuit, with a zip all the way up the front, done up to show off as much of her impressive cleavage as possible. She wore it with black platform mules and a high ponytail. She looked like a soft-porn version of Sandy from *Grease*. She turned round with an elaborate twirl.

'D'you think this is too much, babe?'

I immediately tried to adopt a straight face. 'No, babe, honestly — you look great.'

'Good.' She opened her Fendi clutch bag and pulled out

a small white packet. 'Because I've invited a little friend along to help get us going!'

I was shocked. I guessed it was cocaine – but I'd never done drugs before.

'Babe, I'm not sure . . .'

But Pattii was already sitting at the dressing table and tipping out white powder on to the glass surface, expertly chopping up two white lines with her black Amex card.

'Oh come on, Miss Goody-Two-Shoes. Where's your sense of adventure? With the boys out of the way, we've got the chance to let our hair down properly for once, and I for one am not going to miss out. You got a note?'

'I'm – I'm not sure.' I picked up my purse and shuffled through the receipts I'd shoved in there. I didn't ever really carry cash – Adam paid a certain amount into a bank account for me every month, but it didn't cover anything more than a couple of lunches, a few trips to the hairdresser and a manicure. Instead, I tended just to use my credit cards for everything and then give Adam the bill at the end of the month. It didn't feel like real money – it was all a bit surreal – but Adam insisted it was better than me having cash on me. Sometimes, I secretly wished it wasn't – this way, I felt totally dependent on him. Which, I guess, I was . . . Tucked inside a coffee-bar receipt, I found a crumpled-up five-pound note and handed it to Pattii.

'Oh, don't worry, babe – that's no use!' She reached for her own purse and pulled out a crisp fifty-pound note, expertly rolling it into a tube and snorting up one of the lines. 'Your turn now!'

I stood, uncertainly. I wasn't sure about this. Not sure at all. I'd always looked down on people who did drugs – and, to be honest, I'd never really been offered any before. What if Adam found out? Suddenly, a picture of my dad popped into my head. Lovely, decent Dad. What would he say if he knew I'd taken cocaine?

I thought of all the times I'd talked about this with Mum and Dad, and how they'd taught me to say no and stand up for what I believed in. They'd even made me practise *how* to say no! But suddenly, now, when it really mattered, my mind had gone blank, and all I could do was stare gormlessly at Pattii.

I felt weirdly scared. My hands were sweaty and I rubbed them down my dress. I suddenly didn't want to be here at all. I wanted to be with Adam.

'Come on, Louise, what are you waiting for?' said Pattii impatiently, holding out the rolled-up note. 'What's your problem?'

I swallowed nervously. Maybe it would be OK. Loads of people did it, after all, didn't they? And I didn't want to get into a confrontation with Pattii. Maybe it would just be easier to do the one line, and then she'd shut up about it.

'We're only going to do it in here, aren't we, Pattii? I mean, we're not going to risk doing it anywhere else?'

She stared at me incredulously, insistently holding out the

note to me. 'Babe, once you've had a line of this stuff, you won't care where we do the next one!'

An hour and a half and a bottle of champagne later, we walked through an unobtrusive door off London's Regent Street into the subtly lit surrounds of a private members' club. Pattii had called ahead to make sure we were on the guest list. 'I'd normally prefer to go to Faces in Essex, but Jez'll kill me if I do,' she'd said, again with a naughty giggle. 'There's always loads of journos there and he says we can't afford that kind of publicity with him just started at the club.'

We were shown to a table by the house manager and ordered some more champagne. I wasn't so sure about this drugs business. I'd done two lines at the hotel and I felt great – über-confident in fact – but I was also feeling light-headed and totally unlike me. I never really felt like I needed a confidence boost anyway – so I don't know why I'd said yes to Pattii. It seemed stupid. But I guess there was no harm done. It was only two lines, after all.

Pattii, however, was in her element and prattling on nineteen to the dozen – about what, I wasn't quite sure, but I was quite happy letting her incessant babble wash over me as I took in our smart surroundings. The bar was about half full, with people slouching on the chaise longues, brocade sofas and inviting-looking armchairs that were casually arranged around low-slung wooden tables. The walls were decorated with garishly coloured retro wallpaper, broken up only by the occasional gilt-edged painting. The chrome and glass bar, contrasting with the decadent decor, was lit by subtle neon strips, and a handful of members were perched on bar stools or leaning casually against it. Suddenly I spotted Anthony Hargreaves, one of Adam's old friends from the second team at Cardiff. He'd done really well for himself and had just signed up to a big London team, but because of the other names at the club, he hadn't even made the substitutes bench yet.

I waved at him. He nodded and smiled, and sauntered over.

'Hey, Louise, how's it going?' I stood up and kissed him on each cheek and then went to introduce Pattii, but she was one step ahead of me. Uncoiling herself from the banquette she was reclining on, she pouted, shimmied and stuck her ample chest out at Anthony. 'Well, hello, Mr Hargreaves. I've heard so much about you!'

I looked at her, amazed. I don't think I for one had ever mentioned Anthony, and I was pretty sure Jez and he hadn't crossed paths before. Pattii really was a piece of work.

Just then, over Pattii's shoulder, I spotted Anthony's wife, Julia. My heart sank. I thought Pattii was rough, but Julia wasn't just dead common – she was a psychopath, too. And by the looks of her, as she clocked us talking to Anthony, she was also on the warpath.

Glowering threateningly, she picked up a Bacardi Breezer off the bar and stomped over to where we were standing. As always, she was dressed in expensive designer clothes –

Versace by the looks of it – that were at least two sizes too small for her, making her Amazonian body look bigger than it really was. Her satin shirt clung unflatteringly in all the wrong places, buttons straining to remain shut, and she had a muffin top hanging over her tight black trousers. I mean, it might have cost a fortune, but didn't she realise that just because it was designer didn't mean it was any good?

'Anthony. What you doin', Anthony?' She completely ignored us, instead staring manically at her husband. The other thing about Julia was that she watched Anthony like a hawk, and never let him out of her sight. If he was out, she was out too, and she always made him turn down invites to boys only night. Instead, Adam reckoned he just stayed in, playing computer games. What fun . . .

Anthony opened his mouth to reply, but Pattii Motormouth was in there like a shot. 'We was just passing the time of day with the lovely Anthony,' she gushed, giving Anthony a flirtatious look. 'I was just saying how much I'd heard about him – and all very good, obviously—'

I interrupted, certain that this wasn't going to go down well with Julia. 'Julia, I'm Louise, Adam Jones's girlfriend. We met a few times at . . .'

She swung around to me with a evil look, squaring up so her face was only a few inches away from mine. Her breath smelt of alcopops and stale cigarette smoke.

'I don't give a flying fuck who you are, girlfriend,' she

spat. 'All I know is you're both all over my man and I don't like it.'

I stared at her, dumbfounded. Pattii's hand stretched out and pushed her delicately away from me.

'Err – less of the heavy stuff, *girlfriend*,' she said. 'We were just being friendly. There's no need to get upset.'

Julia turned to her, practically snarling. Suddenly, without dropping her gaze, she raised her bottle and smashed it down on the table, holding the broken neck up to Pattii's face. I was certain if Pattii had moved an inch she'd have slashed her.

'Come near my man again, and I'll bottle you. No second chances. Got that?'

With that, she threw the broken bottle on the floor and pulled Anthony away from us. He looked over his shoulder sheepishly as a bouncer hurried over to intervene, and Pattii and I stood watching in shock.

Typically, Pattii was the first to recover, fluffing her ponytail and laughing theatrically for the benefit of the other punters-turned-onlookers. 'Well, that was an unexpected bit of excitement.' She gestured for a waiter to come over and clear up the debris, and sat down, picking up her glass and taking a long sip. 'Still, no use cryin' over spilt Bacardi. Get stuck in, Louise, I've got another bottle in me yet – that's if I can cope with taking a piss in this thing!'

I giggled, still a bit shaken, my heart racing – from the shock or the drugs, I couldn't tell. Pattii leant in to me conspiratorially. 'Maybe we should take a trip to the loos anyway – and have another cheeky little line?'

I shook my head firmly. 'No thanks, Pattii – I've had enough.' I picked up my glass and drained it. 'That's not to say I couldn't do with another glass of bubbly, though!'

Having finished sweeping up the broken glass, the waiter took the hint and filled our glasses. Pattii raised hers to me. 'OK, babe, I'll let you off. We'll need to save a sneaky one for the game tomorrow, anyhow!'

I laughed – but inside I suddenly wasn't finding this funny. What on earth had I got involved in – and what was I thinking, doing drugs like some kind of junkie? I knew I'd have to think of a good reason not to do any tomorrow. There was no way I'd do that to Adam. I was supposed to be at the game supporting him, not sniffing coke. This wasn't me. At least, it wasn't the person I'd always thought I was . . .

Chapter 5

Jodie swung her legs around from under the breakfast bar and hopped off the chrome and black bar stool. She picked up the zebra-print mugs we'd been drinking from (everything was black, white or zebra in her and Gary's luxury riverside apartment) and padded over to the dishwasher, scuffing her Ugg-alike slippers along the floor.

'To be honest, Louise, I don't see the problem,' she said, in the calm, confident, but slightly wheedling tone I'd often heard her use on Gary when she wanted something. 'It's only one night and the boys don't have a midweek game, so I'm sure you can get something ready in advance for Ad's tea – and it'll be fun! Come on, babe, live a little! How old are you? Twenty, or a hundred and twenty?'

She turned with such a look of sincere concern that I burst out laughing. She'd been on at me now nonstop for over an hour to go with her to London on some magazine shoot. It was the twentieth anniversary of *Temperley Road*, and Jodie had been caught up in a frenetic whirlwind of personal appearances and TV interviews. She was in her element – I'd never seen her so buzzing with excitement – and it had made me realise how much she'd given up to be with Gary. I just hoped he realised it.

But this time Jodie had decided she was going to take me with her, and I was running out of excuses not to go. It wasn't that I didn't want to – I'd always watched *Temperley Road*, and hello, who wouldn't want the chance to meet all the best characters that had ever been in it? But the truth was, since the previous trip to London, I was a bit nervous about girls' nights – or any chunk of time – away from Adam. Pattii and I had come so close to getting into serious bother – imagine if there had been journalists in that club! – and her cocaine antics had had me on tenterhooks all through match day, in case she got caught out and I was tarred with the same druggie brush. I'd made a resolution just to stay put where possible and not get myself into situations that, frankly, were asking for trouble.

Of course, I was more than likely blowing things all out of proportion. This was Jodie, after all, my best friend, and she was going to be working. What on earth could happen to us on one measly night away from our fellas?

'Oh, go on then, Jodie – I'll come. You've got yourself a travel buddy.'

Jodie squealed and ran over to me, enveloping me in an excited hug and nearly ripping my ear off with her rose gold and diamond Jacob & Co. Five Time Zone watch.

'Yay! It's gonna be a blast, Louise – you wait!'

I giggled and extracted myself from her embrace. 'It's going to be work, Jodie, and that's the only reason I'm coming with you.' I swiped my car keys off the shiny black marble worktop and picked up my slouchy Chloé bag. The oversized charms hanging from the zip jangled satisfyingly and I leant forward to give Jodie a kiss goodbye. 'Just make sure we're staying somewhere with a spa – I could do with a facial!'

As I took the lift to the underground car park, I wondered how best to pitch the trip to Adam. The irony was, he probably wouldn't even notice I was gone! Well, maybe at teatime when I wasn't there with his carefully balanced evening meal. He was spending so much time fitting in at the club, I hardly ever saw him these days. If he wasn't training, he was sleeping, or watching videos (football, of course – either old ones of himself playing, to track his performance, or ones of his former hero-turned-team-mate, Davy McNulty, so he could mirror his moves on the pitch). And if he wasn't sleeping or eating, he was out bonding with his new mates.

When I did see him, he tended to be a bit snappy. Like, he'd pull me up on silly things – if I got something wrong about football, or if I made his tea too strong; even if I was chatting when he was trying to watch the telly. I tried not to feel hurt by it, but it was hard. But he'd never been like it before, really, so I had just put it down to all the stress of the new club.

I mean, it was still so surreal for me, so God knows what it was like for Adam! One minute we were in Cardiff, with Adam always saying Davy McNulty does this, Davy McNulty plays like that, if I had half the talent of Davy McNulty . . . And then, all of a sudden, he's playing with him and we're having dinner with him and his wife Holly and everything!

Their house was something else. I thought our penthouse was pretty special – and Jodie and Tara's places were the height of luxury – but Oh. My. God. Davy and his wife Holly's house was big-time beautiful. It was this great big rambling mansion right out in the countryside, and had been decorated top to bottom by one of the best interior designers in the country. Everything was top of the range, gorgeous fabrics, really deep soft carpets and ornate wall hangings. Davy had been a bit of a lad when he first started playing, and everywhere you went there were pictures of him in some fabulous club or other with VIPs and A-list movie stars hanging off his arm. Either that or pictures of Holly from her modelling days – magazine covers, fashion shots, even a black-and-white set she'd had done for one of his birthdays, of her sitting on the back of a motorbike in a leather jacket, hot pants and not much else. Even the downstairs loo was impressive – he'd hung all his medals up, and a gold disc he'd got from some record he'd released with one of his drinking buddies (who also happened to be MC Duke Silver, one of the hottest rappers in Britain). At that point I actually had to pinch myself – how weird that little old me from Cardiff was having a wee surrounded by Davy McNulty's medals!

I mean, it's no wonder it seemed to have gone to Adam's head a bit. Being able to call Davy and some of the other biggest names in football your best mates would change anyone, I reasoned. And he was so paranoid about keeping up with them, bless him – at work and at play – that I was being really patient with him getting a bit cocky and not having so much time for me. I used to be the most important person in the world to him and now, well, now he just seemed weird.

I pressed the button to unlock the car and got in, checking my phone before I started the ignition. In fact, you never knew, having a couple of days away from each other could actually be a good thing for me and Adam. I did sometimes feel a bit like a boring old housewife. On paper, life was so exciting and fun – but now I thought about it, I never felt like I'd actually got anything to talk about! Even if Adam did ever get home and want a chat, I'm not sure what I'd have to tell him. He'd hardly want to know about me and Jodie's lunch, or where Tara and I had gone shopping that afternoon, or what kind of manicure I was going to have done the next day. Even the latest family news of my fellow wives and girlfriends wouldn't interest him, I thought, thinking with horror of some of the mindless gossips me and the girls had to while away the time. Before we moved, I'd always had funny little anecdotes from the salon to entertain him with, or impressions of some of my more colourful clients, but I could hardly send up my best friends, their husbands or our favourite shop assistants, could I – how two-faced!

Nope, a couple of days away would do us both the world of good, I decided.

I decided to broach the subject that afternoon. Adam came in, chucked his kit bag in the corner of the kitchen, as usual, reached inside the fridge for a glass of milk and then slumped on the sofa, flicking through channels on the TV.

I sidled over to him and sat next to him, stroking his tousled mop of hair, curling it over his ear and tickling under his ear lobe. He murmured in pleasure and I smiled to myself. He'd always loved having his hair played with – some nights we'd just curl up on the sofa, watching any old crap on the TV, with me running my fingers through it all night. Though we hadn't done that for ages.

'Adam,' I said tentatively.

'Mmm?' he replied absently, leaning back and taking in the snooker match on TV.

'Adam, baby, Jodie's got a shoot coming up, and she wants me to go along with her.' I bit my lip nervously. Please don't say no!

'Oh, right.' Adam turned and looked at me quizzically. 'Why are you telling me like that?'

'Well,' I continued. 'It's in London. It'll mean an overnight stop. It's midweek, but there's no match, and I can make sure your dinner's—'

'It's fine, babe,' he said, not even taking his eyes off the TV. 'No worries.'

I sat staring at him in shock. Well, that wasn't so difficult, was it?

But for some reason, it didn't make me pleased. It made me uneasy.

Jodie pored over the cocktail menu, absent-mindedly chewing on a French-manicured acrylic nail. She sighed. 'I don't know, Louise. That champ at lunchtime has spoilt me for anything else.'

I smiled. 'Oh, come off it, Jodie, as if a couple of glasses at lunchtime has ever made a difference to your evening boozing!'

I leaned over the small, square wooden table and snatched the menu from her. I scanned the list of drinks, hardly recognising any.

'I'm going to have a lychee martini.'

Jodie wrinkled her nose. 'That sounds disgusting. Why mess with a classic? I think I'll have a Slow Comfortable Screw Up Against the Wall. It's about the only X-rated thing I'll be having tonight!' She laughed her dirty cackle and gestured towards a waiter, who was dressed all in black with a black apron. 'You'd never guess Armani would agree to design those uniforms, would you? I mean, an apron! Mind you, they do look good.'

I smiled absently and leant back. Truth was, I was knackered. We'd been on the go since really early that morning and hadn't stopped for breath once. What with the train journey, hanging around at the shoot all day and two draining hours in Selfridges (Jodie might hate shopping, but she came into her own in a department store – it must have been some instinctive reaction to having everything under one roof), we hadn't had a single minute to relax. And despite a long soak in the bath before we came out, I'd got aching feet and a telltale throbbing behind the eyes. I didn't know how people lived in London – even getting a cab could be a hassle – and frankly, the last thing I needed now was a girls' night out in some swanky members' club where I felt like I had to keep smiling and sucking my tummy in.

The shoot had been an experience too – fascinating for, like, the first hour, and then a bit boring. Well, really boring actually. I'd been dead excited on the journey down – not only at the thought of meeting some famous people but also to see what happened behind the scenes on a glam magazine shoot! We'd got a cab direct from the station to the studio – a huge, draughty old warehouse in east London somewhere. It had wooden floors and two walls made up of huge single-glazed windows – great if we'd been somewhere with a view, but all you could see for miles were rooftops and tower blocks. And it was freezing! After an hour or so I had to rifle through my overnight bag for my bed socks 'cos my feet were so cold.

But to begin with, none of this mattered – I was just gobsmacked by all the frenetic activity around me. There were about twenty soap stars, past and present, milling around – some holding Starbucks coffees or tucking into muffins, others having hair and make-up done, still more rifling through rails of clothes with stylists. A couple of harassed-looking assistants were dashing around with mobile phones glued to their ears, and to one side of the room the photographer and two assistants were setting up a camera and testing lighting for the shoot.

Jodie had disappeared almost immediately, air-kissing and hugging everyone excitedly, and I'd pulled all our bags over to one side and nervously taken a seat on the big leather corner-sofa, smiling politely at another girl sitting there reading a magazine, and then just sat back and watched the goings-on.

But, like I say, after about an hour I had had enough. Yes, there was still lots going on, but it was more of the same – soap stars being fussed over by a variety of assistants, stylists and make-up artists, the occasional tantrum, and the photographer barking orders at everyone. It seemed that unless you were directly involved, magazine shoots weren't that glamorous and exciting after all.

Four hours later, I'd lost the will to live. I'd read every glossy magazine and tabloid paper on the table in front of me, drunk my own body mass in coffee and eaten about three muffins. I hadn't done anything all day, but weirdly I felt really really tired.

Now, the waiter set our drinks down in front of us. Jodie, still buzzing from her day back in the spotlight, held up her tumbler and twizzled the straw around flamboyantly.

'Cheers, Louise!' she said, with a dazzling smile. 'Here's to fame and fortune!'

I laughed. Well, at least Jodie had had a good day – and that was what we were here for, after all.

'Cheers, babes. Here's to fame and fortune – for you. But I'm more than happy staying in Ad's shadow, thank you very much.'

She grinned at me and winked. 'You say that now, Louise – but just you wait until someone wants to make you the star of the show for once. I'm more than happy to leave all that football nonsense behind for a couple of days. I'd forgotten what it was like to live without set pieces and squad rotations for a while.' Suddenly her face dropped. 'Omigod. Oh. My. God.'

I followed her gaze to the staircase, where a group of about five good-looking, well-dressed men were descending from the bar entrance, checking out the room for a free table. I gasped. Right in the middle of them was Danny D'Maio – the ex-lead singer of Gold, one of the biggest British boy bands in history. Jodie had had a brief but passionate fling with him just before she met Gary, and rumours had circulated at the time that there had been an overlap between the two relationships. Jodie always referred to Danny as her 'what if', and I knew that sometimes, when she and Gary had a really bad row, she wondered what would have happened if she'd chosen his love rival.

Now she turned to me with a weird look – part exhilaration, part nervous anticipation. 'Well, it seems you can take the girls away from the footballers . . .' she said, eyes shining. 'Danny's brought all his Goal mates from the club along too.'

Danny regularly hung out with a few of the lads from a rival football club, and their hot looks, flash clothes and Lothario ways had earned them the name 'Goal' in the tabloids, a play on the name of Danny's ex-group.

I laughed and patted her knee. 'What d'you want to do, Jodie? Stay here or go somewhere else?'

She didn't have time to answer before I saw her eyes lock with Danny's. My heart sank. I knew what this would mean. Sure enough, he pointed over and the whole group sauntered across the room towards us. Jodie and Danny's eyes never left each other's. But as the boys approached, that became the least of my concerns. Behind Danny, another pair of eyes were staring just as intensely – and not at Jodie.

At me.

Grey-blue and strangely opaque, they seemed to bore into me from under a floppy blond fringe.

'Good evening, ladies,' said Danny, pulling his white Boss

shirt cuff out from under his sharply tailored jacket and revealing a flash of gold Rolex. 'Mind if we join you?' He gave Jodie a cocky look and I could see her bristle. The air was crackling with the chemistry between them.

'If you must,' she said in an unconcerned tone. 'But before you do, you might want to get some Cristal in.' I gave a sigh of relief. She might be pleased to see him, and I was sure she'd enjoy a bit of a flirt, but she wasn't a cheat.

'Is this seat taken?' said a low Scottish voice in my ear. I jumped and turned round, and saw the eyes looking at me again, this time only inches away and dancing with amusement. I took in the rest of him. Tall, gangly and slightly built, yet with the muscular physique of a professional footballer, he was as fair as Adam was dark and dressed in smart jeans, black T-shirt and black Pringle cardigan. He was so close I could smell his musky aftershave, and I blushed. As I looked down, I noticed his nails were beautifully manicured. I kicked myself for seeming so gauche. Stupid girl – what on earth did I have to be embarrassed about?

'No, no – it's fine,' I stammered, all flustered and feeling awkward. The waiter brought over two bottles of Cristal, complete with ice buckets and sparklers, and The Eyes turned back to me, this time with a cheeky grin attached.

'Champagne? I don't even know your name – but something tells me we've got some celebrating to do.'

I shuffled awkwardly in my seat, suddenly painfully aware

of every movement I made. 'Really?' I looked around at the rest of the group – the other lads, full of high spirits and a bit drunk already, were arranging themselves around us, eyeing up a couple of models at the bar and exchanging boisterous banter. Jodie and Danny were sitting next to each other, already at loggerheads but clearly enjoying some flirtatious sparring. I felt trapped. We were meant to be on a girls' night, away from the lads and the football scene, and what were we doing? We were drinking champagne, in a members' bar, with a load of footballers! Adam would be furious – and I couldn't blame him, either.

The Eyes smiled. 'Oh yes. It's not every day you get to meet a beautiful girl on a night out and find the seat next to her is free!'

I glared at him. 'Look, the seat might be free, but I'm not. I'm happily with someone, and he wouldn't be very pleased to know I was out on my own being chatted up. So back off.'

I cringed. What on earth was I on about?

The Eyes crinkled and he threw his head back and laughed. 'Don't worry, babe, I was just being friendly. I'm a footballer, that's what we do.'

'I know all about footballers,' I replied huffily. 'My other half is Adam Jones. And he wouldn't behave like you just did on a night out.'

The Eyes looked at me appraisingly and whistled between his teeth. 'So, you're the lovely Miss Adam Jones. Yes,

I've heard about you. No wonder we hear Adam keeps his nose clean, even with mates like Davy McNulty. I wouldn't risk losing you.'

I looked at him, confused. 'What do you mean, mates like McNulty?'

The Eyes laughed again. 'Oh, come on, babe, you must know the rumours about McNulty?' He nudged the friend sitting next to him and they both chuckled knowingly. I shook my head, numbly.

'McNulty, the most legendary shagger in the League?' They all roared with laughter, even Danny joining in from mid-argument with Jodie.

'He's even known as Pimp my Premiership McNulty', The Eyes continued, as the group practically fell off their stools laughing. 'He comes down here all the time and blows thousands on high-class hookers!'

I felt sick. An image flashed through my mind of our cosy dinners with Davy and Holly, with her talking lovingly about his frequent 'business trips' down south, and how he was investing and planning for when he retired from football. Jodie looked at me sympathetically, as if to say, what do you expect, Louise, he's a footballer?

'That's when he's not getting his rocks off with the Pleasure Machine, of course.'

I frowned. 'The Pleasure Machine?'

The Eyes looked shocked. 'Don't tell me you've never heard of the Pleasure Machine? The supermodel-turnedsupershag? She's been round half the Premiership. And appeared on most of their bat phones.'

'Bat phones?' I spluttered. I couldn't get my head around all this.

Now The Eyes were incredulous. 'Yes, bat phones. A footballer institution. The number they give to girls they meet out on the pull. The ones the same girls send X-rated pictures to. The ones you wives and girlfriends will never find because they're stashed safely away in the car glove compartment or their locker at the training ground. The bat phone is the key to all the extra-curricular activities players like McNulty get up to.'

My head was spinning now. How awful for Holly! What kind of world had me and Adam moved into? And how would he cope when he found out what his idol and new friend got up to away from home?

To my horror, I felt my eyes well up with tears.

The Eyes suddenly looked concerned. As the rowdy laughter continued around us, he leant forward and spoke softly again. 'Hey, babe, I'm sorry – I didn't mean to upset you. I figured you'd know all about that stuff.'

I looked at him through a veil of tears 'No, I didn't. And I'm sorry, but I still don't believe it. That's not the Davy I know. It's sordid and it's horrid and it's . . . it's wrong.'

The Eyes softened again. 'Well, you know what? I happen to agree with you. And you don't need to worry about me chatting you up, because I've got a girlfriend too.

She's a model and she's also very loyal.' He picked up his glass and angled it towards me as if to chink mine. 'I'm Will Daniels.' I flinched – Will Daniels was a high-profile player, the captain of another team up north. How stupid of me not to recognise him. 'And so for the rest of our time together, let's forget about other people's marital problems and concentrate on how lucky we are – in the first place to have such great relationships, and in the second place to have found a like mind in the big pick-up joint that we call London town.'

I smiled wobbly, still shaken but suddenly relieved. I chinked his glass. 'OK, cheers.'

As the night went on (helped by a few more bottles of bubbly), I totally forgot my initial discomfort. Jodie and Danny were clearly revelling in each other's company, but there seemed to be no ulterior motive on either part. And Will was great company. For a Premiership team captain he seemed to be totally lacking in ego, and when the other lads (Danny aside) went off in search of 'some totty', he said he'd prefer to stay and chat some more. He was attentive, friendly and good fun. And, I had to admit, it was nice to be made a fuss of after the past few weeks running around after Adam – and being largely ignored in return.

At around 1 a.m., I decided we should call it a night – Jodie was a bit the worse for wear and had her magazine interview the next day, after all. When Will asked for my phone number, I looked at him uncertainly. Instinctively I wanted to say yes – but wasn't that against the rules? How would Adam feel if he found out?

Will seemed to sense my confusion and smiled kindly. 'Don't worry, Miss Adam Jones, there's no ulterior motive – we're friends, aren't we? We can all hook up as a foursome if you like. After all, you need as many friends as you can get in football.'

But I still didn't give him my number. Friends in football might be hard to come by, but I figured I was one of the lucky ones.

Wasn't I?

Chapter 6

Jodie sighed and pushed the satin Marchesa dress she'd just bought from our favourite boutique back in its tissue-lined, ribbon-tied cardboard carrier bag. We were having our usual bottle of pink Laurent Perrier champagne (Jodie) and Caesar salad and chips (me and Tara) after our regular Friday shopping trip in town. These days, I was far less tentative with the old plastic and always made sure I'd got the latest designer bag, a gorgeous limited-edition top and the most exclusive boots or shoes (now I knew all the shop girls well, I tended to do quite well in the waiting list stakes. Although I couldn't rival the chairman's wife or Tara for priority, after them I was definitely one of the first to get a call if they'd got something extra special coming in). Trouble was, however much you tried not to care, it really was crucial to turn up looking your best on match day. It was part of our job, if you like – our own mini version of the competition taking place on the pitch.

Home games were the worst, somehow. At away matches, we'd still put the same effort in, of course – but there always seemed a lot of other stuff going on to occupy you. At home, you'd have all morning after the boys left at eleven to get yourself ready and get hyped up. It was a bit weird really. In Wales, Adam and I had always had a bit of lunch and then travelled to the ground together. But here, that wasn't allowed. The club insisted on the lads having their lunch at the ground – there was no way they'd let them play on anything less than top-notch nutrition – and warming up properly and doing kick squats or whatever they did. So you wouldn't see them from breakfast time until after the game! Adam was dead cute, though. In Wales, he'd always send me little notes via a youth player or one of the back room staff, saying 'missing you already' and 'love you babes' and stuff. He said he still tried to do it here every now and again, but it was a lot more difficult and I only got them through occasionally. And although he had his mobile, sending a text before a game would be really frowned upon.

Jodie, of course, didn't give a monkey's what the other girls thought of her – in terms of how she behaved or what she wore – but it didn't stop her caning her plastic every now and then, and today she'd been on mission super-glam from the off. 'It's a total see-me want-me shag-me dress, but where am I going to get Gary to take me in it when us girls aren't even invited on the bloody club Christmas do?' She sighed and tapped her French-manicured acrylics against the side of her champagne flute, probably imagining how she was going to seduce Gary out of his latest huff – they'd had another corker of a row after a red-top tabloid reported that he'd been chatting up a lap-dancer on the last lads' night out on Tuesday. He, of course, had denied it and it turned out they hadn't even been in that particular bar – so for once Jodie's tantrum had ended up being for no reason, and now it sounded as though Gary was milking it for all it was worth.

I frowned. The ban on wives and girlfriends at the players' Christmas do was apparently traditional – it was meant to be yet another bonding session for the boys – but it didn't make it any easier to take. Especially as all we were allowed to know about it was the date – not even the time or venue! As I took a swig of bubbly, Jodie's face suddenly lit up and she looked at me with a wicked glint in her eye. 'Sod 'em! Let's have our own Christmas bash. We'll get all the girls out – on the same night as theirs!'

I nearly choked on my LP. Trust Jodie to think of the most controversial plan she could. The boys would hate it – they'd hate us stealing their thunder and they'd hate us all being out together.

Tara wagged a warning finger at Jodie. 'Now, now, babe, don't go getting carried away,' she admonished. 'The boys' Christmas do is always just for them – we're never invited. I think it's a great idea to get all the girls together, but on the same night? I'm not so sure.'

Jodie tutted. 'Oh come on, Tara. Let yourself go for once! This'll be a giggle, and exactly what we need to encourage a bit of the female bonding you're always telling us is so important. Us against them!'

'We-ell, I guess it would be the best night for it,' acknowledged Tara. 'Although I'm in Florida with my mum and the kids around then . . .'

Jodie gave me a look. She suspected Tara was having a new boob job while she was away, but Tara had flatly denied it. 'Well, you won't need to sully your hands with it then,' she said decisively. 'You're up for it, aren't you, Lou?'

I gave Tara a sidelong glance. She definitely seemed OK with it, and so with her complicit approval, I laughed with glee. Jodie was right – sod 'em! 'Yes, I'm up for it,' I said, chinking my glass against hers. 'But God knows how we're going to talk the other girls into it . . .'

It took two weeks and a lot of hard campaigning to persuade everyone else. But after the boys sulked, me and Jodie plotted, trying to think of a plan that would mean we didn't bump into the boys anywhere, finally we were all set for our big night.

The idea was that the two of us would set off in the early evening for a few drinks, before meeting up with the other girls for more drinks and dinner a couple of hours later. We were both a bit nervous and giggly. I don't know why – I guess it was because we were doing something we weren't strictly supposed to. A bit like at school when you're passing notes or something. So the afternoon seemed to drag by, and even though I'd had my hair and nails done that morning, I still started getting ready with an hour and a half to spare.

Now, though, we were hot to trot, me in tight leather trousers and a Warehouse waistcoat, Jodie in a tiny black sleeveless Biba dress and black over-the-knee boots with five-inch heels. The bar we stopped at first was one of our favourite of the non-members' bars in town – all cool white decor, low lighting and air-con – and it was heaving, with most tables occupied and a pre-Christmas buzz about the place. (No tinsel or party decs, though – not in a bar that cool). I sighed with disappointment as I noticed our usual table was taken – a spot in prime position on a VIP platform towards the top right-hand corner of the room. Perfect for seeing and being seen! But I needn't have worried. The maître d' came rushing over to us as we walked in and led us straight over to it. As we stood at a discreet distance, he had a quiet word with the people at it and whisked them off somewhere else – drinks, nibbles, handbags and all. I chewed on my nail nervously. I always felt a bit funny when this kind of thing happened. Jodie and Tara, on the other hand, were old pros and revelled in it. Pattii, needless to say, was always over the moon too, and would look round and make sure everyone else was watching instead of trying to disappear from view like I did. Stupid really – I suppose such special treatment should have given me a bit of a thrill. Plus, in a way it was a quid pro quo. We were well known in town, and I guess there's nothing as good for business as two high-profile girls, well turned out and a bit glam, occupying your VIP table. When I thought about it, it was a neat little circle – it made other punters hang around more, spend more and talk more, and when all was said and done, it ensured we'd come back again!

As we waited for the table to be cleared, a slim, leggy blonde came rushing over, her pneumatic boobs bouncing conspicuously in an off-the-shoulder pink top, and spray-on hipster jeans hovering dangerously around her navel. She looked like a right slapper, but we knew her from some of the promotions she'd done at matches, and she was all right really.

'Jodie! Louise! How funny – I was just talking about you!'

We dutifully exchanged air kisses, Jodie eyeing her suspiciously and trying to sneak a peek at the bit of paper she was waving around. It looked like an invite, and Jodie prided herself on knowing everything that was going on at any given time.

'I was just saying how pissed off I'd be if I was you! But that I'd be making damn sure that I was out with the girls having an even better time than my other half! Hahahahaha!'

Jodie's brow furrowed, and leaning across me, she snatched the invite from the promo girl's hand.

We both read it in horror.

It was a bit dog-eared – a scrappy ticket, really – with cheap coloured ink detailing our boyfriends' Christmas party at Shimmy, a brand-new 'classy' lap-dancing club. So that's where they were off to! Nice.

But that wasn't the worst bit. Printed in neon along the bottom of the invite was 'Dress code: sexy. NO WIVES OR GIRLFRIENDS ALLOWED!'

I stared at it, not immediately taking in the implications. Adam must have had an invite. He must have seen this. And so he must have made a decision not to mention it to me. But why? I knew the lads occasionally went to lap-dancing clubs, it was the kind of thing that me and Adam would have a little giggle about. Why this time did he feel the need to keep it so secret? And why invite loads of other women in town and not any of us wives or girlfriends? We had no secrets. Did we?

I felt hot and heady, like my blood had started to boil. But Jodie was first to react, the telltale red mist descending over her. 'Where the hell did you get that?' she snarled, her face only inches away from the promo girl's. The promo girl stepped back in alarm.

'They've gone out to every modelling agency in town,' she stammered. 'We're all off there later. That's why—'

'Well, if there's so many invites going around, you won't be needing this one, will you?' snapped Jodie, and shoving it in her Versace bag, she stomped off to our table. I followed, stopping only to give the promo girl a quick kiss goodbye and her arm a conciliatory squeeze – after all, it wasn't the silly tart's fault we were going out with total arseholes, was it?

After a bottle of Veuve Clicquot to calm us down, we set off to meet the other girls. They were all in party spirits, glammed up to the eyeballs in flirty little dresses or skin-tight trousers and tops. Every single one had immaculate, poker-straight hair, strappy heels and lip gloss. You could almost hear the crackle of the nylon hair extensions as they chatted and laughed self-consciously. I checked myself. I mustn't take it out on anyone else. It was none of the other girls' fault I was feeling let down and betrayed.

After a few bottles of bubbly and two carefully timed rounds of B52s, Jodie and I decided it was time to act. I clapped my hands so that everyone fell quiet. Jodie's voice rang out across the private room we'd reserved for cocktails.

'Ladies – can we have your attention, please. We're obviously out tonight because our other halves are having their top-secret Christmas wank-fest. But we've got a secret. We know where they are – and what they're doing!'

As Jodie pulled the invite from her bag and showed it around, the glamorous, fake-tanned, happy faces fell one by one and an angry, hysterical buzz erupted. The girls were all looking at each other in disbelief, and calling their respective partners every name under the sun. In a matter of seconds, it seemed, the air had turned blue.

Jodie looked around grimly, arms crossed and a deter-mined look on her face. Suddenly she took a deep breath and nodded at me. I clapped my hands again and everyone looked at us expectantly. Jodie cupped her hands around her mouth.

'So, girls, what are we waiting for? Let's shimmy on down to Shimmy!'

Immediately the hubbub started again, as we moved en masse past the gaping waiters from the bar into the private cars waiting to take us on to the restaurant for dinner, and headed instead for the lap-dancing club.

When we arrived, all hell broke loose. The club, perched atop a wide, high staircase, was surrounded by bouncers, some of whom I recognised immediately as being employed by the football club to look after the players. But I wasn't the only one clocking familiar faces. In a tidal wave of Gucci, the girls charged out of the cars and up the stairs, and all the bouncers could do was look down in horror as they realised what was happening.

I was last out, and as I charged up the stairs after the rest of the girls, I bumped into Jonnie on his way out. Lucky for him – trust Jonnie to be in the right place at just the right time. He was loping down the stairs, hands in pockets as usual and a white beanie hat pulled down low over his ears – probably in case any paps caught him coming out of such a dive, I reckon. He looked a bit bemused to see us all, but in typical self-absorbed fashion, not too shocked.

'What's going on?' I yelled at him. 'What's happening in there?' He stopped and gave me a weird look.

'Erm . . . Well, you're all right, Louise,' he said. 'But she,' he turned and pointed at Jodie, who was wrestling with a bouncer, 'probably doesn't want to go in there. And she,' he pointed at Craig's wife, Becky, who had got past the bouncers and was now negotiating the steep staircase in her Jimmy Choos, using her oversized Mulberry handbag for balance, 'DEFINITELY doesn't want to go in.'

Just then, Ada – the wife of the new Italian striker, Gianni – practically fell out of the club, pulling her husband with her, screaming blue murder in Italian. I had no idea what she was saying but his sheepish expression and the two strippers following closely behind said it all. One was carrying a pair of handcuffs. I guess the poor cow didn't need an Italian/English dictionary to work THAT one out.

I suddenly felt sick, and sank down on to the marble step. Around me, it was all kicking off – the lads by now had cottoned on and were piling out of the club, some in various states of undress, and pissed husbands and drunk wives, angry fiancés, outraged boyfriends and hysterical girlfriends were screaming blue murder at each other in public. It was all so ugly. And somewhere, Adam was part of it.

It didn't take me long to find him. Or at least, for him to find me. As I sat there with all hell breaking loose around me, I suddenly felt someone grab me roughly by the arm and yank me up off the step. It was Adam. He was incensed with anger, and I was scared. I'd never seen him like this before – his eyes were black with rage and he looked at me like I was a stranger. Ironic, really. After all, it was him who was behaving so out of character – it was like he'd had some kind of personality transplant.

Dragging me down the stairs, he pushed me into a waiting car. I yelped in protest – Adam had never man-handled me before in our whole time together. But he didn't seem to care, or even notice. He just sat as far away from me in the back seat as possible, staring grimly out of the window when he wasn't texting furiously on his phone.

I sat there pitifully, not knowing what to say or how to break this huge, heavy silence between us. Ridiculously, I felt like I should apologise. Like, what had I done wrong? But I just wanted to make things all right again.

Some hope. This was the start of a monster sulk that was to last for days. And judging from my secret texts to some of the girls, Adam, in his new sullen style, had taken it worse than any of the other boys. He wouldn't speak to me, or even look at me.

By Christmas Eve, I was at my wits' end. This was meant to be our dream Christmas – the first we'd spent together in our new home, and because he had a fixture on Boxing Day, the first we'd spent on our own away from our families. Two weeks ago, I'd been so excited – buying presents, getting advice from Mum on cooking the Christmas dinner, and planning our decorations colour scheme (I'd had to hire a company to get the Christmas tree up to the flat – and in the end I'd figured I might as well go the whole hog and get them to decorate the entire place. Now the flat was a gorgeous purple and gold grotto, with a magnificent six-foot Christmas tree in one corner of the living room, and Christmassy flower arrangements and table decorations on every free surface).

Yet Adam still refused to speak to me, and I felt lonelier and sadder than I could ever remember. He was in the living room, playing on his PS3, and I was sat at the dining room table, going over my running order for lunch the next day. Suddenly I burst into tears. Adam looked over his shoulder unconcernedly and turned back to the TV screen.

I stood up, suddenly more desperate than I could ever remember being, and ran over to him, kneeling by his feet. 'Adam, will you just speak to me?' I begged. 'I can't cope with this any more! I've said I'm sorry, I just don't know what else to do.'

I grabbed hold of his leg beseechingly. I was being pathetic, I knew, but I couldn't seem to stop.

Adam looked down at me.

'So, you're sorry now, are you?' he sneered. 'What happened to the horrified girlfriend? The sneaky, secretive girl who went snooping around looking for trouble?'

I blinked hard, shocked. Surely *they* were the ones who'd been secretive and sneaky?

Adam sat up, warming to his theme. 'What happened to the silly little girl who decided to make a show of her boyfriend when he'd only been at the club for five minutes?

Who's doing his best to fit in and succeed and make a lovely life for her?'

I was sobbing now, clutching at his feet in misery.

He shook me off angrily. 'Right now, Louise, I can't look at you, let alone speak to you.'

He stood up and stormed off towards the bedroom.

'But Adam,' I wailed, still kneeling. 'It's Christmas!'

He turned. 'Happy Fucking Christmas.'

Next morning, I got up early, determined that I was going to turn things around and make it a lovely day. My eyes were puffy and red from crying, and I felt wrung out after only a few hours' sleep, but I was hopeful that after his outburst last night, Adam would be willing to forgive and forget. I pushed aside the niggling doubts that really it should be him apologising to me. He was feeling insecure at the moment, after all, and he wasn't reacting rationally. I should be making some allowances for him – and anyway, it was Christmas, wasn't it?

I put a bottle of Veuve Clicquot rosé in the fridge, a Christmas CD on the stereo and, ignoring the butterflies in my tummy, started work on the turkey. I'd have it all lovely by the time Adam got up, and he'd have no reason to still be upset with me.

When I heard him moving around an hour or so later, I wiped my hands on a tea towel, pulled the Veuve out of the fridge and poured two generous flutes. He wandered sleepily into the kitchen, and I held one out to him, smiling shyly.

'Happy Christmas, baby,' I said. 'Peace on earth and all that – how about peace between us two?'

He stared at me like I was something nasty on the bottom of his shoe. 'Didn't you hear me yesterday? I'm not in the mood. And who the fuck has a drink the day before a big match – don't you pay any attention to what I need?'

He opened the fridge door, pulled out a carton of milk and wandered over to the TV. I stared after him in shock. And a Happy Fucking Christmas to you too, I said inwardly. I didn't dare say it out loud. Adam had never behaved like this before, and I was at a loss as to how to deal with it. He was being irrational, unfair and really, really mean – but he seemed hell-bent on ignoring that and instead turning the whole thing round on me.

Dismally, I took a long glug from the glass of champagne I was still holding and turned back to the half-peeled potatoes. We had to eat, after all.

During lunch, we ate silently, the only noise the cutlery chinking on the plates and the sound of the TV in the background. The luxury purple and gold crackers stayed unpulled, and the Saint-Émilion red wine unopened. I was on my fourth glass of pink champagne, but it wasn't having any effect other than to numb the pain a bit.

Once we'd finished, Adam got up and stretched, ready to slouch back through to play yet more computer games.

'Wait, baby,' I said brightly, clearing away the dishes. 'Let me just get rid of these, and I can give you your pressies!' I thought of the carefully chosen and beautifully wrapped gifts under the Christmas tree. There was a signed Leeds City strip from the lead singer of one of the UK's most successful rock bands, who also happened to be one of City's biggest fans. I'd got him the limited-edition Blackberry he'd been banging on about, and a remote-control car – retro but fun, I'd thought, and he'd always loved novelty toys like that.

He looked at me in disgust. 'What's the point in having presents, when I'm the one who's paid for them?' he sneered.

I stared at him as he turned, eyes welling up with hot tears yet again. How cruel could he be? I brushed away the persistent tears as I filled the dishwasher, and decided to phone Jodie. I locked myself in the en suite (with a full glass of bubbly) to make the call. I'd promised Adam I wouldn't speak to her, but I needed someone to commiserate with, and she hadn't responded to any of my sneaky texts. I wasn't surprised – I figured she'd be in even more trouble than me. It had been her idea, after all! And with Gary's temper, he could have done anything, including taking her phone off her completely.

But I couldn't have been more wrong. She was as perky and chirpy as ever.

'Oh, honey, you know what me and Gary are like,' she purred down the phone. 'We're at each other's throats one minute and then all lovey-dovey the next. In fact he bought me that darling diamond Cartier watch I wanted yesterday because he loves me so much!'

I made all the right cooing noises and put the phone down with a heavy heart. I took a deep sip of champagne and leaned back against the bathtub. What a pay-off, I thought. He publicly makes a fool of you and lies to you, and then nips out and spends half his week's salary on a diamond watch and it's all all right. Although at that point I would gladly have swapped the sulks for some tactical sparkle.

But really, what difference did any of it make in the long run? We were all in the same boat at the end of the day. Our other halves had lied to us, deceived us and some had even cheated on us – but instead of them being in the wrong, it seemed we were all in the doghouse for crashing their big night. And I just couldn't shake the feeling that it wasn't right. Or that I was right in the middle of someplace I wasn't sure I really wanted to be – but a place I couldn't see an easy way out of.

Chapter 7

After the Christmas party fiasco, you'd think that the guys might start questioning their own behaviour. That they might realise how hurtful that kind of situation was for all of us wives and girlfriends. Or, if that kind of normal approach was beyond them, that the club would give them a talking-to and remind them of their priorities – like focusing on their jobs and their families! But no. As usual, we were last on the list of things to worry about. The club closed ranks around their stars, and after their mammoth festive match fixtures, the boys all became even closer, spent even more time with each other and had even longer midweek bonding sessions. Weirdly, the same didn't happen to us wives and girlfriends. Instead of us all pulling together, supporting each other through it and being a force to be reckoned with, we all kind of retreated back into our ivory towers, almost as though nothing had happened. Tara, of course, revelling in the fact that Jonnie had come out of the whole thing whiter than white, tried to paint herself as some kind of martyr, inviting some of the girls round to talk things through, like a one-woman marriage counselling service – but I don't think anyone took her up on it. They were too busy trying to forget about it – after taking it out on their credit cards. Carlotta, who'd found her other half Kieron, one of the midfielders, getting a blow job from a lap-dancer in the ladies' loos, even bought a top-of-the-range Subaru on her black VIP Amex card – and then, when Kieron objected, told him he was lucky she hadn't bought herself a new flat! But for the most part, it was kind of like the girls accepted it – it was part of the unspoken contract they'd signed when they moved in with their boyfriends or husbands. The one where the lads got to do exactly what they wanted, whilst the wives and girlfriends stayed sitting pretty at home like gilded lilies.

One of the girls who'd been most pissed off was Becky. When she'd eventually found her errant husband Craig, he was sheepishly doing up his shirt in a dark corner of the club, protesting his innocence. Like the others, he'd eventually turned the tables and had a go at her for ruining their night and showing him up. But apparently she'd not taken any of it, and they too had spent the whole of Christmas in separate rooms – the difference was, she'd demanded it. You had to admire her nerve. As Tara said, 'Well, if you're worried your man is cheating, the last thing you want to do is go and deprive him of sex – he'll be like a bitch on heat and trying to think up all sorts of reasons why he needs to go out after training.'

She had a bloody good point, but Becky and Craig had got two kids – so you couldn't blame her for making him see how out of order he'd been. Anyway, she eventually appeared at a game one Saturday in January with a huge heart-shaped yellow diamond ring from Theo Fennell, so it must have had the desired effect – for a while.

Eventually even Adam came round, thank goodness. He started to thaw out a little bit after Christmas, and by New Year's Eve was almost back to his normal cute self. We had a quiet one at home, as he'd got a fixture the next day, and I cooked and we watched a film and snuggled up on the sofa It was like the old days. Almost.

To be honest, I was trying to be a bit more understanding with Adam's mood swings. After all, it had taken me a little while to settle in, and I'd fallen on my feet with two great new mates almost immediately! I'd had lots to learn – what I was meant to be cooking for Adam and how, for example and despite their special diets and strict nutritional rules, the club never gave us girls any specific instructions, it was like we were just meant to know it instinctively or something! But even though Tara couldn't cook, she knew the rules, and so once I'd got some guidelines, and Mum had emailed me some recipes and given me some lessons over the phone, I felt a lot more confident about what I was doing. No more takeaway pizzas in front of the TV for us – it was a carefully balanced meal every night at six p.m. on the dot! I wasn't the one having to live up to the demands of a

Premiership team and I guess I couldn't blame Adam for getting really stressed. I was sure he'd come around and get back to normal when he felt totally at home with all his team-mates.

As the film finished, Adam yawned and rolled over. 'Big day tomorrow, baby,' he said, nuzzling my neck. 'Start of the transfer window. Wonder who's going to be doing the off?'

I yawned too. 'Wow — I'd forgotten,' I said. 'Isn't that a bit unsettling for you all?'

He shook his head. 'Nah — it's all part and parcel, isn't it?' I flinched at his hard-man act, and he looked at me sheepishly. 'Well, I suppose it is a bit,' he admitted.

I smiled and stroked his hair back from his forehead. 'At least it's unlikely to affect you this time around.'

He sat up indignantly. 'Well, who's to say it won't? I've played pretty well this season.'

I jumped. 'Ad — I wasn't saying you hadn't. I just thought it would be too soon!'

He relaxed and lay back down again. 'You're right. I don't think I'd want to move yet anyway. Unless DD came calling, of course!'

We both laughed. DD stood for David Davidson — legendary manager of Hardcastle United, consistent Premier League front-runners. Adam had always wanted to play for him — and despite his commitment to Leeds City, he still harboured that ambition. The trouble was, even if he ever did attract DD's attention, nine times out of ten he always messed up if someone important was watching.

But that was a long way off happening, if it ever did.

The atmosphere in the players' lounge for the first match of the year was still a bit low, if even more showy than ever – the girls all seemed to be compensating for their emotional downer with even more bling and glossy slap than usual. Jodie and I were sitting at our table, idly helping Delilah arrange her dolls so they could see the television to the right of the bar, and watching Tara flit around the other tables, making sure all the girls and their blokes were back on track. Her OTT smiles and sympathy were creating a kind of Mexican wave of emotion around the lounge.

Suddenly Jodie cackled. 'Look at her, Louise, she's like Mother Bleedin' Teresa!' She clapped her hand over her mouth as Delilah looked up questioningly. 'Don't listen to me, Lila darling, I'm the vocal equivalent of a rubbish dump.' She winked at me. 'Lord knows what will happen if me and Gary ever have kids, eh, Louise? Once we start rowing we turn the air blue – any little ones'll be fluent in four-letter words before they can even say Dada!'

I giggled, and made a big fuss of the nearest doll to try and distract Delilah from remembering (and repeating) Jodie's slip-up. As I did, the subdued chatter suddenly stopped, leaving only the tinny murmur of the football pundits building up matches around the country from the plasma screen on the wall. I looked up expectantly. Standing at the door proprietorially was a tall, olive-skinned woman, flanked by two burly bodyguards, looking imperiously around the room. She was a vision of eighties glamour – her red hair elaborately coiffed into big, voluminous curls cascading over her shoulders, her well-preserved and cosmetically enhanced eyes, cheeks and lips all heavily painted, and big, gaudy jewellery glinting from her ears, throat and wrists. She was wearing a classic black Chanel bouclé suit with oversized gold buttons, her endless legs shown off to maximum effect in miniskirt, sheer black tights and black stilettos. It was statement power-dressing, va-va-voom glamour and the signature style of Gloria Gregoria, the chairman's wife.

Apparently, Gloria rarely honoured us with her presence, preferring instead to entertain the chairman's guests in the lofty surrounds of the plush club boardroom. I'd never been up there – in fact, none of the players or their wives had. Apart from Tara, that is, who had been summoned together with Jonnie for a meeting with the club sponsors on the eve of his appointment as captain. She said it was a world away from the players' lounge – there was a dress code, for a start, and not just demanding the latest limited-edition fashions. No jeans, trainers or open-toed shoes were allowed, the bar was waiter service, and there was a sumptuous buffet on permanent offer. Being part of the chairman's posse meant that in football terms you really had arrived – and Gloria was always happy to let you know it. (Famous for her colourful past life as a cabaret singer, she was better known than her husband, and was seen as something of an eccentric national treasure. She had a range of nicknames including Glo-girl, Glo-bag and Go-Glo, depending on how you felt about her that day or which newspaper you were reading.)

Right now, she opened her arms wide like a preacher welcoming her flock, and started her stroll through the players' lounge, smiling and nodding regally at the girls and their families as she passed.

Halfway round, she stopped beside Tara, who was perched on a chair arm, looking on in shock. As Gloria touched her arm, Tara stood up and kissed her hello.

'Gloria — what a lovely surprise,' she said through gritted teeth. She couldn't stand Gloria — she said it was because the older woman patronised her, but we secretly thought it was more that when Gloria was around, Tara couldn't claim to be Queen Bee — but just now she looked for all the world as though Gloria was her favourite person ever.

Gloria smiled condescendingly. 'Tara, my dear, how shocked I was to hear about the boys' dreadful behaviour at the Christmas party.'

Tara's face set angrily. She was obviously biting her lip as she realised what this visit was all about. A thinly disguised excuse to gloat, and lord it over us unfortunate beings. And anyway, talk about after the event — where had Gloria been when we were all still reeling from it?

'No, it wasn't very pleasant. But I think we've all moved

on now,' Tara replied pointedly. Jodie sniggered and Gloria glared at her before turning back to Tara.

'Well, boys will be boys. And, my dear, it looks like you are coping admirably with the fallout. But I wanted you all to know,' she looked around the room at the hushed WAGs, 'that I am here for you all, if you need any words of wisdom or guidance. I am, after all, the first lady of football.'

As she turned on her heel and swept out the way she'd come, we all stared after her in shock, and then the babble started again, more heartfelt now everyone had something new to gossip about.

Jodie picked up her drink and drained it.

'First lady of football, my arse,' she scoffed. 'First lady in excusing her other half's affairs, more like.' She looked across at Tara. 'Oi, Tara, you OK?'

Tara looked a bit put out at her limelight having been usurped for even a minute, but smiled confidently. 'Oh yes, nice of her to come and visit, wasn't it?'

We knew she was putting on a front for everyone else, so we turned our attentions to one of the apprentices who'd just run in, all hot and bothered and a bit nervous to be in the players' lounge. He spotted me and ran over, handing me a scrappy page from a diary, then ran off again, blushing wildly. My heart leapt. A note from Adam!

Jodie nodded knowingly. 'I told you he'd come round, Louise. What's he say?'

I unfolded the paper.

'Miss u already. DD here – don't want to mess up!'

My heart missed a beat, and my mouth suddenly went dry. Don't screw it up, Ad! I whispered to myself.

'Louise – you OK? What's it say?' Jodie's voice interrupted my thoughts and I screwed the paper up, threw it in my bag and smiled. 'Nothing much, Jodie. Just that he misses me. Y'know – the usual!' I grinned. I wouldn't have cared if the note had been a shopping list – it was a sure sign that Adam was becoming his old self again.

Well, his old self – but better. They won 3–2 – and Adam, far from messing up, scored the winning goal. He'd played one of the best games of his life, and when he appeared in the players' lounge, his face was shining with pride. Jonnie had his arm around him, and people were crowding around him, wanting to shake his hand and congratulate him. I waved excitedly and blew him a kiss. No point in fighting my way through that lot, I thought – I'd let him enjoy the attention. I'd have him all to myself later anyway.

Jodie and Tara were engrossed in a conversation with one of the other footballer's mums about her recent chin implant, and I watched Adam happily from my seat at our usual table as the rest of the team appeared from the changing room, slapping him on the back and reliving moments of the game.

'The First Division boy done good!' marvelled Craig. I frowned. No wonder Adam was so obsessed with fitting in if they still made him feel like a new boy!

'You'll make a Premiership player yet!' laughed Gary. Adam was still smiling, but I could tell he was smarting a bit from their jokes. There was no need for it really, was there?

'Y'know, you really came into your own out there, Ad,' I heard Jonnie say. 'That was one of the best games we've played – and a lot of it was down to you.' I saw Adam smile broadly, and I breathed a sigh of relief.

At last, a footballer who could speak sense.

'Adam! They're here!' I turned from the closed Venetian blind in the living room that I'd been peering through for about the last hour, and threw a cushion at Adam, who was slouched on the sofa in front of the *Match of the Day* from last Saturday, which he'd taped. DD must have been impressed – he'd called Adam's agent immediately and now, just over a week later, they were all set for a top-secret meeting to discuss a potential transfer.

Of course, no manager was allowed to talk about a transfer to a player who was already under contract, so it was all having to be really hush-hush. DD's people had even gone so far as to have *their* people call Ad's agent, and no direct contact must be even hinted at – which was why we were having the meeting at our flat. What I couldn't work out was how they thought the sleek black A-class Merc snaking its way up the drive to our apartment block was going to stay anonymous. I mean, lots of rich people lived here, but surely

DD sitting in the back was going to draw unwelcome attention to it?

Adam got up. He was edgy and a bit nervous. He patted his jeans pockets and wiped his palms down his trouser legs.

'OK, baby – you're still all right to go down to meet them, aren't you?'

'Yes, no problem,' I said, leaning forward and giving him a gentle kiss on the tip of his nose. 'And don't be nervous, you! It's *them* that want *you*, remember?'

From down the corridor came the noise of the toilet flushing, and Adam's agent, Trevor, walked out of the cloak-room – he'd spent most of the morning in there, as far as I could tell – and clapped his hands in a businesslike way. His weaselly little face looked a bit peaky, lacking its usual bright pink cheeks, and he had telltale beads of sweat on his brow. The top button of his blue stripy shirt was undone and his red tie was slightly awry, in stark contrast to the sharp tailoring of his suit. On reflection, the toilet was the best place for him, I thought – although ours was definitely too upmarket for the likes of him. I had never really warmed to him, and though he would always go on to anyone who'd listen about how lovely I was, I was sure that in his heart of hearts the feeling was mutual.

'So, people – ready to make some cold, hard cash?'

I smiled tightly and hurried past him. DD's people had demanded that they get garage access to the flat, rather than risk him being seen entering, and we'd agreed it was best if I let them in (privately I thought this was just as transparent as them being seen with Adam or Trevor, but I had agreed anyway). I took the lift down to the underground car park and waved as the Merc silently pulled in. I counted three people – the chauffeur and what looked like a bodyguard in the front, both wearing shades, and a small, bookish-looking man in the back seat. So where was DD?

As the car pulled into the space we'd reserved for them – right by the lift door – I peered into the back, and there, appearing from underneath an oversized picnic blanket, was DD. One of the most famous managers in the world, all coiled up on the floor of a car – just to come and see my Ad!

I stifled a giggle as he clambered out, and quickly showed them all into the lift without speaking. I was petrified!

Once we'd got up to the flat, DD – who hadn't spoken either – turned to me with a big fatherly smile.

'So, you must be Louise. We must have seemed very rude not saying a word in the lift. But you can never be too careful.' He tapped his nose conspiratorially.

'Please don't concern yourself!' I said, going red and weirdly sounding like the Queen all of a sudden. Get me, putting on airs and graces!

There was an awful lot of hand-shaking and back-slapping and guffawing (mainly from Trevor – I could hear his characteristic snorting laugh above everyone) before they all sat down around the dining room table. I'd carefully laid out water, tea and coffee and some fruit (I had actually also got in some chocolate biscuits, but realised just in time that this wasn't really the image we should be giving them). I was really conscious of not being where I wasn't wanted, so I began to edge my way out of the door.

'Well, I'll get out of your way . . .' I started to say.

DD turned in his seat and looked at me. 'Erm – no, actually, Louise, we're going to need you for this bit, if you don't mind. Please, take a seat.' He gestured towards the one next to Ad and I gingerly sat down. I nearly thanked him before I remembered it was my house. Ad was looking from me to DD nervously.

DD folded his hands and leaned across the table towards us. 'So, are you two married?'

I was taken aback. 'Er . . .'

Adam interrupted. 'No, we're not – yet.' Under the table, he squeezed my leg. 'But it's something we're always talking about.'

I looked at him in surprise. It was something we *had* talked about – but not for ages.

To my left, Trevor cleared his throat self-importantly. 'To be honest, it's been on the cards for a long time, David – but Adam made the decision to concentrate on his game rather than his personal life.'

DD smiled politely. 'Well, that's an admirable approach. But I'm very much in favour of married players. I'm not telling you what to do, of course, but in my opinion, if you're serious about each other, it would be a good idea to get married.' He stared intently at Adam. 'Especially considering the company you've been keeping, son. We don't have incidents like that aberration of a Christmas party at my club. You play for me, you play it my way. A footballer's place is on the pitch or at home with his family, not out gallivanting around nightclubs and strip joints. I train professionals, not playboys, understand?'

Adam nodded obediently, his sweaty hand still on my knee.

DD echoed the nod, his businesslike and decisive. 'Very good. That will be all for now, Louise – thank you.'

It was my turn to nod now, mutely, as I dashed thankfully out of the room, my heart racing. I wasn't expecting that!

By the time DD and his entourage left the building, it was dark, but they still insisted on the whole blanket drama. I had to laugh – it was a bit ridiculous, after all!

Trevor was the next to leave, his mind obviously now firmly on his 20 per cent and figuring exactly how he could maximise his cut.

As I came back upstairs from waving them all off, Adam was stood in the kitchen, clutching a glass of milk and gazing into space. I smiled to myself. Old habits . . . I thought. Just as well there were no cookies or he'd have cracked into those too.

I put my arms around him in a loving hug. 'So, lover boy, I take it that went well?'

He gave me a bewildered look. 'Yeah. Yes, it did. They love me!'

I squealed, and he picked me up and swung me around until I shrieked at him to stop. He laughed and sat me up on the worktop, looking intently into my eyes.

'And I love you, baby. I probably don't tell you that enough.'

I gazed into his puppy-dog eyes, and felt the old feeling of blissful happiness wash over me. 'And I love you, Mr Jones.'

He grabbed my hands, suddenly serious.

'Good. Because . . . because . . .' He stopped, and I looked at him questioningly. What was he on about?

Suddenly he got down on one knee and looked up at me beseechingly.

'Because I think DD's right. I think we should get married! Louise, will you marry me?'

My hands flew from his grasp up to my cheeks and I stared at him in shock. My head was spinning. Had I just heard right?

'Say – say that again, Ad,' I stuttered.

He laughed. 'Louise, will you marry me?'

I stalled. This was everything I'd ever wanted. But from somewhere deep inside me, I felt a niggling doubt. A little voice was whispering 'no'. I shook myself. Don't be stupid, Louise, I told myself. This is Adam, love of your life, the man you've always wanted to marry. You're just overwhelmed.

'Louise, give me an answer!' Adam said insistently,

141

suddenly looking concerned. What was I thinking? This might not be the moment I'd imagined him proposing to me, it might not be the place or the circumstances – but it was my Adam, and I loved him.

'Yes! Yes, you doughnut, of course I will!'

He picked me up again and swung me around, this time till I really was dizzy, and I laughed as he nuzzled my neck. After what seemed like hours, he pulled away and swung open the fridge door, pulling out a bottle of 1995 vintage Krug – a Christmas gift from Tara and Jonnie.

He popped the cork noisily and I giggled as the champagne frothed over the bottle mouth. 'C'mon, baby, we've got some celebrating to do! And then – we'd better get planning. We'll go and get you a ring tomorrow afternoon. We've got to move quick on this!'

As he turned to reach for some glasses, the doubtful little voice inside me nagged away at me again. We hadn't really talked about what the transfer meant other than for his career. A new club meant a new town, a new house, new friends – a new life – when I'd only just begun to feel at home in this one.

But I had no choice, did I? I'd chosen to be with this man, and I knew I had to go wherever he did.

Chapter 8

I closed the thick, catalogue-like wedding magazine and leaned back on the pillows, breathing in the scented Jo Malone candle on the bedside table next to me and holding my hand up so I could inspect my engagement ring for the thousandth time. The facets of the diamond caught the light and I smiled in delight. I'd chosen the Etoile design from Tiffany's, and the round-brilliant diamond bezel-set in a platinum band wasn't as flamboyant as some of the other girls', but I thought it was beautiful – classic, romantic and – well, kind of graceful.

The past week or so had been an exciting social and media whirl, as we announced our engagement to family, friends and finally the media. Everyone seemed thrilled – our families, in particular, who we had seen hardly anything of since we'd moved. Both my mum and Adam's mum were beside themselves, and were on the phone every five minutes wanting to know about venues, dresses, flowers – and what they were going to wear!

I was suddenly rushed off my feet with meetings with

wedding planners and dress designers, and answering all the letters and cards we'd got from Adam's ever-growing fan base. All this, and we hadn't even set a date yet!

Underlying it all, though, I was worried about Adam's transfer, which was looking increasingly likely. Negotiations were still going on between DD's people and Trevor – but despite all the secrecy, someone had leaked the possibility of Adam moving to the press, and the rumours were steadily growing in momentum. I'd managed to put the other girls off the scent, but I felt so guilty about lying to them – not to mention the prospect of leaving them, when I'd practically only just arrived!

But a wedding and the sniff of a scandalous transfer meant we'd even had a few paparazzi camped outside the flat (the security system wouldn't let them any further in than the big iron gates, thankfully).

I couldn't believe it the first time I'd pulled into the apartment and found a few scruffy-looking men with cameras loitering outside the gates. They had rushed over to the car when they realised it was me, and I'd got all flustered, dropped the automatic key to open the gates, and had to scrabble around on the floor of the car for it as they thrust huge, black, fierce-looking cameras in the windows at me. Finally, I'd found the key and accelerated through the slowly opening gates, shielding my face with my hand as I drove. I have to admit, once I got in I'd rushed over to the telly and turned it on to see if I'd made it on screen yet. I hadn't, of course, but I texted Mum and Dad, Sara and all my friends at home telling them to watch the news that night!

But after the initial excitement, actually having them outside day and night was a total nightmare. Not only did we have to keep all the blinds down all the time, but even just nipping out was like preparing for some flipping fashion show. Ironic that now I was busier than I'd been since I'd stopped working, I was having to waste even more time on getting myself glammed up!

I'd never known anything like it. Why was the world interested in me? I knew we were now well known in the area, but living up here in our northern bubble, it had never really dawned on me that people further afield might know who we were, and care what we did. Even though I'd been used to seeing Tara and Jodie on TV and in magazines before we moved, I never thought that I might become even half as high profile as them!

Next to me on the bedside table, my mobile vibrated insistently – it was Tara. No surprise on match day. She often rang round – not, as with the other girls, to discuss outfits (she was far too important for that!), but to give a rallying pep talk to us all and make sure we were on good form and fully supportive of the boys.

'Louise, are you busy this morning?' she gabbled, not waiting for a reply. 'Only I wondered if you could pop round for a spot of lunch. I've spoken to Jodie – she's all set to pick you up at twelve. See you then?'

With that she hung up. I'd barely even said hello! I switched to speed dial to call Jodie, but before I could even press her button, she was already ringing me.

'What's all this about then, Louise?' she cooed excitedly. 'What's the betting she's preggers again? She's been keeping something quiet for weeks.'

I thought back, wincing as I remembered my own little secret. 'Maybe. Why all the urgency to tell us, though? I think it's something else.'

Jodie wasn't in the mood for pondering. 'Well, not long to find out. I'll pick you up in an hour.'

My fork hovered over a king prawn. Jodie, who hadn't even been pretending to eat her salad, nearly choked on a swig of Chablis. We both stared at Tara in disbelief.

'Italy? Jonnie's going to play in ITALY? You're going to live in ITALY?' Jodie was gobsmacked.

'Yes, Jodie, well done, I think you've got the point,' said Tara irritably, sweeping imaginary breadcrumbs on to the floor.

'But that – but that's . . .' Jodie once again was lost for words.

'A different country?' replied Tara sarcastically. 'I'm well aware of that, thank you, Jodie.'

It was my turn. 'But you don't even speak Italian!'

Tara glared at me. 'Well, the fact that fifty per cent of the Premier League don't speak English doesn't seem to stop them having a career here, does it?' she snapped. 'Jonnie's been made a fantastic offer, and it's going to be announced today. That's why I wanted to let you know first. We've thought long and hard about it. We've decided it's now or never. The girls are young enough to make the adjustment fairly easily, and we think it will be an exciting experience for us all. An adventure.'

I stared at her blankly. So this was what life in the Premiership was really like. I'd been worrying about Ad's transfer splitting up our little friendship group, when all along Jonnie was going to wreck it anyway. It didn't seem fair.

Jodie shook her head, and looked up mischievously. 'But what about us? What are we going to do without you?

Tara stood up and took our plates. 'Well, it's clearly not going to affect your appetite,' she said pointedly, looking down at Jodie's barely touched plate. 'Anyway, I'm sure you'll cope.' She rattled the plates on the side, and turned round with an equally mischievous look in her eyes. 'Especially when you hear about the leaving party I've got planned!

At the ground, there were even more paps outside the players' lounge, and we had to fight our way in. Fortunately, Tara had sent the kids to her parents' in anticipation of the press interest after Jonnie's announcement – but, given Adam's own transfer news, I did feel a bit worried that so many journalists and photographers would already be in situ at the ground when Jonnie's news broke. I mean, the press probably knew more about me and Adam than my mates at the moment, I was so busy keeping the possible deal under wraps. I would just have to try my best to act normally and pray nobody raised it.

Instead of stopping for a drink and a chat, I went straight out into the stands. Tara's announcement had shaken me up a bit, and I couldn't face any more questions about the wedding or the transfer rumours at this point. I looked out across the terraces. Somewhere, I knew, DD would have his people waiting, watching Adam's performance, judging their final offer on his on-pitch form today. Touch wood, he seemed to be flying at the moment, with another great game and two goals last week.

As the players made their way out on to the pitch, Jodie linked her arm in mine and gave it a squeeze. 'OK, babe?' she whispered warmly.

I smiled at her reassuringly over my shoulder and squeezed her back.

'This is football, I'm afraid,' she said. 'We'll be all right, you and me!'

I nodded mutely, guilt making me unable to reply.

We watched the first half of the game in companionable silence, only breaking it to scream encouragement to the team below. It was a fast, furious and evenly matched game. Both sides were marking the other closely, and neither seemed to have the upper hand, and as it approached half time, the score was still 0–0. Something out of the ordinary needed to happen to break the stalemate, I thought. Suddenly Adam took possession and sprinted towards the goal. He left behind player after player in his wake. The only one to gain ground on him was Andy Hill, a high-profile but dirty defender, who was giving it everything he had. Extending his right leg, Hilly went for the tackle – and Adam went down. The crowd, worked into a frenzy of excitement, all oohed in sympathy as Adam writhed in agony and was stretchered off the pitch.

Frantic with worry, and struggling to catch my breath from panic, I raced back into the players' lounge and down towards one of the medical rooms where I knew he'd have been taken for treatment. As I hurried along the tunnel, the physio who'd accompanied him off the pitch was walking towards me, shaking his head to stop me going any further. My heart stopped. He looked really grim – what on earth could have happened?

'Sorry, miss, you're not allowed past this point.' So that was it. The problem wasn't Adam – it was their stupid rules about access to the changing rooms!

'Is it serious?' I said, my heart in my mouth.

'Hamstring,' he mouthed, and squeezed my shoulder in sympathy.

I knew what that meant. At least four weeks out of action, and the ever-present worry of it recurring.

Adam injured. On his transfer game. This wasn't good . . .

★

'Louise, will you please just wait up,' moaned Adam, struggling to keep up on his crutches as we walked down the torchlit red, white and green carpet to Tara and Jonnie's La Dolce Vita gala evening. In my long coral Cavalli draped silk dress, and five-inch Gina sandals, I was hardly charging ahead, but I bit back my irritated response and turned to wait for him. Adam's injury had not only put paid to his transfer, but to the new, improved Adam, too. He had plunged into a deep depression, and was bored and crotchety. The media frenzy over Jonnie's defection overseas hadn't helped, and he was struggling to control his jealousy. I realised that a huge glam-tastic party to celebrate this was hardly what he needed, but they were our friends – and anyway, I'd been looking forward to this evening ever since Tara first mentioned it.

Everyone who was anyone was invited tonight – from A-list film stars to politicians, writers to rappers, It girls to theatre luvvies – even minor royalty. All the women were dolled up to the nines in full-length evening dress, and diamonded out of their brains. Lots of the biggest jewellery designers, like De Beers and Asprey & Garrard, had sent out invitations to the female guests to borrow gems for the evening, and by the looks of the bling on show here tonight – not to mention the very obvious security posted at every doorway to guard it all – most people had taken them up on the offer! From the moment we received the gold-leaf invitation to the Italian-themed night, delivered in a white box filled with gold tissue and tied with white silk ribbon, there was no way we were ever going to miss out – even if Adam did seem determined to spoil it for me before we'd even got there.

He'd been sulky all day, trying to delay us leaving by watching football DVDs until the last minute, taking ages to get ready and moaning about having to wear a hired dinner suit. I'd been on at him for days to buy one and in the end had had to pop out to Moss Bros for one – and of course, that wasn't good enough.

'I look like some kind of chav in someone else's suit,' he whined, while I carefully stepped into my dress and struggled with the zip. I'd turned to him for help, only to see him looking at me in disgust.

'What?' I said worriedly. I'd been really excited about my look tonight – my dress was a perfect fit, and although long and regal it showed off my curves and was subtly sexy. In a nod to the Roman theme, my hairdresser had softly curled my hair and pulled some back from my face, in a half-up, half-down kind of style, very romantic but again – I thought – pretty sexy.

But from the look on Adam's face, he thought different.

'You look like an ageing hippy,' he growled, looking at my bare feet sticking out from under the skirt.

I'd laughed nervously. 'I'm going to wear shoes, you doughnut!'

He hadn't laughed back. 'I know – it's just kind of – oh well. I guess there's no time to change it now.'

I'd fought back the tears as I clipped on the diamond shooting-star drop earrings I'd borrowed from Chopard. It was the first time I'd ever worn anything so valuable – they were made up of forty-six diamonds and I was excited but more than a bit nervous about wearing them!

In an effort to enjoy the night, I'd carried on being nice to Adam during the car journey, and had given myself a stern talking-to. Adam was really down, and I'd probably be a bit mean if I was feeling as depressed as him. I'd stolen a few sideways glances at him on the way, though – mood or no mood, he did look really fit in his dinner jacket!

But now, I gasped as we walked through the lemon-tree-lined entrance. Tara had spared no expense in creating an elaborate and sumptuous arena for the bash and the results were incredible – despite the fact she'd only had two weeks to pull it all together. A dome-shaped marquee masqueraded inside as Rome's Colosseum, with images of crumbling amphitheatre walls projected on to the marquee canvas. Olive and lemon trees were interspersed around the marquee, making it feel like an exotic garden – in fact, smoking areas outside were also designed as mini olive groves with intricate wrought-iron benches and ashtrays. The fifty tables, each set for ten guests, had centrepieces of elaborately arranged greenery twisting around heavily scented white lilies, and their fragrance, together with the jasmine candles flickering away all around the room, gave it a heady, sensual air. Buff-as waiters in tuxedos, bow ties but no shirts wandered around with trays of Bellinis, Italian Stallion cocktails and champagne, or platters of exotic-looking canapés that all seemed to be smothered in truffles or olives.

But as we strolled (or in Adam's case, hobbled) around the room, I realised the best was yet to come. Tara, who had kept most of the party details under her hat as a surprise, had told me to look up the Trevi Fountain – one of Rome's most famous landmarks – on the internet (she knew I'd never been to Rome). And as we passed an ivy-entwined balustrade, in the middle of the room was the *pièce de résistance* – only a replica of the Trevi bloody Fountain! I laughed out loud and clapped my hands spontaneously. 'Look, Ad, it's the Trevi Fountain!'

Beside me, Adam grunted, unimpressed. 'If I knew what the Trevi Fountain was, I might be able to appreciate it a bit better. Lou, can you grab me one of those cocktails, please?'

Still entranced with the working fountain in front of me, I reached out for a tumbler from the passing waiter and turned to Adam. He scowled at me, lifting up his crutch-encased wrists. 'God knows how I'm going to drink it, though – can't we go and sit down somewhere?'

Just then, I spotted Tara, mincing around and talking to everyone but looking nothing short of knockout in a strapless black taffeta floor-length dress by Alexander McQueen, split to the thigh, and sky-high Sergio Rossi silver sandals, with delicate straps that wound around her ankles and laced up just below the knee. She spotted me, too, and waved excitedly. Having done my homework, I guessed her look was a modern-day homage to Anita Ekberg, star of the film classic *La Dolce Vita* – Tara had even had her long blonde hair styled away from her face in delicate waves. However, she had also added diamonds to the look. Her throat sparkled with a thirty-carat De Beers diamond cluster necklace, and she wore a matching right-hand diamond cluster ring. The whole lot was worth well over a million pounds. I was speechless – she looked well classy.

Mind you, looking around, it seemed everyone had scrubbed up well – there were celebrities here I'd normally be too petrified to even look in the eye, but somehow, all glammed up and looking like just another party guest, they didn't seem so scary. I wished that I could take pictures, but Tara's mega-bucks deal with a celebrity magazine meant mobile phones and cameras were banned. Imagine what everyone at home would think of us rubbing shoulders with this crowd!

'Lou-lou! Adam!' I turned to see Pattii charging through the crowds, holding one Bellini above her head and another in her other hand, which was slightly askew and splashing champagne and peach juice down oblivious guests' party frocks. She had definitely embraced the Italian theme – but in a more Roman fashion. Her white toga-style one-shoulder Alberta Ferretti dress still managed to reveal its fair share of her ample cleavage, and stopped just short of her knicker line, showing as much fake-tanned leg as possible (and a bit more besides, if she wasn't careful). She was wearing gold Dolce and Gabbana thong platform mules (which bore more than a passing resemblance to lap-dancing shoes) and her hair was pulled back into its customary pony-tail, cascading over her shoulders in big ringlets. Shoulder-dusting diamond earrings glistened almost blindingly, and her arm jangled with diamond bangles, all borrowed from Bulgari. The overall effect was definitely OTT glamour girl – but I had to admire her balls. She wasn't one to try and fit any mould other than her own! Behind her, Jez followed sheepishly, clutching a pint (where had he got that?) and apologising to guests whose toes Pattii was inadvertently treading on in her haste to reach us. 'OMIGOD! Can you BELIEVE this place?'

She giggled as she kissed us both hello, and I took a step back in case her Bellini decided to slop out over my dress, too.

'I know. It's amazing, isn't it,' I said, taking in the surroundings once again. 'Where are you sitting, Pattii?'

She opened her eyes wide. 'OMIGOD, we've got the most amazing table. We're with Terry Tough and his wife – you know, the lightweight, I mean featherweight – the boxer; there's Andrew Fleming, you know, the ice dance judge, and I'm next to Fenella Fluff, the gossip writer – guess who'll be star of her column come Sunday?'

I nearly choked on my champagne. That might be Pattii's

idea of 'amazing', but I knew they were all Tara's least favourite people. If I'd ever been in any doubt about how she felt about Pattii, this was proof!

'I had a look for you too,' she rattled on. 'You're right up there near the top table. You're sitting with Ruby, Alan Ross the TV presenter and his other half, Charlie Townsend and his wife . . .'

'Charlie Townsend?' said Adam, suddenly piping up from his conversation with Jez. 'Come ON! He's on our table? Lou, what are we waiting for – let's go and sit down!'

Pleased to see him snap out of his mood for a while, I raised my eyebrows helplessly to Pattii and started winding my way to our table. I caught Jodie's eye, standing in a group with our club manager and coach. She looked stunning, as usual, but what no one else at the bash would appreciate was how little effort had gone into her look. She'd pulled her yellow Ghost shift dress out of her wardrobe earlier that day with an uninterested sigh. 'That'll do, babe,' she'd said. 'I'll say it's vintage. I think this little number dates back to the 1980s anyhow, and no one will ever know the difference.' I'd giggled – but now I marvelled at her ability to carry anything off and still look amazing. Yellow was a hard colour to wear, but it looked great against her dark skin and set off her green eyes, and with a skinny gold belt cinching in the waist, and huge gold hoops in her ears, the shapeless shift actually looked foxy! Beside her, Gary was in full-on schmooze mode. Probably with an eye to his fading career, he never missed an opportunity to impress his bosses. Jodie crossed her eyes at me in boredom. I giggled. 'You all right?' she mouthed, nodding at Adam. I put my thumbs up and she mirrored the gesture and blew me a kiss. 'See you later,' she mouthed again.

Our table was nearly full when we reached it. Ruby, a respected soul singer, was chatting animatedly with Alan Ross's wife, while Alan was busy talking to someone on the table behind. Across the table, I recognised a pop singer and his boyfriend, both dressed in matching suits – one gold, the other silver – and a Formula One driver. The only seats not taken were Charlie Townsend and his wife's – right next to me and Ad. So that should keep Adam happy for a while, I thought.

Just then, something slapped me hard on my back. 'Get in there, girl! Make room for a little 'un?' Charlie Townsend's wide Essex tones, familiar to me from the many films and TV programmes we'd seen him in, boomed out into my ear as he squeezed behind my chair and slid into the one next to me. 'Come on, Phillys darlin', you can fit through here.' Charlie's well-preserved blonde, tanned wife squeezed through with a smile and sat down. Charlie, who despite the black-tie dress code was wearing a shiny grey suit and matching tie, clapped his big bear hands together. 'Well, well, well, Adam Jones. What esteemed company I'm in!' I nudged my chair back to let them chat, and both Adam and Charlie immediately took advantage of it, leaning across me. Phillys gave me a sympathetic smile. Instinctively, I warmed to her.

'Bit of bad luck there with the old injury, mate,' barked Charlie. 'But you know what, son? Everything happens for a reason. And so I reckon that little transfer deal that I heard about on the grapevine wasn't meant to happen.'

Adam looked mollified by his idol's sympathy.

'And you know what that means?' continued Charlie. 'It means you're not playing at the moment, so tonight we can GEDDONIT!' He laughed and rubbed his hands with glee. 'So sod the wine and champers. I want some proper booze!'

Two hours later, after five courses – basil and mozzarella salad, tuna carpaccio, white truffle risotto, filet mignon with brandy, cream and peppercorns, and tiramisu (all cooked by celebrity chef Giovanni DaLuca) – our table was littered with the debris of Charlie's huge appetite for alcohol, and I, along with everyone else on the table, was starting to feel the effects. I'd stuck to white wine, but vodka, whisky, gin and brandy had joined the bottles of Gavi di Gavi, Montepulciano and still and sparkling mineral water that had been placed on the table – and Charlie had just ordered a bottle of ice-cold limoncello to follow the flaming Sambucas that the rather hesitant waiters were delivering to every table before coffee was served.

It was great fun, though – Charlie was a fabulous raconteur, and though Jodie had told me in the toilets that he had the reputation for being a 'taker' (which meant, she explained patiently, a friend of the rich and famous who was happy to accept 'donations' for creative projects that somehow never materialised), it was obvious that he gave it back in the way of good times and great company. Adam's shining eyes weren't just because of the booze, and I hadn't seen him this happy since we got engaged.

Just then, there was a fanfare from the big band before it broke into the unmistakable opening bars of 'Big Spender'. The lights dimmed and a spotlight swung dramatically around the room. We all looked around us wonderingly before it stopped on the Trevi Fountain, and Truly Scrumptious – famous drag queen and compère of the charity auction – stepped out of the water and slunk her way across the room to the stage. The room erupted into delighted laughter and applause as Truly – resplendent in tight sequinned gown, six-inch sparkly heels and beehive hair – took her place behind the mic.

First up, she introduced the hosts, Tara and Jonnie, who walked regally on to the stage for their farewell speech. Well, for Tara's farewell speech, really – Jonnie just stood there nodding gamely whenever he felt it was appropriate. It was a great speech – emotional, poignant, and also introducing the charity the auction proceeds were going to – and I must admit to feeling a bit misty-eyed at the thought of them leaving.

But once the speech was over, Truly took back the mic and the bidding began. I'd never been to an auction before, and I'd always thought they sounded dead boring. But this was really good fun. Lots of the celebrities had given 'money can't buy' gifts – Ruby had offered a recording session with her, for example, and the Formula One driver had pledged a race circuit with him in a rally car. A top golf player had promised a round of golf, and other local boutiques, hotels and restaurants had offered 'experiences'. Truly was camp and hilarious, and took the mickey out of everyone who was bidding – and some who weren't!

Across the room, Jodie pulled a face at me as a well-oiled Gary got into the spirit, bidding against a famous film producer for a huge framed, signed Bert Stern portrait of Marilyn Monroe. His technique appeared to be pulling more notes out of his wallet with each bid and waving them around ostentatiously. It struck me as a bit weird – Gary was usually such a tight-wad. Adam nudged me, laughing. 'Gal's been splashing the cash a bit recently,' he said under his breath. 'The only thing that normally comes out of his wallet is moths!'

I giggled, and as Gary's final bid of £15,000 sealed the deal, I turned my attention to the next lot – a case of fine champagnes that had apparently been collected over several years by a local businessman. Adam leant over to me. 'That seems like a lovely start to our wedding-day collection, don't you think, babe?' he breathed intimately into my ear.

I looked at him, touched. 'What, you want to bid for it?'

He grinned. 'No, babe, I want you to bid for it!'

I stared at him, horrified. 'I can't!'

Next to me, Charlie nudged me, chortling loudly. 'Course you can, girl. Wot a laugh! Come on, hands up!'

So suddenly I was in on the action – tentatively raising my hand and bidding every time, on either side of me, either Charlie or Adam nudged me. I was aware of Jodie and Tara's eyes on me, delighted but also horrified, as the bids went up and up and up. But I couldn't stop. Everyone was looking, and Adam and Charlie kept the pressure on, until the price had reached over £30,000!

I nudged Adam back. 'Babe! I'm scared! This is too much!' I hissed through gritted teeth. (I couldn't speak properly or it might have counted as a bid!)

Adam squeezed my knee. 'Don't worry, baby! We can afford it.'

But it seemed the other bidder couldn't, and suddenly Truly spoke the words 'Going, going – GONE! To the lovely lady in the peach. For thirty thousand pounds – a case of the finest champagne!'

Adam whooped in delight, kissing my neck in joy, and Charlie nearly fell off his chair in excitement. 'High five, girl! High five, Adam Jones!'

We all laughed as we slapped hands, and Charlie poured us all yet another limoncello shot.

'Well, here's to you two about-to-be-newly-weds,' he said joyfully. 'May your big day be as well oiled as tonight!'

Adam leant across the table, laughing hard, and clinked his shot glass. 'Well, I hope so, Charlie – we'd love you two to be there, of course!'

I stared at him in surprise. We hadn't even discussed a

guest list! I mean, Charlie and Phillys were lovely, but . . .

But worse was to come. Adam necked his drink and slammed it on the table. 'In fact, Charlie – we'd like you to have the champagne.'

We all stared at him in shock. Charlie roared with laughter and slapped him on the back behind me. 'You are a piece of work, Mr Jones! Let's all drink to that!'

And with another shot, my first £30,000 wedding present was given to someone we'd only just met.

Who said romance was dead?

Adam put his hand on my knee and leaned his head back. 'Well – that was a good night in the end, wasn't it, baby?' He squeezed my knee and smiled at me.

I stared at him incredulously. I still hadn't got over him giving away our wedding champagne, but he hadn't even noticed I was upset!

'Oh yes, it was brilliant. I'm not sure which was my favourite bit, though – spending all evening fawning over the biggest ligger in showbiz, or giving away thirty grand's worth of champagne to him,' I replied sarcastically.

Adam sat up like he'd been shot. 'What the fuck are you talking about?' he said angrily. 'He's a mate!'

I laughed. 'Yes, you and everyone else who's stupid enough to flash their cash in front of him! That was a gift for our wedding, Adam, and you giving it away was really hurtful. Not to mention making us a bloody laughing stock.'

As soon as I said the words, I regretted them. If there was one thing guaranteed to make Adam see red, it was the thought that he was in any way an outsider, that people were laughing at him.

'Yeah, well, it's my money and I'll do what I like,' he retorted. 'The day you've got even thirty quid of your own to put towards the wedding is the day you can have an opinion on how we spend it.'

I moved across the huge seat away from him. How dare he? As if I needed to justify my position. He wouldn't be where he was if it wasn't for me running around after him, doing everything for him – including massaging his huge ego. I was shaking with the injustice of it all – but there seemed little point in carrying on the row. Adam just never listened to reason these days.

Back home, we exited the lift in silence. Inside the front door, though, Adam turned to me and grabbed my shoulders passionately.

'Baby, baby love – I'm so sorry,' he slurred. I looked at him through my now sober eyes. Did he mean that?

'I'm sorry, baby, I just got carried away – you know what I'm like when I'm on one. I'll buy you a better wedding present than that. Forgive me – please?' he pleaded.

I shrugged off his hands and tried to walk past him. 'I don't know, Adam – that really upset me.'

He stepped in front of me, looking down at me with a dappy smile. 'C'mon, baby – it was just a silly mistake,' he wheedled. 'Give me a cuddle – let me make it better?'

Seeing his big brown eyes look at me so beseechingly, my heart softened. Sensing he was making headway, Adam grabbed hold of my hands.

'I can make it all better,' he whispered, kissing my neck and pulling me in to him. I felt myself melt. Resistance, it seemed, wasn't going to come easy . . .

But later, after Adam had rolled off me and immediately started snoring, I lay awake, an uneasy feeling washing over me. Adam had not only done something preposterous tonight – he'd insinuated I was only with him for the money. Was that what he really thought of me? And if so, what on earth was I still doing with him?

Chapter 9

The week following the party, I was really down. If I'd been upset at the thought of Tara leaving, the reality of her and the kids not being around was even worse. I hadn't realised quite how central to my life she'd become, and both me and Jodie felt like we'd lost a limb or something. She was so busy with settling them all in, coping with two kids in a hotel, looking for somewhere to live, that since she moved we hadn't even really had time to speak to her.

But then Leeds City won against Liverpool at home, so that helped lift our spirits, and we were on a total high. By the time the boys had made it suited and booted back into the players' lounge after the game, all glowing and damp from the shower, wafting expensive cologne and slapping each other on the back in matey congratulations, us girls had come up with our own celebratory game plan. We were going to head off home, get changed, and then go out with all our fellas to the latest members' club – have a late dinner, a few drinks and a bit of a dance too.

'Were' being the operative word, of course – little did

we know that in the short time it had taken them to shower and change, the lads had made their own plans and were heading out on their own – yep, you guessed it, more 'bonding'.

We were all fuming, and a couple of the girls had a half-hearted strop – but really, there was nothing doing. They'd made up their minds, and the prospect of a night out with their wives and girlfriends sure wasn't going to change matters, far from it in fact. Adam was apologetic, but it was obvious he'd made his mind up too.

'Awww, c'mon, babe – we can all go out any time.' He picked up a lock of my hair, twisting it around his finger playfully, and looked up at me winningly. 'This was a big game for us – we need to celebrate in style!'

I tried to stay cross, but I could feel my resolve melting away. 'I know – it's just that we're excited too, and it would be fun, all of us together.'

He frowned at me. 'And what about the single lads? Don't you think they'd feel a bit left out having to party with all our wives and girlfriends too?'

I opened my mouth to object – there hardly *were* any single players! – but Adam placed his forefinger on my lips to silence me.

'Look, baby, I'll make it up to you, I promise. The gaffer's given us tomorrow off – what say we go for a spot of lunch and some shopping?'

I crossed my arms petulantly and stuck my bottom lip

out. It was an old childhood habit that I recently seemed to have picked up again. The difference was, as a kid I'd either have got a slap across the back of the legs for it, or been ignored. With Adam, I either got an expensive gift or was ignored. I hated myself for doing it, but more and more often recently, it seemed the only way to deal with Adam's selfish whims.

'OK, I guess I haven't got any choice in the matter.'

He whooped with joy. 'Thanks, babe. We'll spend some proper time together tomorrow, I promise.' He gave me a huge sloppy kiss. I gave him a dejected peck on the cheek in return, got in the car and drove back to the flat for another night in, in front of the telly.

I ended up having a long hot bath, and was half asleep in bed when my mobile went off. I always kept it on in case Adam needed to get hold of me – he had a habit of ringing in the early hours on a big night to tell me how much he loved me (I know I'm soft, but I did like to hear it!). Admittedly, those calls were starting to get a bit less frequent, so my heart leapt when I heard it go. But it wasn't Adam – it was Becky. Weird or what?

'All right, babes, what's up?' I said sleepily.

'Lou – have you heard from Adam? Do you know where he is? I'm trying to get hold of Craig.'

Her voice sounded weird – a bit strained, like she'd been crying. Either that or she was dead angry – and having seen her in action on the night of the Christmas party, anything was possible. You wouldn't mess with Becky, that's for sure.

I hadn't heard from Ad, of course – but I thought I knew where they'd all be, so I gave her the name of the nightclub they tended to go to when they were out en masse. It wasn't a members' club – but it had a big VIP section, so I figured they not only got special treatment but got to hang out with other local celebs too.

'Craig'll be all right – they all went out as a group, and you know they always stay together. I'd go to bed and not worry, if I were you,' I said, trying to mollify her. She hung up without even saying thanks, and I thought how odd she was. I almost felt a bit sorry for her, though – imagine having to call someone else's fiancée to find out where your husband was.

Next thing I know, it's 3 a.m. and Adam's come in, absolutely hammered and ranting. I heard a crash as he stumbled through the door, and could hear him calling my name as he made his way up to the bedroom.

'Louise. Lou-ise!' Suddenly, the light went on and I sat up, blinking.

'Ad, what's the matter. Are you OK?'

Adam stood swaying in front of me, dishevelled and looking angry.

'No, I'm bloody not all right!' His words were slurred and his eyes were rolling. Talk about out of it! He started trying to unbutton his shirt, but stumbled and fell into the wardrobe door. 'Humiliated and belittled. HUMILIATED AND BELITTLED, that's what it boils down to.'

I slid out of bed and went around to help him with his shirt, but he knocked my hand away in irritation. 'Not me. Craig! That bloody witch Becky. Stalker. STALKER! You give someone everything you can, and they try to take away your civil rights.'

I sat down on the bed, puzzled. 'Adam, I have no idea what you're going on about. Becky rang me earlier and I—'

He turned around, glaring. 'You? *You* were part of it? Fanfucking-tastic. I should have known. I've warned you, Louise! First Craig and now me. You girls, you're embarrassments, the lot of you. You should be thanking your lucky stars, not turning into moaning bloody stalkers.'

I stared at him in shock and confusion. What on earth was he banging on about? With a dramatic sigh, he lay back on the bed, closed his eyes and passed out. That was obviously as far as we were going to get tonight . . .

After a sleepless night, I couldn't wait to find out the rest of the story but Adam was first dead to the world and then occupied with his Wii, so I had to wait until I left home for a hair appointment to phone Jodie to see what was what. Of course, she knew the whole story.

You won't believe what Becky did. She must have put the phone down from me, woken the kids up and piled them – still bleary-eyed and in their pyjamas, bless them – into the car, then driven into town.

Apparently she went to the club I'd suggested, but the lads weren't there – so she drove all the way around town until she found them at another, really seedy lap-dancing club. She stormed in, dragging the kids along with her – one of them was apparently still clutching his little teddy bear by the paw – and stomped around the club until she found the lads. They were all stood on the dance floor in a big circle, leering at whatever was going on in the middle. Still, she couldn't see Craig, so she pushed through the circle to see if he was on the other side of it. He wasn't. He was in the middle, literally caught with his pants down, wrapped around some girl on the dance floor, doing all sorts. And I mean *all sorts*. I'd heard about these kind of girls before, but never actually known someone to get involved with them. They are vile – they have no shame, and will do anything to get a footballer. Full sex in a nightclub being one of them, it would seem. I mean, you just can't get your breath!

Becky apparently stood there, then picked one of the kids up, shoved him in Craig's face, pointed and said, 'Look. That's your daddy. That's what he's doing when he should be reading you your bedtime story, what he's doing when he's not at home with us.' And then started screaming blue murder at him. Honestly, can you imagine – all the lads were standing around laughing and jeering at him, whilst he's stood there, pissed out of his head, all over some old slapper, gawping in disbelief as his wife and kids, dressed in their nightwear, have hysterics in front of him.

Us girls, of course, gossiped about it for a day or so and then let it drop. It wasn't a good idea to dwell on someone's bad luck. It wouldn't happen to me, Tara or Jodie of course – but we all believed in karma. I was learning that it simply doesn't do to tempt fate: especially when your other half is a Premiership footballer.

I listlessly tossed the gossip magazine I'd been reading to one side and leaned back on the sofa, hugging my knees and straining my ears to hear what Adam, huddled away in the kitchen, was saying on his mobile. Trevor had rung him about fifteen minutes ago and I could tell from his excited tones that it was something good. Thank goodness we were out of the transfer window – at least it wouldn't mean another potential move!

But that was just me, wishful thinking, and being selfish. In reality, Adam needed something to give him a serious boost. Despite recovering from his hamstring injury in record time – just four weeks! – and returning to some of the best form of his career, he'd started suffering from some weird kind of insecurities. It was like all the times he'd worried about not being good enough had suddenly come back to haunt him, and when that happened, it was like he suddenly turned into a different person.

This morning was a classic example. The alarm had gone off and Ad had rolled over and hidden his head under the duvet whilst I'd got up to make him his usual hot water with a squeeze of lemon juice. (I thought this was disgusting – and though the boys swore by it as a fitness tool and the girls said it gave you clear, glowing skin, I was sticking with my builder's tea of a morning.)

But when I'd returned to the bedroom, instead of sitting up in bed sleepily and beginning to come around like usual, he was still submerged under the duvet. I'd shaken him, called him, sat on him – but he'd refused to move. He was behaving like a child!

Eventually I stuck my head under the duvet and boomed at him.

I thought I was being funny, but when he emerged he looked totally distraught. 'I can't go in, Louise. I can't do it.'

I frowned at him. 'What do you mean, you can't go in? You've got training in half an hour, just like normal! What's different about today?'

'I don't know,' he replied, lying back on the pillow and staring blankly into space. 'I just can't do it. I haven't got it in me. I'm not up to it. I'm not good enough.'

I couldn't believe what I was hearing. Adam, who was fast turning into one of the club's major stars, was having some kind of crisis of confidence! 'But – Adam—'

'LOUISE!' He shot back up again, yelling in my face. 'Didn't you hear me? I'm not good enough! I'm a fraud. And it's only a matter of time before they find out.'

Even after I'd pleaded and wheedled and actually tried to physically drag him out of bed, he still wouldn't budge. I ended up having to phone up the club and lie and tell them he was sick, like I was his mum! I wasn't happy about it – but once Adam had made up his mind about something, that was it.

So all day he'd been moping around, firstly in bed, watching old football videos of himself and his favourite players, as if he was trying to soak up all their expertise, and then in the living room, watching the same videos and just staring into space. It had ruined my day – I'd had to cancel my lunch plans with Jodie and a massage I'd had booked for this afternoon – and had played on my mind as I sat there looking at him, willing him to snap out of it. I mean, what on earth was wrong with him?

Now, after a whole day of his weirdo behaviour, I idly picked up the TV remote, and flicked through a series of mindless satellite channels, hoping that it was just a freak day and that the call he was taking right now would be good news that would snap him out of it. The door burst open and Adam stood there in his baggy sweat pants, club T-shirt and socks, eyes shining. It was like some kind of schizophrenic transformation. Where had old moody-boots disappeared to?

'Louise! You'll never guess what.'

I looked at him, a half-smile playing at my lips as I got caught up in his excitement.

'What?'

'I've only been called up for England. FOR ENGLAND!'

I gasped. 'You see! YOU SEE! You *are* good. And everyone knows it.' I stood up and did a little jig in my Juicy Couture tracksuit and slipper boots. 'You're a genius and you're going to play for England!'

Adam grinned. 'So it seems. The game's next Wednesday, against Italy. We'll fly out Monday, train Monday and Tuesday, and play Wednesday night. Then back Thursday morning and I'll be ready to train again at the club on Friday. No rest for the wicked!'

He gave me a sexy lopsided grin and flopped on to the sofa. I felt my heart lurch. Bless him! It was great to see him on top of the world again. And a few days in Italy would be a treat for both of us . . . I could see Tara . . . do some shopping . . . maybe even a bit of sightseeing, depending on where we were staying. Hmmm . . . where *were* we staying?

I sat back on the sofa next to him and reached for a pen and the notepad I'd been filling with wedding 'things to do' lists earlier that day. 'So, Ad, do I need to sort out my tickets and hotel and stuff like when we go to an away match here, or will the England,' my stomach flipped over again with excitement as I said the words, 'organisers sort it?'

Adam looked up from typing a text on his phone, and smiled distractedly. 'Oh, sorry, baby, didn't I say? Trevor thinks it's best if I have no distractions. You'd be better off staying at home. Like all the other girls.'

I stared at him in dismay. 'But — but Ad, I always come

with you to away matches. And this is your first international game. I should be there.'

Adam paused as he sent his text, then picked up the remote, flicking the TV on.

'Well, I'm sure there'll be others,' he said dismissively. 'If I play well in this one, anyway.'

'But me being there is hardly going to stop you playing well, is it?' I was beginning to sound hysterical, but I couldn't help it. 'I'll be in another hotel like normal. You've always said you love knowing I'm there, supporting you.'

'I do,' he said weakly, eyes not moving from the game on the TV screen. 'But Trev reckons I need to focus on this one.'

I couldn't believe what I was hearing. Did Adam not realise how much this meant to me, too? Did he even want me there? My throat felt tight as tears suddenly welled up in my eyes.

'Yes, but Trevor doesn't call the shots for the other players, does he?' I continued mulishly. 'I don't understand why none of the other girls are going. Surely that's not normal. I've seen loads of pictures of wives and girlfriends at England away matches.'

Adam turned to me, a bemused look on his face. 'Baby, what's the big deal? You want me to do well, don't you?' I nodded mutely. He turned back to the TV. 'Then let's just go with the flow on this one.'

As he engrossed himself in the game once more, I sat,

arms crossed, looking at him in disbelief. Once upon a time he'd have been well nervous going to a game without me there to cheer him on. And this was the biggest one of his life. Something in him was different, and I wasn't sure I liked it.

I checked the arrivals board for about the fifteenth time in as many minutes. Adam's flight was still showing 'delayed' but no other information. It was four hours late now, and I was bored rigid. Surprising him off his flight back from Italy had seemed like such a good plan, but I should have known better.

After having spent all weekend pretending I was thrilled to stay at home while Adam went abroad to represent his country for the first time ever, I'd decided enough was enough, and after waving him off on the coach on the Monday morning, I'd driven down to see my folks. They'd been over the moon to see me, and it had done me the power of good. I'd had a heart-to-heart with Mum about all the silly little niggles I'd been having, my feelings about being bored, my worries about Adam's increasing mood swings and my concern over our vague wedding plans. Adam seemed to have lost all interest in it since his injury – well, to be honest, since he asked me in the first place. I mean, we hadn't even set a date yet!

But Mum had been really reassuring. 'Don't worry, my love – he's got a very high-profile job and it's bound to take him a little while to settle down,' she said, kissing my head like when I was little. 'But you must be honest with him – and when you're feeling worried, tell him. That's what being in love is all about – give and take.'

In fact, it had been her idea for me to come and meet him today – as a little surprise. We hadn't been apart for this long since Adam had first moved to the club, and I was hoping he'd have missed me as much as I'd missed him – especially as England had won, so he'd be on a real high. I'd had my hair and make-up and a spray tan done specially – I wanted to look my best. He'd probably be the only one with a wife or girlfriend there, so it wouldn't do to show him up! But more than that – I was sure that having played well for England, he'd be feeling a lot better about himself, and seeing me there looking all lovely and happy to see him would hopefully make him feel better about us, too! It almost felt like a new start for us both. I looked up at the arrivals board again. Bingo! The plane was due in twenty minutes.

I picked up my new white Marc Jacobs handbag, pulled my dark blue skinny jeans down over my new Terry de Havilland platforms, and tottered off to the gate. Just as I reached it, the first few passengers were straggling through, and I noticed a group of paps by customs lifting up their cameras ready to snap the England stars. I strained my eyes, but couldn't make out any of the team yet.

Until . . . around the corner came a couple of buggies, three toddlers, their nannies, and two girls I recognised.

At least, *half* recognised. Because I'd only ever seen these normally super-glam women in magazines, in players' lounges, or at Tara's party. But now they and the straggle of other England WAGs that followed were all looking horrendous. The delay obviously hadn't done them any good – their hair was all over the place, their faces were shiny with make-up sliding down them, and one of them had what looked suspiciously like baby sick all down her top. And what's more, none of them looked happy about it – especially when the paps started lining them up for pictures.

'Louise!' I spun around as I heard a male voice call my name, expecting to see Adam or one of the team. But it wasn't – it was one of the photographers, who'd recognised me and obviously thought I had come off the plane with the rest of them. I looked at them in shock. I wasn't used to being recognised out and about without Tara or Jodie! At the thought of Tara, I pictured how she reacted when she was spotted. Like she would, I sucked my tummy in, pulled myself up tall and smiled. Fluffing my immaculately styled hair, I trotted over and apologetically squeezed into the line-up of England WAGs, smiling sweetly at them and trying to ignore the dirty looks from the more bedraggled women surrounding me. I felt a bit bad about it – I knew if I looked as rough as them I'd be a bit pissed off with some new girl arriving all done up to the nines! – and with the prospect of more England games in the future, I couldn't afford to upset any of them, after all. But I tried to push the guilt from my mind. I was the one who'd missed out, after all. And I may not have been to Italy with them, but I was sure as hell going to look the part in tomorrow's papers.

'Hi, I'm Louise, Adam Jones's fiancée,' I said brightly to a girl I recognised as being the England goalie's wife. 'Do you know what's keeping the boys?'

'They always hang back to sign autographs for the crew and wait for the crowds to die down,' she said, talking through her smile as she continued posing for the photographers. 'So they don't have to do this after a long and tiring flight,' she added pointedly, looking me up and down.

'Oh, right, of course,' I said as if I'd known all along, also talking through my smile. No one would ever have guessed the fury it was hiding – or the rage welling up in me. Right now, I was angrier than I could ever remember being.

What was making me seethe was that Adam had told me none of the girls were going to Italy. But here, to a woman, was every single wife or girlfriend of the British-based England team. And every one of them had been to Italy with their husband or boyfriend.

Every one, that is, but me.

Just then, the lads started to appear, all in their England team tracksuits, some with bags slung over their shoulders. They were all laughing and slapping each other on the back, and I looked on numbly. This should have been one of the proudest moments of mine and Adam's life together. Making the England team, after all, was the pinnacle of years of working and planning and hoping – for both of us. Instead, I'd been completely left out of the whole experience – sidelined like some inconsequential bit player.

Adam was one of the last players to stroll through customs, talking earnestly to one of the older players. His face lit up as our eyes met, then immediately clouded guiltily.

I stood expressionless as he waved sheepishly and shrugged helplessly at the other girls. What the hell did that mean? Sorry I lied to you? Sorry they all happened to turn up unexpectedly and I never thought to mention it to you, or tell you to get a last-minute flight, or anything? I held his gaze coldly for several long seconds, then turned on my heel and walked purposefully towards the car park.

Alone.

I didn't look back.

Chapter 10

I opened the apartment door nervously, and it creaked loudly. I inhaled sharply. It had never done that before – why now? I slipped my boots off and crept through the apartment. Thank the Lord for shag-pile carpet . . .

Even by the half-light of such an early hour (it was still only 5 a.m. – I hadn't been able to sleep, again), the place looked like a bomb had hit it. There were glasses and empty beer bottles everywhere, and a takeaway pizza box with a half-eaten American Hot congealing inside sat on the kitchen worktop. The apartment felt cold and still and unloved. I shivered. Didn't Adam know how to use the central heating, for goodness' sake?

After I'd left the airport, I'd driven straight back to my mum's. My phone, sitting in its little stand on my dashboard, had rung insistently with repeated calls from Adam. I'd ignored them to begin with, but then I'd relented and pulled over and answered the phone.

'Baby? Baby, where are you?' He'd sounded distressed – and confused.

'I'm on my way back to my mum's,' I'd said, coldly. 'I should never have come back, should I?'

'But why? What's the matter?' He sounded genuinely perplexed, and that only made me even madder.

'Adam, you've purposefully – and publicly – excluded me from one of the most important occasions in your career. You've treated me like I don't count. What do you think is the matter?'

He was silent. 'I'm sorry, baby,' he said miserably. 'But Trevor said—'

'Sod Trevor,' I said, harshly. 'If he told you to jump off a cliff, would you? Suddenly take a twenty grand a week pay cut to play in the Third Division, would you?'

'Lou, baby—' he pleaded.

'Baby nothing,' I interrupted. 'I'm obviously not even important enough for you to stand up to your bloody agent every once in a while. You've hurt me and humiliated me, and right now, I need some space.' I'd hung up at that, and turned my phone off, heart racing. I was full of futile anger and eaten up with hurt. Why was he treating me like this?

I turned my phone on again after a while, of course, and it rang after only a couple of minutes. It was Adam again, and this time I ignored him. In fact, I ignored him for a couple of days. When he wasn't training, he rang about five times an hour, leaving voice messages just saying sorry over and over again. He sent me texts, huge bunches of flowers – even a teddy bear with a note saying sorry. With every one, Mum and Dad had given me a look. I knew they felt I was being overly harsh – but something was holding me back from forgiving him.

The last text had arrived at about one o'clock this morning.

'Baby. Can't live without you. Come home. Please. I'm sorry.'

For some reason, that had got to me more than any of the others, and I'd felt an overwhelming urge to go home and sort things out. Without replying, I'd jumped straight in my car and headed back. Everyone makes mistakes, after all. And I knew he was sorry – right now. I just had to be sure he'd mean it for ever.

Until now, though, I hadn't realised the extent of the practical consequences my absence would have had, as well as the emotional effect. Instinctively, I picked up a glass and opened the dishwasher to put it in. As I did, a waft of unwashed plates and rotting food hit me. The dishwasher was overflowing with dirty pots – nice. I gagged, unwrapped a detergent tablet and put the machine on a pre-wash. It was going to take more than a quick rinse to clean up that lot . . .

'Louise . . .' Adam's voice, cracking with sleep or tiredness or emotion – or I don't know what – made me jump, and I dropped the glass, which promptly smashed all over the floor. I looked up at him helplessly.

'Leave it, and come here.' He held his arms out to me beseechingly. He looked dreadful – like he hadn't slept for weeks. His eyes were surrounded by big black rings, his face was framed by a five o'clock shadow and he had a sort of sallow complexion.

Instinctively my heart went out to him and I almost went over to him, but I checked myself. I had to be strong. I didn't feel much better than he looked, after all. But I hadn't spent the past three nights on my own for no reason. Things were going to have to change between us – and no one else was going to demand it but me.

'Adam. I was trying not to wake you.' I bent down and rummaged around under the sink for the dustpan and started furiously sweeping up the broken glass. 'And as for a cuddle, it's not as easy as that, is it?'

'I don't know what you mean, baby. I've told you I'm sorry, I've told you I . . .' He ran a hand through his hair desperately. 'I don't know what else to say. I love you. I can't live without you.'

I carried on with my sweeping, glad to have something to occupy my shaking hands. I stood up and emptied the glass into the pedal bin.

'Well, Adam, that much is clear. Just look at you! And the state of the place!' I gestured through to the carnage we'd once called our living room. 'The question is, are you really sorry? Or are you just missing having a housekeeper? I mean, do you know how to work the dishwasher? Or the washing machine? Do you even know where the bin is?' I was ranting now, but I didn't care. Adam pointed sheepishly at my foot, which was still on the pedal holding open the bin lid. I lifted it off and the lid shut with a clatter.

'*Before* I just showed you, I mean!' I was really angry again. This was not the time or the place for jokes. I'd spent the past six months acting like a wife, mother, cook, house-keeper and punchbag all rolled into one – and what was I getting out of it? All he had to do was concentrate on playing well. Enough was enough – I'd decided it was time to put my foot down.

I stomped across the kitchen but Adam stopped me, holding out his arm to block my way.

'Baby – baby, I love you. I know I've been neglecting you. And I'm sorry about the England game. I honestly thought—'

I glared at him, brushing his hand off my arm. 'Don't even try to blame Trevor again, Adam. You could easily have let me know when you realised all the other girls were going.'

At that, he did at least have the grace to look ashamed.

'OK, baby, you're right. But I was dead nervous. And it's made me realise how much I've been neglecting you. How I've been putting my game above everything. And how I've been behaving like a total arse. But I love you, and I want to put things right. Like, by spending more time together. Moving out, maybe, away from town, away from the party scene.' His voice cracked, and he cleared his throat. 'And by setting a date for our wedding,' he added softly.

I looked up at him, tears spilling down my cheeks. This sounded more like the Adam of old. But I'd been here before . . . 'Do you really mean that? Set a date and actually go through with it?'

He took me in his arms and rocked me gently. 'This is the start of the new me,' he murmured into my ear. 'At least, it's the start of the old me again!' I laughed through my tears. 'It's all going to be different from now on. You wait.'

A couple of hours (and a whole lot of love) later, from my cosy spot way under the duvet, I heard my mobile ring. I groaned inwardly. It was probably Mum – who else would call at this time? I'd told her I'd ring her as soon as I got back. But of course, in the meantime Adam and I had had a lot of making up to do . . .

My Rihanna ringtone stopped, and I breathed a sigh of relief and shut my eyes again. Immediately, it started up again. Whoever was calling was sure as hell keen to get hold of me! I started to wriggle out of the duvet. Adam groaned loudly in protest and tightened his arm around me. 'Where are you going? I've only just got you back!'

I pushed the duvet back and leant down to kiss his forehead.

'I'll be right back, lover,' I said. 'But I need to make sure that's not some kind of emergency.'

I pulled my fluffy white robe off its hook in the en suite and wrapped it around me – the apartment still hadn't warmed up. I yawned widely and padded out to the living room, where I'd left my bag. Just then, my mobile rang again. It was Jodie. I squinted at the clock on the DVD player: 7.23 a.m. What was she doing up before midday?

'Hi, babe, whassup?' I said sleepily.

'Louise? Louise, where are you?' said Jodie urgently. I immediately felt wide awake. Something was very wrong. Very wrong indeed.

'I'm back at home, babe. With Adam. Why, what's wrong?'

Jodie started sobbing huge, gulping sobs down the phone. 'Babe, I'm in the car park. Can I come up?'

I swallowed. Jodie was in our car park? How the hell . . . ? Then I remembered she'd managed to flirt an automatic key fob out of Jim the concierge to save me always having to let her in manually. Not that it was any real hassle – it was more that procuring an illicit way in was a challenge for Jodie.

'Of course – come up now.'

I hung up the phone, heart pounding. What on earth was going on? I looked around at the filthy apartment in dismay. Great time for visitors . . . Automatically, I padded through to the kitchen and put the kettle on. Whatever it was, it seemed a cup of tea was going to be needed.

The door buzzer sounded and I ran to open it. Jodie stood in front of me, a broken mess. She was wearing a faded old hoodie and jeans, and had thick black mascara streaks down her cheeks and mascara bogeys in the corners of her eyes. Her eyes were bloodshot from crying. She looked desperate and – well – wretched, I guess.

'Jodie, babe – what's wrong?' With that, she wailed, and fell into my arms, wafting perfume and stale cigarette smoke. I moved backwards slowly, guiding her towards the nearest chair. Over her shoulder I saw Adam appear at the door, looking sleepy and bemused. I mouthed 'Tea' at him, and he shuffled off obediently to make some.

Once we'd reached the sofa, I propelled Jodie into it, quickly moving a takeaway menu from the seat first, and then gently sat myself next to her. She was racked with huge, snotty sobs, her whole body shaking with the burden of whatever had upset her.

'Gary – Gary's been arrested,' she managed between teary hiccups. 'And I – I'm deep in the shit too!' With that, she fell forward on to my lap and started crying hysterically again.

I stroked her hair comfortingly, but inside I was anything but calm. What on earth had they got themselves into?

Adam brought two steaming mugs of tea and I smiled gratefully. He pointed towards the shower, indicating he was going to get himself washed and dressed, and I nodded in agreement. I was feeling pretty manky myself, but it didn't really seem like the right time to nip and have a bath.

Jodie seemed to calm down a bit with the tea, and though I was dying to ask her what was going on, I made myself hold back and finish my own mug. Finally, blowing her nose noisily, she turned to me.

'So, I'm right in it, Lou. And I haven't got a flying fuck idea what to do about it.'

I patted her knee reassuringly. 'Look, Jodie, I'm sure it's not as bad as it seems. But what the hell has Gary been arrested for?'

I sensed Adam come back into the room and perch on a chair arm. Jodie, master of the pregnant pause, looked around at the pair of us dramatically.

'Drugs!' We both gasped. She laughed bitterly. 'Oh, don't worry – not taking them. He's been selling them, they reckon. And I, unbeknownst to stupid old me, have been his bloody mule, haven't I?'

Adam came over now and sat on the floor in front of us, a concerned look on his face. 'Right, Jodie, you need to tell us exactly what's gone on.'

She took a deep breath, and started her story.

'Well, you know Mitch?' We both nodded. Mitch was Gary's brother-in-law. He was some big shot in 'business' – you know the sort: the big 'I am' with bad taste in business ventures. He'd recently split with Gary's sister, and being really close to Gary, had moved in with him and Jodie, which had been yet another bone of contention between them of late. The thing was, though Mitch was obviously a dodgy bloke, you could never put your finger on anything with him. He covered up his shady side with niceness, like doing stuff for charity, and taking care of Gary's elderly mum when everyone else was too busy to.

Jodie took another deep breath in an attempt to control her hiccups. 'Well, he's had a private line installed in the flat.'

Me and Adam looked at her blankly.

'Right . . .' I said, uncertainly.

'And he's been taking calls at all hours. He's always on the bloody phone. And he's always got bloody cash! And him and Gary have been really secretive together. So I've been getting dead suspicious. But Gary says there's nothing to worry about, Mitch would never try to stitch us up, blah. But I'm still worried. So we have a huge row about it. And another huge row about it. And then on Wednesday, Gary says right, he's going to take me out to treat me because he's fed up of seeing me upset about it. Which I thought was really sweet.'

I nodded encouragingly, even though I couldn't really see where this was going.

'So we get in the car and drive into town, but we went a really weird way. And so I asked Gary and he said, well, babe, I just need to drop something off for someone. In fact, he says, as you're in the passenger seat, why don't you jump out and run it in for me?'

Jodie paused again to blow her nose noisily. Adam shook his head despairingly, as if he already knew what was coming. I was getting a bit impatient. Why couldn't she just get to the point?

'So, Gary gives me this parcel. All gift-wrapped it is, like a birthday present or something. I said to him, this had better not be a bung! 'Cos it felt like a load of notes wrapped up. And he laughed like I'd said something really funny, so I shut up. And when we got to this dodgy council estate and this deserted car park and he told me to get out and go and give it to this bloke in a beat-up old motor right across the road, I did!'

She looked at us incredulously. 'How stupid is that? I bloody did it!'

I must admit, I was pretty shocked. It sounded like a crazy thing to ask anyone to do. Odd, at the very least. But then, crazy things did sometimes happen living with footballers – so who was I to judge Jodie?

Adam tapped her on the leg. 'C'mon, Jodie, don't beat yourself up about it. How has this led to Gazza being arrested?'

'Well, I got back in the car and we went out as planned. And we had a lovely evening and got a bit jolly and had to book a cab back. And I hadn't got any cash, and I knew Gary probably didn't, so I was about to mention it when I saw him paying the bill in notes!'

Adam and me both gasped again. It was even rarer for Gary to carry cash than any of us wives or girlfriends. Until lately, anyway.

Jodie looked at us, pleased with the impact of her story. 'I know. So I start rattling on to Gary about why he's got some great big wad in his wallet, and he gives me some cock-and-bull story, which I don't believe but for once I can't be arsed to argue with. Instead, as we're going home in the cab, I start thinking about the past few weeks. And it occurs to me that there has been an awful lot of cash hanging around the house. Like, drawers full of it. Literally! But still, I can't put my finger on what might be going on. Can you believe I didn't link it with the incident in the car park?'

Again she looked at us for confirmation. Again I agreed with her – I couldn't believe she hadn't questioned that little incident, but I didn't really feel now was the right time to point that out. Instead, I nodded encouragingly. 'Go on, babe.'

'So anyway, it kept bugging me, But I still didn't mention it. Until this morning, when there's a knock at the door at about four o'clock. Like, who knocks at that time in the morning? So no one answered. And then they keep knocking, so eventually I go down to answer it. And when I do, there's these two guys in suits. They say they're from CID, and does Mitch live here? Of course I said yes. And then they say, is Gary there? So again I say yes. By this time, I can hear them up and about and probably getting dressed, and all kinds of banging and commotion coming from Mitch's room. Then this bloke says he's got a warrant to search the flat, and pushes his way in, followed by his mate and two more who've turned up. I'm just shaking, babe, I can't believe it, and when I walk through to the lounge, he's got both

Gary and Mitch in handcuffs and a dirty great packet of I don't know what – but he says it's drugs!'

Jodie, who hadn't breathed for the past few minutes, took in another huge lug of oxygen. Adam and I sat, mouths open, transfixed.

'So – so Gary's been selling drugs?' said Adam, aghast. His brow furrowed. 'He should know better. Getting mixed up with all that kind of crap. They mess you up. Not only that, they mess your career up. Paps, journalists – they're every-where, and they know everything. If the drugs don't cock up your pitch performance, the press'll crucify you anyway. It's a lose–lose situation – for losers.'

A picture of me and Pattii snorting cocaine on our girls' night out flashed through my mind, and I felt myself go white as a sheet. I was dizzy with panic. What if this came out now too – what would happen then? I took a sly look at Adam to see if he'd noticed my reaction, but he was totally preoccupied with Jodie.

'Noooooooooooo!' responded Jodie, and she started crying again. I shook myself and tried to concentrate on what she was saying, even though I was pondering my own guilty secret. 'It's Mitch! It's all Mitch! I'm sure my Gary wouldn't get involved in something like that intentionally! You know he'd do anything to help Mitch out, no questions asked.' She reached for another tissue blindly. 'Our lawyer's down there now. He says the *News of the World* set Mitch up. They fake-sheiked him. They arranged a business meeting with him under some other guise, and then tried to buy drugs. They filmed it all.'

She blew her nose noisily, and threw the tissue on the floor to join the rest of the detritus of Adam's time home alone. 'They recorded him on the phone speaking to someone about dropping a package off. They reckon it was Gary on the other end of the phone. The only thing they can't work out is who actually dropped it off. Somehow they know it wasn't Gary – but they reckon it was a close associate of his.' She looked at us wildly. 'But what if it was me? What if it was meeeeeeeeeeeeeee? What if people think I'm a drugs pusher? I'll never be able to show my face again. I'm finished. I'm broken. How could he do this to me?'

Sobbing out of control again, she buried her face in the cushions. Adam and I looked at each other helplessly. What on earth were we meant to do now?

'Jodie – have you thought about getting Raymond Moore involved?' Adam said hesitantly. Jodie had always scoffed at Tara and Jonnie's use of Raymond's skills, and was never anything but derogatory about him. 'Strikes me Gary needs as much help as he can get here.'

Jodie glared at him. 'Oh fuck off, Adam. What Gary needs is legal advice and a brain transplant, not some predatory pensioner who spends his life wooing the gutter press.'

Adam shook his head vehemently. 'No way, Jodie. I reckon you need both. It's not just the police that will want to get to the bottom of this, is it? The press are going to be all over us all, trying to find out who's doing what. Not that any of us are into the filthy drugs scene, of course,' he said, smiling over at me trustingly. 'But if Mitch is – and maybe Gary – then you might need someone who understands how the press work to protect you.'

Jodie picked up another tissue with a flourish. 'Well, Adam, I think I understand the press well enough to know I can handle them without the help of Grandad Raymond. I'm innocent, and Gary better sure as hell be, and somehow I'm going to prove it.'

At the mention of Raymond's name, my heart started racing again and my rising panic returned. If the press really did start rooting around, would they find out about me and Pattii? Was I going to be the next football drugs scandal? What would Adam say? How would my mum and dad react? And what would happen to me?

Never mind giving Jodie and Gary advice, what on earth was *I* meant to do now?

Chapter 11

Jodie wriggled her toes delightedly as she inspected her newly painted crimson nails. She picked up the champagne flute on the table next to her and raised it to her manicurist. 'You've done a good job there, love. Cheers!'

'It was my pleasure,' said the beautician proudly, as she stood up, straightened her regulation shirtdress, and busied herself with tidying the files and polishes. Jodie adjusted her fluffy white robe theatrically and stretched languidly.

'Ooh, I feel all put back together now, don't you, babe?'

I snuggled down further into my own robe and glanced out of the window at the indoor pool our treatment room looked out over. The sun was shining across the still-frosty garden and casting a yellow wintry mid-morning glow over the water.

'I'll say.' I took a deep, contented swig of my bubbly. For once, I'd persuaded Jodie to come to a spa with me, and we'd abandoned our usual Friday champagne-and-shopping agenda for – well – a champagne-and-spa agenda. We'd arrived last night, exhausted after all the dramas of the previous couple of weeks, and overdone the cocktails – and after a few restorative spa treatments today, we were now about to overdo the bubbly, too.

But sod it, we deserved it! We'd been through hell on earth over the past couple of weeks, ever since that awful Sunday when Jodie had appeared on our doorstep. She hadn't actually left, as it turned out – she'd stayed nearly a whole week, not even bothering to go back to the flat and pick up her stuff.

Gary had been charged with being concerned in supply, but had made bail on the Monday and come straight round for the mother of all barneys with Jodie. She blamed him for putting her in a compromising situation and they'd screamed blue murder at each other whilst me and Adam had taken refuge in the bedroom. I was a bit surprised Adam didn't have a pop at Gary too, to be honest – he'd been so hacked off with him about it all – but it seemed he'd forgiven and forgotten a bit quicker than Jodie.

Jodie, thank God, had escaped any kind of finger-pointing – though it didn't stop me lying awake worrying about my own cocaine incident all night every night, or being unable to eat or drink anything through worry.

Anyway, despite Mitch still being in jail on charges of possession with intent to supply, come Thursday Gary suddenly had all the charges dropped, and according to a text from Adam had apparently been at the club all afternoon awaiting the results of his drug tests.

Adam was late back from training that day. Jodie – who was still staying at ours – and I had had an afternoon in, and were watching the final moments of *Dirty Dancing* when the intercom indicated he was in the lift. I looked at my watch.

'Jesus, it's half five!' I said, leaping up. 'I haven't even thought about dinner yet!'

Jodie yawned and changed channels as I jogged over to the kitchen. I was just surveying the contents of the fridge when I heard Adam come in, whooping.

I popped my head out of the kitchen. He was standing in the middle of the living room, on his mobile and making triumphant 'come on' gestures. He hung up, and looked from me to Jodie, eyes shining.

'Gal's had his club suspension lifted!' he grinned. 'He's back on the team – and in training from tomorrow!'

'That's fantastic!' I squealed and ran over to give Adam a hug. 'Isn't it, babe?' I looked over at the sofa, where Jodie had gone back to watching the TV, feigning indifference at the news. She and Gary hadn't spoken since their row on Monday – even the news about him getting out had come via their lawyer.

'Yeah, I guess so,' she said unconcernedly. 'So he can get back to doing what he does best. Fucking things up for other people.'

I smiled sympathetically. 'At least now you know he was innocent!'

'Do I?' she replied, raising an eyebrow sceptically. 'Seems a pretty fast turnaround to me. Wonder if he used some of that plentiful cash to secure himself a quick exit.'

I gasped. 'Jodie! You're not suggesting he paid off the police?' I must admit, I couldn't understand how the police had one minute thought he was guilty and the next decided he wasn't, but all the same – a pay-off seemed pretty far-fetched to me! I looked at Adam searchingly. 'That wouldn't happen, would it?'

He smiled softly at me. 'Nah,' he replied. 'I doubt he would've tried to pay anyone off. That's the point of having a kosher investigation, for him to be found in the clear and put it all behind him.'

'You see!' I said brightly to Jodie. 'He *is* innocent!'

She tutted. 'Hmm, maybe of the drugs thing, although it's all pretty bloody convenient. But of fucking me over time after time, I'm afraid Gary is well and truly guilty.'

I'd raised my eyebrows at Ad and retreated back to the kitchen to make dinner. Before I started cooking, though, I did take a moment to breathe a sigh of relief. With Gary out of the woods, maybe I could stop worrying about me and Pattii's 'little weekend away with Charlie' (as she liked to refer to it) being found out?

But as it turned out, none of that had stopped the papers sniffing around us all for more dirt, and Jodie and Gary were at the centre of some pretty hideous headlines. The tabloids delved into all their past relationships (which for both of them were numerous and some pretty shameful). Even today, the floor around us was scattered with papers containing a kiss-and-tell from Jodie's first boyfriend, Keith, now a refuse collector in Chingford, and an air stewardess who claimed Gary had tried to join the mile-high club with her on a flight to an England game. Nothing, as yet, had come out about me and Pattii – though during several sleepless nights I'd wondered whether I should approach Raymond Moore to make sure it never did. The only problem was, how would I keep it secret from Adam?

Jodie blew on her nails. 'So?' she said, with a wicked look. I steeled myself for some lewd anecdote or other. She'd eventually got back together with Gary, of course, and I'd had to endure stories of their passionate reunion. Not that I minded – for a start, it meant that she was finding the newspaper stories easier to deal with, and I was just glad to have everything back to normal!

But this time, it seemed, I was safe. 'What are you and Adam up to tonight after the match?'

I frowned. 'I'm not sure, babe. I still haven't spoken to Ad.'

For some reason, Adam's phone had been off all last night. At least, I hadn't been able to get through – despite its penthouse position right at the top of the apartment block, the flat had a rubbish reception, and Adam was also really bad at forgetting to charge his phone up. The fact that he hadn't answered the landline either frankly meant nothing – if he was home alone he'd either have his stereo or the TV up so high he couldn't even hear the door go, or he'd be in bed, dead to the world. He'd sent me a lovely text earlier today but I'd been in a massage, and I knew he would've been at the ground ever since.

Jodie hugged her knees. 'Well, Gary wants to go out and celebrate.' She threw me a crafty sidelong glance.

I stared at her suspiciously. 'Celebrate what – the charges being dropped? I thought he was getting you a new car to say sorry as it is?'

Jodie did pretty well in apology gestures from all their heated fall-outs. Particularly as from what I could tell, when she was in the wrong, all it cost *her* to say sorry was a blow-job.

She narrowed her eyes at me. 'He is. And he doesn't know we've got anything to celebrate yet.'

She paused again for effect. I sighed and hit her with a chair cushion in frustration. 'We haven't got time for this, Jodie! Quit the big mystery act and tell me what you're celebrating!'

She leant forward conspiratorially.

'Well, before I came away, Gary,' she opened her eyes wide, relishing the moment, 'asked me to marry him!'

I looked at her, gobsmacked. 'But – but why haven't you mentioned this before now?'

She winked and grinned. 'I hadn't made up my mind. But looking in that mirror there,' she nodded towards the soft-green wall of the treatment room, 'it suddenly occurred to me – well, girl, you're approaching your sell-by date!'

I tutted in disagreement, but she shook her head at me. 'No, Louise, you can't argue with nature. The fact is, after thirty-five you're looking at a shrinking window of opportunity. Marriage, kids – it all seems pretty straightforward at your age. But me' – she smiled brightly, but I was sure I could detect some despair in there too – 'me, I'm no spring chicken. Just like my Gary, really! In that sense, we're bloody made for each other.'

She laughed at her own punchline and I pretended to find it funny too. Then, she turned to me earnestly. 'So anyway, I figure I love the stupid bugger, so why not? And you know what?' She picked up the bottle and reached across to top up my glass. 'You're going to be my bridesmaid!'

I stared at her in a mixture of shock and delight. I was going to be a bride, and a bridesmaid for my best friend, all in the same summer! This was what dreams really were made of. But deep down inside, I felt a twinge of worry, and the return of that by now familiar niggling feeling. Was this really going to be the dream life we both wanted it to be?

The game that day was a big one. It was the quarter-finals of the FA Cup. The players' lounge was bursting at the seams with family and friends of the players on both sides, and the atmosphere was highly charged. Girls on either side were looking each other up and down far less subtly than normal, and you practically couldn't move without getting a judgemental look or bitchy aside from someone. I could only imagine what it was like in the changing rooms.

It was also the first time Adam had played against Andy Hill since the defender had taken him out and Adam had been injured. Adam had been seething ever since – he now held a huge grudge against Andy, and I knew he felt like there was a score to be settled.

Jodie, of course, was buzzing with her engagement decision and I could tell she was bursting to tell someone – even though she hadn't even given Gary the good news yet! Pattii was even more OTT than usual – and I felt guilty that I'd neglected her a bit over the past couple of weeks. At least I had Jodie and Gary's split as an excuse. Practically the only time I ever saw Pattii now was on match days or during our joint gym sessions.. The few times I had called her to arrange a shopping trip or a lunch, she'd either been busy or hadn't answered. Now she ran over, the stack of bangles on her wrists jangling loudly.

'Babes! How was your *spa trip*?' She emphasised the last two words as if we'd been up to something we shouldn't.

Jodie waved her question away airily. 'Oh, the usual. Pretty momentous.' She raised her eyebrows at me knowingly, referring to her secret decision to marry Gary, and I giggled. Pattii frowned. She hated being excluded from anything.

'Yes, well, it was quite a night all round from what I've heard,' she said, and patted my knee absent-mindedly. I gave her a sharp look. She was obviously stirring it about someone – but who? However, at that moment the commentary indicated we were close to kick-off, so we dutifully traipsed out on to the stands.

It was a hard-fought game, with no love lost between the two teams. Right from the first whistle, I could tell by Adam's body language that he wasn't going to let Andy Hill get away with anything. On camera, it was obvious they were exchanging increasingly heated banter too. (This often happened during a game. One player would start the ball rolling by elbowing the other, or insulting him, and by the end of the game it would generally have descended into 'I've done your missus' – that kind of really charming stuff.)

Anyway, the game was a draw – and we expected the lads to come out and want to get off pretty sharpish. Unusually, though, both teams seemed to take forever to come out of the changing rooms.

Jodie was deep in conversation with one of the lads' mums, and I pushed my way through the melee to where Pattii and some of the other girls were chatting animatedly.

'OK, that sounds like a plan!' said Pattii, her back still to me. 'High five!' Becky slapped hands with her, and I laughed, squeezing into the group next to Pattii.

'What's the plan?' I said brightly. 'I was just going to see what you were all up to tonight.'

Pattii turned to me, looking slightly put out. 'Oh – Louise,' she said. She hesitated, and I felt my smile slip. 'Erm – yeah, well we were just saying we should meet up for a few drinks tonight. Y'know, while the lads go out to celebrate Brighty's birthday.'

Brighty was coming through from the youth team and popular with all the players, but he was a bit young to want to do the drinks-and-dinner thing, and I knew Adam had mentioned they were all going out for a few early-doors drinks with him tonight.

'Oh, right,' I said. I felt strangely uncomfortable. It went without saying that if some of the girls did something en masse, we were all invited — but right now, I wasn't feeling very welcome. 'So, erm — is everyone cool with that?'

The girls all looked at Pattii. 'Of course!' she said falsely, giving me a stiff hug.

I arranged to meet them all in a bar in town and wandered back over to Jodie, mulling over why Pattii was being so weird. Had I done something to upset her?

Finally, at least half an hour later than usual, the players started to file out into the lounge, bringing the acrimonious on-pitch atmosphere with them. They all seemed really edgy, and no one seemed keen to leave. I tugged at Jez's elbow. 'Jez, where's Ad? He's usually first out!'

Jez frowned. 'He's had a bit of a dust-up, babe. With Hilly. He's in with the gaffer now.'

Just then, Adam emerged. Instead of his usual swagger, he was walking with his head slightly bowed and looked like he'd been ten rounds with Ricky Hatton. His right eye was all swollen and bruised, and he had a cut lip. I looked at him in shock, and then went as if to move over to him.

He put his hand up to stop me. 'Get your stuff, we're going,' he mouthed sullenly.

'What's going on?' I mouthed back.

'I'll tell you later. Just get your stuff.' He turned and stormed out of the lounge. Quickly I picked up my coat and bag from the chair and waved goodbye to Jodie and Pattii. As I pushed through the other team by the exit, I caught sight of Andy Hill chatting to two of his team-mates, and he winked cheekily at me.

Maybe better not tell Adam that one, I thought, hurrying out after him.

'Ad! Wait up!' I cried, tottering on my Louboutins as I tried to keep up with him stalking across the car park. He was in one of the blackest moods I'd ever seen, and his eyes were flashing with anger. His face was closed and looked kind of impenetrable.

'What's going on? What happened with the gaffer?'

'Nothing,' mumbled Adam irritably. 'Let's just get home.'

I caught up with him and grabbed his elbow. 'Adam! Tell me what's up!' I pleaded.

He stopped and turned, looking down at me (even though I had stacked heels on, he was still taller than me).

'Well, I've spent the last two hours having my ear bent about you,' he said accusingly.

'About me?' I was flummoxed. How could I have anything to do with it?

'Yeah. That prick Hill was on about you all through the game. How he fancies the arse off you, what he likes about you, how he's gonna get you off me.'

My insides turned to marshmallow. Bless him – Adam had ended up in a fight over me!

'Oh, Ad, baby,' I said soothingly.

'Ad baby nothing,' he snapped. 'You try having someone tell you exactly which way they're going to shag your fiancée – and it got a lot more graphic than that, I can tell you – while you're trying to concentrate on a crucial Cup tie.' He turned and carried on walking towards the car, and again I practically had to run to keep up with him.

'Anyway, by the end of the game I'd had enough,' growled Adam. 'He made one comment too many in the tunnel and it all kicked off – I landed him one and we had a full-on scrap.'

'In the tunnel?' I repeated. That was a first.

'Yes, Louise, in the tunnel,' Adam mimicked irritably. 'Do you have to repeat everything I say? The other lads weren't going to let it go, so they were egging me on.' We were by the car now, and he ran a hand through his hair distractedly and fished around in his pocket for his keys.

He looked at me over the bonnet of the Hummer. 'We got pulled apart in the end,' he said, in a resigned monotone. 'But the gaffer's not happy. Gave me the full hairdryer treatment. I've been fined three weeks' pay – but I'm due up in front of the FA on Monday.'

I bit my lip nervously. With yet another focus on football hooligans going on in the media, apparently the FA was taking a dim view of violence between players. 'What does that mean?'

Adam glared at me. 'Worst-case scenario, suspension. And if either of us press charges, the police could get involved.'

He opened the driver-side door and clambered in, leaving the full impact of his words to sink in.

All in all, Adam's ruck couldn't have come at a worse time for him.

A few weeks later, I sat toying with my champers, trying to get into the spirit of things, but behind my stuck-on smile my heart felt heavy. All I really wanted to do was curl up on the sofa with Adam and shut the world out. He was really down at the moment – his suspension had hit him hard, and he was just moping around at home. I kept trying to tell him he should be grateful that the police weren't involved, but it made no difference. Strangely, when I thought of 'home', I still pictured our little house in Cardiff, not the penthouse. Funny that. But instead, I was out in town counting the hours until the lads joined us and Adam and I could go home together.

'Oi, cloth-ears! I'm talking to you!' Pattii, half-cut already, mobile in hand, leaned over to whisper something in my ear, her left boob nearly escaping from her pink lamé Moschino dress, and knocked most of the glasses on the table over with a loud crash. A cheer went up from a nearby table and she stood up, grinning broadly, and took a staggery bow.

'I thank you!' She turned back to me. 'Babe – look at this! The buggers are blowing us out!' She thrust her open mobile in my face to show me a text from Jez.

'P – goin on 2 a club. Boyz celebration. Love ya. J'

My heart sank. This evening was going from bad to worse. Instinctively, I checked my own phone for a message from Adam. There was none. Maybe he wasn't going out with them? I could slip away and we could have an early night. I sent him a text.

'Wot u up 2 baby?'

Across the table, Pattii was winding herself up for a big night, and it looked like the other girls weren't far behind her.

'C'mon, Lou, we're going to Pampas Moon. What a laugh! We're gonna show those boys we know how to party – with or without them!'

I looked at her, horrified. Pampas Moon was what my dad might call 'a high-class knocking shop' – it was a flash club where a lot of the single boys liked to hang out, along with wannabe WAGs who went out with the sole purpose of pulling a footballer. I made a face.

'Really? Can't we think of anywhere better?'

Pattii gave me a strange look. 'Like where? Don't be such

a stuck-up cow! And cheer up, can't you? You don't think Adam's going to be moping around on their lads' night out, do you? Well, from what I've heard he won't anyway!' She cackled loudly and winked at the other girls. Holly McNulty, for one, looked uncomfortable, and a couple of the others smirked knowingly.

A hot, angry flush came over me. I'd never seen Pattii quite this drunk or quite this out of control, and I wasn't sure how to respond. But one thing was for sure – she wasn't going to get away with making lewd insinuations about my fiancé.

'And what exactly do you mean by that?' I said, narrowing my eyes and taking a deep breath. However angry I was, it wouldn't do to make a scene.

Pattii laughed, but a bit less assuredly this time. I guess she wasn't used to anyone challenging her silly drink-fuelled behaviour. She flipped her hand at me dismissively. 'Oh, you know what the boys are like when they're out, Lou – they're nightmares! There's always talk, no matter what they actually get up to.'

Now I was seething. 'Well, Pattii, then it's just as well I don't listen to talk, isn't it? After all, there are reasons not to stray other than not being able to pull, aren't there?'

At that reminder of her reasons for trusting her own husband, Pattii's face hardened. 'Aw, c'mon, Lou. Adam's a footballer. Play the game, babe! Don't you think that's what he wants you to do? This is what it's all about!'

Chuckling, she drained her glass, pulled the last bottle of

champagne out of the bucket to check it was finished, linked her arm in Becky's and led the way out of the club and down the street to Pampas Moon. I hesitated before following them. Every bone in my body wanted to go home – but I knew after that little exchange it would fuel whatever petty rumours Pattii's pissed stupidity might have started. And I knew her pretty well by now – she always got out of order at some point during a night out; I'd just never been on the receiving end of it before now. Best just to put it behind us. Inside, though, I was still raging. I trusted Adam implicitly – I'd never had any reason not to, and I was going to marry him, after all! – but that kind of talk was enough to make anyone a bit edgy.

The night didn't get any better when we arrived. The club – which now described itself as a 'retro homage' (making a virtue out of the fact it apparently hadn't been decorated since 1982) – had a louche, debauched air. It was pitch black, with black walls that were damp and seemed to be sweating. Its low-slung tables were also black, and surrounded by little red pouffes. Neon strip lighting on every other wall was crafted into images of margarita glasses and champagne flutes, and waitresses in tight black dresses twirled around with little drinks trays held high above their heads. It was full of British girls with dark orange tans, stunning Eastern European girls in tiny dresses, drunk men in expensive, crumpled suits and the smell of dirty money.

There were no tables free when we arrived, so we stood

at the bar waiting to be served. Pattii, lapping up all the openly lechy stares behind the DJ booth, squealed as a favourite song blasted out, and dragged the other girls on to the dance floor.

'Get the bubbly in, babe,' she yelled back at me, lifting her arms above her head and gyrating like a lap-dancer.

I pulled myself up on to a bar stool and leaned back against a pillar. I was wearing a tiny halterneck top, and the marble felt cool against my bare back. I checked my phone for more nonexistent messages from Adam and closed my eyes. Why was Pattii being such a bitch? I thought we were friends, but she was acting more like I was her worst enemy.

'You don't look like a lady who's enjoying herself,' said a familiar low Scottish voice in my ear. I opened my eyes with a jolt. In front of me, wearing carefully distressed jeans, a grey polo shirt, black jacket and a cute, caring smile, was Will Daniels!

'We really must stop meeting like this, Miss Adam Jones,' he said, turning and leaning on the bar. 'You got a drink?'

I shook my head.

'Well, would you like one?'

That made me laugh. 'Yes, a glass of champagne, please. What are you doing here?'

He gestured for the barman and looked at me out of the corner of his eye. 'I'm sidelined at the moment. Tail end of a metatarsal.' He pointed at his foot. Like a child, I looked down curiously – but of course, as he was up and about, it was no longer in plaster. Instead, all I could see were two smart black shoes sticking out the bottom of his trousers. 'But I should be asking you the same question,' he said, The Eyes twinkling. 'What's a lovely girl like you doing in a joint like this?'

I laughed and looked over at Pattii and Co., still strutting around the dance floor, all hair and teeth and legs and heels. 'I've been dragged out on another girls' night out.'

Will whistled through his teeth. 'Mr Adam Jones is a fool to let you out on your own so often. Doesn't he realise what might happen to a lovely girl like you without a man to look after her?'

My face clouded over as I pictured Adam, out with the boys and with no thought for where I was, what I was up to, or even how worried I might be about him.

'Oh, I'm sure Adam knows what he's doing,' I said tightly. 'Anyway, I'm not the only one out on my own, am I – where's your other half?'

Will looked startled, and then his face relaxed. 'Oh – we broke up,' he said quietly. I made a sympathetic face. 'Hey, there's no drama,' he said. 'Turns out we weren't exactly compatible.'

The barman returned with a bottle of Dom Perignon, and poured us a glass each.

'Cheers!'

'Cheers!' I said, raising my glass.

Once again we fell into easy conversation with each other. He was so attentive, so chatty, so – well – interested, I thought as I stared out of the taxi window a couple of hours later. Unlike my fiancé. And unlike my fiancé, he'd also already texted me to thank me for a lovely night and to make sure I was safely on my way home.

Because this time, I'd given him my number. I wasn't sure why. I pondered the possible reasons as I got out of the lift outside the flat and stood gazing at the picture of me and Adam. What would make me give my phone number to another man when I was due to marry the love of my life in just a few months? True, Will was pretty good-looking – he must have loads of girls falling at his feet – but I didn't fancy him . . . much. The thing was, he was just so – well – nice! I felt a twinge of guilt. No wonder people like Pattii were starting to make little digs about me and Adam, with the pair of us out separately all the time, and me chatting to another man all night and texting him on the way home.

Inside, I lay on the bed miserably, in the pitch darkness, and tried Adam's mobile. I was being eaten up by guilt and I just wanted him home. He didn't answer and I hung up without waiting to be put through to his voice mail. I rolled over to his side of the bed, and breathed in his smell. Underneath my cheek, a piece of paper crinkled up and scratched my skin. My heart stopped. It was a note I'd left for Adam to find the previous night, when I was away at the spa.

It told him how much I'd be missing him. It told him how much I loved him.

It hadn't been moved.

Adam hadn't slept here last night.

Chapter 12

Adam gave me a long, slow, sweet kiss goodbye and pulled up the zip on his tracksuit top. His big brown eyes stared up at me. I caught my breath. God, he was cute! He could still give me butterflies just with one look.

'See you later, birthday girl,' he said, saluting me with two fingers to his forehead. Cheerfully he threw the car key fob in the air and caught it again.

'Don't be late!' I grinned, waving him off down the little stairs, and shut the door happily behind me. Who'd have thought that just over two weeks ago I was convinced he'd been cheating on me? I'd been really quick to judge him after the night I thought he'd stayed away from home. I should have known it was something easily explainable like his phone not working, which was why I'd been unable to get through to him when me and Jodie had been at the spa, and why I'd never got all the texts he'd sent from the night out with Jez. When I woke up the morning after that dreadful evening, under the duvet but still fully dressed, my face crispy and my eyes puffy from having cried so much, I'd found him lying next to me, like nothing had happened. And when he'd explained about his phone, and how he'd slept on the sofa because he didn't want to sleep in our bed on his own, I guess it hadn't, really. He'd found it really cute that I'd written him the little note, and had been loving and caring since – with no hint of the mood swings he'd suffered from earlier in the year.

And as far as Pattii was concerned, well, I'd decided all her stirring wasn't worth bringing up with her. Things weren't all rosy with her and Jez, from what I could tell – Jodie swore he was up to no good. She reckoned she'd seen him looking very friendly with their nanny on more than one occasion, and Pattii was all over anything in trousers whenever she got the chance. And thinking about it, Pattii was just the type who if she wasn't completely happy had to take it out on people who were.

Nope, the only thing playing on my mind as far as me and Adam were concerned was me – and how I'd given Will my number. Not that I'd done it for any untoward reasons, of course – but it felt like a betrayal, and every time he texted me (which was, when I thought about it, quite a lot), I'd jump guiltily and make sure Adam hadn't noticed. What a nutter.

Anyway, I didn't have to worry about all that today, I thought, as I strolled back into the living room. I picked up my birthday cards one by one, and read the messages for about the zillionth time. Twenty-one today – and living in the lap of luxury, with the love of my life. It didn't get much better than that, did it? And whilst all my old friends and the girls I went to school with were slogging their guts out doing some dead-end job, probably moaning about having the Monday blues, all I had to do today was go to the hairdresser, get a bikini wax and get ready for my special birthday meal out with Adam tonight.

Well, this afternoon, really, I thought, looking at the new Raymond Weil 'Tango' diamond watch he'd given me this morning with delight. Adam had gone out to organise a special birthday surprise – but he'd told me to be ready by five, so I'd better get a move on. Tonight I wanted to look the best I'd ever looked!

At 6.30 I was still waiting. All glammed up, hair and make-up on, new Roland Mouret dress, new Jimmy Choo shoes. And I was furious. Adam had apparently bumped into some of the lads out on their usual Monday drinking sessions, and had stopped 'for a cheeky one'. He was now ringing me, on the half-hour, every half-hour, promising he was 'just having one more' and he'd be back 'a bit later on' to take me out. I couldn't believe it.

Right on cue, the phone rang.

'Adam – are you on your way yet?' I sounded like a nag, I knew, but right now I couldn't care less.

Adam was shouting into the phone and I could tell he was already drunk. 'Look, babe, I'm coming in a bit. It's just a few drinks with the lads, nothing to worry about. I'll be back soon.'

I put the phone down, seething. Why today, of all days? I should have gone for the party he'd offered me, I thought. At least then he wouldn't have been able to mess me about – it would have been too public. But silly old me, I'd figured that with a big wedding coming up it would have been nicer to spend my special birthday with just Adam. We'd seen my family at the weekend, and I'd been full of what a romantic night Adam had promised me. What a mug.

I shuffled miserably over to the fridge and pulled out a bottle of Chablis, pouring myself a huge glass. Well, if Adam was going to be half cut, I might as well start myself.

My phone beeped and I looked down, half expecting a conciliatory text from Ad.

'21 2day! Happy Birthday gorgeous – have a good one. xx'

It was from Will. Before I could stop myself, I sent one back.

'Sum hope. Miserable bloody day.'

The phone rang, and I started – I hadn't meant Will to call me! But it was Adam, and my spirits immediately lifted. At last!

But not for long.

'Babe, I've been thinking. Can we do this another night? I know it's your birthday, but maybe Monday wasn't the best night to plan something on.'

I couldn't believe what I was hearing. 'But Adam – you

promised. It's my twenty-first birthday and I'm here on my own—'

He cut in apologetically. 'I know, babe. But there's this party – and look, we can eat out tomorrow.'

I sank back on to the sofa, defeated. 'Well, how about I come out and join you?' I said in a small voice.

'No, it's just the boys, babe. I'll make it up to you!' In the background, I could hear shouting. There were obviously more than just a few lads – I could make out girls' voices, too.

'So that's it.' I stared at the phone in disbelief. 'You're leaving me here on my own on my twenty-first birthday?'

The significance seemed to be lost on Adam. 'Yeah, babe, I'm sorry. You know I love you. Call you later. Bye!'

I was stunned. How insensitive was that? But before I could dwell on it, the phone rang again. This time it was Will. I hesitated for a minute and then answered. Sod it! Why should I feel guilty after how Adam had just treated me? Anyway, we were only friends, weren't we?

'Whassup, gorgeous? Just got your text and I was kinda worried. What could make you so miserable on your birthday?'

Well, that was it. The floodgates opened and I started crying, wailing to Will about how Adam had left me in on my own.

'I just don't understand it.' I sobbed. 'I'd rather spend time with Adam than anyone. Why doesn't he feel the same? It's my twenty-first birthday, for God's sake! Why can't he see how important this is to me and leave the bloody boys alone for one measly night? It's so unfair . . .'

I trailed off, and there was silence on the line, apart from my sobs.

Then Will spoke. 'Well, gorgeous, no one stays in on their twenty-first – and as luck would have it, I'm footloose and fancy-free. Be ready in half an hour.' He hung up.

I poured another glass of wine, shocked. This is so wrong, I thought. Or was it? Me and Will had been friends for a while now. Why shouldn't he take me out on my birthday when my fiancé so obviously wasn't bothered? I sipped my wine and looked in the mirror above the fireplace. I was pretty dressed up for a girl going out for a meal with a friend. Maybe I should get changed?

Or maybe not.

Thirty minutes later, the intercom rang. I looked on the CCTV expecting to see Will – but instead there was a chauffeur there, in full uniform, hat and everything!

'Madam, your chariot awaits,' he announced in a deep voice. I practically fell down the stairs in my haste to get to the lift. He was still standing in reception when I got down there.

'Your car is outside, madam,' he said, and led me out of my own front door. There, in front of our apartment block, was a huge stretch limo, with blacked-out windows, the lot. I clapped my hands in delight and I saw the chauffeur try not to smile in response. He opened the door and I gasped.

Inside, there were twinkling lights all over the black ceiling, a state-of-the-art stereo and plasma TV screen, a bottle of champagne, two glasses, and red roses scattered absolutely everywhere over the leather seats. 'Omigod!' I squealed. 'Omigod, omigod, omigod!' Then I looked around at the chauffeur, suddenly confused.

'Is Will not here?' I asked.

'Please, make yourself comfortable, madam,' he said, smiling, and shut the door on me.

OK, I thought – fine. Obviously all part of the surprise – let's run with it!

Just as I had cleared a rose-free space to sit on, Adam called. It was almost as if he was telepathic. My heart started palpitating and I felt like I was going to pass out. What the hell was I going to say? As I answered the phone, a wall of thumping music and background party noise assaulted me. Adam's voice was hoarse and high-pitched.

'Babe, babe, I'm sorry – I'm at this party still but I'm thinking how wrong it is. I should be with you. I'm coming back.' My heart was thumping even harder now. I tried to swallow but it felt like my throat had seized up.

'Sorry, Ad, I'm going out.'

There was a shocked silence on the other end. 'With who?'

'Oh you know, just some of the girls.' My voice sounded weird even to my ears. I wasn't used to lying, wasn't good at it.

'Oh.' Adam sounded really put out. 'But – if I jump in a cab I can be with you in half an hour.' I felt torn – and guilty. I'd never, ever lied to him before. But then I looked at the roses, and all the effort Will had gone to, and grew angry again.

'Sorry, you had your chance! It's now coming up for eight o'clock on my twenty-first birthday and you're only now telling me you want to see me?'

'Of course I do, babe! I love you!'

He seriously thought that was enough! I don't know what I was thinking, but that just made me even more determined not to give in.

'Well, like I say, babe – you're a bit late.' My voice softened in spite of myself. I hated disappointing him, whatever the circumstances. I checked myself – it was a shame he didn't feel the same way, really, wasn't it? 'I've made other plans now. See you later!' I hung up, and pressed my head against the cool window to try and calm down a bit. I was all in a fluster – again – and it just wasn't fair. Nope, I was going to enjoy tonight. Adam could wait for tomorrow. I started to gather roses up to make a bouquet – it seemed such a waste to leave them lying around.

Ten minutes later, the car pulled up outside another smart-looking apartment block, and I saw Will step outside. He was wearing a dark grey suit and looked really smart – I'd never seen him that dressed up before!

As he clambered into the car, he gave me a kiss on the cheek and I felt goose bumps run down the back of my neck. Suddenly this felt really intimate – and I was starting to feel uneasy again.

'Evening, gorgeous!' he said breezily, sliding across the seat beside me, casually pushing a stray rose to one side. 'Hope you're hungry – we're going to my favourite restaurant, and I can't abide fussy eaters!'

I giggled. 'Will – I can't believe the trouble you've gone to! How—'

He winked and put his finger over his lips. 'Friends in the right places,' he grinned, picking a bottle of Laurent Perrier rosé out of the ice bucket and pouring me a glass. 'Now, did someone mention a birthday?'

Inside the restaurant, things just got even better. The staff all obviously knew Will well and led him to a beautiful, secluded table covered in more red roses and with an elaborately wrapped box of chocolates on my seat. Champagne was already chilling in a bucket, and a bottle of red stood ready on the table. I looked at Will, delighted, and then to my horror suddenly felt my face crumple and tears start to roll down my cheeks.

Will grabbed my arm and guided me on to my chair. 'Louise, don't cry! What's the matter?'

The maître d' moved away to a discreet distance and I wiped under my eyes with my napkin, cursing myself for such a pathetic show. I looked up to see Will gazing at me across the table with such a look of concern that I nearly started all over again.

'Oh, Will – I'm sorry,' I sniffed. 'This is lovely. I guess it's all just a bit much. It's great being here with you, but I was expecting to be sitting somewhere like this with Adam, and I . . .' and there I was, off again. What was wrong with me?

Will smiled kindly. 'Look, Louise, you've really been through the mill today. Adam is an absolute prat for treating you like that, birthday or no birthday, but boys will be boys. And who am I to complain? It gives me a good excuse to treat a beautiful woman' – I glared at him unintentionally and he grinned ruefully – 'a beautiful woman *and good friend* to a lovely time and get to enjoy her company all night.'

The maître d' returned and filled our glasses with champagne.

'So, Miss Adam Jones, let's drink to being twenty-one and start enjoying ourselves!'

I gave him a hesitant smile, clinked his glass and turned my attention to the menu. He was right. It was my birthday, and sod Adam – I was bloody well going to enjoy myself!

The meal was delicious, and Will was good fun, telling me funny stories about places he'd been – he was really well travelled – and restaurants he'd been to around the world. He knew so much, and I couldn't believe how quickly the evening was flying by. After dessert and coffee, he looked at his watch.

'Well, Cinderella, it's getting on for midnight. I should really be taking you home. But – I can't help but feel your birthday treat shouldn't end yet. How about we go for a little nightcap first?'

I laughed. 'I think a little drink would be fine. After all, I want to enjoy every single second I've got left of my birthday!'

Suddenly I remembered Adam. It was the first time I'd thought about him for a good three hours. What would he say if I was seen in a club with Will?

As if reading my mind, Will gave me a conspiratorial wink. 'I've got somewhere very discreet in mind,' he said as we walked back towards the limo. 'The perfect place for birthday girls who want to celebrate in secret.'

I giggled in relief. 'OK then. Let's go!'

As we walked across the street, though, a group of girls coming the other way stopped, gawping at Will. 'Omigod, it's Will Daniels,' shrieked one of them, and with that they all came clattering across to us. Will made a face. Over dinner he'd said he felt uncomfortable with being famous, and I could see that he wasn't entirely at ease with this situation. The girls were overdressed and overstyled and all seemed to be wearing the same cloying kind of perfume — a whole group of Pattii clones. I grinned at my own joke. But as I stood to one side, watching them actually physically stroke Will as he signed autographs, politely declining a boob that one of them offered him to scrawl on, I suddenly had a vision of Adam out on the town with his friends. Was this the kind of adulation he got wherever he went? And was this why he never wanted me around with him — because he enjoyed it in some kind of sick way? I felt like I was having an epiphany. Suddenly, through Will, I was seeing what my fiancé must have turned into – and I didn't like it.

The rest of the evening passed in the same companionable way. I still couldn't work out exactly what was behind Will's kindness, but other than the big fuss he'd made over my birthday, he certainly wasn't giving me signs that he wanted anything other than friendship – he wasn't being flirty at all, just nice, which made me feel totally at ease with him. Plus, he was an amazing guy to be around. He seemed to know everyone in the club, too – wherever we went, people appeared to treat him in the same kind of respectful way. He was obviously well liked, and it made me feel good that he seemed to think highly of me, too.

Come about 2 a.m., I was ready to go. We'd had some more to drink, we'd had a bit of a dance, and I'd had a lovely time, but the emotion of the day – not to mention all the booze tonight! – suddenly hit me, and I longed to be at home in my pyjamas. With Adam, I thought, and then pushed the idea to the back of my mind. There was time enough to deal with him tomorrow.

Not for the first time, Will seemed to read my mind, and led me to the limo – out of the back door this time, as the club owner had warned him there were now some paps outside. The lights in the car had been turned down to a soft glow, and I felt safe and warm and happy cocooned inside as we drove home.

At the apartment, Will made as if to get out with me and see me to the door. I pulled an apologetic face at him. 'Sorry, Will, do you mind if you don't? It's just – if Adam . . .'

He nodded understandingly. 'Hey, gorgeous, don't worry about it. My job is to make you feel better, not worse, remember?' He kissed me softly on the cheek. 'I guess that means you won't be taking these with you, either?' He pointed at the roses, which at some point during our absence had been magically arranged in a proper bouquet and tied up with twine, and smiled. 'I'm just glad you've had a lovely birthday in the end.'

'I have,' I said, squeezing his hand earnestly. 'The best.'

With that, I tottered unsteadily towards the apartment. I felt my phone buzz as I walked, and pulled it out. It was Adam – and, by the looks of it, not for the first time. My phone was showing eleven missed calls.

Suddenly sober again, I hesitated a moment before deciding whether to answer it or not. And as I pressed 'reject', it felt like something more momentous than ignoring someone's call. It felt like a huge step – a step too far, really.

But that was it. I couldn't go back now.

Chapter 13

'C'mon, Louise! Don't give up. Think of all those glasses of champagne and WORK IT!'

Desperately I tried to lift the hand weights above my head again, but I just had no strength. I managed a half-stretch and then my arms flopped down by my sides.

'What about those bingo wings? They'll be creeping up on you if you're not careful – four more, now!'

I scowled at Shane, my personal trainer, in the long studio mirrors. An Australian ex-champion surfer and fitness fanatic, he rippled with toned muscles and outdoorsy good health. I bet he'd never struggled with an exercise in his life. And anyway, what was he talking about? Looking at myself in the mirror, there didn't seem to be any hint of bingo wings!

Next to me, Pattii – in full make-up, matching pink-and-white leotard, knee-length leggings and platform trainers, was effortlessly lifting her weights, not breaking a sweat and even managing to pout seductively!

That was it for me. I dropped the weights on to the mat with a huge thud and flopped down next to them.

'Awww, bless her, Shane – she's probably hung over from her birthday bash last night!' said Pattii, smiling indulgently at me.

I smiled blankly at her. 'Not hung over, Pattii, just not really up for it today.' I looked at Shane. 'Sorry, Shane. I don't know what's up with me.'

Shane looked at me, an out-of-character expression of concern on his face. 'Well, maybe you'd better call it a day, Louise. You look exhausted. Emotional stress can affect your physical performance, you know.' He nodded at me, pointedly ignoring a lewd wink from Pattii as she took a double meaning from his words. 'There's no point pushing yourself if you're not into it. Pattii, shall we . . . ?'

Pattii shook her head. 'I think I might sit this one out as well,' she said, making very unsubtle faces about her concern for my mental health. Shane, for once, nodded understandingly, and busied himself putting away the weights, steps and fitness paraphernalia that had created our training circuit. Pattii embarked on a series of elaborate stretches, whilst I continued to sit there gratefully, unable to do anything else but stare into space.

The truth was, I was exhausted. Mentally and emotionally whacked out from living the roller-coaster existence that had been mine and Adam's life ever since we moved up north. I'd lain awake practically all night worrying about it. Adam, of course, had come in at some ungodly hour absolutely plastered, and then this morning had slunk in to have his breakfast later than usual, obviously still the worse for wear and contrite about his behaviour. I'd said very little – I didn't want to lie again, and anyway I didn't have the energy to deal with his constant but empty apologies. I couldn't cope any more – with the mood swings, the letdowns and, now – on my part anyhow – the lies. I hadn't done anything wrong on my birthday, but even having done something behind Adam's back felt like cheating. And the trouble was, I just didn't know what to do about it.

'Come on, you,' said Pattii, pulling herself out of some kind of downward cat-back stretch. 'Let's go back to mine and get a coffee. Looks like you could do with a chat.'

I laughed a hard, bitter laugh that didn't really sound like me. 'I could do with a lot more than that,' I said. 'Starting with a life transplant!'

Pattii looked shocked. 'That doesn't sound like the words of someone who's just turned twenty-one!' she tutted. 'I'm gonna have to do something about this!'

Despite its five-star plushness, we never showered at the gym – it wouldn't do to find yourself towelling yourself dry next to one of the WAG wannabes from town, or worse still, a gossip journalist. Today we'd not done enough to work up a sweat anyway, so we picked up our bags from our lockers and left, driving back to Pattii's house in companionable silence. Pattii obviously didn't want to start the ball rolling with the therapy session until we could be sure of no interruptions, and I felt a bit numb, like I'd had all the life sapped out of me. It was a while since we'd done this – when I'd first offered to share training sessions with Pattii, we'd always had a coffee or lunch afterwards. But I'd hardly seen her at all lately. I stared into space as we drove down the familiar street, my mind full of blank thoughts.

Once back at Pattii and Jez's sprawling faux-Tudor mansion in a gated development just outside of town, we settled into the huge raffia conservatory chairs with fat, cosy cushions and basked in the spring sunshine pouring in through the glass panels.

'So, what's this all about? I thought you'd had some kind of amazing love-fest last night. I would have expected you to be bouncing off the walls.' Pattii took a sip of her coffee. 'Or at least showing off your new watch, hahaha!'

I looked down at my naked wrist and then out of the window, winding my hair around my fingers distractedly.

'No, babe. I didn't get my love-fest. Adam didn't turn up.' I knitted my eyebrows when I saw Pattii's shocked face. Somehow, telling her wasn't making it any easier, as I'd hoped – instead, it seemed to be making it more painful. Probably because it was making it seem more real.

'What do you mean, he didn't turn up?' she parroted. 'Where was he?' She looked at me questioningly at first, and then her eyes widened. 'He wasn't – he wasn't with McNulty and those, was he?'

I shrugged. 'Who knows where he was? All I know is, it was somewhere he was very keen for me not to follow him to. I asked if I could join him,' I explained as Pattii looked confused. 'It was my twenty-first, after all!' Suddenly I felt total despair. 'There was no way I was going to stay in on my own.' I started to cry.

Pattii nodded understandingly and sighed deeply. 'Oh, Louise, honestly, babe – these boys. They do put us through the bleeding wringer, don't they? Give them a cushy job, a shedload of money and a gorgeous gal sitting at home waiting for them to finish kicking a poxy ball around, and they still have to go out sniffing out skirt.'

I shook my head vehemently, 'Oh no, Pattii, he wasn't out with other girls. Well, there were other girls there, I'm sure – it was a party, you see – but he wouldn't have done that. That's not his style. I trust him. He trusts me.'

Pattii snorted. 'Yeah, right, and the rest, Louise.'

'No, Pattii, honestly, that's not like Adam. He's not the same as other footballers, not like—' I bit my lip, remembering Jodie's theory about Jez's fidelity. It probably wouldn't be a good idea to start analysing individual behaviour right now. 'He's not unfaithful, he's just thoughtless. And carried away with his glamorous new life. It's like he wants to love me but all his new friends are getting in the way.' I sobbed wretchedly, desperately trying to wipe away my tears. What had I done? I'd deceived and made a fool of the person I loved most in the world!

Pattii laughed cruelly. 'Yep, Adam and all the others, babe,' she said. 'What makes you think he's any better than anyone else? Seems to me he's classic philanderer material. Working-class boy made good, doting childhood sweetheart waiting unquestioningly at home.' She took a deep breath, and gave me a weird look – almost like she was jealous of me. 'He's from the same stock as Gary, as Craig, even McNulty!' she continued. 'The only thing that separates them is when and how they do the dirty – the rest is inevitable. If only my Jez had the looks, I'm sure he'd be up to no good as well.'

I stood up angrily. 'Look, Pattii, you asked me here when I was feeling really low – and I came because you're my friend, and I need some advice. But if all you're going to do is slag off Adam, then I'd better get myself home.'

I slammed the coffee cup down on the side table, sloshing mocha latte all over the faux-mahogany surface.

Pattii held her hand out. 'Louise, I'm sorry, gel. You know what I'm like – my mouth runs away with me! I was just saying, don't blow things out of proportion. So Adam's been a bit silly? Well, aren't we all sometimes. It's not the end of the world. Sit down and let's chat it through.'

I looked out the window, suddenly wishing I was talking to Jodie or Tara about this. They weren't quite so black and white about everything and actually gave me some comfort rather than winding me up!

But they weren't here. Pattii was. And annoying though she could be, she was my friend and so I guessed her advice should count for as much as that of the others.

I sat down hesitantly. Pattii laughed, softer now. 'Don't

look so bleeding scared! I'm not gonna bite you. So, naughty old Adam went out on the piss when he should have been taking you out for your big birthday night, leaving you all on your own. How the hell is he going to make this one up to you?'

I stared at my knee, picking at an imaginary thread on my tracksuit. When I looked up, Pattii was looking at me inquisitively.

'I didn't stay at home on my own, though, Pattii. I went out with Will.'

Later that afternoon, Mum called. I picked up the phone with a sinking feeling. How was I going to explain away last night to her? Last time I'd spoken to her was when I was getting dressed for my night out with Adam. It was less than twenty-four hours ago – but it felt like weeks.

'Hello, love!'

'Hi, Mum,' I said, trying to sound happy.

'So . . . ?' she said excitedly. 'How was your birthday night? Did Adam totally spoil you?'

'I – I had a lovely time,' I said truthfully. 'I – oh, Mum, sorry – there's another call coming through. It could be him now – can I ring you back?'

'Well, yes, love – of course,' she said, sounding a bit put out. I didn't blame her, but I couldn't lie to her – and I didn't know how to tell her the truth.

I picked up the other call – it was Jodie. She sounded

breathless, like she'd been running. But this was Jodie, whose most strenuous form of exercise was going to the fridge for a Diet Coke or a glass of champers, and I knew it could mean only thing. Gossip, with a capital G.

'Louise! Where've you been?'

I was puzzled. 'Oh, you know. Shopping. Hanging out at home. I was gonna call you but I've had a lot on my mind, I kind of needed to download it all a bit.'

'Oh, right.' Jodie didn't really sound like she believed me. 'And how was physio?'

I laughed. My physio appointments for a strained foot had finished weeks before. Mind you, she always went to visit Gary's mother on a Tuesday lunchtime, so she wouldn't necessarily have known that. 'Jodie, you are so, like, two months ago. I haven't had physio for ages!'

'Oh, right.' Now it was her turn to sound puzzled. 'So why don't you go to any of Fatty Pattii's "sushi and Chablis" lunches? I would have thought that was right up your street.'

I had no idea what she was talking about. 'Sushi and Chablis? Pattii's never mentioned that to me. Who goes? And how do you know about them?'

Jodie was silent for a moment. 'Hmmm. Not sure what's going on here. Gary's mum wasn't feeling up to visitors today, and so I went into town, bumped into Susie and she invited me along. Seems to be a regular thing. All the girls go – there was quite a turnout. Fatty seems to be Queen Bee of it all – she definitely organises it – it's meant to be an antidote to the boys' Tuesday afternoon boozing, sorry, bonding sessions.'

But I was in no mood for jokes. My head was swimming. Why had Pattii left me out of something like this? 'Right,' I said slowly. 'Well, I've never been invited.'

'How weird,' Jodie mused. 'She told me you were having physio.'

'Pattii and I train together, babe,' I snapped. 'She's well aware of my physical health.'

Jodie, sensing she'd put her foot right in it, but obviously feeling bad at having upset me, tried to change the subject. 'Of course, she was over the moon to see me there . . .' she said sarcastically. 'Anyway, babe, that's not why I was ringing. What's this I hear about you and Will Daniels?'

I froze. What on earth . . .

'What do you mean?' I stammered. 'We're mates – you know that. You were there when we first met!'

'Oh, come on, Louise. Pattii was full of it. It's all anyone talked about all lunchtime. Well, except me, 'cos I didn't know anything about it.' She sounded hurt, and I cursed myself again for not confiding in her like I normally would. 'You blow Adam out on your twenty-first and go out partying with another man, and say there's nothing going on?' She sounded concerned rather than critical, and when she put it like that, I could understand why. 'This isn't like you. What's going on?'

I felt like the room was spinning around me. I sat on the

nearest surface — the coffee table — and tried to swallow. I couldn't. I looked at my watch. Adam would be home any minute. There was no doubt the rumours would reach him, either before he got home or just after. I needed to deal with this — and fast. Panic overwhelmed me. I hadn't done anything wrong! Why did everyone seem hell-bent on believing I had? 'Jodie, you have to believe me. Nothing happened. Adam blew *me* out. I was left all on my own at home on my twenty-first — and Will was just there.' It sounded feeble even to my ears. 'You believe me, don't you? I wish someone would.'

'I wish they would too,' said Jodie slowly. 'I also wish you'd told me and not Pattii. But most of all, I wish you'd called me up last night and gone out with me and not some playboy footballer. You've been in the game long enough to know what it's like, Louise. You can't just do something like that and hope to keep it quiet.'

'Do something like what?' I practically screamed at her. 'I haven't done anything wrong! Nothing happened between us! We're just friends. And anyway, I'd be lucky if Adam did notice. Him even remembering my name is a miracle these days.'

'Oh, babe, honestly,' sighed Jodie. 'Just listen to yourself. If you heard Adam'd been out for dinner with someone else on his birthday, and he'd lied to you about where he was — I'm assuming you didn't 'fess up this morning? No, I thought not — but if all that happened, would you honestly believe him when he told you nothing had happened?'

'I guess not.' I massaged my forehead despairingly. 'Oh Jodie, what am I going to do?'

'Babe, I can't decide that for you,' she said soothingly. 'But from the sounds of it, there's an awful lot wrong with you and Adam at the moment and you're going to have to make some changes one way or the other.' She paused. 'And I could say the same about some of your friends, too.'

I nodded miserably. 'Yep. Point taken.'

I heard Jodie sigh heavily on the other end of the phone. 'I still don't understand why you couldn't have called me.'

'I wish I had!' I cried out passionately. 'I didn't plan on telling Pattii! It just came out. I was upset – confused – I—'

'Babe, calm down.' interrupted Jodie. 'Sounds to me like your life is totally out of control – no wonder you're all in a pickle. Don't move. I'm coming round right now.'

I put the phone down beside me. I felt like someone had punched me in the stomach with a fire extinguisher and then beaten me around the head a few times with it for good measure. That bitch Pattii! What was her game? And how dare she treat me like that? I'd confided my closest secrets to her, and she'd not only told everyone else, she'd changed the story to make it as scandalous as possible. What else had she told the others, hoping to ingratiate herself amongst them all?

I couldn't believe she'd tried to exclude me from everything, either. How vindictive was that? She must have started the lunches around the time that Tara and Jonnie had left. It all fitted – that was the time when I'd hurt my foot, and when I thought back, also the time that my weekday friendship with Pattii had cooled (she was still always very friendly of a Saturday night, but with hindsight, that probably had more to do with needing a party posse than being a loyal friend). Tara would never have allowed such a regular group fixture to take place without being the organiser, but since she'd gone, no one had really picked up the baton and become chief WAG. Pattii obviously felt that this was her role for some reason, but why it should have to be at my expense, I had no idea. I mean, hadn't I done everything I could to make her feel welcome since she arrived? Introduced her to everyone, included her in our plans, got her discounts, been her friend? Some friendship she offered back. Jodie had been right about her all along.

But right now I had more important things to worry about – like my relationship and my future. What was I going to do? It was high time I listened to my gut instinct – and to Jodie – and really tried to sort this mess out. Maybe a huge inescapable drama was what me and Adam needed to really decide if we were going to make a go of this or not.

I combed my fingers through the ends of my hair thoughtfully. Well, *I* needed to decide. Adam was quite clearly happy to mosey along as we had been doing, but I couldn't do that any more. It was eating away at my self-esteem and my self-confidence, and definitely at my happiness. But did I have the guts to leave him? And did I – a small but insistent voice inside me persisted – did I have the guts to leave all this?

I looked around me at the luxurious flat, the door that led through to our bedroom and my walk-in wardrobe full of designer clothes, the Hermès handbag that held the keys to the Audi. I'd never gone out with Adam for all this – but could I leave him despite it?

My phone rang again, and I looked at it fearfully, expecting Adam. The number was unknown – but not thinking, I picked it up straight away.

'Hullo?'

A tinny female voice came down a crackly line. 'Is that Louise Gayle?'

'Yes, speaking.'

'The fiancée of Premiership footballer Adam Jones?'

I was suspicious now. 'Yes, who is this?'

'Louise, this is the *News of the World*. We've heard about your affair with Will Daniels and we'd like to make you a substantial offer for your story exclusive.'

I dropped the phone in shock, then bent down to hang up properly. In a daze, I turned the phone off. How had the papers found out about this already? I had a weird, dizzy feeling, of being out of control in my own life. Suddenly, I just wanted to be back at home in Cardiff – at Mum and Dad's house, where nothing bad ever happened and the most trouble you'd ever get into would be for not doing the washing-up properly.

I heard the intercom click as Adam turned the key in the lift to access our floor. I braced myself. Would he have found out yet, or did I have a few hours' grace?

I didn't have to wait long to find out. As he let himself in, he dumped his kit bag, then stomped across the hall and swung the living room door open. He was wearing his team tracksuit, the zip-up top obviously slung on in a hurry. His face was thunderous, and his eyes were wild with anger.

'What the fuck is this about Will Daniels, you little slag?'

I flinched, paralysed with fear. This was it. The worst-case scenario.

Will was wrong. There were no friends in football, after all.

Chapter 14

My body heaved as my sobs turned into hiccups. I felt like I'd been crying all my life. In fact, it was only a matter of hours – a short time on a normal day, but today it had been long enough to change my life for ever.

I looked around our bedroom forlornly and tried to squeeze another top into my already bulging suitcase. It seemed such a small bag to fit my life with Adam into. At the thought that it was all over between us, I fell to my knees and started crying hysterically again. Yes, I'd been wondering what to do about us. Yes, I'd considered leaving him. But the reality of the break-up – the nastiness, the hurt and hatred in Adam's eyes, the vile things he'd called me – was something else entirely.

Adam had, predictably, blown his top at me. I'd never seen anything like it – his face was contorted with rage and he was almost purple with anger and betrayal. Apparently, the 'news' was all around the club – but he hadn't been fortunate enough to hear it from a friend, like I had. Nope, the first he'd heard of his relationship crisis was from the

News of the World, who'd bypassed Trevor entirely and phoned Adam direct. The leak must have come from an insider who had access to Adam's phone number – no three guesses who, I thought, as a grim image of Pattii popped into my head.

But Adam wasn't interested in any of that – instead he'd ranted and ranted, shouting accusations right in my face and refusing to listen to my side of things as I'd cried and begged. Finally, he'd broken down himself. 'How could you do this to me, Lou?' he'd cried, his voice cracking with emotion. 'All I ever did was love you. I've given you everything you could ever have dreamed of. I proposed to you. We were getting married, for Christ's sake!'

With that, he'd upended the coffee table, sending mugs and glasses and candles flying, and stormed out of the flat. He'd paused at the door before he left, looking back at me, his face both menacing and crushed at the same time. 'I want you out of here by the time I get back, Louise. I don't want to set eyes on you ever again.'

I shuddered as I thought back to how devastated he'd looked, and picked myself and my suitcase up. I took one last, longing look around the flat and then left slowly, dragging my case along behind me.

In the car park, I stared at my little two-seater convertible in defeat. Although the weather was still pretty cold, I'd pulled the roof down so I could fit more stuff in, but even so it was overflowing. I had no idea where the suitcase was going to fit. The boot was stuffed full of Louis Vuitton bags containing my shoes and clothes, and a pile of coats still on their hangers was perched precariously across the tiny back ledge. A huge potted tiger lily sat on the passenger seat – it had been a housewarming gift from my late grandpa when we'd first bought the house in Cardiff, and there was no way I was leaving that behind. There was only one thing for it. I was going to have to wear as many of the coats as I could, sit on the rest and put the suitcase where they had been.

Just as I was working out which jacket would fit under which best, a horrific thought hit me. I hadn't checked to see if there were any paps outside – but if word had got out about me and Will, there were bound to be some waiting there. I couldn't leave in an open-top car wearing ten coats and driving a pot plant! It would be all over the papers tomorrow – upsetting for our families as well as me and Adam. Thank goodness for an underground car park, or I'd have been caught out already. I'd have to call Jodie and get her and Gary to put as much as possible in the Range Rover, and then take the rest myself. Jodie had done an about-turn when she'd got to the flat and realised Adam was already there, but I'd spoken to her since and had arranged to stay at hers for a few days. All my things were going to end up there one way or another – better to do it in the most low-key way possible.

I pulled my phone out of my bag, but just as I was about to hit Jodie's number on speed dial, it rang. It was Will.

I inhaled sharply. I hadn't had a chance to consider how this must be affecting Will – presumably the papers would have called him, too. I was almost too scared to answer. What if *he* was angry with me as well?

Then I pulled myself together. Will was the only one who knew the truth, after all – and it sure as hell seemed like he was the only one who believed it.

'Hi, Will,' I said softly as I pressed 'answer'.

'Hey, gorgeous,' he replied, equally softly. 'Guess I don't need to ask how things are, eh?'

'No, not really. In fact, I'm just leaving the flat now,' I said bravely. But I wasn't fooling anyone – least of all myself. 'For the last time . . .' I finished lamely, bursting into tears again.

'Where are you going?' said Will, suddenly sounding a lot more masterful and businesslike.

'I'm on my way to Jodie's,' I wailed. 'But my plant won't fit in my car and I've had to pull the top down and I'm sure all the paps are outside and I don't know what to do.'

'And where's Adam in all this?' asked Will briskly.

'I don't know – out somewhere,' I sobbed.

'Right, gorgeous, stay right where you are. I'm coming to get you.'

I sank down on to my coat-covered driver's seat and cried, out of both sorrow and relief – and I wasn't sure which was strongest.

*

I let out a gasp of awe as I climbed out of my car on to the circular gravel driveway of the mansion Will had brought me to. It was idyllic – a huge ivy-covered farmhouse with sweeping manicured lawns on either side and lead-shot windows that twinkled welcomingly in the twilight with the glow of the lights behind them.

I'd been a bit confused when Will's E-Type Jaguar had led me a different way entirely from where the limo had driven last night to pick him up. But I was hardly in a position to stop and ask him, so I'd followed as he'd driven out of town and into a sleepy village about thirty minutes from the city centre.

He smiled as he noticed my tear-stained delight. 'Like it?' he asked, unnecessarily in my opinion.

Just then a white van pulled into the driveway. It was one of Will's mates – he'd pitched up with Will at the flat and all hell had broken loose when I asked the concierge to let *two* extra vehicles into the car park. But seeing my distress, he'd given in, even though I'd protested to Will that we didn't need a van.

'I haven't got that much stuff!' I'd said, but when he'd made me go back up to the flat and make sure, it was amazing how much I'd come back down with. Like pictures and things, all my jewellery, which I hadn't liked to take but which Will had said I should – and even the odd chair or bit of furniture I'd fallen in love with.

'But I haven't got anywhere to store it,' I'd protested.

'Don't you worry about that,' he'd said, touching my cheek tenderly. 'It's time to take care of number one, Louise. You've been putting Mr Jones first for far too long.'

Will directed his mate around the back of the house, and turned to me, smiling excitedly and dangling a key.

'So, want to have a look round your new house?'

I giggled. 'Come on, Will, who lives here really?'

He stopped smiling, suddenly serious. 'I do. It's my latest property investment – for me. It's commuting distance from the club but a much nicer area. This is the business that's kept my mind occupied whilst I've been injured. Well, that and a certain young lady.'

I looked up at him uncertainly. Was he saying what I thought he was saying?

He smiled again, softly this time. 'Look, I know you've only just broken up with Adam, Louise, but I would have thought it's quite clear how I feel about you. So, look on this as your shelter, your refuge, and whenever you're ready – and if you want it to be – your home.'

I felt my legs buckle, and Will grabbed me to stop me falling over right there in the driveway. This was all too much, too soon. Jodie was right. My life was out of control. Way, way out of control. But there seemed no way of getting back on top of it.

By Saturday, things seemed to be calming down at bit – on the face of it. Will had got me a new phone and instructed me only to give the number to people I really trusted, like family and Jodie, so that the papers couldn't get hold of me. There had been a media frenzy over the story, and there were apparently photographers 24/7 outside the club, outside mine and Adam's flat, outside Will's flat, even outside Mum and Dad's house in Cardiff. (None, however, outside the mansion — apparently Will had bought it in an assumed name and I hadn't set foot outside the garden, so up until now, no one had twigged that that was where I was.) I guess I could see why it made such a good story — not only did it involve footballers and infidelity, but the rivalry between Will and Adam's teams was the stuff of tabloid poetry. 'ONE–NIL TO WILL' one headline had screamed; 'ADAM DUMPS LOU' was another. The worst was 'I WILL, SAYS LOUISE', claiming that Will had proposed to me and we were planning to head off abroad and marry next week. My mum and dad loved that one . . .

Otherwise, to be honest, my parents seemed completely bemused by the whole thing. Apart from the trauma of telling Mum that me and Adam — the only boyfriend I'd ever had — had split up, I had to tell her that instead of going to the safety of their house, I was staying with a man they'd never met or even heard me mention.

'But who *is* he, love?' Mum had asked, totally perplexed. 'And how do you know him? Are you sure he's all right?'

I could understand her confusion, to be honest. Even to me, in the middle of the whole thing, it felt a bit surreal —

God knows how it felt for Mum and Dad, still safely cocooned in Cardiff.

Well, kind of cocooned. Because with the arrival of the paps when the story broke, Mum and Dad – and Adam's mum and dad – had been given a taster of what it felt like to live under the media spotlight. Which helped them understand why I actually had no choice but to be at Will's.

'They're just always there, Lou!' Mum had said in shock. 'We wake up in the morning, they're there. We get home from work, they're there. We can't understand why. Lord knows how they're making any money, taking pictures of your father scratching his armpit of a morning!'

Mum had apparently started to feel sorry for them, and was spending a large part of her free time taking out tea and biscuits to them. For the first time ever, I envied the paps. I ached for a cuppa and a chocolate digestive at Mum's cosy kitchen table, and some of her own brand of TLC.

Not that I was short of support. Jodie had been round every morning since I'd left the flat, for coffee and gossip while Gary was training. Well, nearly every day. Apparently, a couple of times Will had answered the door and told her I was resting and shouldn't be disturbed. I couldn't understand that. The last thing I needed was rest – I wanted distractions! But when I'd questioned him about it, he'd said he felt I needed a bit of a break from that whole lifestyle, to come to terms with everything. I could see his point – I just couldn't understand why it meant not seeing my best mate! But I'd let it go – for now. Time enough for that kind of conversation in the future – right now, I was more concerned with the present.

Tara, of course, had been straight on the phone the very night Adam had asked me to leave, before I'd even told her what had happened. Distance didn't seem to have affected her ability to be right there in the thick of every story, and between Jodie, Raymond Moore, and I guess several other contacts I might never know about, she had the whole story and some. And she was revelling in it – whilst being worried about me, of course.

'So, babe, what is *really* going on with you and Daniels?' she'd pressed, obviously convinced I was lying and that Will and I had been lovers all along.

'Nothing!' I insisted.

'Well, just you watch yourself,' she'd warned. 'You don't find footballers of that age without any baggage.'

'Look, babe, if there was anything going on between me and Will, I would tell you – and if there was anything going to happen you'd be the first I'd turn to for advice!' I said. 'Right now, he's offering me friendship and a place to live that no one seems to have found out about – yet.' A horrible thought hit me. 'Tara, don't go telling Raymond or anyone where I am, will you?' I regretted it the moment I'd said it. Tara was one of my best friends, after all, and she might be a gossip, but I knew she'd never drop me in it.

'Of course not, babe,' she said huffily. 'As if ! Information is a one-way street with me – in one ear and out into yours. But if you don't trust me, then . . .'

'Of course, I do, babe,' I said hurriedly. 'I'm sorry.'

'It's OK,' she said, relenting immediately. 'Obviously mixing with people like Pattii Steadman has made you think no one can be trusted.'

Ouch. I'd asked for that one. And Tara, like Jodie, had always hated Pattii. She'd warned me, so she deserved her 'I told you so' moment.

'But,' she continued happily, 'I'm sure that karma will sort that one out.'

'What do you mean?' I'd asked curiously.

'Oh, nothing, babe. Just wait and see. I know the ways these things work. There's skeletons in that girl's cupboard, believe me – and she's asking for them to come out.'

I'd even heard from Sara – bless her. Even though Will had told me to get rid of my old mobile phone, I'd kept hold of my SIM card. She'd texted me the day the story broke after she'd seen it in the papers. There was no chance of getting home to Cardiff to see her, but it felt good to know she still cared.

Adam hadn't got off scot-free, either. Not only had the story been an excuse for the papers to rehash the fight-in-the-tunnel incident, but some photographs of him on a night out with the lads had appeared in yet another red-top, out of his skull with drink and with vomit all down his shirt. 'LOVE SICK' had been the headline on that, but the story had portrayed him as some self-destructive party boy, and hinted that it was this kind of behaviour that had led to my 'affair' with Will.

But even though to the outside world it might seem like things were blowing over – after all, they just needed to move on to another story and in their heads it was all fixed – for me it was only getting worse. Once the drama of me and Adam breaking up had passed, I was now having to deal with the fact that I'd lost the person I loved most in the world. I felt like someone had died. Every time I managed to put the thought of him, his smell, his feel, his voice, out of my head, something would remind me of him and I'd get the by now familiar jolt of hurt and longing and despair back again.

And the worst thing was, it was all for nothing. I'd done nothing wrong. Pattii's lies and the papers' pick-up had made an urban myth of my relationship with Will, and there was nothing I could do about it.

Well, I had tried. Jodie – even though I still didn't think she was a hundred per cent convinced of my story – had promised to speak to Adam, and I'd given her a letter for him, explaining everything that had happened. But although she'd given it to him directly, she'd said he'd refused point blank to discuss it. The club had carpeted him after the pictures of him out on the lash had come out, and she said that the time he wasn't spending training, Gary reckoned he was at home with the curtains drawn watching football videos or playing on his PS3 or Wii. So some things didn't change, then.

Will was doing his best to cheer me up, though, and had tried to make me feel as at home as possible. Well, as at home as I could be with very little furniture anywhere! Weirdly, although I had a few bits from mine and Adam's flat which would have at least got us by for a couple of weeks, Will had put them in storage, claiming they didn't work with the house. I guess I was glad in a way – I'm not sure I could have coped with seeing reminders of my life with Adam all around Will's house.

I was sleeping in a lovely room with views all over the surrounding countryside, and Will had promised to get an interior designer in next week so that I could get it redecorated to my taste – and so that I could start revamping the whole property! He'd begun coming home from training with piles of interior decorating magazines. I'd been slightly taken aback – it was a bit much considering I was still reeling from my break-up with Adam. I'd hardly even come to terms with that yet, let alone got over it and decided how I felt about Will!

Of course none of this had gone unnoticed, and Will had been really cool about it. 'Look, gorgeous, don't panic. If you're unhappy thinking of it as an investment in your future home, consider it something to do while you're bored out of your brains and unable to leave the house. Secretly it's my underhand method of making you pay your way!'

That had made me giggle. It was odd really: despite him being a good ten years older than me, he was really fun and could be dead silly. He was worried about me having to be cooped up in the house all the time, so last night he'd arranged for a catering company to send a cook and a butler to serve us up a three-course meal in his fancy formal dining room (he reckoned it was to celebrate the arrival of the huge mahogany table and chairs – plus he could only get away with having a slap-up meal and a bottle of wine on a Friday because he wasn't fit after his injury. However, I still think he was trying to make me feel better). So we'd had a gorgeous dinner of foie gras followed by venison with celeriac mash, and were just tucking into an amazing gooey chocolate fondant when he sat back and called over the butler.

'Mate – can I have a blob of vanilla ice cream with this?'

The butler had look surprised, but nodded. Will looked at me. 'Louise – do you want some?'

I giggled. 'Erm – yes please.'

The butler hurried off to get the ice cream, and Will leaned over. 'This is gorgeous – but don't you sometimes just wish you could have a McFlurry?' he whispered.

I giggled again. 'I've never had a McFlurry!'

Will looked gobsmacked. 'What? You've never had a McFlurry? I thought your generation was brought up on McDonald's?'

I'd laughed out loud at that one. 'All right, Grandad. So maybe my mum would never let me eat fast food. She said it was bad for my skin. And what you've never had, you never miss.'

Will had pointed his spoon at me. 'Wise words indeed. But in my opinion, people who've never had a McFlurry have never lived.'

At this point the butler had returned with the ice cream. Will was right, it did make the pudding taste even sweeter. If he was right about that, maybe he was right about the McFlurrys. And if he was right about the McFlurrys, maybe he was right about us . . .

Right now, I looked at my watch. He'd be due back from the match in a couple of hours – maybe I could go for a run and then be showered and changed by the time he got home. I was fidgety and restless today – it was the first Saturday in the season for years I'd not been to a match, and I honestly didn't know what to do with myself.

I changed into my running gear and set off on my now regular jog around the mansion gardens. Two laps took about forty minutes, and that was it for me at the moment. I must call Shane, I thought, to see if he'd come out here. If meals like that one last night were going to become a regular thing, I was going to have to up my exercise! But then again, maybe Shane wasn't the best bet – if he was still training Pattii, how could I be sure that my private life wasn't going to end up all over the tabloids again? Tara had tried to instil in me how careful I'd need to be about putting myself in 'situations'.

She'd had to learn that the hard way – she'd even been betrayed by her cleaner in the past – and I was beginning to understand what she meant.

I groaned out loud as I approached the house for the second and last time. This bit was the worst – a sharp incline out of a pretty wooded area – and on the second lap it was always a bit of an effort. Still, no pain, no gain and all that! I could hear Shane's voice in my head as I panted up the hill. 'Come on, Louise, if it's hurting, it's doing you good. Put some muscle into it!'

As I jogged down the hill, I spotted Will's car in the driveway. He was home early – damn, I hadn't planned for him to arrive back to find me all red-faced and sweaty! Suddenly the sunlight caught something shiny on the steps leading up to the imposing front doors. In fact, as I got closer, there were lots of what looked like ice buckets, sitting on each of the steps.

I jogged a bit faster, intrigued by this delivery. I wondered if Will knew about it, or if he'd got home before it arrived. Crunching up the drive, I could tell they were definitely ice buckets, with something brightly coloured in each one. I counted at least ten – what on earth were they?

But as I stopped in front of the steps, panting, hands on hips, it all became clear and I laughed out loud. I clapped my hands excitedly and looked around for Will. He must be watching somewhere . . . I spotted his face at the lounge window, looking out expectantly. I picked up an ice bucket and waved it at him delightedly, and I could see him laughing along with me. He opened the window and leaned out. 'You can make up for lost time now, gorgeous!'

On the steps were twelve mini champagne buckets filled with crushed ice. In each one was a shiny silver spoon . . . and a McFlurry! I guessed there was every flavour here that had ever been created – I spotted a Munchies one, a Mini Egg one, an M&Ms one, a Rolo one . . .

I looked back up at Will's twinkling smile, and my eyes filled with tears. It was years since Adam had done anything half this thoughtful. In fact, I hadn't really seen that side of him since we left Cardiff. What on earth had happened to that Adam and Louise, who'd fallen so deeply in love and thought they'd be together for ever? And was there ever any chance of finding them again – or them finding each other?

Chapter 15

'Well, it couldn't have happened to a nicer person, as far as I'm concerned,' said Jodie, leaning back on her chair with a satisfied grin and inspecting her newly painted nails. 'I guess somebody else did want her bloke after all!'

I nodded in agreement, surveying the newspapers spread around us on the kitchen table detailing Jez Steadman's passionate affair with their nanny. The stories were lurid and explicit, and made me glad that despite everything, Adam hadn't slept with anyone else. Because however painful our break-up, I was sure that kind of betrayal would be even harder to deal with.

Jez's infidelity was splashed over the front page of every newspaper. One carried the original scoop of the story itself, and had details of secret liaisons, text messages and furtive voice mails. Another had paid the nanny for her story, and alongside a photograph of her in black lacy underwear and suspenders had detailed Jez's rampant sexual appetite, some of his sexual preferences and details of how as well as where and when they had had sex.

Just then, my phone rang. 'It's Tara!' I told Jodie excitedly, who feigned surprise and then blew elaborate kisses at me, indicating I should send her love to Tara.

I grinned, and answered. 'Ciao, bella!'

Tara giggled. 'Hi, babe. You can quit with the cosmopolitan act, too. Just because you're living with a man of the world doesn't mean you have to show the rest of us up!'

It was my turn to giggle. 'Jodie's here, babe. She sends hugs. And kisses,' I added, as Jodie started the air-kiss pantomime again.

'Ooooh, how fabulous, babe, put me on loudspeaker!' I fumbled with my phone, trying to find the 'conference' facility, and placed it ceremoniously in the middle of the table, where both Jodie and I could hear and speak into it.

'Hey, Tara, now you're on top of all the tabloids – just where you like to be best!' quipped Jodie, and we all laughed.

'So, girls, are you toasting Fatty Pattii's bad news with a bottle of bubbly?' asked Tara gleefully. I gasped. It was very unlike Tara to be so openly hostile about someone. 'Anything on her rather than her heartthrob husband?'

Jodie leaned forward excitedly, pulling out the most downmarket paper on the table. It, having missed out on the scoop of the month, had embellished quotes from both stories and added details of Pattii's colourful past.

'Oh yes babe. And so it begins. Fatty Pattii is going DOWN!'

I shifted uncomfortably on my seat. As far as I could tell,

this was a case of trial by tabloid – but I couldn't work out who the papers thought was the villain and who the victim. I mean, Jez and the nanny were in the wrong, surely – but it was almost as though Pattii was at fault for her page-three past!

Since Mitch's drugs bust, and mine and Adam's split, the tabloids had become hungry for the next football scandal, and had been sniffing around for weeks.

The next casualty had been Anthony Hargreaves, the footballer with the rough wife, Julia, who'd threatened me and Pattii on our London night out. The one who'd made him spend all his time at home, with only the internet for entertainment, thinking she was superior because her hubby was never out partying. Well, he'd been caught having an affair and had moved out, leaving her with their four kids. The irony of it was, he'd met his new girlfriend in an online chatroom!

Now, the daily coverage was bordering on a witch hunt for footballer gossip. Jodie said that every Saturday there seemed to be more and more snappers outside the club, and although I still hadn't been to a game with Will, he said it was the same scenario at his club. Every morning I woke up terrified that they'd have found out where I was, and that I was living with Will – in every sense of the word now – and that they'd dredge the whole thing up again, painting me in the worst possible light. Because of course, now that Will and I really were an item, my protestations that I was innocent all along would fall on deaf ears – in fact, I was pretty sure no one believed me now at all.

Life with Will felt so secure after the madness that Adam had surrounded himself with ever since we moved up north – but I still *really* missed Ad. Maybe it was too soon after we split to be starting up with someone new, or maybe you never get over your first love – but the way it had all happened still filled me with horror. I just wanted to see him, to apologise, to make him understand that I never would have cheated on him.

So unlike Jodie, I didn't feel triumphant about the latest scandal to hit the headlines – I just felt a bit sick and, well, sad. Even though Pattii had ruined my life, I now knew how it felt and I was sure that being faced with the revelation that Jez had been having an affair with their nanny was going to crucify her.

'I told you, anyway, babe,' continued Jodie. 'Weeks ago. Remember, when we saw Jez and that little slapper out shopping? There had to be something going on. I mean, no footballer would voluntarily spend time with the kids unless he was up to something. They looked as thick as thieves. I knew something was up.'

'Going out shopping is one thing, but what about all those X-rated text messages the papers reckoned he sent?' I cringed as I picked up one of the tabloids and scanned a section for the umpteenth time. It read like soft porn. 'Imagining your other half with someone must be hard enough, but knowing what he wanted to do to her, and what they ended up doing together, is even worse. Look, this paper has even blanked out some of the cruder stuff. Which means that half of the UK is going to be discussing what Jez *might* have said to his mistress – I think that's even worse than knowing the exact words!

'I don't get it,' I went on, poring over another page. 'I mean, when Pattii and Jez got together, everyone said he was punching above his weight and he'd done pretty well for himself. Yet he's risked it all by shagging someone else – under the same roof!'

'Well, maybe once Jez had lived every ugly boy's silicon dream, he realised that he actually preferred au naturel after all,' mused Jodie, studying the picture of the nanny. 'If you can ignore the "hit me, I'm Russian" expression, she's quite pretty after all. Or, more likely, he got sick of Fatty spending more time hungover than pampering him, and looked for someone who could give him the attention he thinks he needs. Or, even more likely, he's thought he can have his cake and eat it too. Like every other footballer before him, gawd love 'em,' she added, almost as an afterthought.

'Yes, OK, that's true,' I conceded. 'But now he's been playing away, it's almost like the press are slapping him on the back for having got one over the glamour model!'

'Oh, babe, haven't you learnt anything over the past few weeks?' said Tara affectionately down the phone. 'The more the press love you one minute, the harder the fall when they decide your time is up. They loved Pattii when she was one of them, and getting her tits out all the time, but the minute she met Jez and stopped working, they decided she was too big for her boots and couldn't wait to bring her back down again. It happens all the time,' she added authoritatively. 'Anyway, what are you worried about her for? She's had this coming to her for a long time. Number one: she's a bitch. Number two: she got too comfortable. And number three: how bloody stupid must you be to employ a stunning sex-mad Russian teenager to live with you and look after your kids? Like I say, karma. Anyway, I've got to go, babes. Keep me posted!'

We blew kisses down the phone and hung up. I could see Tara's point. But that didn't make it right, did it? 'So what do you think will happen?' I persisted to Jodie. 'After everything she's said, about how Jez would never have an affair? Do you reckon she'll leave him? She's going to look really stupid if she doesn't.'

'Babe, I'm not sure Fatty Pattii has ever really worried about looking stupid, has she?' said Jodie. 'Anyway, enough about her. You know what this means for us, don't you?'

I looked at her, puzzled. 'Erm – no?'

Jodie laughed and punched me on the arm. 'It means the heat's off you! No one's going to care about you and Adam while this story's running. It means you, me, Gal and Will can finally go out as a foursome and start having some fun again!'

I smiled and bit my lip uncertainly. Even though I'd been living with Will for over three weeks now, I still hadn't dared go out in public. Not only was I scared about starting up a whole load of unnecessary hurt and scandal by being seen out with him, he felt that I shouldn't even go out with Jodie or any of the other girls. 'It's too soon,' he said. 'People will still be wondering where you're living and who with, so you'll have photographers following you around, analysing what you're doing, saying, eating, wearing. They'll follow you everywhere, follow you home even – best bet is to stay safe here for a while longer.'

Not that I'd needed to leave home, in many ways – my hairdresser, nail technician, beauty therapist, fake-tan man and new personal trainer were all happy to come to the house, and I'd got into internet shopping in a big way. Although I had no need for cash, Will had given me three credit cards – including a black Amex – and every day a succession of delivery vans brought huge parcels from John Lewis, Habitat, Marks and Spencer and Laura Ashley (for the house) and netaporter.com, Topshop.com, Figleaves.com and any online shoe retailer you care to mention (for me). Additionally, we'd come to a fantastic agreement with some of the boutiques in town whereby they'd bring racks of clothes over after hours so I could choose from home and under the cover of darkness! It was genius.

The only thing was, I now had a wardrobe of clothes to replace those that I hadn't been able to bring from the flat, and nowhere to wear them. And, secretly, the beautiful mansion was starting to feel more like a prison, and I was longing to get out and about somewhere – anywhere!

I chewed the inside of my cheek thoughtfully. Maybe Jodie was right. Maybe now was the time.

Sensing she was making headway, Jodie picked up her phone and started texting, expertly using the pads of her fingertips rather than her newly applied acrylic tips. 'Babe, you know what? Gary's got a table at Circle tonight. Let me see if he can make it for four. We should celebrate Fatty's demise.'

I relented. 'OK. I'll ask Will. But I'm not promising anything. And I am not celebrating someone else's relationship trauma.'

I could tell that Will was unsure about going out, and he did try to put me off, but once Jodie had left, just before lunch, I'd had ample time to think about it. I was bored, bored, bored of being hidden away – and I missed seeing Jodie and, well, actually, there was no one else. After all Pattii's stirring, Jodie was the only friend I'd got left in Leeds. I mean, did Will really think I was going to spend the rest of my life locked up like Rapunzel in his tower?

'All right, gorgeous – you win,' he'd said, smiling at me indulgently. 'I guess I should be glad of the opportunity to show you off.'

I squealed with delight and hugged him. He looked a bit

uncomfortable at that – he was great with outlandish gestures but not so good with spontaneous shows of affection – and untangled himself from my arms.

'Just one thing, though, gorgeous,' he said, kissing my hand as he unwound it from around his neck. 'I'm not going to Circle. It's a bloody media circus. Tell your friends I'll book somewhere else.'

I felt stung. I knew how hard it was to get tables at Circle, even midweek, and how much Jodie had been looking forward to going there. But looking at Will's face, I sensed there was no point objecting – and I knew Jodie would prefer to be out with us at another restaurant than not at all. When I rang to tell her, she hardly even seemed to register that they'd have to change their plans – even though I knew it would be a different story when Gary found out, but I'd just have to hope that they were going through one of their loved-up phases rather than being constantly at each other's throats.

So now, I was buzzing with excitement as I rifled through my lush new clothes, deciding what to wear. I was tempted to go super-sexy – it felt like so long since I'd been out! – but instinct told me to tone it down a bit. I wasn't sure if all the press *would* have forgotten me so quickly, and I didn't want to give them an excuse to slag me off any more. Eventually I decided on a gorgeous new Chloé white chiffon baby-doll dress. It came to just above the knee, with a plunging neckline and long, billowing chiffon sleeves, and looked great with my new white peep-toe Louboutins. I went easy on the accessories, wearing just the Patek Phillipe diamond watch Will had bought me in place of Adam's birthday Raymond Weil one (not that I wanted to replace it, but Will thought it might be upsetting, bearing in mind that was the day that had begun our break-up), and the simple silver Tiffany locket that my mum and dad had bought me. I left my hair down, emphasising its natural wave. It was the perfect combination of foxy and innocent, I thought.

Will whistled appreciatively as I walked downstairs. 'Wow!' he said, smiling and kissing me on the neck. 'That's a lot of leg to be showing for a meal out, isn't it?'

I looked down. I didn't think my dress was that short – what was he on about? I looked back up at him, confused.

'Don't worry, babe, I'm only joking,' he said lightly. 'I just don't want you to catch your death, that's all!'

I tried to laugh along with him, but couldn't help but think what a crap and weird joke it was. We were going from house to car to restaurant to car again – I'd never be outside for longer than twenty seconds! It was more like something my dad would say. But I decided to ignore it. Maybe he was nervous about going out with one of Adam's best mates.

By the time we arrived at the restaurant, Jodie was already seated – but there was no Gary. My heart sank. I could tell from her posture that something was up, and I guessed there had been 'words' about the change of venue – or worse. I looked at Will nervously. His jaw was set and he didn't look happy. I suddenly felt ridiculously nervous.

'No Gary?' I asked Jodie as I leant over to kiss her hello.

'No,' she said abruptly. 'I'm sorry, he was, er – taken ill.'

'At the thought of spending a night with his best mate's ex-girlfriend's new bloke?' said Will lightly, but I could tell he was furious.

'No, of course not!' said Jodie, overly brightly. 'He's really sorry.' She shrugged apologetically. From the look on her face, I could tell Will had got it spot on. How stupid of us to ever think Gary would betray one of the lads – especially Adam.

But as it turned out, the night was still fun. Any frostiness melted away with the first couple of drinks, and the first two courses passed jovially, with Will entertaining us with his funny stories as usual.

As the main-course plates were cleared away and the dessert menus arrived, I took the chance to slip away to the loos with Jodie. I was dying to hear what she thought of Will. Although she'd met him several times at home, this was the first time she'd spent any real time with him.

We were the only people in the ladies', so as I washed my hands I looked at her in the mirror and plunged straight in. 'So, what do you think?'

She finished drying her hands on the individual towels piled up by the sink, and reached for her Fendi baguette handbag. 'Well, babe, as long as you're happy, I think Will's just great,' she said, pulling out a Mac nude-coloured lipstick.

I was a bit disappointed – she didn't exactly seem over the moon about him – but before I had time to probe further, the door opened and a familiar figure walked through. Despite the day's headlines, the revealing outfit, pneumatic chest, OTT hair and garish make-up were all as normal – it was only the aggressive attitude that was a little more deflated than usual.

There in front of us stood Pattii.

Me and Jodie stopped, open-mouthed, me with my hands under the still-running tap, Jodie poised ready to apply her lippie. Pattii, too, was stood stock still, staring like a rabbit in headlights. Just as suddenly she cast her eyes low, took a wide berth around us and without saying a word sped into the nearest cubicle.

Me and Jodie, still gawping, looked at each other in the mirror.

'Of all the bare-faced . . .' I mouthed. I stopped, lost for words. Firstly, I couldn't believe she was out at all – she really did have some nerve. I supposed I should admire her for it, but I couldn't help but think it just proved how thick-skinned she was. Secondly, how dare she just walk straight past without even trying to apologise for all the upset she'd caused me?

I gestured at Jodie to hurry up. I had no desire to spend more than a split second around that girl, and no intention of still being here when she came out.

Jodie shook her head. 'Wait,' she mouthed, and winked wickedly. My heart sank. What was she up to now?

'God, I can't believe how GORGEOUS Will is,' she said loudly, rifling unnecessarily through her make-up, pulling out a compact and dabbing at her nose. 'Which just goes to prove my point, doesn't it? You reap what you sow. I mean, think about all that horrible heartache you had to go through for no reason. You'd found yourself a lovely bloke and then other, jealous people had to go and mess it up for you. But babe – just think! You've shown them all by only going and finding ANOTHER lovely bloke, who's fit and minted and head over heels in love with you too! Honestly, if ever I didn't believe in karma, after this week, I truly do.'

I grinned, but gestured again, frantically. I had no wish to come face to face with Pattii again.

But Jodie was enjoying herself too much. 'Babe, can I borrow your mascara?'

I sighed pointedly. 'Yes, but hurry up, I want some pudding.'

She winked again and turned to the toilet attendant, who was rearranging the selection of fragrances lined up alongside the washbasins.

'I hear you had a big drugs bust in here recently,' she said conversationally. 'Do you reckon that's going to be a regular thing? I'm sure Will said he was sure he saw some police in here earlier.'

There was a sudden frantic shuffling in the cubicle that Pattii had gone into, and I stuffed my fist in my mouth to stop myself laughing out loud. There was a flushing noise – presumably Pattii had decided she couldn't put off the inevitable any longer.

Jodie linked arms with me. 'Come on then, you, let's get back to Will. He'll be wondering what's happened to us.' She giggled loudly. 'But he's going to have to get used to it. After all, not many people get to have such loyal friends, do they?'

Suddenly the cubicle door opened and Pattii shot past, not even bothering to wash her hands. The door banged shut behind her, and we looked at one another and laughed.

Jodie gave my arm a comradely squeeze. 'Oooh, I feel better for that. Let's go back out now. I could do with a cheeky drink to celebrate that one!'

I squeezed her back and we returned happily to the table. As we arrived, Will had his phone in his hand and was in urgent conversation with the waiter.

'What's up?' said Jodie as we approached. 'I'm sure when we went to the loo a couple of minutes ago we were having dessert – but now it looks like you're about to leave!'

Will turned round grimly. 'We are. The manager is a friend of mine and he's just told me there's a load of paps outside. We'll need to go out another exit, Louise. I can't have you appearing all over the papers again tomorrow.'

I looked at him in surprise. Did Will know every manager

in every restaurant in town – and why did we always have to leave secretly?

I didn't have to wonder for long. He frowned at me.

'It's all thanks to your mate Pattii,' he said, deadpan. 'Seems Jez Steadman isn't the only one who's been enjoying a bit of extramarital action.' He pointed at his phone by way of explanation. 'The story's just broken. She's been having an affair with her personal trainer!'

Chapter 16

Will checked his watch, folded the newspaper over and drained his juice.

'Well, I'd better be making a move,' he said, leaning over to kiss me. 'And leave you to get ready for the big game!'

I smiled nervously and sipped at my own juice. Big was the operative word. Today Will's team were playing Leeds City. It would be the first time I'd seen Adam since we'd split, and I was really nervous, but at the same time I really wanted to see him.

Will pulled out his wallet, took out a couple of ten-pound notes and placed them carefully on the table.

'You won't need any more than that today, will you, sweetheart?'

I shook my head. Will didn't seem to think I had a clue about money, and other than the credit cards he'd given me and the bit of cash he threw my way every now and again, I never saw any. He guarded his finances very carefully, and never discussed with me what he earned or how much things cost. I wasn't even allowed to discuss fees or prices with any of the interior designers or tradesmen that I'd hired to do up the house! I just told them what we needed and they were instructed to invoice Will. It was a bit odd, and made me behave weirdly – like, I'd started putting the odd tenner aside for a rainy day. What was all that about?

Will selected a couple of CDs from the stereo cabinet and slung them in his kit bag. He liked to get himself pumped up on gangsta rap music before a game, and would apparently arrive at the club with the car stereo blasting, windows shut and not a smile for anyone (their club was a bit more open, and you'd often get fans or photographers hanging out at the entrance). Most of the players would stop, even on match day, and sign autographs and stuff, but Will claimed that when he was 'in the zone' before a match, any break to his concentration would affect his play.

'Derek's going to pick you up at two, so make sure you're ready, sweetheart,' he said over his shoulder as he left.

Derek was Will's best mate – an ex-player-turned-pundit who also had a reputation for being a bit of a meathead. Fortunately, he lived down south now so we hardly ever saw him. 'Oh, but Will, I'd arranged to pick up Jodie on the way – we were going to go together, like old times!' I protested. 'There's no need for Derek to go out of his way just for little old me.'

Will turned slowly and unsmilingly, with a hard look in his eyes. 'Well, I don't think that's particularly appropriate, do you?' he said coldly. 'Turning up with someone from the home team, when you were engaged to one of their players? No, it's all arranged. Derek's coming up for the match anyway, and it's no bother for him to pick you up. I think it's better if you tell Jodie you'll see her in the players' lounge.'

I scowled and stuck out my lip sulkily. 'But . . .'

Will came over and kissed me again. 'No buts, gorgeous. Derek's picking you up, end of. I'll see you later.'

He turned and walked out of the huge breakfast room, and I watched from the wide bay window as he crunched across the grand drive to his car. I had a weird feeling of not being able to breathe, like someone was standing on my chest.

I was happy with Will, I really was. But sometimes, every now and again, I was beginning to feel a bit suffocated. I didn't ever seem to be able to do anything on my own. If I'd felt neglected by Adam, then it was the exact opposite with Will. Apart from when he was training or playing (when I was supposed to be getting the house done up), we spent every waking moment together. Ever since the meal out, he'd been less keen on me spending time with Jodie – not that it had stopped me, of course, but I did have to try and fit seeing her into mornings rather than long lunches now. He even insisted on me waiting for him to finish at the training ground and us leaving together!

I knew it was because he was smitten, and I knew I should be grateful – but sometimes I felt like a prisoner in my own life.

My phone beeped with a voice mail, and I keyed in my security code. It was Mum. My heart sank. I wasn't avoiding her – she just asked lots of questions that I couldn't answer. Like how I was feeling, and what my plans were. The truth was, I didn't know.

'Hi, Lou, it's your mother,' she said, a touch narkily. 'I was wondering if I needed to set up an appointment to speak to you – it's so hard to get hold of you these days. Give me and your father a call sometime – when you're not too busy with your fabulous new life.'

I padded upstairs guiltily. I couldn't blame her for being upset with me. *I* was upset with me. I just hadn't got a clue what to say. I started running a bath, then walked through to my amazing new walk-in wardrobe. I wasn't sure what to wear today. Normally I'd have had a couple of days with the girls and a multitude of shopping trips to give me a clear idea of what look I was going for – but without my little network I had no idea how to gauge what everyone else was going to turn up in. Also, I'd lost a lot of weight in the past few weeks. Whether it was the stress of leaving Adam or the lack of champagne-fuelled lunches, I was definitely only half the girl I'd been just a couple of months earlier. Also, Will was a bit funny about what I wore sometimes. He hated me wearing anything too revealing, or too casual, like jeans to matches or – well, actually what he liked or didn't like was pretty unpredictable. Today would be even worse – he was as paranoid about me seeing Adam as I was, but it was exactly because I was seeing Adam that I wanted to look extra special!

I pulled out a pair of soft grey tweed trousers, a white shirt and a black jacket. Will would approve of that, I thought – conservative but subtly sexy. But then I thought of Jodie's face if I turned up in anything that dowdy, and I sighed and threw the lot on the floor in desperation. It was more like an interview outfit than a match-day outfit for a twenty-something WAG! I stomped out of the wardrobe towards the bathroom. Maybe after a good soak I'd be in a better frame of mind to choose.

I waved at Jodie across the stands. She gestured excitedly as Derek and I walked down the steps. He'd been a bit late, so we'd only just got here in time for kick-off.

'Look, Derek – over there.' I pointed over at Jodie and made as if to join her. Derek put his hand in the small of my back and guided me in the opposite direction.

'Er, no, darlin', I don't think that's a good idea, do you?' I looked at him in shock. Who did he think he was, my bodyguard? As if he could read my mind, he bent his head and spoke softly into my ear.

'Don't get any ideas today, Louise. I'm with you for the afternoon, and I don't plan to leave your side for the duration.'

I looked at him in shock. So *that* was what this was about. He was here to stop me speaking to my friends – or, more likely, Adam! I couldn't believe it. But before I could object, the whistle blew for kick-off.

By the time the game was over, I was beside myself. I'd planned to try and say hello to Adam at some point, and I'd thought that when the lads all came back into the lounge would be my best opportunity. But if Derek wouldn't even let me go and speak to Jodie, what chance did I have?

Right now, I was focused on seeing Adam. Out of the corner of my eye I saw his team-mates come into the lounge. I caught Davy McNulty's eye, and smiled, but to my horror he pulled a face at me. 'Slag,' he mouthed.

I felt like I'd been slapped in the face. Then, behind McNulty, I saw the familiar profile of Adam's curly hair. He looked up, and we caught each other's eyes. I saw raw hurt in his, and immediately he cast his eyes downwards. My heart leapt. It was now or never. I touched Derek on the shoulder. 'I'm just going to the loo, Derek,' I said, and stood up before he had time to object. I wasn't quick enough. He stood up with me and grabbed my hand, smiling nastily.

'You don't think I'd fall for that one, do you, Louise?' he said nastily. 'I'm coming with you. I told you, I'm not leaving your side today.'

I looked at him in disbelief. He was even going to follow me to the *toilet*? I tried to laugh it off. 'Derek, don't be a prat! I'm going to the *ladies*'!'

My tone of voice seemed totally lost on him. 'Well,

I can wait for you. But I'm coming up there with you. We wouldn't want you making a fool of yourself, would we?'

I was speechless. Will must have put him up to it – but why? And what did he hope to achieve by it?

But for some reason, I didn't fight it. There seemed no point. I wasn't going to win. I'd just do what he wanted – it seemed the easiest way.

So I went along with the pantomime. I went to the loo, and Derek stood outside. When I emerged, he was still standing there by the door on his own. The lounge was packed. Friends and family of both teams jostled for space as wives and girlfriends waited eagerly for their other halves to come out. Bored of being with just Derek, I looked around at the familiar scene – from which I suddenly felt horribly detached. I glanced around anxiously. Derek, still glued to my side, seemed to relax. He was obviously satisfied that I couldn't wait to see Will. I bit my lip guiltily as I realised I wasn't looking for Will at all. I was looking for Adam.

My phone beeped, and I practically jumped out of my skin. Both Derek and I looked down at it at the same time. 'It's Jodie,' I snapped accusingly. He grunted and looked away.

'Babe. If you get away from your minder, we're going to 7-11 tonite. xxx'

Bless her. She knew how nervous I was about today and obviously thought she'd give me a way out of having to go over to her and see all the other girls in public. But instead of feeling relieved about it, I was suddenly totally, unbearably sad. 'No can do. Catch up wiv u l8r xxx.'

I gave Derek a sidelong glance and hit send.

I saw Adam again, he looked all cute, like he always did after a game – a bit dishevelled, but with bright pink cheeks and wet curls plastered to his head. But my excitement was short-lived. Behind him I could see Will's razor-sharp green eyes glinting in the afternoon sunlight. Behind me I could still feel Derek breathing down my neck. Tears welled in my eyes. I'd lost my last chance to say hi to Adam – to say sorry, to say anything that would make things better between us. I was trapped.

That night, Derek stayed over and he and Will sat up drinking late into the night. I couldn't bring myself to spend another moment with them, so I went upstairs and lay on the bed, watching *Love Actually*. But for once even my favourite rom-com couldn't cheer me up. Somewhere in town, all my friends and my ex-fiancé were out on their usual Saturday night, having fun, whilst I was stuck here in my ivory tower with three old men – my boyfriend, his sidekick and Hugh Grant. I cried like I'd never cried before.

When I opened my eyes again, it was mid-morning and I was staring straight into Will's concerned face. He was sitting on top of the duvet, stroking my hair lovingly and looking at me with a worried expression.

'Morning, gorgeous,' he said softly. 'Feel better for a bit of a sleep?'

I blinked and stretched. A ray of sunshine squeezed through a tiny gap in the curtains and caught something shiny and brightly coloured on my pillow.

I sat up, frowning sleepily and trying to work out what it was. Will smiled indulgently.

'Happy Easter, gorgeous. It's a beautiful day, so I thought we might go out for lunch somewhere later. That's if you're not too busy, of course!' He smiled mysteriously and kissed me again, more passionately this time. I pulled away and feigned a yawn. Will was dead good-looking, and I did fancy him – but quite often I'd find myself making excuses not to sleep with him.

He stood up, tying his dressing gown tighter around him in a businesslike fashion. 'Meanwhile, I'm going to have a shower.'

'OK, babe.' I yawned, reaching out for the foil-wrapped parcel. Inside the wrapping was a beautiful jewellery box. My heart beat fast as I inspected it, though I was secretly a bit miffed. Why hadn't Will stuck around to see me open it? Eagerly, I pulled the lid off and laughed in delight. Inside was a mini Crème Egg – my favourite – and a note. 'There are 300 of me around the house – find them all and get your REAL Easter gift!'

I looked around the room to see if I could see any others, and spotted a movement by the door. Will was lurking outside it, watching me! I laughed again and threw a pillow at him. '*Three hundred* mini Crème Eggs?' I said incredulously. 'Are you sure I'm going to be able to fit in lunch?'

Will poked his head around the door. 'Well, you don't have to eat them all this morning!' he said, laughing too. 'Happy hunting!' He disappeared off to the bathroom, and I lay back on the bed, re-reading my note.

What on earth had been up with me the last couple of weeks? Here I was, with a lovely man, a beautiful house, and a life most girls would give their right arm for, and I was still finding reasons to be unhappy.

It was all very well for me to hanker after seeing Adam – but I missed the old Adam, not the new Premier League Adam who acted like he couldn't give two hoots about me. I was missing a man who had long since ceased to exist. So from now on, I decided as I pulled on my slippers and padded off on my Easter egg hunt, I was going to try to forget that horrible haunted look I'd seen in Adam's eyes and get on with enjoying life with Will.

As predicted, the Easter egg hunt took up most of the morning, and by lunchtime I was still forty-three short of the three hundred. Will had certainly been inventive – they were hidden in cupboards, in shoes, in my jewellery case – I even found one in my hairspray lid as I was getting ready for lunch! He had spent all morning at the breakfast table, reading the papers and keeping count as I delivered my finds to him, an amused smile on his face each time he announced how many more I had to find.

'Come on, gorgeous, you've still got seventy-eight to go – and counting,' he'd say, slapping my bum as I ran off to find some more. By lunchtime I was a bit bored of it, to be honest, but I was desperate to find out what my 'real' Easter gift was. 'Oh come on, Will,' I wheedled. 'I've done so well . . .'

But he was unrelenting, and as I mooched around the house waiting for him to come off the phone and take me out, I wondered where on earth else he could have thought to hide forty-three more bloody chocolate eggs!

Suddenly I had a brainwave. I hadn't looked in Will's office at all! I pounded down the stairs in excitement and ran through the kitchen to the study room beyond. I never went in here – it was a tiny room about ten feet square containing a huge old-fashioned mahogany desk, which practically filled half of it, an executive leather desk chair, his computer, and boxes of files and papers, I guessed containing all his many property deals and the other little business concerns he seemed to have so many of.

The air in the office seemed heavy and cold – it was hardly ever used, after all – and I suddenly doubted my hunch. Will would never have hidden anything in here! Just as I turned to leave, a pile of papers in the corner caught my eye. It looked like it had been recently disturbed – maybe there'd be some eggs behind it. Excitedly I knelt down and moved the papers out of the way. There was nothing there –

but the second sheet in the pile caught my eye. It was a bill, an electricity bill by the looks of it, and it had 'reminder' stamped across it in red. Puzzled, I started to flick through the rest of the pile. Every piece of paper was an unpaid bill or invoice of some description. Some were months old. Why had Will, who earned tens of thousands of pounds a week, not paid any of them?

'So, Miss Marple, checking up on me already, are you?'

I jumped out of my skin. Will was standing in the doorway, mobile in hand, with a thunderous expression on his face.

'Will! No, I – I was . . . I thought . . . I was looking for eggs,' I finished lamely.

'But you found something much more interesting, eh?' he said, bending down and snatching the papers out of my hands. 'Go and get your coat and keep your nose out of things that don't concern you.'

I stood up meekly. I felt like a small child who'd been caught stealing cookies. 'But – I don't understand why—'

'Who asked you to understand?' he interrupted brusquely. 'I ask you to dress nicely and look pretty and be cute, not to *understand*. I pay people when *I'm* good and ready, not when *they* are. Now go and get ready.'

I ran off, chastised but still curious. Why would someone on a Premiership salary refuse to pay people what they were owed?

★

After a gorgeous lunch in a posh restaurant in the country, an evening spent finding the rest of the eggs, and a beautiful Fabergé egg pendant gift at the end of it, I'd stopped worrying. I was lucky not to ever have to think about where my next dollar was coming from, so why make problems where there weren't any? Will had been looking after himself and his businesses for years before I came along, and I didn't see any reason to doubt him.

The trouble was, I was still feeling fractious, and on Tuesday morning I decided to give Jodie a treat for being such a great friend. We were due to have a dress fitting for her fast-approaching wedding, so I suggested the dressmaker come to Will's house on the Thursday and we would have a brunch afterwards. It was perfect – something special to say thanks, an excuse for a glass of bubbly even before lunchtime, and, most importantly, something Will would never find out about.

It was genius. Will left as always at 9.30 a.m. and Jodie turned up at eleven, by which time I'd had a chance to get ready and make the table look really pretty, with flowers and some posh champagne flutes, coffee and bagels (these were decoration only, of course, as Jodie never touched anything before lunchtime other than a skinny latte).

Right on cue, she pulled into the drive, beeping her car horn loudly. As she got out, she pulled out a huge file bursting with magazine cuttings, spreadsheets and brochures. She waved it at me cheerily.

'Don't mind me bringing along a bit of wedding admin, do you, babe?' she yelled as I stood at the front door, giggling as her little frame struggled with the weight of it. 'Only I could do with a bit of help. I'm way behind schedule and the wedding planner's about to have a hernia! Not to mention the bloody magazine people. They pay for coverage of your wedding and all of a sudden they think they can tell you what to wear, think, do and say.'

I laughed and skipped out to help her with it. 'Well, if you're missing anything, I've still got half of mine and Adam's booked,' I said, trying to make light of it. 'Though I'm not sure what kind of karma that'd be!'

We both laughed over-brightly at my bad joke and traipsed through to the living room, where the dressmaker had the calico versions of our dresses laid out ready for us to try on.

After the fitting, we moved back to the dining room and sat in the capacious, throne-like dining chairs. 'How's it going with the in-laws?' I asked, nudging her and smirking. Gary's parents had been invited to stay with him and Jodie for Easter, and turned up with enough luggage for two months – which, it turned out, was exactly how long they intended to stay. Right up to the wedding and beyond, house-sitting when the newly-weds were on honeymoon.

Jodie rolled her eyes dramatically, dumping her file on the table noisily and nearly toppling the vase of flowers over.

'Oh my God, I want to kill them,' she moaned. 'Big as that

flat is, it still isn't enough space for us all. Marge keeps trying to take over everything and it's really stressing me. And on top of that, Gary is still insisting Mitch is going to be his best man. But he's not turning up for fittings, or if he does, he's late, and they're all waiting for him. Being on bloody bail is no excuse. If anything, it should make him more punctual! There's always something with that one. He drives me up the wall. So I've told Gary he's gonna have to promote Adam.'

I laughed uneasily. 'What do you mean, promote him?'

'Well, to second best man. Gal's gonna have to have two best men. One he wants, and one *I* want. I mean, Mitch can hardly string a sentence together, let alone deliver a speech!' Jodie looked at me, eyes nearly popping out of her head as she realised what that would mean. 'Oooooh, babe, I didn't even think! That means Adam'll be best man and you'll be bridesmaid!' She giggled guiltily. 'Are you cool with that?'

'Of course I am,' I said, feigning a confidence I didn't necessarily feel. 'It'll be fine.'

I buried my face in a wedding magazine to hide the flush that had started to creep up over my face when she'd mentioned Adam's name. The truth was, I wasn't at all sure I was happy about standing at the altar alongside a man I'd been planning to marry until recently. And I was pretty sure Will wouldn't like it either . . . But it was Jodie's day, and she was having enough hassle with it without me adding to it. I'd just have to find a way to cope.

We spent the next couple of hours leafing through

wedding magazines and discussing her 'hen' – she'd decided not to have a party night (which I was secretly thankful for; I could just imagine having to explain that one away to Will) but had opted for drinks in a private room in a club in town. It's surprising how long you can spend discussing the minutiae of cocktails and guest lists when you put your mind to it.

At just after 1 p.m., there was a sharp rap at the door. I looked up, startled. Will wasn't due back for hours – who could that be? Looking out of the big bay window, I could see a black Rover parked next to Jodie's Mini. Relief that it definitely wasn't Will was mixed with intrigue at who it could be, and I stood up hurriedly and scuttled out to the front door.

I opened it to a short, balding man in a beige rain mac, with a big burly guy in a black bomber jacket standing next to him.

'Mrs Daniels?' said the small guy self-importantly. I don't know why, but I had an inkling this was Not Good.

'Yes, er, no, I mean – I'm his girlfriend,' I said nervously.

'Well, I have something for you and Mr Daniels. It's a repossession notice. You're in arrears for non-payment of utilities bills. I've been instructed to remove belongings up to and above the amount owed.'

I gasped. 'I don't understand,' I stammered. 'You're bailiffs?' I heard a scuffle from the next room, as Jodie, no doubt earwigging, stood up and dashed through towards where all the action was. 'Will earns loads of money. Of course he can't be in debt. I'm sorry, you can't come in.'

The man brandished a letter in my face. 'It's all here, madam. I suggest you contact Mr Daniels immediately. This is extremely serious. We are not leaving without payment.'

I closed the door on them slowly, and turned to Jodie, horrified. Bailiffs. The shame. I'd never got into debt, even when I was at my most skint in Cardiff. How had it happened now I was living in the lap of luxury?

Chapter 17

I sprayed my Evian in-flight rehydration spray all over my face, popped it back into my Louis Vuitton in-flight bag and checked my make-up in my compact mirror.

'Come on, gorgeous, we haven't got all day, you know.' Will was standing by his first-class seat over to Portugal, impatient with excitement.

I turned and smiled calmly at him. 'Don't rush me, Will! I don't want to turn up looking like a dog's dinner.'

Ever since the bailiffs incident, I'd felt our relationship change ever so slightly, and I no longer felt so young and silly and – well – irrelevant. Will's brush with the bailiffs had shown me that he could fuck up too, and his obvious horror and sorrow at the whole nasty incident were well on their way to making up for all the upset that his arrogance had put me through.

Of course, he'd only experienced the half of it. When we got the knock, Will was still training so I had to call the club and fake some kind of family emergency. There I was again, lying to them about my boyfriend – different bloke, different scenario, but the end result was the same.

And then there was the small matter of Jodie, our illicit brunch and what Will was going to say about it. The irony wasn't lost on me — I was more worried about all this than the fact that the bloody house and everything in it was being repossessed. My boyfriend's control freak personality meant that we were about to lose everything, but that reality was paling into insignificance against the fact that I'd had my best friend round to visit without having asked his permission first.

But I'd managed to clear everything up and wave goodbye to a protesting Jodie in the half-hour it took Will to get back home, and was back to nervously eyeballing the bailiffs in their parked-up Rover by the time Will's Jag crunched along the drive and up to the house. More lies, more cover-ups. I was turning into some kind of girl.

Will had emerged briskly from his car, glowering but also looking uncharacteristically nervous. I'd expected him to be aggressive and angry, but weirdly he seemed quite subdued, almost submissive. He'd gone straight to the bailiffs' car, exchanged words through the window, and after about ten minutes had reached into his pocket for his wallet, fishing out a wad of notes and handing it over.

The Rover had driven off and Will had come into the house, head hunched and brow furrowed.

I'd rushed at him. 'Will, what was all that about? Who did you owe money to? How did you get rid of them?'

He ruffled my hair and tried to smile. 'Nothing for you to worry about, gorgeous,' he'd said over his shoulder as he climbed the grand curved staircase. 'It's all sorted now.'

'But,' I called impotently up after him, 'but I want to know what happened. I was worried. I was *scared*! Who were they?'

He leaned over the banisters and blew me a kiss. 'Like I said, gorgeous, nothing for you to worry about. All sorted.'

I was infuriated. How dare he put me through all that and then refuse to explain himself to me? Just exactly what did he expect me to do after I'd been threatened by two dodgy geezers who claimed they had the right to raid our house and take all our beloved belongings?

After kicking the banister and hurting my toe, I went for a pounding run around the grounds to try to calm down. Maybe this was Will's way of dealing with the embarrassment of the whole episode. After all, he wasn't the kind of person I imagined would find it easy to have to admit he was crap at anything, let alone managing his own money. And he, like most blokes, was rubbish at expressing his feelings – so perhaps I should cut him a bit more slack.

He'd behaved really apologetically over dinner, and had been lovely ever since. Now, three weeks later, he was taking me away to his house in Portugal to make it up to me. I couldn't wait. He had bought the Algarve retreat in Quinta Do Lago the previous year, and planned eventually to spend half the year there and half in the UK. He was immeasurably proud of it – I'd heard so much about it, and was really excited about seeing it for myself. It also felt good to be leaving the mansion – much as I loved it, it was beginning to feel like a proper prison.

I snapped my compact shut and stood up. 'Come on then, handsome, show me your Portuguese paradise!'

He grinned and I edged past him into the aisle to exit, jumping as he pinched my bum.

Twenty minutes later, the air-conditioned Mercedes left the coastal road we'd been following almost since the airport and drove along a palm-fringed road, through some imposing iron gates and up a short, leafy drive to the house. I gasped. Set in palm-rich gardens and surrounded by a small green lawn was a beautiful peach-coloured villa, comprising two two-storey buildings with a one-storey entrance in the middle. The tall, thin windows were bordered with white paint that shone brightly in the Portuguese sun. It was absolutely stunning. Will sure seemed to have good taste in houses – home *and* away!

Will's driver – who lived out here and was on duty permanently, ready for whenever he was needed – pulled up and Will jumped out.

'Come on, gorgeous, wait until you see inside!'

I giggled excitedly and leapt out after him, stumbling a little as my gold Miu Miu wedges hit the cobbled path.

'Wait, then!' I grabbed his hand and we walked under the arched doorway together, and through the door into a kind of open-air porch which acted as a reception room, with low rattan easy chairs and a coffee table nestled into one corner. It led on to a stunning shady courtyard, with cobbled floor and trickly stone fountain in the centre. Under a leafy pagoda was a pretty mosaic table and chairs, with two place settings and a bottle of rosé chilling in an ice bucket. Will looked at me, green eyes shining.

'I phoned ahead to make sure lunch was ready.' He took a deep breath. 'So, what do you think, gorgeous?'

'I love it!' I shrieked. 'Can I see the rest before we eat?'

He laughed. 'Of course! Follow me.'

We wandered through the villa. It went on and on and on. It had a huge open-plan living space, kitchen, dining room, eight bedrooms, seven bathrooms, a gym, sauna – even a cinema room! Through the windows overlooking the back I could see the azure blue of the marble-edge pool and a Jacuzzi, and beyond that, one of the town's famous golf courses. It was a lovely place, but I felt a rising panic in my chest. It was so – well – 1980s! The location, the decor – the decor! It was all OTT glitz – gold taps, marble floors, huge elaborate drapes, the lot. I didn't mind a bit of pizzazz, admittedly – but here I felt like I was in a Jackie Collins novel. I could only imagine what the other people who lived in the area were like. I felt I'd aged fifty years in five minutes.

As we arrived back at the courtyard, this time down a winding stone staircase from the smallest and cutest of all the bedrooms, Will strode purposefully over to the table and poured two glasses of rosé.

'So, here's to our lovely Portuguese home!' he said triumphantly, and held out his glass to me.

I raised mine half-heartedly and tried to raise a smile to go with it. 'Here's to Portugal,' I mumbled. I took a large swig of my wine and looked around the courtyard. As I felt the cool liquid slip down my throat, I thought thankfully how this at least had escaped the clutches of the interior designer. Or maybe – I stared closer at the fountain's ornate base, covered in Cupids – maybe it hadn't.

'I'm glad you like it, Louise,' said Will, in a weird tone that I didn't recognise. It brought me right back into the moment, and I turned to him sharply. To my horror, he'd put his glass down and was kneeling in front of me. My heart stopped. He wasn't – he wasn't going to . . .'

As if he could read my mind, Will grabbed hold of my hand. 'Because I want it to be your home. For ever. Louise, will you marry me?'

He pulled out a beautiful diamond ring from his pocket. I recognised it immediately as a Van Cleef and Arpels 'Couture' ring – I'd seen it when Adam and I were looking for wedding bands. It was platinum, with two pavé diamond rows that encircled a one-carat diamond solitaire. It was meant to represent a loving embrace. I looked from it to him and back to it again in shock, head spinning. How was my luck? Only a few months ago my childhood sweetheart had asked me the very same thing. Two questions, and two very different lives – but only a matter of weeks apart.

I couldn't do this. It was the right man – I was pretty sure – but it was too soon. But to my horror, when I opened my mouth to tell Will this, the word that came out wasn't 'no'.

It was 'yes'.

Will was full of it over lunch. He'd planned this for weeks, it seemed, and had had it all worked out.

'You see, Louise, I don't know why, but I guessed you'd say yes,' he said proudly, 'and so I thought I'd go one better than most people. So not only have I set up the proposal – I've set up the wedding, too! We can get married tomorrow – all we need to do is shop for your dress this afternoon!'

I nearly choked on my seafood. 'Tomorrow?' I managed. 'But – but – we can't get married that quickly!'

'Why not?' he said, genuinely perplexed. 'It's all arranged. There's a perfect spot on a stunning island just off the coast. I'll show you it from shore, later. I've booked the registrar already. We'll get a boat out there early tomorrow morning. It's just magical at that time of day. The sun will have just risen and—'

'What about my family, Will?' I interrupted quietly. 'They haven't even met you yet! And I'd want them there for my wedding . . . there's no way I'd get married without Mum and Dad there.'

He grabbed my hand and looked into my eyes earnestly.

'And they can be there – at our British wedding! This one is all about us. Just think about it, gorgeous – you and me, exchanging our vows on a tiny island in the middle of the Med. You can see it from the attic room. We'll be able to look at it for the rest of our lives together!'

I shifted uncomfortably. Again, I had the disturbing feeling that my life was in everyone else's hands but my own.

'Well, OK,' I said. His eyes were so intense they were making me feel uneasy. 'Let's talk about it later.'

But we didn't talk about it later. Instead, we went shopping to a smart boutique in town and bought a beautiful knee-length chiffon dress, pale cream and floaty – perfect for a chic but romantic wedding. Will had already bought matching bands from the same jewellers who'd made my engagement ring – he'd thought of everything, it seemed – so after a quiet dinner, we made our way back to the villa.

By morning, I had kind of convinced myself this was what I wanted. After all, I was very lucky to have Will, I knew he would make a perfect husband and father, so why not go along with his romantic notion? He was right, we could celebrate with our families properly back at home.

But as I lay awake, half aware dawn was breaking, I heard Will tut as he got up to go to the toilet. I sat up to see what was the matter – but one look out of the window over his shoulder told me all I needed to know. It was raining.

The second morning, I had crippling period pains, so we couldn't go again. We laughed about it, but I could tell Will was finding it increasingly unfunny.

'Well, gorgeous, tomorrow's our last chance!' he said over dinner in the courtyard. His smile didn't reach his eyes.

I laughed and grabbed his hand. 'It's not our last chance!' I said gaily. 'Even if something does happen tomorrow to stop us getting married, which it won't, we've got the rest of our lives to do it.'

Suddenly all I could think about was that only a few months ago I'd been planning my wedding with Adam.

I was so overcome, I almost missed what Will said next. Almost, but not quite.

He leaned back proudly. 'Yep, I promised myself when we first met that I'd marry you within six months. And here we are!'

I was certain I must have misheard. Surely he hadn't said what I thought he just had? 'What?'

He grinned proudly, a dazzling, white-toothed smile that only hours ago would have made me smile right back. Now it filled me with slowly unravelling horror.

'When I first met you, I knew we'd be together. I could just feel the connection. But I couldn't wait for fate, so I decided to give it a helping hand.'

My mouth felt dry and claggy, and my forehead was damp and cold. 'What are you saying, Will?' I asked slowly.

He laughed, carried away with his own cleverness. 'Well,

it helped that you had a crap friend like Pattii,' he chuckled.
'I knew that once she had a sniff that something was going
on between us, it wouldn't be long before the rest of the
world found out. Though even I couldn't have guessed she'd
go straight to the bloody papers!'

I looked at him, suddenly filled with a deep loathing. 'But
nothing was going on with us then, Will,' I said, slowly and
deliberately. 'I was still with Adam. Engaged to Adam.'

Will smiled softly and grabbed my hand. 'In name only,
gorgeous. You were already mine – believe me.'

I wiped my brow. I was sweating properly now, and my
breath had turned shallow and panicky. I suddenly longed to
be alone. 'Will, do you mind if I head off to bed? We've got
another early start tomorrow and,' I squeezed his hand with
a certainty I didn't feel, and pulled it away, 'a big day.' Putting
all the effort I had left into my smile, I stood up. Will stood
up with me, hugging me tenderly and rocking me gently.

'Of course not, gorgeous. I won't be long behind you.
Like you say, it's a big day tomorrow.'

With a heavy heart I climbed the stairs and mechanically
went about my normal Clinique three-step pre-bed routine.
Then I cleaned my teeth and lay down between the cool
linen sheets. When Will came to bed half an hour later, I
pretended I was asleep – even though I was anything but.
My head was racing with the enormity of what I'd just
found out, and what I was about to do. I was going to get
married, for goodness' sake. I was going to promise to be

with Will for the rest of my life. I was going to pledge myself to him and embark on that huge journey that my mum and dad had – successfully, if not always smoothly – without them ever having met him and hardly even having heard about him. The same Will who, knowingly, had played a hand – a huge hand – in splitting me up from my previous fiancé. That he'd done it for love was not in question – but did I really want an obsessive, destructive love like this, that had been based on lies from the very start?

I spent a restless night, and when Will leaned over to wake me the next morning, I felt as though I hadn't slept for weeks. It was as if I had the weight of the world on my shoulders.

He shook me gently. 'Louise. Wake up, gorgeous! It's our big day!'

I turned to him, eyes full of tears, unable to speak.

He frowned, his face darkened and he let out a heavy sigh. 'Louise . . . ?' Still words were beyond me. 'You don't want to do this, do you?'

I shook my head sadly. 'I'm sorry, Will. I really am. I want a proper wedding.'

He turned his back to me and sat on the edge of the bed, his naked back bent over, his head in his hands. After what seemed like an age, he turned back to me. I couldn't fathom his expression in the half-light, and I felt unnerved and a bit exposed, lying under a linen sheet and wearing only a silk nightdress.

'Why?' he asked.

I took a deep breath. 'I don't know, Will. You've kind of bamboozled me.'

He frowned. '*How* have I bamboozled you? We meet, we fall in love, we get married. How difficult is that? It's what most girls dream of.'

I swallowed hard and spoke softly. 'It's what I dream of, too. But we're doing this too fast.'

He nodded slowly, then looked up at me again, brighter this time. 'So we'll be engaged for a while. Don't worry about this wedding, gorgeous, we'll have the wedding you want – when you want it. Maybe this was all a bit fast.'

He leaned over to kiss me, and I flinched. He stopped, and looked at me questioningly.

'Will – I'm sorry – it's not the wedding I don't want. It's us. I don't want us.'

So that was that. From that second, Will went into total control-freak mode, and any doubts I'd had overnight about losing the amazing man I thought I'd fallen for went in a flash. Will's cruel, arrogant, manipulative side came out in force, as if to prove to me I'd made the right decision. His personal assistant back home booked us on separate flights – me first, Will two hours later – and me a hotel for when we got back. Ironically, it was the hotel Adam and I had stayed in when we'd first moved to Leeds what seemed like a lifetime ago. I received a text telling me in no uncertain terms that my 'effects' would be sent on there in due course.

I felt numb. I was upset about hurting Will and losing what I thought I'd found, but in my heart of hearts I knew this was the right thing. There was so much to Will that I didn't understand – and so much that I was starting to dislike – that I needed to get out before I lost sight of who I was completely.

And who I wanted, I added to myself, as Adam's face popped into my head.

Will didn't see me off when his driver came to pick me up for the flight, and as we pulled away from the villa, I took one morose glance over my shoulder at the life I could have had. Someone else's life, I thought, shaking myself inwardly as we set off on the short drive to Faro.

I had only moments to wait to board my flight, thanks to my first-class priority booking and the online check-in Will's assistant had also arranged for me. I was thankful I had no time to reflect. However, there was one thing I needed to do before I boarded.

I pulled my phone from out of my bag.

'Babe, it's me.'

'Babe!' Jodie's voice seemed so close – bizarre, considering how far away she felt right at this moment. 'What are you up to? How's the golf?'

I giggled. Jodie had been obsessed with the idea that Will

and I were holidaying in some kind of retirement home for ex-pro golfers.

'It's awful. I'm coming home!' I tried to swallow my tears. I had to stop crying all the time. Plus, I was starting to attract attention from various bored and nosy passengers. I tried to shield my face with my hand on the pretext of keeping my phone call private. 'Babe, I'm so unhappy! I've messed everything up, haven't I?'

'Lou – where are you?' said Jodie, suddenly full of concern.

'I'm at the airport. I'm about to get on a flight. Will asked me to marry him, but I've left him. I didn't love him.' I stopped, willing myself not to break down again. 'Jodie, I still love Adam! What am I going to do?'

'You're going to sort it out, that's what you're going to do,' she said briskly. 'You two are made for one another. But right now, you're going to get on that plane and get back here. I'll make sure there's someone to meet you at the airport.'

Three hours later, I wearily picked up my luggage from the carousel and loaded up my trolley. I couldn't wait to get to Jodie's flat – I felt like I needed to sleep for a month.

I pulled my DVB sunglasses down over my eyes in case there were any photographers – you could never tell at Heathrow, and it had become second nature to me now – and searched the crowd of chauffeurs and excited relatives for Jodie or Gary. Neither of them were there . . .

Suddenly I saw a familiar face, standing shyly off to one side, and I walked over slowly, heart in my mouth.

'Hi,' I said nervously.

'Hi, baby,' said Adam. 'I've come to take you home.'

Chapter 18

In the end, it took Adam, of all people, to persuade Jodie to marry Gary. He came up to the room and told her everything he'd told me, and swore on his life that he was telling her the truth. (How Adam could be so certain when he hadn't even been with Gary, I wasn't sure, but seeing him sitting there in front of her, looking earnestly into her eyes and holding her hands, so handsome in his grey morning suit, I wasn't surprised she believed him. I would have.)

'Jodie, I wouldn't let you get married to him if I thought for one moment that he had been in a brothel, I promise.' She stared at him intensely. Adam didn't even flinch under her direct gaze.

'Are you sure?' she said sternly.

'Dead sure,' he replied.

'Swear on Louise's life?'

'I swear,' he'd said earnestly.

'OK, let's do it,' she said, clapping her hands decisively.

Adam cleared his throat. 'The only thing is, Mitch has just arrived downstairs.'

Jodie turned her head sharply. 'You know what? You guys sort that out,' she said. 'If he's there, he's there. Whatever. I've got more important things to think about than that loser.'

So then it was a mad rush to get us all ready – but finally it was fun, like it was meant to have been all morning. Jodie's nieces, the little flower girls, were allowed up to the room and were running everywhere, the *Hello!* people came in and got their interview – with strict instructions from Raymond not to discuss the brothel story, or the potential wedding cancellation – and in between organising everybody, even I managed to get ready (although I had to get my hair and make-up done in like half an hour).

Just as we were all leaving, behind me I heard Jodie stop her dad.

'Dad – will you wait a bit?' Her voice wobbled, and as I pulled the door to behind me, I stopped to listen to what she was going to ask him. Surely she wasn't going to pull out again at this late stage?

'Will you read your speech to me before we go down?' She sounded like she was going to cry, and my heart went out to her. Poor thing – she must be running on empty by now.

'Of course, darlin',' I heard her dad reply. 'Why?'

''Cos if I'm going to cry at some crap story from when I was a kid, I want to do it here in my own room!' she said. 'If I start when I'm down there, I'll never bleeding stop!'

I smiled to myself and hurried downstairs to help get everyone together for the first set of pictures while Jodie and her dad did what they had to do. We had to change plans for the *Hello!* pictures of Jodie and me and the flower girls and her family because we couldn't actually get to where they were originally supposed to be taken, thanks to all the TV vans outside. But the wedding planner found a gorgeous staircase with an antique chandelier hanging just in the frame, so everyone seemed happy with Plan B.

The only problem was that now we were really late – not, of course, that Jodie seemed to care.

'The way I see it, babe, he's bloody lucky I'm gonna be there at all – so he can wait until midnight for all I care!' she said, holding up her skirts and stepping carefully down the stairs. A *Hello!* assistant wrapped a black cape around her – even though we weren't going anywhere exposed, they were taking no chances that her dress might be snapped by anyone other than the official photographer.

And after all the sordid goings-on of the night before, and the dramas of today, it really was a beautiful ceremony. Following Jodie and her dad, I led the two flower girls along an external corridor (carefully covered with tarpaulin, of course, to prevent any paps sneaking in and taking unauthorised pictures that might scupper the *Hello!* deal) through to the olde-worlde chapel.

I gasped as I got a glimpse through the door, which had been left slightly ajar. The pretty chapel – bursting at the seams with its unusually large congregation – had tiny stained-glass windows which let in hardly any daylight, and the whole room was lit just by candles. They were everywhere – on windowsills, on the altar, on wrought-iron stands at the end of alternate pews. Red roses adorned the end of every other pew, arranged in elaborate glass vases in wrought-iron holders. Jodie's mum and dad had brought ivy from their own garden in Essex the previous night and had arranged it around the candles wherever there was space. The effect was gothic, dramatic, and one hundred and ten per cent romantic.

The only thing to spoil the atmosphere were the four burly security guards who had been drafted in by *Hello!* following this morning's shenanigans and who even had to accompany Jodie down the aisle. That, and the pitying looks from the guests who were obviously just feeling sorry for her rather than being in awe of how great she looked. It did feel a bit strange.

As Jodie took her place by the altar, I clocked Gary for the first time. He looked tired and about ten years older than the last time I'd seen him, but he was beaming at her, unadulterated love shining from his eyes, and I relaxed a bit. Maybe this was for the best after all. I gave Adam a secret smile as he slipped me a wink, and tried to ignore Mitch's gormless grin. Mitch, I just wanted to kill.

Gary leaned forward to give Jodie a kiss, despite an exaggerated frown from the vicar, and I read his lips as he whispered, 'You look beautiful.'

Jodie smiled back, but even before I heard her reply, 'I'll talk to you later,' I could tell it was through gritted teeth.

Gary wasn't having any of it. Raising his voice slightly, so we could all hear, he leant in and did a stage whisper in her ear: 'Your tits look really fine in that dress.'

Me and the vicar looked on in shock, and Adam and Mitch tried to hide a snigger. Jodie, however, just gave Gary a totally expressionless stare. For a split second I thought she was going to punch his lights out. All of a sudden, though, she threw her head back and let rip one of her trademark cackles. She didn't stop. I started to laugh then, and so did the vicar, and the first few rows of the chapel, and eventually we were all laughing, even though only a handful of us knew what we were laughing about! But it didn't matter. The ice was broken, and now the wedding could really begin.

After the ceremony and the photographs, Peter Quick, Gary's agent, came running over. A short man with bright pink cheeks and thinning grey hair, he seemed even pinker today – I couldn't tell whether it was with stress or self-importance.

'Look, Gal, Jodie, the hotel are going nuts. It's crazy out-side, the staff can't get in or out – if you don't say something, they won't go away and you won't get your reception party, 'cos there'll be no one to work it.'

Gary turned to Peter self-importantly. 'Look, mate, not today. Can you speak to Raymond about it? The Silver Fox'll sort it, surely!'

Peter coughed delicately. 'It was his idea, Gary.'

Jodie looked at Gary in horror. 'I'm going to have to speak to the press? On my wedding day?'

Gary rubbed her back reassuringly. 'Maybe it's for the best, darlin',' he said, though he didn't sound very certain of it to me. 'Let's face it, if you're going to have your picture all over the world's papers, you might as well look knockout for it!'

Jodie stared at him disbelievingly. 'If I was ever in any doubt as to whether you'd read the *Hello!* contract, I know for sure now,' she snarled. 'We can't be pictured anywhere. I'm going to have to talk to the press wearing a fucking cape!'

She turned to me. 'Lou, babe, will you come with us?'

I looked around uncertainly. 'Well, I'll come as far as I can for moral support,' I promised. 'But I'm not coming out front. I don't think there's enough capes to go around for all of us!'

Through a chink in the huge old iron-shot door that Jodie and Gary inched through, I saw thousands of flash bulbs go off as the baying crowds of press finally got their picture. I'd never seen Jodie look so nervous – or so beautiful. Her fixed smile looked almost serene, and Gary held her hand protectively, but he may as well not have been there. It wasn't him they wanted to talk to, it was her. The club might treat us girls as *persona non grata*, but when it came to the press, without us wives and girlfriends the boys would never make the front pages for anything other than some dirty scandal or other.

The questions, once they started, were loud, direct and unrelenting.

'How you doin' Jodie?'

'How d'you feel that Gary was outside Madam Ho's last night?'

'Separate rooms tonight?'

'D'you think the honeymoon's gonna be fun?'

Jodie held up a hand to silence them, and for once, they all fell silent. She's still got it, I thought with a smile.

She cleared her throat dramatically. With her hair all done up in ringlets and that huge cape over her amazing dress, she looked like a queen, I thought. Well, a drama queen at the very least . . .

'Thanks for coming, all of you,' she said, her voice clear and unwavering. 'It's nice to know you all still care.'

A titter ran through the crowd.

'As you'll all know, Gary and I are the unfortunate victims of a rather enormous misunderstanding, but we're both good, we've sorted everything out, and we're now husband and wife!'

I don't know if she expected a cheer, but none came. Just the same sea of blank, expectant faces.

'But we can't hope to celebrate this with all your bloody great trucks in the way, so we've come up with a solution. Call it a compromise, if you like. You've got your pictures, you're gonna get some drinks and grub, and once you've had that, will you please all FUCK OFF!'

There was a roar at that one, and Jodie blew them all a kiss and then ducked back through the door, pulling a bemused Gary with her. She swiped her half-empty champagne glass off the table she'd left it on and grabbed my arm.

'Right, babe, that's it. Let's go fucking party.'

'She never! What is she like?' It was a few weeks after Jodie's wedding and my voice had just gone about six octaves higher than usual in shock. I hoped Tara didn't have anything else up her sleeve – I'd go off the scale!

'I know, babe.'

I shook my head wonderingly and rearranged myself on my sunbed. The penthouse balcony could just about hold a proper wooden sunbed, but keeping in line with the sun without getting railing marks was a full-time occupation. And with our wedding only a couple of weeks away, I couldn't afford to have anything that would spoil the effect of my very expensive but very gorgeous designer dress that was being created especially for me right at this moment. (The timing was so tight that I'd had to sign an agreement that I wouldn't put on or lose any weight in between my first fitting and the wedding – so not only was I having to obsessively monitor my tan lines, I was also having to watch what I ate like I had some kind of eating disorder, too.)

Tara had missed out on Jodie's wedding, thanks to one of

Jonnie's sponsorship commitments which had involved a photo shoot with her and the kids, too. (Since Tara and Jonnie had moved, they had become fair game for the British press and were occasionally accused of cashing in unnecessarily on his success — and commercially exploiting their family unit. However, she always got around this by explaining it away as 'setting a good example'.) The next chance they'd have to get back here was mine and Adam's wedding at the end of July, so I was being kept busy with lengthy phone conversations updating her on my versions of all the latest stories. With the way things had been going recently, these calls had been getting more and more frequent, and longer and longer. They were generally interrupted two or three times by one child or the other having some kind of crisis, like throwing cereal everywhere, falling over or having a fight with the nanny. Imagine if Tara had no help, I often thought — you'd never get past 'hello'!

But I was glad of any opportunity for a chat. I still missed Tara terribly, and with Jodie away, I was feeling a bit lonely.

No sooner had I finished on my (very hung over) call to Tara the day after the wedding than my phone had rung again — this time it was Jodie.

Intrigued, I'd picked up immediately. 'What are you doing phoning me, you nutter?' I laughed. 'You said thanks about a trillion times last night. Aren't you meant to be in some just-married post-coital bliss?'

But Jodie hadn't laughed. Instead she'd sounded weird,

distant, almost robotic. 'Babe, I'm not with Gary. I'm on my own. I'm on my way to the airport. Without him.'

I'd gasped. After everything that had happened yesterday, Jodie was now on her own?

'What on earth's going on?' I'd asked, totally shocked.

She sounded tired, disenchanted – fed up with life. 'I dunno, babe. We got back to the room, shagged, shagged again, and he went to sleep. I couldn't. Instead, I got a call from Raymondo. Turns out the bloody *News of the Screws*'ve got a prostitute ready to talk about how she spent all of Friday night humping my husband. I just looked at him lying there snoring and thought: you little fucker. I just lost it. So I packed up my stuff and moved rooms – he's still asleep, mind – and sat up until this morning, when I did the off. Irony is, babe, he's given me my getaway.'

'What d'you mean?' I'd asked, puzzled.

'My wedding present. It's only a bleeding apartment at The Palm Jumeirah in Dubai.'

True to form, the *News of the World* printed the prostitute's story the same day. Gary, of course, vehemently denied it. But that was a whole five weeks ago now, and the last I'd heard from Jodie – she hadn't replied to any of my texts or voice messages, or Tara's texts or voice messages.

Now, however, for the first time in ages, it wasn't Jodie who was occupying me and Tara's phone conversation. It was Pattii. She'd been videoed by the *Sun* snorting coke at a private party and promising the reporter she could get him some 'hot shit' (which, of course, had been interpreted to mean girls as well as cocaine). According to Tara (who'd got the story ahead of publication from Raymond Moore), tomorrow's paper was going to run the scoop on her 'confession' and promises to clean up.

But deserved though her latest scandal was, I'd received Tara's news with trepidation. Was this going to blow the lid on my own coked-up night with Pattii?

'So tell me again,' I said nervously. 'Why is Pattii going to 'fess up?'

Tara sighed patiently. 'The paper did the sting, right? They've got the video. There's no way out – this story is going to come out tomorrow, whatever Pattii does. But she – with Raymond's help, of course – can try and manage the situation to make her look as good as possible. In the circumstances.'

She sniggered. 'So, she gives the papers a warts-and-all interview about her drug habit, thanking them for bringing it to the public's attention and allowing her to get professional help. She trots off to rehab – and a month later, the scandal's over, her reputation's not so in tatters as it might otherwise have been, she can show her face in public, Jez gets to hold his head up on the pitch again – bingo, all boxes ticked.'

Pattii and Jez had stayed together through their respective infidelity scandals, but I could only imagine what effect this latest blow was having on their home life.

I shook my head wonderingly. The world of public relations was still a bit of an enigma to me. But if Pattii was going to be trying to deflect attention away from herself, didn't that mean she might try and incriminate others? Like – like me?

'So, who d'you reckon were her partners in crime?' I ventured. 'Do you think there'll be any other casualties?' I drew a sharp intake of breath. Please, please say no.

'Oh, I'm not sure,' said Tara casually. 'I guess we'll have to wait and see!'

A week later, Pattii was safely tucked up in rehab and there had been no mention of me in her interviews, giving me more head space to think about Jodie. I was really concerned about her, even though I knew where she was and that she could get hold of me any time she wanted. She had really loved Gary, and though the allegations had shaken all of us, they'd never really been proven, had they? It was just the word of a dirty old whore against his. Still, Jodie had a pretty damning view of footballers in general, and had always said that at the faintest proof of any dodgy behaviour from Gary she'd be off.

And despite his faults, Gary really loved her too. Ever since she'd been gone, he'd been totally lost. He'd been straight out to Dubai, trying to get her back, but she apparently was having none of it. He'd come back heart-broken, and had spent a couple of nights with us, pacing the flat for hours, unable to settle. It was awful to see him like that.

'But Lou – I didn't do anything,' he'd say over and over, beseechingly, holding my phone out to me. 'Tell her! Phone her now! Text her!'

I'd sent a couple of texts on his behalf, but when she hadn't responded even to me, I think he'd known the fight was up and he'd gone back home, where, reverting to type, he'd proceeded to go right off the rails.

Normally, out of season, the boys would try and keep fit even if they weren't doing really full-on training, but without the discipline of having to be at the ground every day with the rest of the lads, Gary had been dealing with losing Jodie by partying hard. Too hard. He'd been going on all-night benders with Mitch, starting fights – he'd even headbutted a cabbie last week, but according to Adam had paid him off so he wouldn't press charges. At that point, even Adam, who was never critical of any of his mates' behaviour, had started to really worry. At first, he'd just been really angry with Jodie.

'Bloody gold-digger,' he'd said angrily – more than once. 'Just like all the rest. She saw her chance and she legged it. The courts won't look favourably on that, you know.'

I frowned as I remembered that line of thinking – when had Adam suddenly become an expert on divorce law? And didn't he remember how cut up Jodie'd been to find out Gary might have been visiting prostitutes? Didn't he realise it was all Gary's fault – guilty or not – and that Jodie had done what any self-respecting, if admittedly hot-headed, woman would do in that situation?

But Gary's total devastation had shaken Adam up a bit – maybe it reminded him of losing me – and after a few days' brooding on it he had taken him out for a beer and a frank chat.

I'd been eagerly waiting for Adam when he got back, reasonably sober for once, and before midnight! He'd sloped into the bedroom thinking I'd be asleep, but the minute I heard him the light went on and I sat bolt upright in bed.

'So?' I'd demanded. 'What's the score?'

Adam had sat on the edge of the bed and sighed wearily. 'He's going out there again, babe. Tomorrow. And this time he reckons he's going to bring her back.'

We'd heard nothing from either of them for two days, until this morning – when I'd got a text from Jodie.

'BABE. COMING HOME WITH GAL. CAN'T WAIT 2 C U. BIG KISS X X X X X'

I'd tried calling immediately but she hadn't replied, and I'd sent text after text, but she hadn't sent any more.

Instead, I'd rung Tara to give her the newsflash. Frustratingly, I kept getting 'user busy'.

Eventually I gave up, and within seconds my phone rang – with a call from Tara.

'Babe! I've been trying to get through to you for ages!' she said excitedly.

'Me too!' I shrieked. 'I kept getting the engaged tone. Must have been you calling me!'

'Anyway' she said dramatically, 'I've got some news. You're gonna love it!'

I laughed. 'Me too! You're gonna love this more! You go first.'

She tutted. 'No, I'll save mine. It's a corker. You go first!'

I grinned. Tara still always had the upper hand when it came to news.

'Jodie's coming back! With Gary!'

She gasped. 'No way! When? How? Have they made it up?'

I cursed my lack of any other information. 'Erm – that's all I know at the mo,' I said lamely. 'But it's great news, isn't it?'

'It's great – as long as he behaves himself,' she said sagely. 'I guess we'll find out more pretty soon if she's on her way back.' She paused dramatically. 'She'll be glad to hear she won't have to bump into Fatty Pattii for a little while longer, anyway!'

'What do you mean?' I asked. 'I thought she was due out of the Priory next week?'

'Well, it seems she's going to be in there a little while longer than she thought,' she said gleefully. 'But Raymond's managed to bury this story – so you're not to tell anyone, ever!'

Tara didn't normally revel in other people's misfortune quite to this level, but her dislike of Pattii really did seem deep-rooted. And after all the trouble Pattii had caused me, I agreed, it couldn't have happened to a nicer person.

'She's apparently been getting sent flowers from a mystery admirer the whole time she's been in there,' she said.

I scoffed disdainfully. 'Who'd waste their money on her after all that's happened?' I said.

'Well, exactly,' Tara said, spinning out the punchline. 'No one, as it turns out. Pattii's been paying her dealer to send them. Attached to every one of them was a little foil packet of cut flower food. Except it didn't contain flower food. It contained cocaine . . .'

After I'd hung up on Tara, I mooched around the flat, thanking my lucky stars I'd got away with my night of debauchery, and promising myself I'd never get caught up in anything like that again. It wasn't just the public shame – imagine if Adam ever found out . . .

Just then, I heard him come in, and immediately picked up a magazine and sat down on the sofa, trying to look like that was what I'd been doing all day.

'Hiya, baby,' he said casually, flinging his kit bag down as usual and going straight to the fridge for his milk. 'What are you looking so guilty about?'

I cursed under my breath. Nothing seemed to get past him these days!

He downed a pint straight from the carton. I pursed my

lips and tried not to nag at him, even though it was probably the one habit of Adam's that really wound me up.

He turned round and smiled wickedly, licking off his milk moustache.

'So, Lou, heard the latest?'

I smiled. Gary must have let him know too. 'Yep. Great news Gary and Jodie are back together again, isn't it?'

He flopped over the back of the sofa next to me. I leaned in for a kiss but he put up a finger to stop me.

'I don't mean Gal and Jodie. I mean that fuckwit you ran off with.'

Now it was my turn to be confused. 'Will?'

'Yes, *Will,*' said Adam, mimicking me bitterly. He had a weird look in his eyes – a mixture of hatred, cold amusement and, oddly, admiration. Suddenly he leered at me. 'You didn't tell me he'd got such specific tastes.'

I looked at him nervously. 'What do you mean, *specific tastes?*'

Adam laughed harshly. 'Oh come on, Louise, you must know what I'm talking about. In bed! Sex!' He almost spat the words. 'You did *have* sex, didn't you?'

I recoiled and tried to move further away from him. 'Ad – why would we talk about . . . it's not something I . . .'

The truth was, my sex life with Will hadn't been anything to talk about at all – it was missionary all the way. Not that I would ever have discussed it with Adam, of course. That would be just plain wrong!

'Well if he wasn't getting his kicks with you, he must have been getting them elsewhere the whole time you were together,' said Adam cruelly. 'I hear he's into – how shall we put it – visual stimulation? A bit of al fresco action? Sex with strangers?'

I stared at him, horrified. 'What are you talking about?'

Adam looked at me wildly. 'It's all over the club. The dirty bastard's been caught dogging. Picking up women and taking them to car parks and getting off on them shagging some old perv in a Cortina. While he looks on. He's a fucking weirdo, Louise. And you lived with him!'

Chapter 19

'Two Caesar salads, please,' I said, smiling. 'And two glasses of champagne. Unless' – I winked at Jodie – 'we should get a bottle?'

It was Jodie's second day back in the UK, and the first time I'd seen her since her wedding. She'd rung the minute they'd landed, but just to say she was there, everything was cool between her and Gary, and was I free for lunch today.

Was I? I wouldn't miss it for the world.

So here we were, in one of our favourite lunchtime haunts. She looked incredible – glowing skin, sparkling eyes and a deep tan – and somehow softer than she was before. All over, too! Instead of her usual skin-tight tops, she was wearing a soft chiffon smock, bare brown legs and woven-sole wedges, and I was sure her boobs were looking bigger than usual – had she treated herself to another boob job while she'd been away? Clearly we had a lot to catch up on, so I figured we deserved a bottle of bubbly at least!

But to my surprise, Jodie shook her head firmly. 'Just mineral water for me, please.'

I looked at her incredulously. Jodie, not drinking?

'Oh — and could we have some bread, please?'

I stared aghast at her. 'Babe, you're not — are you ill?'

Jodie smiled coyly. 'Only a bit sick in the mornings . . .'

My eyes opened wide. 'You're pregnant?' I shrieked. 'That's amazing!'

'Yep, nearly five months.'

Suddenly it all made sense. She hadn't had a boob job — she was pregnant. And she hadn't suddenly had a personality transplant — the baggy top was to cover up her bump.

As if reading my mind, she squeezed my hand. 'Babe — can you believe it?'

I shook my head, eyes welling up with happy tears. Beneath all her bravado, Jodie was a real softie, and I knew a family was something she'd hankered after for a long time.

'So — so how did it happen?' I asked tentatively.

Jodie rolled her eyes as she spread butter thickly over a bread roll and bit into it. 'Babe, if I've got to explain the birds and the bees to you at this age . . .'

I laughed. 'No, stupid, I mean — weren't you on the Pill?'

Jodie swallowed and shook her head triumphantly. 'I'd come off it — me and Gal were gonna start trying for a family on honeymoon, remember? Who would have thought it would happen straight away — especially with my old lifestyle!'

I smiled. She seemed thrilled. But . . . 'And you're sure it's Gary's?' I ventured tentatively.

She stared at me in shock. 'Babe, what kind of girl do you think I am?

She reached for a chunk of focaccia. I'd never seen her even touch bread before, let alone tear into it like this!

'I know,' I said hurriedly. 'I was just thinking . . .'

'I know what you're thinking,' she interrupted. 'You're thinking that if I'm five months pregnant, then why aren't I showing more. You're thinking that if I'm five months pregnant, that gives me at least three months of heavy drinking and the odd smoke too whilst I was carrying my child. You're thinking that if I'm five months pregnant now, why the hell didn't I notice beforehand and do something about it?'

She stopped when she ran out of breath, and took a long glug of water. I stared at her, speechless.

'Babe, I hadn't thought about any of that. I—'

'No?' she shot back. 'Well, I have. I've thought long and hard about it. About how I put off having children for so long because I fell in love with some no-mark good-time footballer who couldn't ever commit properly to me, never mind kids. About how I'd battered my body to fit my lifestyle so much that when I finally was pregnant my cycle was in such a state that it took me three months to even notice. And how when I found out I was pregnant and decided I did really love Gary and was going to give it a go with him, he decided he wasn't sure he wanted kids after all and left me stewing in Dubai while *he* made up *his* mind.'

I gasped. 'What? You mean – Gary knew you were pregnant, and knew you wanted him back, but stalled?'

Jodie nodded grimly. I thought back to Gary's sudden change from desperate depressive to head–in–the–sand party boy. It made perfect sense. I reached my hand out to hers and squeezed it. It felt small and frail and cold.

I decided a slight change of tack might be a good idea. It wouldn't do for her to get stressed out now, after all.

'Well, in a way that's even better,' I said brightly. 'You've had a chance to think about what you really want, and Gary's had a chance to think about what he really wants, and you've both ended up in the same place!'

She shrugged. 'For now, maybe. But what about when I'm all fat and tired after it's born? I know what I'm talking about. Ask anyone married to a footballer. Well, anyone except Tara,' she conceded. 'Everything's fine until a baby comes along. And then, suddenly, it stops being all about them. Your world doesn't revolve around your man. They're not the sole centre of your universe. They're not number one any more. And that's when the trouble *really* starts.'

I shrugged, brushing off her damning summary of, let's face it, the guy I was about to marry, but somewhere deep inside, her words had struck a chord. Was that how it would be if *I* ever got pregnant?

I shook myself. Adam was different. We'd always talked about having kids sometime in the future, and I knew he'd make a great dad if we did. Now Jodie was trying to justify finding fault with Gary, everything about footballers was wrong. Just because he hadn't wanted kids, she was coming up with theories as to why no other footballer would want them.

'I mean, look at Becky and Craig,' she continued. 'I bumped into her last week – she was down at the Portland having her scans done. Craig, let's not forget, was almost the model hubby until she started popping sprogs. When she found him in the club that time, shagging that girl, she must already have been a few weeks pregnant with their third. And now he's broken her down, begging her to take him back, she's agreed, and he's said great, but he's not sure if he wants the baby. Like, just what exactly does he think she's going to do about it at seven months gone?'

I bit my lip nervously. She did have a point.

Adam kissed me softly and squeezed my bum affectionately. 'All right, gorgeous, see you later, yeah? Behave yourselves!'

I smiled up at him. 'You two too!'

It was a little while after I'd first seen Jodie, and me, her, Adam and Gary had come down to London for a couple of days – ostensibly so that we could all do some shopping before our wedding, but really so that me and Jodie could have a pretend hen celebration for me. She was being ultra careful with her pregnancy and, being Jodie, didn't feel like she could come out on my real hen with the girls and not drink, so after our lunch with the boys we were going back to our hotel for an afternoon of pampering in the spa, and a girls' night in the suite, whilst the boys went out and had a few drinks.

Truth was, I'd been a bit nervous about the trip – it was the first time we'd all been out since Jodie and Gary had got back together, and I was worried it might feel weird. But nothing could be further from the truth. For all her wobbles the other day, Gary and Jodie were properly loved up again (bar the odd heated word, of course), and I put her concerns about Gary's paternal potential down to hormones. So the four of us had fallen back into an easy camaraderie.

After a bit of half-hearted shopping, we'd gone for lunch at Le Caprice, where Adam and Gary had spent the whole time talking shop and exchanging wisecracks whilst me and Jodie gossiped and talked weddings and babies. Well, babies mostly – Adam and I had decided on a pretty low-key wedding after all the fuss over Jodie and Gary's. We'd decided to take our families and one or two close friends away to Italy, and with the dress in progress and Tara helping me with the venue for the ceremony and party, there really wasn't that much for me to talk (or worry) about.

After coffee, the boys'd settled up and we'd emerged back into the late June sunshine to go our separate ways.

Adam ran into the road to flag down a passing cab for me and Jodie, and I grabbed her hand as she was smooching goodbye with Gary.

'Come on, you, let's get to that spa! My back's crying out for a massage!'

Gary winked at me over her head. 'Look after her, Louise. Remember, the only bubbles she's allowed are in the jacuzzi!'

I laughed and we jumped in the cab, waving at the boys as we drove off.

'Well, no need for us to worry about those two – talk about separated at birth!' I said, turning to squeeze Jodie's knee affectionately. 'Hey – are you all right?'

She was leaning on the cab window, rubbing her bump and breathing heavily. In the sunlight, she suddenly looked really tired. Her face had lines I'd never seen before, and despite her bright, strappy smock top and huge hoop earrings, her complexion looked – well – grey.

'I'm fine, babe, I just need to get back to the hotel. I think all the excitement's got to the baby a bit!'

I frowned. Jodie had been under a lot of pressure recently. What with all the emotional stress over getting back with Gary, a long flight back from the Emirates and settling back into life in England, she had been through the mill a bit. She needed a good rest – and an afternoon's pampering in the spa was just what was called for.

Once we were inside the cool, calm, surrounds of the hotel spa, and she'd turned her phone off, she seemed to relax a bit. By the time we'd both got undressed, wrapped ourselves in fat, fluffy robes and met in the relaxation room, she seemed much more like her normal self.

'Ooh, it feels good to be here,' she said, sipping at a glass of iced water and letting the tinkling of the miniature fountain wash over her.

I sighed, settling back into my relaxation bed, and closed my eyes. 'It sure does. What's your first treatment? Jodie?'

When she didn't respond, I opened my eyes to find her bent over double. She gasped and looked up at me, her eyes hollow with pain. 'Babe – get someone – I'm in agony!'

I touched her reassuringly on her back. As I did, I looked down and noticed a dark patch creeping up the back of her white robe. She was bleeding.

I ran through to spa reception. 'Help! Ambulance! My friend – she's pregnant – she's in pain – I think she's bleeding!'

The next few minutes seemed to take hours. Everyone appeared to be moving in slow motion, even though I knew they were acting as quickly as possible. In less than ten minutes we were in a private ambulance, hurtling our way to a private hospital affiliated to the Leeds one Jodie was due to give birth in. I'd grabbed all our clothes from our lockers and was changing into mine as best I could as the ambulance raced around corners. Jodie, however, was lying on the stretcher, ashen-faced and crumpled up with pain.

Once I was dressed, I fumbled around in her bag for her mobile. I found it – but of course it was turned off and I had no idea of the pin code. I didn't want to ask her now –

instead I thought I'd text Adam and then call when Jodie was safely with a doctor.

'On way to hospital. J bleeding and in pain. Pls tell Gary and call me. xxx'

The second I pressed send, it seemed, we arrived. The hospital reception was bright and welcoming, with comfy chairs and indoor plants – kind of like a country-house hotel, I thought. It was clean and clinical but softly lit, without the harsh striplights and smell of disinfectant of the huge NHS hospitals I had been in before. Jodie was hustled into a consulting room with a concerned doctor whilst I was left outside.

I paced up and down and called Adam's number. It went straight to voice mail. Cursing silently, I left an urgent message.

I tried to peer through the blinds and work out what was going on, but couldn't see anything. Suddenly the door opened, making me jump, and a nurse popped her head out.

'Louise? Would you like to come in a moment?'

I nodded nervously, heart pulsing loudly in my chest. I walked quickly across to where Jodie was lying on a bed, wearing a white hospital gown open at the midriff, and looking anguished. A middle-aged, bespectacled doctor was scanning her tummy and looking up at a screen, a grim expression on his face.

Jodie reached out a shaking hand to me. 'Babe – babe. There's no heartbeat. They can't find a heartbeat!'

I gasped and squeezed her hand, looking to the doctor for confirmation. He nodded sympathetically.

'I'm afraid it's not good.' He placed a kindly hand on Jodie's shoulder. 'I'm so sorry.'

Jodie's grip on my hand tightened, but she looked at him resignedly. 'So what now?' she asked numbly.

The doctor started to explain in great medical detail the process Jodie would now have to undergo. At her stage of pregnancy, it wasn't going to be simple – she was going to have to be induced, and give birth to her own stillborn child. It was too painful even for me to hear – I couldn't imagine the ordeal this was going to be for her. I sat down in the chair next to her, mind racing. I had to get hold of Gary.

Suddenly Jodie squeezed my hand. 'Isn't that right, babe? You can make sure Gary gets here all right while I'm in surgery? Have you told him already?'

I cleared my throat nervously. 'I've told Adam,' I said truthfully. 'But I need to use your phone, as I'd like to speak to Gary directly. I'm sure he's in a right state.'

Apparently glad of something to do, Jodie occupied herself with turning her phone on for me. The doctor took me aside and spoke to me in low tones. Jodie's miscarriage, it seemed, was almost undoubtedly stress-related, and he wanted to ensure that her recovery would be totally stress-free.

'The father – is that Gary? – he'll need to be clear on appropriate post-surgery care, both physical and psychological,' he murmured. 'Are we expecting him here at the hospital?'

'Oh yes, absolutely,' I assured him confidently, inwardly cursing Adam again. Why was he always so crap at answering his phone?

'Very good,' he nodded, satisfied with my answer, and went back to Jodie.

I shot outside and transferred Gary's number into my phone, then called it. It rang and rang – and then abruptly went through to voice mail. I stared at the phone, too shocked to leave a message. Had he just rejected my call?

I dialled Adam's number, this time from my phone. It, too, rang and then went through to voice mail – but earlier than it normally would if he'd missed a call. He, too, had rejected my call.

My head spun with anger and panic. How dare they ignore my calls! They knew it was urgent from the messages I'd left Adam. Outraged, I rang Adam straight back. This time it went directly through to voice mail as if he'd now turned his phone off. I left a curt message, and called Gary's number. He'd also turned his phone off, so I spoke equally strongly.

As I went to open the door to Jodie's room again, I took a deep breath and tried to calm down. How the hell was I going to explain this one away to her?

More than eight hours later, a nurse popped her head around the door of the visitors' room where I'd been holed up with a pile of magazines.

'If you'd like to come and see your friend, she's ready for you now.' She smiled kindly, and leaned in intimately. 'She's had quite an ordeal. The birth was very complicated – and as you can imagine, very emotionally draining.'

I leapt up and almost ran after her in my haste to see Jodie.

As I stepped into the room nervously, I nearly burst into tears at the sight of Jodie. For a start, I'd rarely seen her without her make-up on, and lying there in the bed, leaning on a pile of plumped-up pillows, so pale and wan, she seemed tiny. She looked like a little girl.

Her face lit up as she saw me, and then fell again when she realised it was just me.

'No Gary?' she croaked through dry lips.

I shook my head. There was no point lying – this was Jodie, my best friend, after all. 'I can't get hold of them,' I said.

'Oh, right,' she said, nodding matter-of-factly. It was as if she was on autopilot – she seemed numb, like she wasn't capable of processing any kind of reaction or emotion.

'How are you feeling?' I asked, and kicked myself. What a bloody stupid thing to say.

'Like I need to put some slap on,' she responded, quick as you like.

I gave her a half-smile. 'There's time enough for that,' I said. 'Just rest up for now.'

She leant across to her bag and pulled out a compact. Opening it with a snap, she looked in the mirror like she didn't recognise herself. To be honest, *I* didn't recognise her.

'Right, bird, you're gonna have to pull yourself together,' she said to herself firmly.

I moved up next to her and squeezed her shoulder. She looked haunted.

'Listen to me, talking to myself like a bloody idiot,' she said quietly. 'You know what, though, babe,' she said weakly, looking up at me with wide eyes.

'What?' I replied, stroking her hair away from her face.

'That's God dealing me a way out, isn't it?'

Her words nearly ripped my heart out. 'Out of what?'

'Out of having my husband's baby when he didn't really want one at all.'

I swallowed hard. 'Don't be silly, babe. You're not yourself. Gary will be devastated when he finds out – which will be soon. And then it'll be his turn to look after you, instead of you worrying about him. Now, for once in your life, you need to be taken care of.'

I sat down then and she laid her head on my shoulder, and we both stared into space, thinking about everything and nothing.

Much later, I walked slowly back to reception, my mind racing. I'd tried to call Adam and Gary at intervals all evening and into the early hours, and either their phones were turned off or my calls were rejected. I was fuming – and confused. Why would they do that?

I sat blindly watching Sky Sports on the plasma TV

screen. Some much-hyped big fight had taken place in town – the boys had been on about it the previous lunchtime, and how tickets were like gold dust – from the highlights they were showing, it looked like it was a packed house.

Suddenly I sat up like I'd been shot. I screwed my eyes up and peered closer at the screen. I couldn't believe what I was seeing. There, in the front row, obviously pissed out of their heads, were Gary and Adam.

Chapter 20

I woke with a start. It was 6 am – meaning I'd had little over three hours sleep. I could hear my phone ringing – but where was I? Slowly, as I came to, I remembered. Jodie, the miscarriage – I was at the hospital. My wrist was stiff where I'd fallen asleep propping my head up, and I flexed it sleepily.

I picked up my still-ringing phone, and saw Adam's name flashing on the LED screen. Like a bolt, I remembered. The boys, the no-show, the TV coverage of the fight.

'Adam.' I said, deadpan.

'Babe! Where are you?' He sounded concerned – and, would you believe it, put out.

'I'm at the hospital,' I sighed. 'Which you'd know if you'd read any of the zillion text messages I sent you last night.'

'What are you still doing there?' he said, genuinely puzzled. 'I thought Jodie would be out by now.'

Trying very hard to keep my temper, I counted to ten before replying. It would do no one any good to blow my top in the middle of a hospital.

'Adam, Jodie had a miscarriage. She lost her baby. She

had to go into labour and give birth to a stillborn child.' I swallowed hard with the pain of the memory. 'It was traumatic, painful and exhausting and she is still very poorly, and I have stayed with her in the absence of the next of kin.' I thought sarcasm was probably the best way to get across the seriousness of the situation. I hadn't wanted to tell either of the boys the extent of what had really happened over the phone, but he'd pushed me into it.

'Oh no, babe, that's dreadful,' said Adam. He paused, and I couldn't tell if he was shocked. 'But babe, when are you going to be back?'

Before I could bring myself to respond, Jodie's phone rang. Gary had obviously just arrived in his hotel room, and found Jodie was missing too.

'Ad, I've got to go. I'll be back soon,' I promised and hung up. It might do him good to have to wait for me for once. I switched phones and pressed 'accept call' on Jodie's blinging Nokia.

'Hey, darling, how are you feeling? I thought you'd be back by now! I'm lone-ly.' Gary was obviously still half cut, and full of pissed self-pity. It seemed the words 'hospital', 'pain' and 'bleeding' weren't urgent enough to interrupt their boys' bonding session – but getting back to their respective quarters to find me and Jodie were missing constituted a national emergency.

It wasn't ideal – but I was going to have to break the news to him now.

'Gary, it's Louise,' I said quietly.

'Louise?' He sounded perplexed. 'Where's Jodie?'

Anger boiled up in me again, and I took a deep breath. 'Gary, I've been leaving you messages all evening. Jodie's in a very bad way. She needs you here at the hospital. I suggest you get in a cab and get here as soon as possible.'

Within half an hour, Gary wandered through the reception doors, crumpled-looking and with heavy, bloodshot eyes – but brandishing an enormous bouquet of flowers and a huge, soft teddy bear. Where had he managed to find those at this hour?

I gestured to him and he rushed over, holding his arms out expansively, already full of proprietorial bluster.

'I'm here. Where is she? Where's my girl?'

Firmly, I took the teddy bear out of his hands and steeled myself to explain what had happened overnight. 'She's still sleeping. You can see her when she wakes up, Gary. But first I need to—'

Gary waved me away. 'I need to see the doctor, Louise. Tell me who's in charge here. I want to know exactly what's happening to my girl and my baby.'

He stalked off towards – well, I wasn't sure, really – and I sank back down into the chair. Gary might well have spent years saying he didn't want kids, but it was clear this was going to hit him hard. The only problem was, at the moment, I could tell it was all going to be about him.

Once a footballer, always a footballer, I guess . . .

★

I was so exhausted – and Adam so hungover – that we didn't leave London until late afternoon the next day.

'I'm so worried about her, Adam,' I said, as we pulled out of the hospital car park. 'I wish I could stay a bit longer with her.'

Adam squeezed my knee lovingly as he went to change gear, and blew me a kiss. (Ever since he'd surfaced this afternoon he'd been super-lovely to me to make up for his super-crapness last night.) 'She's a tough old bird, that Jodie,' he said. 'She'll get through it all right. You were with her when it really counted, but right now you need to be up north with me – organising our wedding!'

I chewed the inside of my cheek and looked out of the window as we drove along the leafy, nameless north London streets towards the A1. Soon, I knew, we'd hit Archway and the grimmer part of the journey out of the city, so I made the most of soaking up this more picturesque part. Or appearing to, anyway. In reality my mind was on much more important things.

'Ad . . .' I ventured hesitantly.

'What, baby?' he said absent-mindedly, one eye on the road, the other on flicking through CD tracks on the car stereo.

'I – I still don't understand how you and Gary didn't get any of my messages. It's not like your phones were even off all the time – they both definitely rang a couple of times. It was as if you'd rejected my calls.'

Adam sighed and then started talking really slowly and deliberately, as if to a small and particularly stupid child.

'Look, how many more times, Louise? We went to meet a couple of Gary's mates for a beer. Then some of their friends joined us and there was no way we could have heard our phones. Then one of the lads with us said he could get us into the fight, so we went to a club for a couple and then straight on to the fight. Tickets were like—'

'I know, I know – they were like gold dust,' I repeated, parrot fashion. 'I just can't believe that you didn't think to check your phone even once during that whole time.' I was whining now, but even though his explanation added up, I couldn't get rid of the suspicion that they had known we were trying to get hold of them, and that they'd just chosen to ignore us.

'Well, babe, sorry, but that's just the way it is,' said Adam, thumping the steering wheel in time to the r'n'b blasting out of the stereo. 'But you got us in the end, didn't you? Shame it turned out the way it did, though. I just hope Gal's back in time for my stag tomorrow!'

Sometimes, words failed me.

I went back to staring out of the window.

The credits rolled up over the screen indicating the end of another rubbish film. I turned the TV off with the remote and listlessly rolled over on to the other side of the bed. The pillows on this side were crisp and cool, and I sank my cheek deep into them. Breathing in, Adam's scent filled my senses and my eyes snapped open, wide awake once again. Where was he?

I peered over the edge of our wooden sleigh bed to look at the alarm clock: 06:05, and he still wasn't back from his stag, and I still didn't have any of the promised texts or voice messages. I fumbled around on the floor for my mobile to double-check — nope, nothing.

I sat up, mind racing. I flicked through my contacts on my phone, wondering which of the girls might know where they'd gone. I, of course, had no idea — as far as I was concerned, Adam's stag had been shrouded in total secrecy. Gary was Adam's best man, and although he'd made it back from London for the bash, leaving Jodie recuperating in hospital, with the way the final day in London had gone, I hadn't even been able to press him for any clues.

Not that I would have tried. After the miscarriage debacle, Adam had promised me faithfully that he would never go off radar again, and his stag night was his first opportunity to prove it to me. I hated feeling like a nag, but I really felt he needed to show me that he could put me first for once.

Shaking myself, I put the phone down. How sad was I? Only a few months earlier, I'd been the one secretly thinking Becky was off her rocker to be phoning round after Craig, and now I was doing exactly the same thing to Adam — but on his stag!

I lay back down and tried to calm myself, but the more I thought about it, the more irate I got. Then it hit me. Gary was out with them – and I had Gary's number. There was no guarantee he'd pick the phone up, of course, but still . . .

I dialled his number. It rang, and rang, and I was about to hang up when suddenly he answered.

'Ycl–lo.' said Gary. He was clearly plastered.

'Gary, it's Louise,' I said, as calmly as I could. 'Is Adam still with you?'

'Louish? Adam?' he said, obviously taken aback. 'Adam – well, yes, he is – but, erm . . .' He petered off uncertainly. 'He's not allowed to talk to you on his stag!' he finished triumphantly. 'Nope, that's the rule – no contact with the fiancée on the stag!'

'Oh, right,' I said, through gritted teeth. Well, at least that went some way to explaining the lack of contact throughout the night. 'But technically, it's not his stag now, is it? It's the morning after. And as I was expecting him home some time ago, it would be nice if I could have a quick word.'

'Oh, well, that wouldn't be possible, Louish,' slurred Gary, obviously over his shock now and enjoying his role as Protector of the Stag. 'Because he's asleep!'

'And where would he be asleep, Gary?' I said coldly. 'Only, he normally sleeps here.'

Gary laughed like I'd cracked the funniest joke he'd ever heard. 'Don't worry, Lou, he's at mine. I'll make sure he gets home all right.'

I put the phone down without bothering to say goodbye. So, Adam was at Gary's, was he? After all his promises to come home, he hadn't even managed to make it back across town. Some husband-to-be he was turning out to be.

Suddenly I was consumed by anger. How dare he? After everything he'd said? Did he really think so little of me that he could forget his promises just as soon as he'd made them? Well, not this time. Adam was going to fulfil his promise to come home to me – and if the only way to bloody make him was to go and get him myself, then that was exactly what I was going to do.

I snatched my bag up off the kitchen worktop, pulled out my car keys and rushed out of the flat.

There was a fine summer mist over the city as I drove flat out to Gary's apartment. Everywhere was still and calm – the total opposite to the boiling cauldron inside my head. I pulled up in one of the parking spaces outside the apartment block and rushed up to the entrance, not even bothering to lock the car. All I wanted was Adam – whatever state he was in – in the car and coming home with me. My finger hovered over the intercom buzzer, but for some reason I withdrew it without pressing it. I don't know why, but something in me wanted to give them a shock, so instead of announcing my arrival, I felt in my pocket for the key to the building's main front door. Jodie had left a set at my place, in case of an emergency. I let myself in and stopped on the second landing, trying to catch my breath before I buzzed at Gary's door. What was I playing at? Did I think I was some kind of modern-day Anneka Rice, racing against the clock to get my man back?

I stood up straight and walked to the door to the flat, and pressed the buzzer. Almost immediately, Gary answered. He was naked apart from a tiny white towel wrapped around his waist. When he saw me, the dappy pissed smile he was wearing suddenly dropped.

'Louise!' he exclaimed. 'What are you doing here?'

'I've come to collect my fiancé,' I said matter-of-factly, and stalked past him into the corridor. Most of the doors off it were shut, but I could hear giggling coming from somewhere, and music and shrieking coming from somewhere further off – the lounge, I thought, as I stood momentarily taking it all in.

Gary followed me like a little sheep. 'Louise – Louise, it's not what you think,' he was saying meekly.

I turned sharply. 'What's not what I think, Gary?' I snapped. 'And what do you think I think?'

He opened his mouth to reply and then shut it again, looking confused. 'It's not what you think,' he repeated, pathetically.

I pushed open the door nearest to me – the bedroom he shared with Jodie – and an empty bottle of Veuve Clicquot clattered against it and rolled into the centre of the room. Two girls, lying naked on the duvet, giggled and tried to roll under it. One was brunette, the other a blonde. They were both heavily made up, skinny, with fake tits as far as I could tell, and one looked all of fifteen years old.

I took in the scattered debris in disgust. A bottle of vodka stood on one of the bedside tables, and I could see coke paraphernalia next to it and the telltale signs of left-over white lines. Tarty lingerie was flung in various corners of the room. A picture of Jodie lying in the hospital bed having just lost Gary's baby flashed through my mind, and I gagged.

'Louise – it's not what you think. Adam's not involved,' continued Gary.

'He'd better fucking not be,' I stormed, pulling the door shut behind me. I carried on down the corridor towards the music and laughter. I had a strong feeling of impending doom, and I knew that I really should be turning back right now – but some invisible force was pulling me on, towards the living room.

I opened the door, and nearly collapsed.

There, in the centre of the room, was Adam – my Adam! – bent over the glass coffee table. He was wearing red French knickers and a black bra and gyrating to the hip hop blasting out of Gary's Bang & Olufsen speakers. Behind him, a bottle blonde wearing no bra (I guess that's where Adam had got his), a black thong and hold-ups, was whipping him with a cat-o'-nine tails. In the corner, Davy McNulty, topless, with a young Chinese girl on her knees in front of him, had his eyes shut and was clearly engrossed in the blow job he was getting through what appeared to be a grass skirt.

I felt my mouth fill with bile, and my eyes burned with shame and humiliation.

'Louise,' whimpered Gary at my elbow.

'DON'T TELL ME IT'S NOT WHAT I FUCKING THINK!' I screamed at him. At that, everyone in the room turned round to me in shock – except the Chinese girl, who carried on with the job in hand.

Adam looked at me, pissed out of his head and apparently unable to fathom what was going on. 'Lou, babe – what . . .'

'DON'T FUCKING BABE ME!' I screamed, insane with anger and hurt and – well – embarrassment. I turned wildly, and grabbed the nearest thing – a jug full of wilting lilies. Pulling the flowers out, I threw them aside, stalked over to where Adam was still bent over and threw the stinking, stagnant water over him.

'Pap–p-p,' he spluttered, and the girl behind him sniggered. Incensed, I turned on her and threw the jug at her. It missed, instead hitting the floor and smashing loudly and messily.

'Well, I've really caught you on the off this time, haven't I, Adam?' I spat. 'Thank God it was before I married you – you spineless, cheating, lying SHIT!' I spun around and pushed Gary out of the way, hot, heavy tears of humiliation blinding me as I rushed out of the flat.

I could hear Adam running behind me, shouting that he hadn't cheated, but I was way beyond listening.

As I reached the front door, desperate for fresh air and to be anywhere away from this depraved madness, I heard a now familiar giggle behind me. I slammed open the bedroom door, and the two girls stopped mid-laugh as they saw my thunderous face.

'And you two little slags can fuck off as well!'

It wasn't big, and it certainly wasn't clever. But right now, I wanted them to feel every bit as bad as I did.

Epilogue

'God, I just can't believe it!' mused Tara on the other end of the phone. I smiled fondly. I could tell she'd be sitting there, watching the kids, twiddling her hair around her fingers like she did when she was computing gossip or some huge piece of news. 'So you're really not going back to him?'

'I just don't know,' I said, more confidently than I felt. The truth was, I knew there was no way I should even be thinking about going back to Adam, but the reality of life without him had begun to hit me and it was pretty scary.

I looked up and checked the departures board. My flight still wasn't showing 'boarding'.

'And what will you do?' she continued, wonderingly.

I laughed uncertainly. 'I dunno! One thing's for sure, I can't stay at Mum and Dad's for much longer. They're being so lovely it's doing my head in.' There was a limit to how much tea and sympathy a girl could put up with, after all, and after four weeks of Mum fussing around me, I figured I'd just reached it.

After the hideousness of turning up at Adam's stag night, I didn't think things could get any worse. I'd gone back to the flat, packed up my stuff – again – and fitted what I could into the car. I'd taken the Hummer this time. There was no way I was making a return trip and so I was taking as much as I could in one go.

I'd arrived back at Mum and Dad's in bits, and stayed in my old room for days, keeping the curtains shut and my phone off, not even crying – just feeling totally numb. I could hear Mum, obviously fretting about wedding arrangements and the like, having hushed phone conversations with various people – Tara, I presumed, and maybe Adam – who knew? I didn't have the energy to ask. I didn't want to talk to anyone, and for three days no one had any inkling as to why I'd left.

Until, that is, the *Sun* told the story for me. Four days after the horror of visiting Gary's flat, I got to relive it all again, thanks to pictures someone at the flat that night had taken on their phone. There, splashed all over the front page, in unmistakable black and white, was the man I'd been due to marry in just a few days, wearing women's underwear and being whipped by a whore. No one had known what to say to me. Dad couldn't meet my eyes. Mum, in her 'look-on-the-bright-side' way, had pointed out that the paper stressed Adam hadn't actually *slept* with anyone, as if that somehow made it better.

It might have for everyone else, but for me it didn't. Even

though in my heart of hearts I knew that despite everything Adam was just a gullible prat and wouldn't ever cheat on me. When I looked around, there were many more women worse off than me in the Premiership – and beyond. Ad's only crime was to get carried away with every little boy's dream and have shit mates.

The trouble was, he'd gone too far. He'd humiliated himself, and me, and both our families. If he'd loved me like I loved him, he never would have done it. As far as I was concerned, he'd put some sordid part of his new life above everything I thought we both believed in – and I couldn't overlook it.

'The thing is, Tara, what *can* I do?' I said, voicing the biggest fear I had. 'I gave up work at the beauty salon to be with Adam, and how am I going to explain away a whole year of doing nothing to a future employer?'

'Oh, I don't know. There must be lots of things you can do!' she said brightly. 'Like, you could work in a Supermarket!'

I frowned. I was still only twenty-one, for goodness' sake – surely there were more options than that? Typical Tara.

A good-looking, casually but expensively dressed guy carrying a briefcase walked past and pulled a face at me, sitting there looking so cross. It made me smile, and he winked back.

'Or . . .' Tara said theatrically, like she'd just had the best brainwave ever 'you could do my nails for me! Oh, go on,

Louise! You could come out here and be my nail technician, and you could travel around with me and Jonnie and everything!'

And you know what? For one split second she nearly had me convinced. But that was Tara. She really did have the perfect life, and who knew, she probably had found the one footballer you could rely on. The trouble was, her main aim in life now was making sure everyone else fitted into her own personal nirvana – to better their own lives, but more importantly, to improve the convenience of hers.

I looked up at the departures board. My gate number had been called.

'Tara, babe, I've got to go – my flight's boarding!' I said, gathering my bits and pieces up.

'OK babe,' she trilled. 'Give my love to Jodie!'

'I will,' I promised, hanging up and breaking into a run as I remembered how far it was from the departure lounge to the gates. I scrabbled for my boarding pass as I ran, and suddenly had an overwhelming feeling of being free. I was going out to Dubai to see my best mate – to have some fun, to get some sun, and more importantly, to escape all this bloody gloom and doom that had been following me around for what seemed like for ever.

It took me so long to get to the boarding gate that I was flushed and breathless when I arrived, and passengers were already queuing for the plane. I was thirsty, and I eyed the vending machine before deciding against it. Adam had very kindly cancelled all my credit cards – no doubt on the well-meaning instructions of his agent and the club management as they closed ranks around one of their own – and so by now I was beyond skint. We'd get a drink on the plane – better wait until then.

Before I boarded, I checked my phone one last time for messages. As I suspected, there was one from Adam – he was leaving them about once every four and a half minutes on average – and I tried to feign indifference as I listened to it.

'Baby – please call me. Come back. You know I didn't cheat on you. Yes, I was stupid, no, I shouldn't have done it – but we can get over that, can't we?' As his voice broke on the last few words, my heart ached. Why had he had to go and mess things up? Why couldn't we just have carried on as we used to be, before we got mixed up in this ridiculous world?

As if he read my mind, Adam's message continued: 'I'm sorry I haven't sent you flowers. I'm sorry I haven't bought you any jewellery. It's just – it's just – nothing seems right. This isn't about stuff. This is about you and me. You and me, and how we used to be. I want that back. And I don't care about anything else.'

I hung up, eyes streaming with tears.

As I glanced to my left at first class I looked longingly at the wide, comfortable seats, the snug blankets and the glasses of champagne waiting to be served. Economy for you now, babe, I told myself firmly, as I was ushered to the right and you'll be all the better for it.

I tried to keep cheerful as I squeezed into my tiny aisle seat and attempted to squash my handbag under the seat in front of me. It wouldn't fit, and just as I was about to get up and put it in the overhead locker, a stewardess started heading straight for me. I smiled brightly.

'It's OK, I'm just about to put it up there,' I said, pointing above my head and pre-empting her request. My new-found feeling of freedom wouldn't last very long if I started getting bossed about, after all.

She smiled and then stopped, doing a double-take. 'Don't I recognise you from somewhere?' she said, peering more closely at me. 'I know! You're Adam Jones's ex-girlfriend, aren't you? Fiancée, I mean,' she said, hurriedly correcting herself. Then she smiled sympathetically and lowered her voice. 'I admire you so much for taking a stand. I mean, most girls would put up with that kind of behaviour just for the lifestyle. You're better than that.' She patted me on the shoulder. Then she loomed still closer. I could smell her cloyingly musky Obsession perfume and see the pores under her thickly applied foundation. I tried not to flinch. She was only being sweet, after all. 'Are you all right, though?'

I smiled. 'Yes, I'm doing OK,' I managed.

She looked furtively right, and then left. 'You know what,' she said, somewhat dramatically, 'why don't you come with me? We still have space in first class. I'm going to upgrade you. After all you've been through, you deserve it!'

She gave a tinkly laugh and pulled out my bag for me. I followed her gratefully, suddenly overcome by her kindness.

As I settled into my expansive first-class seat, she leaned in again. 'At some point during the flight, do you think . . .' She cleared her throat. 'Do you think you could do me an autograph? Only me and the girls think you're great, and—'

I smiled. 'Of course I can.' I pulled a page out of the tiny pink Smythson notebook I carried in my handbag. 'What's your name?'

'Carrie,' she breathed excitedly.

I wrote: 'Dear Carrie – thanks for a first-class flight! Lou xxx', then ripped it out and handed it to her.

She thanked me profusely and I buried my head in my bag for a couple of minutes on the pretext of looking for something – in reality, I was secretly hiding the tears that had suddenly threatened to spill out. I was torn between despair over everything I'd lost – Adam, the lifestyle, the fame – and guilt over what I'd become, and why. I mean, I might have made it, had the clothes, the car, the credit cards, but what for? For all the wrong reasons, that's what for.

When I emerged, I felt someone's eyes on me, and looked around curiously. In the row in front of me, in the seat just to my left, the good-looking guy from earlier was peering through the gap between his seat and the next, blue eyes twinkling in amusement and face creased in an interested smile.

I blushed and turned away, accepting a glass of champagne from a cute but effeminate steward and leaning back. Cheers to me, I thought, raising my glass, and giggled to myself. Again I felt the man in the row in front turn to look at me. No chance, mate, I said under my breath, and turned to the in-flight entertainment magazine.

A few hours, two films and a snooze later, the stewardess who'd upgraded me brought round hot towels. As she picked one up between her tweezers and gave it to me, she smiled conspiratorially and nodded at the good-looking guy's seat. 'He's definitely got the hots for you.' I looked over in horror, thinking he must have heard, but his seat was empty.

I shook my head. 'I don't think so. Anyway, I'm off men for the time being.' I made a face and she nodded understandingly.

'It's a shame, though,' she said. 'If you were on the market, you could do worse than him. We see him a lot – he's a very frequent flyer – and he's always dead polite, never lechy like a lot of them.' She nodded knowingly. 'Loaded as well, I hear. Anyway, if you're not in the market you won't be interested, will you?' Her mouth twitched in a half-smile.

It made me laugh. 'What makes you think he's so interested in me anyway?' I said curiously.

'He asked about you when you were asleep earlier. Must have seen me chatting to you. Anyway, like I say, if you're not interested . . .'

I *wasn't* interested, I told myself sternly. I smiled politely at her and picked up the duty free brochure in the pocket of the seat in front of me. When the good-looking guy sat back in his seat a few minutes later, I tried to get another glimpse of his face. He did seem nice – but who on earth meets someone on a plane?

As we landed, I couldn't wait to turn on my phone to see if there were any more messages. I wasn't disappointed. Adam had left more voice mails, and had sent a text. 'PS I 4got to tell u sumfin. I luv u baby.'

My heart melted and I snapped the phone shut with a bittersweet smile. As I waited to pull my bag down from the locker, I heard someone clear their throat respectfully to my right. It was him, standing with his luggage, waiting to leave. Or – was he waiting for me?

'Erm – I'm sorry, you must think I'm very forward,' he said shyly. My heart went out to him. He was dead nervous! 'And believe me when I say I don't normally do this kind of thing, but – I'd really like to take you out.'

He looked at me bashfully, and I got the full force of those crinkly clear blue eyes again.

'I'm in Dubai for a short business trip only – but maybe when we're back in the UK . . . ?'

He left the sentence unfinished, but his hopeful look

made my heart go out to him again, and made me think twice about saying no.

I found myself nodding and smiling. 'Yes – yes, I'd like that,' I said. I held out my hand. 'Louise.'

He shook my hand, and we both laughed. It felt so formal – but kind of nice. 'I'm Robert.'

We looked at each other for a long moment. 'Errr – I guess I should take your number!' he said, as we both became aware of the emptying plane. He patted his blazer pockets. 'But I don't seem to have . . .' We laughed again, and he pulled out a business card.

'I'll tell you what. You take that, and give me a call when you're back home.'

I nodded. 'OK,' I said. 'Maybe,' I added under my breath.

It wasn't until I'd left baggage reclaim and was on my way through customs that I thought to look at the card.

Robert Andrews, I breathed. Nice name. And then I saw the rest of the card.

'Robert Andrews. Chairman. Rotherham FC.'

Another bloody footballer.

How was my luck?

I thought of hapless, hopeless Adam, waiting for me to return from Dubai and take him back. I thought of how cosy our life together would be, once he'd learned his lesson and understood exactly how important it was to keep it real, and not forget who we were or where we came from.

As I walked past a dustbin, I held the business card over

it. But something stopped me chucking it away forever – it's always worth saving for a rainy day after all.

Another footballer indeed. Well, I'd already got one of those, waiting for me back at home, I thought as I tucked the card safely into my purse.

Better the devil you know, I reckon. But then again, a girl should always have options . . .

LINDA GREEN

I Did A Bad Thing

Sarah Roberts used to be good.

Then she did something bad. Very bad.

Now, years later, she's trying to make up for her past
by leading a respectable life, working as a local newspaper reporter and living with her saintly boyfriend
Jonathan. She has no intention of ever doing a bad
thing again.

Until Nick walks back into her life.

And suddenly, what's good and bad isn't so clear to
Sarah any more.

I Did A Bad Thing is dark, funny, wicked and true.
Because haven't we all got a guilty secret?

978 0 7553 3341 7

headline
review

LOUISE BAGSHAWE

Glamour

California, 1980s. Texan honey Sally Lassiter, English rose Jane Morgan and shy Jordanian Helen Yanna are best friends at an exclusive girls' school. They form a bond which, they swear, will never be broken . . .

The girls grow up, becoming co-founders of the exclusive GLAMOUR chain – a runaway success the world over. They are fabulously wealthy, adored and blissfully happy. Or are they?

For all is not as it seems. The empire is on the verge of collapse and the former friends are now embroiled in a bitter feud.

So what went wrong? What has changed? And, in the final showdown between three powerful beauties, who will emerge as the queen of GLAMOUR?

Louise Bagshawe's gloriously addictive new bestseller is a glossy blend of glitzy women, handsome men, tragedy and triumphs. Because every woman needs GLAMOUR in her life . . .

Praise for Louise Bagshawe:

'This glittering blockbuster of a novel will have you hooked from the very first page' *Heat*

'Her novels are action-packed; her heroines gorgeous; and her writing punchy . . . I love it' *Daily Mail*

'Mouth-wateringly addictive' *OK!* magazine

'Britain's younger, smarter answer to Jackie Collins' *Mirror*

978 0 7553 3669 2

headline
review

PENNY VINCENZI

An Absolute Scandal

WHEN YOU'VE HAD EVERYTHING

It's the glittering eighties and Lucinda Cowper, Elizabeth Beaumont and Flora Fielding feel happy and secure in the power and pleasure of wealth. Nothing could have prepared them for a devastating financial scandal, which turns the boom to bust.

AND SUDDENLY YOU HAVE NOTHING

For these women and their families it isn't just a case of losing the luxuries and the lifestyle. The crash takes away their hope, their self-respect and, for some, it destroys even more . . .

YOU'LL DO ANYTHING

Facing bleak futures, affairs begin, lies are spun, relationships are pushed to breaking point, and within the year someone will be dead. But who? And why?

'Guilty pleasures? We certainly all have them and this is better than most' *Daily Express*

'Highly addictive. Don't even think of opening unless you've got a lazy week to fill' *Daily Telegraph*

A Penny Vincenzi is:

'Like a glass of champagne: bubbly, moreish and you don't want it to end' *Daily Express*

'Deliciously readable' *Mail on Sunday*

'The literary equivalent of a huge box of beautiful handmade chocolate truffles – a total indulgence' *Ideal Home*

978 0 7553 3680 7

headline
review